DOGFIGHT IN SPACE

Both sides put out jamming frequencies. Communication was out. Training and experience took over.

"Battle systems in," Kerry rapped as his hands flew. 39 was a kilometer ahead, diving at a polyp plane—a slender dart powered by a fission jet and armed with a fixed-forward electrostatic cannon, primitive but dangerous at close range. The other fighters of the squadron were also diving.

"Get out of my way!" Orloff shouted at the unhearing STADEX dot representing 39, locked in its attack run between 37 and the polyp.

"Target opportunity at eight o'clock," Kerry cut in urgently. A polyp was slicing at them almost dead-on, already firing but missing 37's foreshortened hull.

"My turn, creep!" Orloff took the helm, lined up the shot, and touched the black-rimmed switch . . .

—from *Gambler's War*
by Eric Vinicoff and Marcia Martin

SPACE-FIGHTERS

**EDITED BY
JOE HALDEMAN**
WITH CHARLES G. WAUGH
AND MARTIN HARRY
GREENBERG

ACE BOOKS, NEW YORK

SPACEFIGHTERS

An Ace Book / published by arrangement with
the editors

PRINTING HISTORY
Ace edition/April 1988

ISBN: 0-441-77786-4

Ace Books are published
by The Berkley Publishing Group,
200 Madison Avenue, New York, New York 10016.
The name ''Ace'' and the ''A'' logo are trademarks
belonging to Charter Communications, Inc.

TABLE OF CONTENTS

INTRODUCTION

by Joe Haldeman

The stories in this collection range from a couple of straightforward tales of space aces to a delicate use of the Luke Skywalker imagery in life-preserving child psychology. Most of them, to me, have a pleasantly anachronistic feel. If and when we ever do fight ship-to-ship in space, there won't be any *"Alien meatball at ten o'clock!"* derring-do. We've already gone beyond that.

Last year I was invited to Wright-Patterson Air Force Base to participate in a "think tank" about the future of weaponry. Most of the people were professional futurists or Air Force researchers and pilots, but they threw in a few science fiction writers to give the thing a pleasant nut-like flavor. (I hope nobody would be surprised to learn that the futurists were rather stodgy and conservative, and the Air Force people gratifyingly freewheeling-to-gonzo.)

We saw the future there, and a lot of the pilots didn't like what they saw: their obsolescence. At least in terms of being people who button up in machines and take to the sky to place their lives between their loved ones and the war's desolation. That's going the way of the leather jacket and white scarf flapping in the propeller backwash.

We were shown a computer simulation of an advanced "heads-up" system for a helicopter pilot. Heads-up displays are already in use now; in their simplest form they're simply projections of instrument data onto the inside of the cockpit, making bright reflections so the pilot can check this or that without having to take his eyes off what he's doing. More sophisticated systems project an aiming point for the pilot's guns and rockets.

In the heads-up system we saw demonstrated, the pilot never even sees outside the cockpit. He's looking at a cathode ray tube that shows a simplified representation of what he would see if he could look outside. If he turns his head, the image shifts to show what's to the left or right or behind him.

The computer's image of the world is like the scrawling of an autistic child. This cone is a mountain. These squares are a city. That curvy line is a river. The blinking X's are enemy planes; the blinking O's are friendlies.

Uh-oh. Here comes a pencil. Don't let that pencil touch you.

The images aren't simplified because of the computer's graphic limitations. Flight simulators that train people for driving aircraft and spacecraft are able to generate pictures of forests where each tree is different; show waves breaking on the shore; people running for cover. All in detail with realistic color.

Of course all that detail is distracting, in real life or on a computer screen; what the pilot's really interested in are his targets and the things that are trying to get in his way. So a mountain becomes a cone; a SAM becomes a pencil.

You don't have to be a hotshot futurist or science fiction writer to take this process to its next step: why put the pilot in the plane at all? It's all TV images. Why not just beam them down to the ground, where the pilot's sitting in a safe bunker with his heads-up display around him? After all, the pilot is the most expensive component in the system, and the one that takes longest to replace (even though they're made by unskilled labor, as several people pointed out).

Carry it further—"ask the next question," as Theodore Sturgeon was always saying. If you take the pilot out of the plane, how does that change the plane? You don't need any elaborate life-support apparatus, so you can either replace that weight with more fuel and ammunition, or you can make the plane smaller—thus harder to hit—and more maneuverable.

You can also throw human factors out of the plane's design limitations. If the other components can take a fifty-gee dive, go ahead. Make it so it stops and turns on a dime. Come screaming toward the enemy at ten kilometers a second, one meter off the ground.

But wait. If you're pretty good, you can make a simple response, like pushing a button, to a visual stimulus in about a tenth of a second. At ten kilometers a second (which is less than Earth's escape velocity) that's a whole kilometer eaten up before you can start putting on the brakes. If a missile is coming toward you at the same speed, its distance closes almost a mile and a half in that tenth of a second. Think of how small a person's head looks, a mile and a half away. That's the cross-section of the missile that's going to be in your lap before you can push the button. If you ever see it at all.

So the next step is to take slow human reflexes out of the business. Have human pilots train special computers, using some "expert system" algorithm. Once they know what to do, let the computers do it at their own speed, or whatever slower speed is dictated by the aircraft's propulsion and weapons systems.

Then when we humans want to fight a war, we just turn on our machines and go underground and play Canasta until it's over. Whichever side has the most toys at the end, wins.

Well, that doesn't give you much of a story, unless you're the kind of writer who can make a gripping drama out of a Canasta game.* None of the people in this anthology picked up that particular gauntlet, though all of them did investigate one aspect or another of the "space fighters" question: given X years of development, how would the circumstances of aerial/ aerospace combat change? Of course the best stories are about considerably more than the evolution of weapons.

The stories you don't see here, the ones that were considered but not selected for this book, form an interesting set, and they have a lot in common with the stories rejected from the two

*An interesting challenge. I once saw an unintentionally hilarious television program, the supposedly live telecast of the World Series of Poker. It was like a cross between *Wide World of Sports* and a Harold Pinter play: long close-ups of people who had been practicing since childhood to show absolutely no emotion.

companion volumes *Body Armor: 2000* and *Supertanks*. All the rejects ought to be assembled into a "How Not to Write a Science Fiction War Story" collection, a guaranteed worst-seller but of some interest to students of the genre. The stories would fall into three main groups:

1. The straight hardware extrapolation, with tactics, personalities, and military goals unchanged from present-day models.

2. Old-fashioned or contemporary politics transplanted whole into the future: usually those nasty Russkies still being Russkies.

3. The story where the aliens have us outnumbered and outgunned, but we beat them anyhow, because humans are the roughest toughest critters in the universe.

(Here's a parenthetical pop quiz. When I teach writing, I like to make up lists of rules, but not so the students will slavishly follow them. Instead, they're supposed to turn the rule inside out, and make the breaking of it central to a story. Of the three "don'ts" above, the first one could, in the hands of a genius, yield Harry Harrison's *Bill, the Galactic Hero*. What about the other two?)

So I suppose the stories in these three volumes, conversely, add up to a "How to Write a Science Fiction War Story" collection—or at least one that demonstrates how to write an sf war story that will be selected by Haldeman, Waugh, and Greenberg. (Don't send me any! When I finish this page, I'm out of the collecting-war-stories business!) What do the chosen stories have in common?

It may be a symptom of thematic burnout, but the two that I like best in this collection seem to use war as a source of conflict, without actually, thematically, being about war. "The Game of Rat and Dragon" is about a particular kind of love. "Empire Dreams" is about coping with memories, hideous memories.

Two other favorites are straightforward war stories, in that their plots describe combat missions in the expected "preparation/mission/aftermath" pattern. "Wings Out of Shadow" stands out for the cleverness of its plot twist and Saberhagen's berserkers, which always grab you tight by the Jungian backbrain. "Common Denominator" is impressive in its well-thought-out descriptions of future war.

These four come immediately to mind, but the others aren't

chopped liver, either. (Some of the rejected ones *were* chopped liver, rather too literally.) The only overall criticism I have is that none of the stories is set in the future that I saw coming at the Wright-Patterson think tank, with individual combat becoming obsolete *a fortoriori* because of the relentless march of technology.

Maybe I'll have to write it myself. Brush up on my Canasta.

THE GAME OF RAT AND DRAGON

by Cordwainer Smith

I.
The Table

Pinlighting is a hell of a way to earn a living. Underhill was furious as he closed the door behind himself. It didn't make much sense to wear a uniform and look like a soldier if people didn't appreciate what you did.

He sat down in his chair, laid his head back in the headrest, and pulled the helmet down over his forehead.

As he waited for the pin-set to warm up, he remembered the girl in the outer corridor. She had looked at it, then looked at him scornfully.

"Meow." That was all she had said. Yet it had cut him like a knife.

What did she think he was—a fool, a loafer, a uniformed nonentity? Didn't she know that for every half-hour of pinlighting, he got a minimum of two months' recuperation in the hospital?

By now the set was warm. He felt the squares of space around him, sensed himself at the middle of an immense grid, a cubic grid, full of nothing. Out in that nothingness, he could sense the hollow aching horror of space itself and could feel the terrible anxiety which his mind encountered whenever it met the faintest trace of inert dust.

As he relaxed, the comforting solidity of the sun, the clockwork of the familiar planets and the moon rang in on him. Our own solar system was as charming and as simple as an ancient cuckoo clock filled with familiar ticking and with reassuring noises. The odd little moons of Mars swung around their planet like frantic mice, yet their regularity was itself an assurance that all was well. Far above the plane of the ecliptic, he could feel half a ton of dust more or less drifting outside the lanes of human travel.

Here there was nothing to fight, nothing to challenge the mind, to tear the living soul out of a body with its roots dripping in effluvium as tangible as blood.

Nothing ever moved in on the solar system. He could wear the pin-set forever and be nothing more than a sort of telepathic astronomer, a man who could feel the hot, warm protection of the sun throbbing and burning against his living mind.

Woodley came in.

"Same old ticking world," said Underhill. "Nothing to report. No wonder they didn't develop the pin-set until they began to planoform. Down here with the hot sun around us, it feels so good and so quiet. You can feel everything spinning and turning. It's nice and sharp and compact. It's sort of like sitting around home."

Woodley grunted. He was not much given to flights of fantasy.

Undeterred, Underhill went on, "It must have been pretty good to have been an ancient man. I wonder why they burned up their world with war. They didn't have to planoform. They didn't have to go out to earn their livings among the stars. They didn't have to dodge the Rats or play the Game. They couldn't have invented pinlighting because they didn't have any need of it, did they, Woodley?"

Woodley grunted, "Uh-huh." Woodley was twenty-six years old and due to retire in one more year. He already had a farm picked out. He had gotten through ten years of hard work pinlighting with the best of them. He had kept his sanity by not thinking very much about his job, meeting the strains of the task whenever he had to meet them and thinking nothing more about his duties until the next emergency arose.

Woodley never made a point of getting popular among the

Partners. None of the Partners liked him very much. Some of them even resented him. He was suspected of thinking ugly thoughts of the Partners on occasion, but since none of the Partners ever thought a complaint in articulate form, the other pinlighters and the Chiefs of the Instrumentality left him alone.

Underhill was still full of the wonder of their job. Happily he babbled on, "What does happen to us when we planoform? Do you think it's sort of like dying? Did you ever see anybody who had his soul pulled out?"

"Pulling souls is just a way of talking about it," said Woodley. "After all these years, nobody knows whether we have souls or not."

"But I saw one once. I saw what Dogwood looked like when he came apart. There was something funny. It looked wet and sort of sticky as if it were bleeding and it went out of him—and you know what they did to Dogwood? They took him away, up in that part of the hospital where you and I never go—way up at the top part where the others are, where the others always have to go if they are alive after the Rats of the Up-and-Out have gotten them."

Woodley sat down and lit an ancient pipe. He was burning something called tobacco in it. It was a dirty sort of habit, but it made him look very dashing and adventurous.

"Look here, youngster. You don't have to worry about that stuff. Pinlighting is getting better all the time. The Partners are getting better. I've seen them pinlight two Rats forty-six million miles apart in one and a half milliseconds. As long as people had to try to work the pin-sets themselves, there was always the chance that with a minimum of four hundred milliseconds for the human mind to set a pinlight, we wouldn't light the Rats up fast enough to protect our planoforming ships. The Partners have changed all that. Once they get going, they're faster than Rats. And they always will be. I know it's not easy, letting a Partner share your mind—"

"It's not easy for them, either," said Underhill.

"Don't worry about them. They're not human. Let them take care of themselves. I've seen more pinlighters go crazy from monkeying around with Partners than I have ever seen caught by the Rats. How many of them do you actually know of that got grabbed by Rats?"

Underhill looked down at his fingers, which shone green and purple in the vivid light thrown by the tuned-in pin-set, and counted ships. The thumb for the *Andromeda*, lost with crew and passengers, the index finger and the middle finger for *Release Ships 43* and *56*, found with their pin-sets burned out and every man, woman, and child on board dead or insane. The ring finger, the little finger, and the thumb of the other hand were the first three battleships to be lost to the Rats—lost as people realized that there was something out there *underneath space itself* which was alive, capricious, and malevolent.

Planoforming was sort of funny. It felt like—

Like nothing much.

Like the twinge of a mild electric shock.

Like the ache of a sore tooth bitten on for the first time.

Like a slightly painful flash of light against the eyes.

Yet in that time, a forty-thousand-ton ship lifting free above Earth disappeared somehow or other into two dimensions and appeared half a light year or fifty light years off.

At one moment, he would be sitting in the Fighting Room, the pin-set ready and the familiar solar system ticking around inside his head. For a second or a year (he could never tell how long it really was, subjectively), the funny little flash went through him and then he was loose in the Up-and-Out, the terrible open spaces between the stars, where the stars themselves felt like pimples on his telepathic mind and the planets were too far away to be sensed or read.

Somewhere in this outer space, a gruesome death awaited, death and horror of a kind which Man had never encountered until he reached out for interstellar space itself. Apparently the light of the suns kept the Dragons away.

Dragons. That was what people called them. To ordinary people, there was nothing, nothing except the shiver of planoforming and the hammer blow of sudden death or the dark spastic note of lunacy descending into their minds.

But to the telepaths, they were Dragons.

In the fraction of a second between the telepaths' awareness of a hostile something out in the black, hollow nothingness of space and the impact of a ferocious, ruinous psychic blow against all living things within the ship, the telepaths had sensed entities something like the Dragons of ancient human lore, beasts more clever than beasts, demons more tangible than demons, hungry vortices of aliveness and hate compounded by unknown means out of the thin tenuous matter between the stars.

It took a surviving ship to bring back the news—a ship in

which, by sheer chance, a telepath had a light beam ready, turning it out at the innocent dust so that, within the panorama of his mind, the Dragon dissolved into nothing at all and the other passengers, themselves non-telepathic, went about their way not realizing that their own immediate deaths had been averted.

From then on, it was easy—almost.

Planoforming ships always carried telepaths. Telepaths had their sensitiveness enlarged to an immense range by the pin-sets, which were telepathic amplifiers adapted to the mammal mind. The pin-sets in turn were electronically geared into small dirigible light bombs. Light did it.

Light broke up the Dragons, allowed the ships to reform three-dimensionally, skip, skip, skip, as they moved from star to star.

The odds suddenly moved down from a hundred to one against mankind to sixty to forty in mankind's favor.

This was not enough. The telepaths were trained to become ultrasensitive, trained to become aware of the Dragons in less than a millisecond.

But it was found that the Dragons could move a million miles in just under two milliseconds and that this was not enough for the human mind to activate the light beams.

Attempts had been made to sheath the ships in light at all times.

This defense wore out.

As mankind learned about the Dragons, so too, apparently, the Dragons learned about mankind. Somehow they flattened their own bulk and came in on extremely flat trajectories very quickly.

Intense light was needed, light of sunlike intensity. This could be provided only by light bombs. Pinlighting came into existence.

Pinlighting consisted of the detonation of ultra-vivid miniature photonuclear bombs, which converted a few ounces of a magnesium isotope into pure visible radiance.

The odds kept coming down in mankind's favor, yet ships were being lost.

It became so bad that people didn't even want to find the ships because the rescuers knew what they would see. It was sad to bring back to Earth three hundred bodies ready for burial and two hundred or three hundred lunatics, damaged beyond repair, to be wakened, and fed, and cleaned, and put to sleep, wakened and fed again until their lives were ended.

Telepaths tried to reach into the minds of the psychotics who had been damaged by the Dragons, but they found nothing there beyond vivid spouting columns of fiery terror bursting from the primordial id itself, the volcanic source of life.

Then came the Partners.

Man and Partner could do together what Man could not do alone. Men had the intellect. Partners had the speed.

The Partners rode their tiny craft, no larger than footballs, outside the spaceships. They planoformed with the ships. They rode beside them in their six-pound craft ready to attack.

The tiny ships of the Partners were swift. Each carried a dozen pinlights, bombs no bigger than thimbles.

The pinlighters threw the Partners—quite literally threw—by means of mind-to-firing relays directly at the Dragons.

What seemed to be Dragons to the human mind appeared in the form of gigantic Rats in the minds of the Partners.

Out in the pitiless nothingness of space, the Partners' minds responded to an instinct as old as life. The Partners attacked, striking with a speed faster than Man's, going from attack to attack until the Rats or themselves were destroyed. Almost all the time it was the Partners who won.

With the safety of the interstellar skip, skip, skip of the ships, commerce increased immensely, the population of all the colonies went up, and the demand for trained Partners increased.

Underhill and Woodley were a part of the third generation of pinlighters and yet, to them, it seemed as though their craft had endured forever.

Gearing space into minds by means of the pin-set, adding the Partners to those minds, keying up the mind for the tension of a fight on which all depended—this was more than human synapses could stand for long. Underhill needed his two months' rest after half an hour of fighting. Woodley needed his retirement after ten years of service. They were young. They were good. But they had limitations.

So much depended on the choice of Partners, so much on the sheer luck of who drew whom.

II.
The Shuffle

Father Moontree and the little girl named West entered the room. They were the other two pinlighters. The human complement of the Fighting Room was now complete.

Father Moontree was a red-faced man of forty-five who had lived the peaceful life of a farmer until he reached his fortieth year. Only then, belatedly, did the authorities find he was telepathic and agree to let him late in life enter upon the career of pinlighter. He did well at it, but he was fantastically old for this kind of business.

Father Moontree looked at the glum Woodley and the musing Underhill. "How're the youngsters today? Ready for a good fight?"

"Father always wants a fight," giggled the little girl named West. She was such a little little girl. Her giggle was high and childish. She looked like the last person in the world one would expect to find in the rough, sharp dueling of pinlighting.

Underhill had been amused one time when he found one of the most sluggish of the Partners coming away happy from contact with the mind of the girl named West.

Usually the Partners didn't care much about the human minds with which they were paired for the journey. The Partners seemed to take the attitude that human minds were complex and fouled up beyond belief, anyhow. No Partner ever questioned the superiority of the human mind, though very few of the Partners were much impressed by that superiority.

The Partners liked people. They were willing to fight with them. They were even willing to die for them. But when a Partner liked an individual the way, for example, that Captain Wow or the Lady May liked Underhill, the liking had nothing to do with intellect. It was a matter of temperament, of feel.

Underhill knew perfectly well that Captain Wow regarded his, Underhill's, brains as silly. What Captain Wow liked was Underhill's friendly emotional structure, the cheerfulness and glint of wicked amusement that shot through Underhill's unconscious thought patterns, and the gaiety with which Underhill faced danger. The words, the history books, the ideas, the science—Underhill could sense all that in his own mind, reflected back from Captain Wow's mind, as so much rubbish.

Miss West looked at Underhill. "I bet you've put stickum on the stones."

"I did not!"

Underhill felt his ears grow red with embarrassment. During his novitiate, he had tried to cheat in the lottery because he got particularly fond of a special Partner, a lovely young mother named Murr. It was so much easier to operate with Murr and she was so affectionate toward him that he forgot pinlighting was hard work and that he was not instructed to have a good time with his Partner. They were both designed and prepared to go into deadly battle together.

One cheating had been enough. They had found him out and he had been laughed at for years.

Father Moontree picked up the imitation-leather cup and shook the stone dice which assigned them their Partners for the trip. By senior rights he took first draw.

He grimaced. He had drawn a greedy old character, a tough old male whose mind was full of slobbering thoughts of food, veritable oceans full of half-spoiled fish. Father Moontree had once said that he burped cod liver oil for weeks after drawing that particular glutton, so strongly had the telepathic image of fish impressed itself upon his mind. Yet the glutton was a glutton for danger as well as for fish. He had killed sixty-three Dragons, more than any other Partner in the service, and was quite literally worth his weight in gold.

The little girl West came next. She drew Captain Wow. When she saw who it was, she smiled.

"I *like* him," she said. "He's such fun to fight with. He feels so nice and cuddly in my mind."

"Cuddly, hell," said Woodley. "I've been in his mind, too. It's the most leering mind in this ship, bar none."

"Nasty man," said the little girl. She said it declaratively, without reproach.

Underhill, looking at her, shivered.

He didn't see how she could take Captain Wow so calmly. Captain Wow's mind *did* leer. When Captain Wow got excited in the middle of a battle, confused images of Dragons, deadly Rats, luscious beds, the smell of fish, and the shock of space all scrambled together in his mind as he and Captain Wow, their consciousnesses linked together through the pin-set, became a fantastic composite of human being and Persian cat.

That's the trouble with working with cats, thought Underhill.

It's a pity that nothing else anywhere will serve as Partner. Cats were all right once you got in touch with them telepathically. They were smart enough to meet the needs of the fight, but their motives and desires were certainly different from those of humans.

They were companionable enough as long as you thought tangible images at them, but their minds just closed up and went to sleep when you recited Shakespeare or Colegrove, or if you tried to tell them what space was.

It was sort of funny realizing that the Partners who were so grim and mature out here in space were the same cute little animals that people had used as pets for thousands of years back on Earth. He had embarrassed himself more than once while on the ground, saluting perfectly ordinary nontelepathic cats because he had forgotten for the moment that they were not Partners.

He picked up the cup and shook out his stone dice.

He was lucky—he drew the Lady May.

The Lady May was the most thoughtful Partner he had ever met. In her, the finely bred pedigree mind of a Persian cat had reached one of its highest peaks of development. She was more complex than any human woman, but the complexity was all one of emotions, memory, hope, and discriminated experience—experience sorted through without benefit of words.

When he had first come into contact with her mind, he was astonished at its clarity. With her he remembered her kittenhood. He remembered every mating experience she had ever had. He saw in a half-recognizable gallery all the other pinlighters with whom she had been paired for the fight. And he saw himself radiant, cheerful, and desirable.

He even thought he caught the edge of a longing—

A very flattering and yearning thought: *What a pity he is not a cat.*

Woodley picked up the last stone. He drew what he deserved—a sullen, scarred old tomcat with none of the verve of Captain Wow. Woodley's Partner was the most animal of all the cats on the ship, a low, brutish type with a dull mind. Even telepathy had not refined his character. His ears were half chewed off from the first fights in which he had engaged. He was a serviceable fighter, nothing more.

Woodley grunted.

Underhill glanced at him oddly. Didn't Woodley ever do anything but grunt?

Father Moontree looked at the other three. "You might as well get your Partners now. I'll let the Scanner know we're ready to go into the Up-and-Out."

III.
The Deal

Underhill spun the combination lock on the Lady May's cage. He woke her gently and took her into his arms. She humped her back luxuriously, stretched her claws, started to purr, thought better of it, and licked him on the wrist instead. He did not have the pin-set on, so their minds were closed to each other, but in the angle of her mustache and in the movement of her ears, he caught some sense of the gratification she experienced in finding him as her Partner.

He talked to her in human speech, even though speech meant nothing to a cat when the pin-set was not on.

"It's a damn shame, sending a sweet little thing like you whirling around in the coldness of nothing to hunt for Rats that are bigger and deadlier than all of us put together. You didn't ask for this kind of fight, did you?"

For answer, she licked his hand, purred, tickled his cheek with her long fluffy tail, turned around and faced him, golden eyes shining.

For a moment, they stared at each other, man squatting, cat standing erect on her hind legs, front claws digging into his knee. Human eyes and cat eyes looked across an immensity which no words could meet, but which affection spanned in a single glance.

"Time to get in," he said.

She walked docilely to her spheroid carrier. She climbed in. He saw to it that her miniature pin-set rested firmly and comfortably against the base of her brain. He made sure that her claws were padded so that she could not tear herself in the excitement of battle.

Softly he said to her, "Ready?"

For answer, she preened her back as much as her harness

would permit and purred softly within the confines of the frame that held her.

He slapped down the lid and watched the sealant ooze around the seam. For a few hours, she was welded into her projectile until a workman with a short cutting arc would remove her after she had done her duty.

He picked up the entire projectile and slipped it into the ejection tube. He closed the door of the tube, spun the lock, seated himself in his chair, and put his own pin-set on.

Once again he flung the switch.

He sat in a small room, *small, small, warm, warm,* the bodies of the other three people moving close around him, the tangible lights in the ceiling bright and heavy against his closed eyelids.

As the pin-set warmed, the room fell away. The other people ceased to be people and became small glowing heaps of fire, embers, dark red fire, with the consciousness of life burning like old red coals in a country fireplace.

As the pin-set warmed a little more, he felt Earth just below him, felt the ship slipping away, felt the turning Moon as it swung on the far side of the world, felt the planets and the hot, clear goodness of the Sun, which kept the Dragons so far from mankind's native ground.

Finally, he reached complete awareness.

He was telepathically alive to a range of millions of miles. He felt the dust which he had noticed earlier high above the ecliptic. With a thrill of warmth and tenderness, he felt the consciousness of the Lady May pouring over into his own. Her consciousness was as gentle and clear and yet sharp to the taste of his mind as if it were scented oil. It felt relaxing and reassuring. He could sense her welcome of him. It was scarcely a thought, just a raw emotion of greeting.

In a tiny remote corner of his mind, as tiny as the smallest toy he had ever seen in his childhood, he was still aware of the room and the ship, and of Father Moontree picking up a telephone and speaking to a Go-Captain in charge of the ship.

His telepathic mind caught the idea long before his ears could frame the words. The actual sound followed the idea the way that thunder on an ocean beach follows the lightning inward from far out over the seas.

"The Fighting Room is ready. Clear to planoform, sir."

IV.
The Play

Underhill was always a little exasperated the way that Lady May experienced things before he did.

He was braced for the quick vinegar thrill of planoforming, but he caught her report of it before his own nerves could register what happened.

Earth had fallen so far away that he groped for several milliseconds before he found the Sun in the upper rear righthand corner of his telepathic mind.

That was a good jump, he thought. *This way we'll get there in four or five skips.*

A few hundred miles outside the ship, the Lady May thought back at him, "O warm, O generous, O gigantic man! O brave, O friendly, O tender and huge Partner! O wonderful with you, with you so good, good, good, warm, warm, now to fight, now to go, good with you . . ."

He knew that she was not thinking words, that his mind took the clear amiable babble of her cat intellect and translated it into images which his own thinking could record and understand.

Neither one of them was absorbed in the game of mutual greetings. He reached out far beyond her range of perception to see if there was anything near the ship. It was funny how it was possible to do two things at once. He could scan space with his pin-set mind and yet at the same time catch a vagrant thought of hers, a lovely, affectionate thought about a son who had had a golden face and a chest covered with soft, incredibly downy white fur.

While he was still searching, he caught the warning from her.

We jump again!

And so they had. The ship had moved to a second planoform. The stars were different. The Sun was immeasurably far behind. Even the nearest stars were barely in contact. This was good Dragon country, this open, nasty, hollow kind of space. He reached farther, faster, sensing and looking for danger, ready to fling the Lady May at danger wherever he found it.

Terror blazed up in his mind, so sharp, so clear, that it came through as a physical wrench.

The little girl named West had found something—something immense, long, black, sharp, greedy, horrific. She flung Captain Wow at it.

Underhill tried to keep his own mind clear. "Watch out!" he shouted telepathically at the others, trying to move the Lady May around.

At one corner of the battle, he felt the lustful rage of Captain Wow as the big Persian tomcat detonated lights while he approached the streak of dust which threatened the ship and the people within.

The lights scored near misses.

The dust flattened itself, changing from the shape of a stingray into the shape of a spear.

Not three milliseconds had elapsed.

Father Moontree was talking human words and was saying in a voice that moved like cold molasses out of a heavy jar, "C-a-p-t-a-i-n." Underhill knew that the sentence was going to be "Captain, move fast!"

The battle would be fought and finished before Father Moontree got through talking.

Now, fractions of a millisecond later, the Lady May was directly in line.

Here was where the skill and speed of the Partners came in. She could react faster than he. She could see the threat as an immense Rat coming directly at her.

She could fire the light-bombs with a discrimination which he might miss.

He was connected with her mind, but he could not follow it.

His consciousness absorbed the tearing wound inflicted by the alien enemy. It was like no wound on Earth—raw, crazy pain which started like a burn at his navel. He began to writhe in his chair.

Actually he had not yet had time to move a muscle when the Lady May struck back at their enemy.

Five evenly spaced photonuclear bombs blazed out across a hundred thousand miles.

The pain in his mind and body vanished.

He felt a moment of fierce, terrible, feral elation running through the mind of the Lady May as she finished her kill. It was always disappointing to the cats to find out that their enemies disappeared at the moment of destruction.

Then he felt her hurt, the pain and the fear that swept over both of them as the battle, quicker than the movement of an eyelid, had come and gone. In the same instant there came the sharp and acid twinge of planoform.

Once more the ship went skip.

He could hear Woodley thinking at him. "You don't have to bother much. This old son-of-a-gun and I will take over for a while."

Twice again the twinge, the skip.

He had no idea where he was until the lights of the Caledonia space port shone below.

With a weariness that lay almost beyond the limits of thought, he threw his mind back into rapport with the pin-set, fixing the Lady May's projectile gently and neatly in its launching tube.

She was half dead with fatigue, but he could feel the beat of her heart, could listen to her panting, and he grasped the grateful edge of a "Thanks" reaching from her mind to his.

V.
The Score

They put him in the hospital at Caledonia.

The doctor was friendly but firm. "You actually got touched by that Dragon. That's as close a shave as I've ever seen. It's all so quick that it'll be a long time before we know what happened scientifically, but I suppose you'd be ready for the insane asylum now if the contact had lasted several tenths of a millisecond longer. What kind of cat did you have out in front of you?"

Underhill felt the words coming out of him slowly. Words were such a lot of trouble compared with the speed and the joy of thinking, fast and sharp and clear, mind to mind! But words were all that could reach ordinary people like this doctor.

His mouth moved heavily as he articulated words. "Don't call our Partners cats. The right thing to call them is Partners. They fight for us in a team. You ought to know we call them Partners, not cats. How is mine?"

"I don't know," said the doctor contritely. "We'll find out for you. Meanwhile, old man, you take it easy. There's nothing but rest that can help you. Can you make yourself sleep, or would you like us to give you some kind of sedative?"

"I can sleep," said Underhill. "I just want to know about the Lady May."

The nurse joined in. She was a little antagonistic. "Don't you want to know about the other people?"

"They're okay," said Underhill. "I knew that before I came in here."

He stretched his arms and sighed and grinned at them. He could see they were relaxing and were beginning to treat him as a person instead of a patient.

"I'm all right," he said. "Just let me know when I can go see my Partner."

A new thought struck him. He looked wildly at the doctor. "They didn't send her off with the ship, did they?"

"I'll find out right away," said the doctor. He gave Underhill a reassuring squeeze of the shoulder and left the room.

The nurse took a napkin off a goblet of chilled fruit juice.

Underhill tried to smile at her. There seemed to be something wrong with the girl. He wished she would go away. First she had started to be friendly and now she was distant again. *It's a nuisance being telepathic*, he thought. *You keep trying to reach even when you are not making contact.*

Suddenly she swung around on him.

"You pinlighters! You and your damn cats!"

Just as she stamped out, he burst into her mind. He saw himself a radiant hero, clad in his smooth suède uniform, the pin-set crown shining like ancient royal jewels around his head. He saw his own face, handsome and masculine, shining out of her mind. He saw himself very far away and he saw himself as she hated him.

She hated him in the secrecy of her own mind. She hated him because he was—she thought—proud and strange and rich, better and more beautiful than people like her.

He cut off the sight of her mind and, as he buried his face in the pillow, he caught an image of the Lady May.

"She *is* a cat," he thought. "That's all she is—a *cat!*"

But that was not how his mind saw her—quick beyond all dreams of speed, sharp, clever, unbelievably graceful, beautiful, wordless and undemanding.

Where would he ever find a woman who could compare with her?

THE IMMORTAL

by Gordon R. Dickson

The phone was ringing. He came up out of a sleep as dark as death, fumbled at the glowing button in the phone's base with numb fingers and punched it. The ringing ceased.

"Wander here," he mumbled.

"Major, this is Assignment. Lieutenant Van Lee. Scramble, sir."

"Right," he muttered.

"You're to show in Operations Room four-oh-nine at four hundred hours. Bring your personals."

"Right." Groggily he rolled over on his stomach and squinted at his watch in the glow from the button on the phone. In the pale light, the hands of his watch stood at twelve minutes after three—three hundred ten hours. Enough time.

"Understood, sir?"

"Understood, Lieutenant," he said.

"Very good, sir. Out." The phone went dead. For a moment the desire for sleep sucked at Jim Wander like some great black bog, then with a convulsive jerk he threw it and the covers off him in one motion and sat on the edge of his bed in the darkness, scrubbing at his face with an awkward hand.

After a moment, he turned the light on, got up, showered and dressed. As he shaved, he watched his face in the mirror.

It was still made up of the same roughly handsome, large-boned features he remembered, but the lines about the mouth and between the eyebrows under the tousled black hair, coursely curling up from his forehead, seemed deepened with the sleep. It could not be drink, he thought. He never drank even on rest-alert nowdays. Alcohol did nothing for him any more. It was just that nowdays he slept like a log—like a log water-soaked and drowning in some bottomless lake.

When he was finally dressed, he strapped on last of all his personals—his side-arm, the x-morphine kit, the little green thumbnail-square box holding the cyanide capsules. Then he left his room, went down the long sleeping corridor of the officers' quarters and out a side door into the darkness of predawn and the rain.

He could have gone around by the interior corridors to the Operations building, but it was a shortcut across the quadrangle and the rain and chill would wake him, drive the last longing for sleep from his bones. As he stepped out of the door the invisible rain, driven by a light wind, hit him in the face. Beyond were the blurred lights of the Operations building across the quadrangle.

Far off to his left thunder rolled. Tinny thunder—the kind heard at high altitudes, in the mountains. Beyond the rain and darkness were the Rockies. Above the Rockies the clouds. And beyond the clouds, space, stretching beyond the Pole Star to the Frontier.

Where he would doubtless be before the dawn rose, above this quadrangle, above these buildings, these mountains, and this Earth.

He entered the Operations building, showed his identification to the Officer of the Day, and took the lift tube up to the fourth floor. The frosted pane of the door to room four-oh-nine glowed with a brisk, interior light. He knocked on the door and went in without waiting for an answer.

Behind the desk inside sat General Mollen, and in a chair facing the general was a civilian of Jim's own age, lean and high-foreheaded, with the fresh skin and clear eyes of someone who has spent most of his years inside walls, sheltered from the weather. Both men looked up as Jim came in and Jim felt a twinge of sudden and reasonless dislike for the civilian. Perhaps, he thought, it was because the other looked so wide awake and businesslike this unnatural hour of the morning. Of course, so did General Mollen, but that was different.

As Jim came forward, both of the other men stood up.

"Jim," said the general, deep-voiced, his square face unsmiling. "I want you to meet Walt Trey. He's from the Geriatrics Bureau."

He would be, thought Jim grimly, shaking hands with the other. Walt Trey was as tall as Jim himself, if leaner boned. And his handshake was not weak. But still . . . here he was, thought Jim, a man as young as Jim himself, full of the juices of living and with all his attention focussed on the gray and tottering end years of life. A bodysnatcher—a snatcher of old bodies back from the brink of the grave for a few months or a few years.

"Pleased to meet you, Walt," he said, in a neutral tone.

"Good to meet you, Jim."

"Sit down," said the general. Jim pulled up a chair and they all sat down once more around the desk.

"What's up, sir?" asked Jim.

"Something special," answered Mollen. "That's why Walt here's been rung in on it. Do you happen to remember about the Sixty Ships Battle?"

"It was right after we found we had a frontier in common with the Laggi, wasn't it?" said Jim, slightly puzzled. "Back before we and they found out logistics made space wars unworkable. Sixty of our ships met forty-some of theirs beyond the Pole Star, and their ships were better. What about it?"

"Do you remember how the battle came out?" It was the civilian, Walt Trey, leaning forward with strange intensity.

Jim shrugged.

"Our ships were slower then. We hadn't started to design them for guarding a spatial border, instead of fighting pitched battles. They cut us up and suckered what was left into standing still while they set off a nova explosion," he said. He looked into the civilian's eyes and spoke deliberately. "The ships on the edge of the explosion were burst up like paper cutouts. The ones in the center—well, they just disappeared."

"Disappeared," said Walt Trey. He did not seem disturbed by Jim's vivid description of the nova and death. "That's the right word. Do you remember how long ago this was?"

"Nearly two hundred years ago," said Jim. He turned and looked impatiently at General Mollen, with a glance that said plainly, *what is this?*

"Look here, Jim," said the general. "We've got something to show you." He pushed aside the few papers on the surface of the desk in front of him and touched some studs on the edge of the desk. The overhead lights dimmed. The surface of the table became transparent and gave way to a scene of stars. To the three men seated around the desk top it was as if they looked down and out into an area of space a thousand light years across. To the civilian, Jim was thinking, the stars would be only a maze. To Jim himself, the image was long familiar.

Mollen's hands did things with the studs. Two hazy spheroids of dim light, each about six hundred light years in diameter along its longest axis, sprang into view—bright enough to establish their position and volume, not so bright as to hide the stars they enclosed. The center of one of the spheroids was the sun of Earth, and the farthest extent of this spheroid in one direction intermixed with an edge of the other spheroid beyond the Pole Star, Polaris.

"Our area of space," said Mollen's voice, out of the dimness around the table, "and the Laggi's, Walt. They block our expansion in that direction, and we block theirs in this. The distribution of the stars in this view being what it is, it's not practical for either race to go around the other. You see the Frontier area?"

"Where the two come together, yes," said the voice of Walt.

"Now, Jim—" said Mollen. "Jim commands a wing of our frontier guard ships, and he knows that area well. But nothing but unmanned drones of ours have ever gotten deep into Laggi territory beyond the Frontier and come back out again. Agreed, Jim?"

"Agreed, sir," said Jim. "More than ten, fifteen light years deep is suicide."

"Well, perhaps," said Mollen. "But let me go on. The Sixty Ships Battle was fought a hundred and ninety-two years ago—here." A bright point of light sprang into existence in the Frontier area. "One of the ships engaged in it was a one-man vessel with semianimate automatic control system, named by its pilot *La Chasse Gallerie*—you said something, Jim?"

The exclamation had emerged from Jim's lips involuntarily. And at the same time, foolishly, a slight shiver had run down his back. It had been years since he had run across the old tale as a boy.

"It's a French-Canadian ghost legend, sir," he said. "The legend was that voyageurs who had left their homes in eastern Canada to go out on the fur trade routes and who had died out there would be able to come back home one night of the year.

New Year's night. They'd come sailing in through the storms and snow in ghost canoes, to join the people back home and kiss the girls they wouldn't ever be seeing again. That's what they called the story, *La Chasse Gallerie*. It means the hunting of a type of butterfly that invades beehives to steal the honey.''

"The pilot of this ship was a French-Canadian,'' said Mollen. "Raoul Penard.'' He coughed dryly. "He was greatly attached to his home. *La Chasse Gallerie* was one of the ships near the center of the nova explosion, one of the ones that disappeared. At that time we didn't realize that the nova explosion was merely a destructive application of the principle used in trans-light drive. . . . You've heard of the statistical chance that a ship caught just right by a nova explosion could be transported instead of destroyed, Jim?''

"I'd hate to count on it, sir,'' said Jim. "Anyway, what's the difference? Modern ships can't be anticipated or held still long enough for any kind of explosion to be effective. Neither the Laggi nor we have used the nova for eighty years.''

"True enough,'' said Mollen. "But we aren't talking about modern ships. Look at the desk schema, Jim. Forty-three hours ago one of our deep unmanned probes returned from far into Laggi territory with pictures of a ship. Look.''

Jim heard a stud click. The stars shifted and drew back. Floating against a backdrop of unknown stars he saw the cone shape of a one-man space battlecraft, of a type forgotten a hundred and fifty years before. The view moved in close and he saw a name, abraded by dust and dimmed, but readable on the hull. He read it.

La Chasse Gallerie—the breath caught in his throat.

"It's been floating around in Laggi territory all this time?'' Jim said. "I can't believe—''

"More than that,'' Mollen interrupted him. "That ship's under power and moving.'' A stud clicked. The original scene came back. A bright line began at the extreme edge of the desk and began to creep toward the back limits of Laggi territory. It entered the territory and began to pass through.

"You see,'' said Mollen's voice out of the dimness, "it's coming back from wherever the nova explosion kicked it to, nearly two hundred years ago. It's headed back to our own territory. It's headed back, toward Earth.''

Jim stared at the line in fascination.

"No,'' he heard himself saying, "it can't be. It's some sort of Laggi trick. They've got a Laggi pilot aboard—— ''

"Listen," said Mollen. "The probe heard talking inside the ship. And it recorded. Listen——"

Again, there was a faint snap of a stud. A voice, a human voice, singing raggedly, almost absent-mindedly to itself, entered the air of the room and rang on Jim's ears.

". . .*en roulant ma boule, roulant*—" the singing broke off and the voice dropped into a mutter of a voice in a mixture of French and English, speaking to itself, mixing the two languages indiscriminately. Jim, who had all but forgotten the little French he had picked up as a boy in Quebec, was barely able to make out that the possessor of the voice was carrying on a running commentary to the housekeeping duties he was doing about the ship. Talking to himself after the fashion of hermits and lonely men.

"Now, then," said Jim, even while he wondered why he was protesting such strong evidence at all. "Didn't you say they had the early semianimate control systems then? They used brain tissue grown in a culture, didn't they? It's just the control system, parroting what it's heard, following out an early order to bring the ship back."

"Look again," said Mollen. The view changed once more to a closeup of *La Chasse Gallerie*. Jim looked and saw wounds in the dust-scarred hull—the slashing cuts of modern light weapons, refinements of the ancient laser beam-guns.

"The ship's already had its first encounter with the Laggi on its way home. It met three ships of a Laggi patrol—and fought them off."

"Fought them off? That old hulk?" Jim stared into the dimness where Mollen's face should be. "Three modern Laggi ships?"

"That's right," said Mollen. "It killed two and escaped from the third—and by rights it ought to be dead itself, but it's still coming. A control system might record a voice and head a ship home, but it can't fight off odds of three to one. That takes a living mind."

A stud clicked. Dazzling overhead light sprang on again and the desk top was only a desk top. Blinking in the illumination, Jim saw Mollen looking across at him.

"Jim," said the general, "this is a volunteer mission. That ship is headed dead across the middle of Laggi territory and it's going to be hit again before it reaches the Frontier. Next time it'll be cut to ribbons, or captured. We can't afford to have that happen. The pilot of that ship, this Raoul Penard, has too much to tell us, even beginning with the fact of how he happens to be alive at over two hundred years of age.'' He watched Jim closely. ''Jim, I'm asking you to take a section of four ships in to meet *La Chasse Gallerie* and bring her out.''

Jim stared at him. He found himself involuntarily wetting his lips and stopped the gesture.

''How deep?'' he asked.

''At least a hundred and fifty years in toward the heart of Laggi territory,'' said Mollen, bluntly. ''If you want to turn it down, Jim, don't hesitate. The man who pulls this off has got to go into it believing he can make it back out again.''

''That's me,'' said Jim. He laughed, the bare husk of a laugh. ''That's the way I operate, General. I volunteer.''

''Good,'' said Mollen. He sat back in his chair. ''There's just one more thing, then. Raoul Penard is older than any human being has a right to be and he's pretty certainly senile, if not out and out insane. We'll want a trained observer along to get as much information out of contact with the man as we can, in case you lose him and his ship getting back. That calls for a man with a unique background and experience in geriatrics and all the knowledge of the aging process. Walt, here, is the man. He'll replace your regular gunner and ride in your two-man ship with you.''

It was like a hard punch in the belly. Jim sucked in air and found he had jerked erect. Both men watched him. He waited a second, to get his voice under control. He spoke first to the general.

''Sir, I'll need a gunner. If there was ever a job where I'd need a gunner, it'd be this one.''

''As a matter of fact,'' said Mollen, slowly, and Jim could feel that this answer had been ready and waiting for him, ''Walt here is a gunner—a good one. He's a captain in the Reserves, Forty-Second Training Squadron. With a ninety-two point six efficiency rating.''

''But he's still a week-end warrior—'' Jim swung about on the lean geriatrics man. ''Have you ever done a tour of duty? Real duty? On the Frontier?''

''I think you know I haven't, Major,'' said Walt, evenly. ''If I'd had you'd have recognized me. We're about the same age, and there aren't that many on Frontier duty.''

''Then do you know what it's like—what it can be like out there?'' raged Jim. He knew his voice was getting away from him, scaling upward in tone, but he did not care. ''Do you know how the bandits can come out of nowhere? Do you know you can be hit before you know anyone's anywhere near around? Or the ship next to you can be hit and the screens have to stay open—that's regulation, in case of some miracle that there's something can be done? Do you know what it's like to sit there and watch a man you've lived with burning to death in a cabin he can't get out of? Or spilled out of a ship cut wide open, and lost back there somewhere . . . alive but lost . . . where you'll never be able to find him? Do you know what it might be like to be spilled out and lost yourself and faced with the choice of living three weeks, a month, two months in your suit in the one in a million chance of being found after all—or of taking your cyanide capsule? Do you know what that's like?"

"I know it," said Walt. His face had not changed. "The same way you do, as a series of possibilities for the most part. I know it as well as I can without having been wounded or killed."

"I don't think you do!" snapped Jim raggedly. His hands were shaking. He saw Walt looking at them.

"General," said Walt, "perhaps we should ask for another volunteer?"

"Jim's our best man," said Mollen. He had not moved, watching them both from behind the desk. "If I had a better man—or an equal man who was fresher—I'd have called him in instead. But what you're after is just about impossible, and only a man who can do the impossible can bring it off. Jim's that man. It's like athletic skills. Every so often a champion comes along, one in billions of people, who isn't just one notch up from the next contenders but ten notches up from the nearest. There's no point in sending you and five ships into Laggi territory with anyone else in command. You simply wouldn't come back. With Jim, you . . . may."

"I see," said Walt. He looked at Jim. "Regardless, I'm going."

"And you're taking him, Jim," said Mollen, "or turning down the mission."

"And if I turn it down?" Jim darted a glance at the general.

"I'll answer that," said Walt. Jim looked back at him. "If necessary, my Bureau will requisition a ship and I'll go alone."

Jim stared back at the other for a long moment, and felt the rage drain slowly away from him, to be replaced by a great weariness.

"All right," he said. "All right, Walt—General. I'll head

the mission.'' He breathed deeply, and glanced over Walt's civilian suit. ''How long'll it take you to get ready?''

''I'm ready now,'' said Walt. He reached down to the floor behind the desk and came up with a package of personals, side-arm, med-kit and cyanide box. ''The sooner the better.''

''All right. The five ships of the Section are manned and waiting for you,'' said Mollen. He stood up behind the desk and the two younger men got to their feet facing him. ''I'll walk down to Transmission Section with you.''

They went out together into the corridor and along it and down an elevator tube to a tunnel with a moving floorway. They stepped onto the gently rolling strip, which carried them forward onto a slightly faster strip, and then to a faster, and so on until they were flashing down the tunnel surrounded by air pumped at a hundred and twenty miles an hour in the same direction they traveled, so that they would not be blown off their feet. In a few minutes they came to the end, and air and strips decelerated so that they slowed and stepped at last into what looked like an ordinary office, but which was deep in the heart of a mountain. This, the memory returned to Jim, was in case the Transmission Section blew up on one of its attempts to transmit. The statistical chance was always there. Perhaps, this time . . .?

But Mollen had cleared them with the officer of the duty guard and they were moving on through other rooms to the suiting room, where Jim and Walt climbed into the unbelievably barrel-bodied suits that were actually small spaceships in themselves and in which—if they who wore them were unlucky and still would not take their cyanide—they might drift in space, living on recycled air and nourishments until they went mad, or died of natural causes.

—Or were found and brought back. The one in a million chance. Jim, now fully inside his suit, locked it closed.

''All set?'' It was Mollen's voice coming at him over the audio circuit of the suit. Through the transparent window of the headpiece he saw the older man watching him.

''All set, General.'' He looked over at Walt and saw him already suited and waiting. Trying to make points by being fast, thought Jim sardonically. With the putting on of the suit, the old feeling of sureness had begun to flow back into him, and he felt released. ''Let's go, bodysnatcher.''

''Good luck,'' said Mollen. He did not comment on the name Jim had thrown at the geriatrics man. Nor did Walt answer. Together they clumped across the room, waited for the tons-heavy explosion door to swing open, and clumped through.

On the floor of the vast cavern that was the takeoff area, five two-man ships sat like gray-white darts, waiting. Red "manned" lights glowed by each sealed port on the back four. Jim read their names as he stumped forward toward the open port of the lead ship, his ship, the *Fourth Mary*. The other four ships were the *Swallow*, the *Fair Maid*, the *Lela*, and the *Andfriend*. He knew their pilots and gunners well. The *Swallow* and the *Andfriend* were ships from his own command. They and the other two were good ships handled by good men. The best.

Jim led the way aboard the *Fourth Mary* and fitted himself into the forward seat facing the controls. Through his suit's receptors, he heard Walt sliding into the gunner's seat, behind and to the left of him. Already, in spite of the efficiency of the suit, he could feel the faint, enclosed stink of his own body sweat, and responding to the habit of many missions, his brain began to clear and come alive. He plugged his suit into the controls.

"Report," he said. One by one, in order, the *Swallow*, the *Fair Maid*, the *Lela*, and the *Andfriend* replied. . . .

"Transmission Section," said Jim, "this is Wander Section, ready and waiting for transmission."

"Acknowledged," replied the voice of the Transmission Section. There followed a short wait, during which as always Jim was conscious, as if through some extra sense, of the many-tons weight of the collapsed magnesium alloy of the ship's hulls bearing down on the specially reinforced concrete of the takeoff area. "Ready to transmit."

"Acknowledged," said Jim.

"On the count of four, then," said Transmission Section's calm, disembodied voice. "For Picket Nine, L Sector, Frontier Area, transmission of Wander Section, five ships. Counting now. Four. Three . . ." the unimaginable tension that always preceded transmission from one established point to another began to build a gearing-up of nerves that affected all the men on all the ships alike. "Two . . ." the voice of Transmission Section seemed to thunder at them along their overwrought nerves. "One . . ."

". . . Transmit!"

Abruptly, a wave of disorientation and nausea broke through

them, and was gone. They floated in dark and empty interstellar space, with the stars of the Frontier Area surrounding them, and a new voice spoke in their ear.

"Identify yourself," it said. "Identify yourself. This is Picket Nine requesting identification."

"Wander Section. Five ships." Jim did not bother to look at his instrument to find the space-floating sphere that was Picket Nine. It was out there somewhere, with twenty ships scattered around, up to half a light year away, but all zeroed in on this reception point where he and the other four ships had emerged. Had Jim been a Laggi Wing or Picket commander, he would not have transmitted into this area with twice twenty ships—no, nor with three times that many. "Confirm transmission notice from Earth? Five ship section for deep probe bandit territory. Wander Section Leader speaking."

"Transmission notice confirmed Wander Section Leader," crackled back the voice from Picket Nine. "Mission confirmed. You will not deship. Repeat, not deship. Local Frontier area has been scouted for slipover, and data prepared for flash transmission to you. You will accept data and leave immediately. Please key to receive data."

"Major—" began the voice of Walt, behind him.

"Shut up," said Jim. He said it casually, without rancor, as if he was speaking to his regular gunner, Leif Molloy. For a moment he had forgotten that he was carrying a passenger instead of a proper gunman. And there was no time to think about it now. "Acknowledge," he said to Picket Nine. "Transmit data, please."

He pressed the data key and the light above it sprang into being and glowed for nearly a full second before going dark again. That, thought Jim, was a lot of data—at the high speed transmission at which such information was pumped into his ship's computing center. That was one of the reasons the new computing units were evolved out of solid-state physics instead of following up the development of the semianimate brains such as the one abroad the ancient *La Chasse Gallerie*. The semianimate brains—living tissue in a nutrient solution—could not accept the modern need for sudden high-speed packing of sixteen hours worth of data in the space of a second or so.

Also, such living tissue had to be specially protected against high accelerations, needed to be fed and trimmed—and it died on you at the wrong times.

All the time Jim was thinking this with one part of his mind,

the other and larger part of his thinking process was driving
the gloved fingers of his right hand. These moved over a bank
of one hundred and twenty small black buttons, ten across and
twelve down, like the stops on a piano-accordion, and with the
unthinking speed and skill of the trained operator, he punched
them, requesting information out of the body of data just
pumped into his ship's computing center, building up from this
a picture of the situation, and constructing a pattern of action
to be taken as a result.

Evoked by the intricate code set up by combinations of the
black buttons under his fingers, the ghost voice of the computing
center whispered in his ear in a code of words and numbers
hardly less intricate.

"... transmit destination area one-eighty ell wye, Lag Sector
L forty-nine c at point twelve-five, thirteen-two, sixty-four-five.
Proceedings jumps ten ell wye, at inclination zforty-nine degrees
frontier midpoint. Optimum jumps two, point of three error
correctible. ..."

He worked steadily. The picture began to emerge. It would
not be hard getting in. It was never hard to do that. They could
reach *La Chasse Gallerie* in two transmissions or jumps across
some hundred and eighty light-years of distance, and locate
her in the area where she should then be, within an hour or
so. Then they could—theoretically at least—surround her, lock
on, and try to improve on the ten light-years of jump it seemed
was the practical limit of her pilot's or her control center's
computing possibilities.

With modern translight drive, the problem was not the ability
to move or jump any required distance, but the ability to compute correctly, in a reasonable time, the direction and distance
in which the move should be made. Such calculations took in
of necessity the position and movement of the destination area—
this in a galaxy where everything was in relative movement,
and only a mathematical fiction, the theoretical centerpoint of
the galaxy from which all distances were marked and measured,
was fixed.

The greater the distance, the more involved and time-consum-
ing the calculation. The law of diminishing returns would set
in, and the process broke down of its own weight—it took a
lifetime to calculate a single jump to a destination it would not
take quite a lifetime to reach by smaller, more easily calculable
jumps. It was this calculation time-factor that made it imprac-

tical for the human and Laggi races to go around each other's spatial territory. If we were all Raoul Penards, thought Jim grimly, with two hundred and more years of life coming, it'd be different. The thought chilled him; he did not know why. He put it out of his mind and went back to the calculations.

The picture grew and completed. He keyed his voice to the other ships floating in dark space around him.

"Wander Leader to Wander Section," he said. "Wander Leader to Wander Section. Prepare to shift into bandit territory. Key for calculations pattern for first of two jumps. Acknowledge, all ships of Wander Section."

The transmit section of his control board glowed briefly as the *Swallow,* the *Fair Maid,* the *Lela,* and the *Andfriend* pumped into their own computing centers the situation and calculations he had worked out with his own. Their voices came back, acknowledging.

"Lock to destination," said Jim. "Dispersal pattern K at destination. Repeat, pattern K, tight, hundred kilometer interval. Hundred kilometer interval." He glanced at the sweep second hand of the clock before him on his control board. "Transmit in six seconds. Counting. Five. Four. Three. Two. One. Transmit——"

Again, the disorientation, and the nausea.

Strange stars were around them.

"Check Ten," whispered Jim. It was the code for "make next jump immediately." "Three. Two. One. Transmit——"

Once again the wrench of dislocation. Nausea.

Darkness. They were alone amongst the enemy's stars. None of the other ships were in sight.

"*Swallow . . .*" came a whisper in his earphones as from somewhere unseen as a tight, short-range, light-borne beam touched the outside of the *Fourth Mary,* beaming its message to his ears. "*Fair Maid. Lela . . .*" a slightly longer pause. "*Andfriend.*"

Andfriend was always a laggard. Jim had braced her pilot about it a dozen times. But now was not the hour for reprimands. They were deep in Laggi territory, and the alien alert posts would have already picked up the burst of energy not only from their transmit off the Frontier, but from the second jump to over a hundred light-years deep in Laggi territory. Communication between the ships of the Section must be held to a minimum while the aliens were still trying to figure out where the second jump had landed the intruders.

Shortly, since they must know by now of the approximate position of *La Chasse Gallerie* and have ships on the way to kill her, they would put two and two together and expect to find the intruders in the same area. But for the moment Wander Section, if it lay low and quiet, could feel it was safely hidden in the immensities of enemy space.

Jim blocked off outside transmission, and spoke over the intercom to Walt.

"All right, bodysnatcher," he said. "What was it you wanted to say to me back at the Frontier?"

There was a slight pause before the other's voice came back.

"Sir——"

"Never mind that," said Jim. "I don't count Reserve officers as the real thing. As far as I'm concerned you're a civilian. What was it you wanted, Wa—bodysnatcher?"

"All right, Major," said the voice of Walt. "I won't bother about military manners with what I call you, and I won't bother with what you call me." There was a slight grimness of humor in the voice of the geriatrics man. "I wanted to say—I'd like to get in close enough to *La Chasse Gallerie* so that we can keep a tight beam connection with her hull at all times and I can record everything Penard says from the time of contact on. It'll be important."

"Don't worry," said Jim. "He'll be along in a few minutes, if my calculations were right, and I'll put you right up next to him. We're going to surround him with our ships, lock him in the middle of us with magnetics, and try to boost out as a unit at something more practical than the little ten light-year at a time jumps that seem to be all he's able to compute."

"You say he'll be along?" said Walt. "Why didn't we go directly to him?"

"And make it absolutely clear to the Laggi he's what we're after?" answered Jim. "As long as they don't know for sure, they have to assume we don't even know of his existence. So we stop ahead in his line of travel—lucky he's just plugging straight ahead without trying any dodges—and wait for him. We might even make it look like an accidental meeting to the Laggi"—Jim smiled inside the privacy of his suit's headpiece without much humor—"I don't think."

"Do you think you can lock on him without too much trouble——"

"Depends," answered Jim, "on how fast he starts shooting at us, when he sees us."

"Shooting at us?" There was incredulity in Walt's voice. "Why should he—oh." His voice dropped. "I see."

"That's right," said Jim, "we don't look like any human ship he could know about, and he's in territory where he's going to be expecting bandits, not friends."

"But what're you going to do to stop him shooting?"

"They dug up the recognition signals of the Sixty Ships Battle," said Jim. "Just pray he remembers them. And they've given me a voice signal that my blinker lights can translate and flash at him in the code he was working under at the time of the battle. Maybe it'll work, maybe it won't."

"It will," said Walt, calmly.

"Oh?" Jim felt harshness in his chest. "What makes you so sure?"

"It's my field, Major. It's my business to know how the aged react. And one of their common reactions is to forget recent events and remember the events of long ago. Their childhood. High points of their early life—and the Sixty Ships Battle will have been one of those."

"So you think Penard will remember?"

"I think so," said Walt. "I think he'll remember with almost hypnotic recall."

Jim grinned again, mirthlessly, privately in his suit.

"You'd better be right," he said. "It's one order of impossibility to pick him up and take him home. It's another to fight off the Laggi while we're doing it. To fight Penard at the same time would be a third order—and that's beyond mortal men."

"Yes," said Walt. "You don't like to think of man as anything but mortal, do you, Major?"

"Why, you—" Jim bit back the rest of the words that flung themselves into his throat. He sat rigid and sweating in his suit, his hand lying across the accessible flap that would let him reach in and draw his side-arm without losing atmosphere from inside the suit. This crum—this *crum*—he thought, who doesn't know what it's like to see men die. . . ! The impulse to do murder passed after a moment, leaving Jim trembling and spent. There was the sour taste of stomach acids in his mouth.

"We'll see," he said shakily over the intercom. "We'll see, bodysnatcher."

"Why put it in the future, Major?" said the voice of the other. "Why not tell me plainly what you've got against someone working in geriatrics?"

"Nothing," said Jim. "It's nothing to do with me. Let'm all live forever."

"Something wrong with that?"

"I don't see the point of it," said Jim. "You've got the average age up pushing a hundred. What good does it do?" His throat went a little dry. *I shouldn't talk so much,* he thought. But he went on and said it, anyway. "What's the use of it?"

"People are pretty vigorous up through their nineties. If we can push it further . . . . Here's Penard who's over two hundred——"

"And what's the use of it? Vigorous!" said Jim, the words breaking out of him. "Vigorous enough to totter around and sit in the sunlight. What do you think's the retirement age from Frontier duty?"

"I know what it is," said Walt. "It's thirty-two."

"Thirty-two." Jim sneered. "So you've got all these extra vigorous years of life for people, have you? If they're all that vigorous, why can't they ride a Frontier ship after thirty-two? I'll tell you why, bodysnatcher. It's because they're too old— too old physically, too old in the reflexes and the nerves! Snatch all the ancient bodies back from the brink of the grave, but you can't change that. So what good's your extra sixty-eight years?"

"Maybe you ought to ask Raoul Penard that," said Walt, softly.

A dark wave of pain and unhappiness rose inside Jim, so that he had to clench his teeth to hold it back from coming out in words.

"Never mind him," Jim said huskily. For a second it was as if he had been through it himself, all the endless years, refusing to die, beating his ship back toward the Frontier, and the Solar System, at little jumps of ten light-years' length apiece—and home. I'll get him home, thought Jim to himself— I'll get Penard to the home he's been after these two centuries if I have to take him through every Laggi Picket area between here and the Frontier. "Never mind him," Jim said again to Walt, "he was a fighter."

"He still is——" Walt was cut suddenly short by the ringing of the contact alarm. Jim's fingers slapped by reflex down on his bank of buttons and a moment later they swam up beside a dust-scarred cone shape with the faded legend *La Chasse Gallerie* visible on its side.

In the same moment, the other ships of Wander Section were appearing on other sides of the ancient spaceship. Their magnetic beams licked out and locked—and held, a fraction of a second before *La Chasse Gallerie* buckled like a wild horse and tried to escape by a jump at translight speeds.

The mass of the five other ships held her back.

"Hold—." Jim was whispering into the headpiece of his suit, and circuits were translating his old-fashioned phrases into blinking signal lights beamed at the cone-shaped ship. "Hold. This is Government Rescue Contingent, title Wander Section. Do not resist. We are taking you in tow—" the unfitness of the ancient word jarred in Jim's mouth as he said it. "We're taking you in tow to return you to Earth Headquarters. Repeat. . . ."

The flashing lights went on spelling the message out, over and over again. *La Chasse Gallerie* ceased fighting and hung docilely in the matching net of magnetic forces. Jim got a talk beam touching on the aged hull.

". . . home," a voice was saying, the same voice he had heard recorded in Mollen's office. "Chez moi . . ." it broke into a tangle of French that Jim could not follow, and emerged in accented English with the cadence of poetry, ". . . *Poleon, hees sojer never fight—more brave as dem poor habitants—Chenier, he try for broke de rank—Chenier come dead immediatement . . ."*

"La Chasse Gallerie, La Chasse Gallerie," Jim was saying over and over, while the blinking lights on his hull transformed the words into a ship's code two centuries dead, "can you understand me? Repeat, can you understand me? If so, acknowledge. Acknowledge . . ." There was no response from the dust-scarred hull, slashed by the Laggi weapons. Only the voice, reciting what Jim now recognized as a poem by William Henry Drummond, one of the early poets to write in the French-accented English of the French-Canadian in the late nineteenth century.

". . . *De gun day rattle lak' tonnere,"* muttered on the

---

*From "De Papineau Gun," by William Henry Drummond, in *The Habitant And Other French-Canadian Poems*, copyright 1897 by G.P. Putnam's Sons.

voice, *"just bang, bang, bang! dat's way she go—"* abruptly the voice of Raoul Penard shifted to poetry in the pure French of another poem by a medieval prisoner looking out the tower window of his prison on the springtime. The shift was in perfect cadence and rhyme with the earlier line in dialectical English.

"Le temps a laissé ton mantau—de vent, de froidure, et de pluie . . ."

"It's no use," said Walt. "We'll have to get him back to Earth and treatment before you'll be able to get through to him."

"All right," said Jim. "Then we'll head——"

The moan of an interior siren blasted through his suit.

"Bandits," yelped the voice of *Andfriend*. "Five bandits, sector six——"

"Bandits. Two bandits, sector two, fifteen hundred kilometers—" broke in the voice of *Lela*.

Jim swore and slapped his fingers down on the buttons. With all ships locked together, his jump impulse was sorted automatically through the computer center of each one so that they all jumped together in the direction and distance he had programmed. There was the wrench of feeling—and sudden silence.

The siren had cut off. The voices were silent. Automatic dispersal had taken place, and the other four ships were spreading out rapidly to distances up to a thousand kilometers on all sides, their receptors probing the empty space for half a light year in each direction, quivering, seeking.

"Looks like we got away," Walt's voice was eerie in its naturalness, breaking the stillness in Jim's headpiece. "Looks like they lost us."

"The hell they did!" said Jim, savagely. "They'll have unmanned detector probes strung out all the way from here to the Frontier. They know we're not going anyplace else."

"Then we'd better jump again——"

"Not yet! Shut up, will you!" Jim bit the words off hard at his lips. "The more they collect to hit us with here, the more we leave behind when we jump again. Sit still back there and keep your mouth shut. You're a gunner now, not a talker."

"Yes sir." There was no mockery in Walt's voice. This time Jim did not comment on the "sir."

The seconds moved slowly with the sweep hand of the clock in front of Jim. Inside the headpiece his face was dripping with perspiration. The blood creaked in his ears——.

Moan of siren!

"Bandits!" shouted the *Fair Maid*. "Four bandits——"

"Bandits!" "Bandits!"—Suddenly the helmet was full of warning cries from all the ships. The telltale sphere in front of Jim came alive with the green dots of Laggi ships, over and beyond the white dots of his own Section.

They came on, the green dots, with the illusion of seeming to spread apart as they advanced. They came on and——

Suddenly they were gone. They had winked out, disappeared as if they had never been there in the first place.

"Formation Charlie," said Jim tonelessly to the other four ships. They shifted their relative positions. Jim sat silent, sweat dripping off his chin inside his suit. He could feel the growing tension in the man behind him.

"Jump!" It was a whisper torn from a raw throat in Walt. "Why don't you jump?"

"Where to, bodysnatcher?" whispered back Jim. "They'll have planet-based computers the size of small cities working on our probabilities of movement now. Anywhere we jump now in a straight line for the Frontier, they'll be waiting for us."

"Then jump to a side point. Evade!"

"If we do that," whispered Jim, "we'll have to recalculate." He suddenly realized the other's whispering had brought him to lower his own voice to a thread. Deliberately he spoke out loud, but with transmission of the conversation to the other ships of the Section blocked off. "Recalculation takes time. They'll be using that time to find us—and they've got bigger and better equipment for it than the computing centers aboard these little ships."

"But what're we waiting for? Why'd they go away? Shouldn't we go now——"

"No!" snarled Jim. "They went away because they thought there weren't enough of them."

"Not enough? There were twice our number."

"Not enough," said Jim. "They want to kill us all at one swat. They don't want any of us to escape. It's not just *La Chasse Gallerie*. Enemy ships can't be allowed to get this deep into their territory and live. We'd do the same thing if Laggi ships came into our space. We'd have to make an object lesson of them—so they wouldn't try it again."

"But——"

"Bandits—Bandits! Bandits!"

Suddenly the pilots of all the vessels were shouting at once. Jim's hand slammed down on a button and four screens woke to life, showing the interior of the other four ships. The sight and sound of the other pilots and gunners were there before his eyes.

The sperical telltale was alive with green dots, closing in from all sectors of the area, racing to englobe the Wander Section.

"James! Pattern James!" Jim heard his own voice shouting to the other ships. "James. Hit, break out, and check Ten. Check Ten. . . ."

They were driving toward one group of the approaching green lights. *La Chasse Gallerie* was driving with them. Over the shouting back and forth of the Wander Section pilots came the voice of Raoul Penard, shouting, singing—a strange, lugubrious tune but in the cadence and tone of a battle song. As if through the winds of a nightmare, Jim heard him:

> *Frainchman, he don't lak to die in de fall!*
> *When de mairsh she am so full of de game!*
> *An de leetle bool-frog, he's roll veree fat . . .*
> *And de leetle mooshrat, he's jus' de same!*

The slow and feeble lasers of the old ship reached out toward the oncoming Laggi lights that were ships, pathetically wide of their mark. Something winked up ahead and suddenly the soft, uncollapsed metal of the point of the primitive, dust-scarred hull was no longer there. Then Wander Section had closed with some eight of the enemy.

The *Fourth Mary* suddenly bucked and screamed. Her internal temperature suddenly shot up momentarily to nearly two hundred degrees as a glancing blow from the light-weapon of one of the Laggi brushed her. There was a moment of insanity. Flame flickered suddenly in the interior of *Fair Maid*, obscuring the screen before Jim, picturing that ship's interior. Then they were past the enemy fifteen and Jim shouted hoarsely "Transmit!" at the same time that he locked his own magnetic beams on the chopped hull of *La Chasse Gallerie* and tried to take her through the jump alone.

It should not have been possible. But some sixth sense in the singing, crazed mind of Raoul Penard seemed to understand what Jim was attempting. The two ships jumped together under the *Fourth Mary*'s control, and suddenly all five ships floated within sight of each other amid the peace and darkness of empty space and the alien stars.

Into this silence came the soft sound of sobbing from one of the screens. Jim looked and saw the charred interior of the *Fair Maid*. Her pilot was out of his seat and half-crouched before the charred, barrel-suited figure in the gunner's chair.

"*Fair Maid*!" Jim had to repeat the call, more sharply. "*Fair Maid*! Acknowledge!"

The pilot's headpiece lifted. The sobbing stopped.

"*Fair Maid* here." The voice was thick-tongued, drugged-sounding. "I had to shoot my gunner, Wander Leader. He was burning up inside his suit. I had to shoot my gunner. He was burning up inside his——"

"*Fair Maid*!" snapped Jim. "Can you still compute and jump?"

"Yes . . ." said the drugged voice. "I can compute and jump, Wander Leader."

"All right, *Fair Maid*," said Jim. "You're to jump wide—angle off outside Laggi territory and then make your own way back to our side of the Frontier. Have you got that? Jump wide, and make your own way back. Jump far enough so that it won't be worth the Laggi's trouble to go after you."

"No!" The voice lost some of its druggedness. "I'm staying, Wander Leader, I'm going to kill some——"

"*Fair Maid*!" Jim heard his own voice snarling into his headpiece. "This Section has a mission—to bring back the ship we've just picked up in Laggi territory. You're no good on that mission—you're no good to this Section without a gunner. Jump wide and go home! Do you hear me? That's an order. Jump wide and go home!"

There was a moment's silence, and then the pilot's figure moved slowly and turned slowly back to sit down before his controls.

"Acknowledge, *Fair Maid*!" snapped Jim.

"Acknowledged," came the lifeless voice of the pilot in the burned interior of the ship. "Jumping wide and going home."

"Out then," said Jim, in a calmer voice. "Good luck getting back. So long, Jerry."

"So long, Wander Leader," came the numb reply. The gloved hands moved on the singed controls. *Fair Maid* vanished.

Jim sat back wearily in his pilot's chair. Hammering into

his ears came the voice of Raoul Penard, now crooning another
verse of his battle song:

> . . . *Come all you beeg Canada man*
> *Who want find work on Meeshegan,*
> *Dere's beeg log drive all troo our lan',*
> *You sure fin' work on Meesh——*

In a sudden reflex of rage, Jim's hand slapped down on a
button, cutting off in midword the song from *La Chasse Gallerie*.

"Major!"

The word was like a whip cracking across his back. Jim
started awake to the fact of his passenger-gunner behind him.

"Well, bodysnatcher!" he said. "Who's been feeding you
raw meat?"

"I think I've got my second wind in this race," answered
the even, cold voice of Walt. "Meanwhile, how about turning
Penard back on? My job's to record everything I can get from
him, and I can't do that with the talk beam between us shut off."

"The *Fair Maid*'s gunner just died——"

"Turn the talk beam on!"

Jim reached out and turned it on, wondering a little at himself.
I should feel like shooting him at this moment, he thought.
Why don't I? Penard's voice sang at him once again.

"Look," Jim began. "When a man dies and a ship is
lost——"

"Have you looked at Penard's ship, Major?" interrupted the
voice of Walt. "Take a look. Then maybe you'll understand
why I want the talk beam on just as long as there's any use."

Jim turned and looked at the screen that showed the cone-
shaped vessel. He stared.

If *La Chasse Gallerie* had been badly cut up before, she was
a floating chunk of scrap now. She had been slashed deep in
half a dozen directions by the light beams of the Laggi ships.
And the old-fashioned ceramet material of her hull, built before
collapsed metals had been possible, had been opened up like
cardboard under the edge of red-hot knives. Jim stared, hearing
the voice of Penard singing in his ears, and an icy trickle went
down his perspiration-soaked spine.

"He can't be alive," Jim heard himself saying. If a hit that
did not even penetrate the collapsed metal hull of the *Fair Maid*
could turn that ship's interior into a charred, if workable, area—

what must those light weapons of the enemy have done to the interior of the old ship he looked at now? But Raoul still sang from it his song about lumbering in Meeshegan.

"Nobody could be alive in that," Jim said. "I was right. It must be just his semianimate control system parroting him and running the ship. Even at that, it's a miracle it's still working——"

"We don't know," Walt's voice cut in on him. "And until we know we have to assume it's Raoul himself, still alive. After all, his coming back at all is an impossible miracle. If that could happen, it could happen he's still alive in that ship now. Maybe he's picked up some kind of protection we don't know about."

Jim shook his head, forgetting that probably Walt could not see this silent negative. It was not possible that Penard was alive. But—he roused himself back to his duty. He had a job to do.

His fingers began to dance over the black buttons in their ranks before him, working out the situation, planning his next move.

"K formation," he said automatically to the other ships, but did not even glance at the telltale sphere to make sure they obeyed correctly. Slowly, the situation took form. He was down one ship, from five to four of them, and that reduced the number of practical fighting and maneuvering formations by a factor of better than three. And there was something else. . . .

"Walt," he said, slowly.

"Yes, Major?"

"I want your opinion on something," said Jim. "When we jumped out of the fight area just now, it was a jump off the direct route home and to the side of nearly sixty light-years. I had to try to pick up *La Chasse Gallerie* and bring her with us. Penard let me do that without fighting me with his own controls. Now, what I want to know is—and it's almost unimaginable that he's got power on that hulk, anyway, but he obviously has—will he let me move him from now on without fighting me, once I slap a magnetic on him? In other words, whether he's a man or a semianimate control, was that a fluke last time, or can I count on it happening again?"

Walt did not answer immediately. Then . . .

"I think you can count on it," he said. "If Raoul Penard is alive in there, the fact he reacted sensibly once should be an indication he'll do it again. And if you're right about it being just a control center driving that ship, then it should react consistently in the same pattern to the same stimulus.''

"Yeah . . ." said Jim softly. "But I wonder which it is—is Penard in there, alive or dead? Is it a man we're trying to get out? Or a control center?"

"Does it a matter?" said the level voice of Walt.

Jim stiffened.

"Not to you, does it, bodysnatcher?" he said. "But I'm the man that has to order men to kill themselves to get that ship home." Something tightened in his throat. "You know that's what hit me when I first saw you in Mollen's office, but I didn't know what it was. You haven't got guts inside you, you've got statistical tables and a computer."

He could hear his own harsh breathing in the headpiece of his suit as he finished talking.

"You think so?" said Walt's voice, grimly. "And how about you, Major? The accidents of birth and change while you were growing up gave you a one-in-billions set of mind and reflexes. You were born to be a white knight and slay dragons. Now you're in the dragon-slaying business and something's gone wrong with it you can't quite figure out. Something's gone sour, hasn't it?"

"Shut up!" said Jim, sweating. He felt his gloved hand resting on the access flap to his side-arm inside the suit. *I'm within my rights,* the back of his mind told him, crazily, *regulations provide for it. The pilot of a two-man ship is still the captain with the power of life and death in emergency over his crew even if that crew is only one man. If I shot him and gave a good reason, they might suspect, but they couldn't do anything. . . .*

"No," said Walt. "You've been going out of your way ever since you laid eyes on me to provoke this—now listen to it. Your nerves are shot, Major. You've a bad case of combat fatigue, but you won't quit and you're so valuable that people like Mollen won't make you quit."

"Play-party psychiatrist, are you?" demanded Jim through gritted teeth. Walt ignored him.

"You think I didn't have a chance to look at your personal history before I met you?" said Walt. "You know better than to think that. You're a Canadian yourself, and your background is Scotch and French. That's all anyone needs to know to read the signs—and the signs all read the same way. Your ship's named the *Fourth Mary*. And the *Fourth Mary* was the one that died, remember?" Abruptly he quoted from the old Scots ballad: "*Last night there were four Marys—tonight there'll be but three——*"

"*Shut up!*" husked Jim, the words choking in his throat.

"The signs read 'dead,' Major. All of them, including the fact you hate me for being in the business of trying to make people live longer. It was victory over evil you wanted in the first place—like the evil that makes men burn and die in their Frontier ships. Victory, or death. And now that you've been worn down to the conclusion that you can't win that victory, you want death. But you're not built right for suicide. That's the trouble. . . ."

Jim tried to speak, but the strained muscles of his throat let out only a little, wordless rasp of air.

"Death's got to come and take you, Major," said Walt. There was a trace of something like brutality in his voice. "And he's got to take you against the most of your strength, against all your fighting will. He's got to take you in spite of yourself. *And Death can't do it*! That's what's wrong with you, isn't it, Major?" Walt paused. "That's why you don't want to grow old and be forced to leave out here, where Death lives."

Walt's voice broke off. Jim sat, fighting for breath, his gloved fingers trembling on the access flap to the side-arm. After a little, his breath grew deeper again, and he forced himself to turn back to his computations. Aside from the habit-instructed section of his mind that concerned itself with this problem, the rest of him was mindless.

I've got to do something, he thought. *I've got to do something*. But nothing would come to mind. Gradually the careening vessel of his mind righted itself, and he came back to a sense of duty—to Wander Section and his mission. Then suddenly a thought woke in him.

"Raoul Penard's got to be dead," he said quite calmly to Walt. "Somehow, what we've been hearing and what we've been watching drive and fight that ship is the semianimate control center. How it got to be another Raoul Penard doesn't matter. The tissue they used kept growing, and no one ever thought to keep one of them in contact with a man twenty-four hours a day for his lifetime. So it's the alter-ego, the control center we've got to bring in. And there's a way to do that."

He paused and waited. There was a second of silence, and then Walt's voice spoke.

"Maybe I underestimated you, Major."

"Maybe you did," said Jim. "At any rate, here it is. In no more than another half hour we're going to be discovered here. Those planet-based big computers have been piling up data on our mission here and on me as Leader of Section, and their picture gets more complete every time we move and they can get new data. If we dodged away from here to hide again, next time they'd find us even faster. And in two more hides they'd hit us almost as soon as we got hid. So there's no choice to it. We've got to go for the Frontier now."

"Yes," said Walt. "I can see we do."

"You can," said Jim. "And the Laggi can. Everybody can. But they also know I know that they've got most of the area from here to the Frontier covered. Almost anywhere we come out they'll be ready to hit us within seconds, with ships that are simply sitting there, ready to make jump to wherever we emerge, their computations to the forty or fifty areas within easy jump of them already computed for them by the big planet-based machines. So, there's only one thing left for me to do, as they see it—go wide."

"Wide?" said Walt. He sounded a trifle startled.

"Sure," said Jim, grinning mirthlessly to himself in the privacy of his suit. "Like I sent *Fair Maid*. But there's a difference between us and *Fair Maid*. We've got *La Chasse Gallerie*. And the Laggi'll follow us. We'll have to keep running—outward until their edge in data lets them catch up with us. And their edge in ship numbers finishes us off. The Laggi ships won't quit on our trail—even if it means they won't get back themselves. As I said a little earlier, enemy ships can't be allowed to get this deep into their territory and get home again."

"So you're going wide," said Walt. "What's the use? It just puts off the time——"

"I'm not going wide." Jim grinned privately and mirthlessly once more. "That's what the Laggi think I'll do, hoping for a miracle to save us. I'm going instead where no one with any sense would go—right under their weapons. I've computed two jumps to the Frontier, which is the least we can make it in. We'll lock on and carry *La Chasse Gallerie*, and when we come out of the jump we'll come out shooting. Blind. We'll blast our way through whatever's there and jump again as fast as we can. If one of us survives, that'll be all that's necessary to lock on to *La Chasse Gallerie* and jump her to the Frontier.

If none of us does—well, we've done our best."

Once more he paused. Walt said nothing.

"Now," said Jim, grinning like a death's head. "If that was a two-hundred-year-old man aboard that wreck of a ship there, and maybe burned badly or broken up by what he's been through so far, that business of jumping and coming out at fighting accelerations would kill him. But," said Jim, drawing a deep breath. "It's not a man. It's a control center. And a control center ought to be able to take it. . . . Have you got anything to say, Walt?"

"Yes," said Walt, quietly. "Officially I protest your assumption that Raoul Penard is dead, and your choice of an action which might be fatal to him as a result."

Jim felt a kind of awe stir in him.

"By—" he broke off. "Bodysnatcher, you really expect to come out of this alive, don't you?"

"Yes," said Walt, calmly. "I'm not afraid of living—the way you are. You don't know it, Jim, but there's a lot of people like you back home, and I meet them all the time. Ever since we started working toward a longer life for people, they've turned their backs on us. They say there's no sense in living a longer time—but the truth is they're afraid of it. Afraid a long life will show them up as failures, that they won't have death as an excuse for not making a go of life."

"Never mind that!" Jim's throat had gone dry again. "Stand to your guns. We're jumping now—and we'll be coming out shooting." He turned swiftly to punch the data key and inform his four remaining other ships. "Transmitting in five seconds. Five. Four. Three. Two. One. Transmit——"

Disorientation. Nausea. . . .

The stars were different. Acceleration hit like a tree trunk ramming into Jim's chest. His fingers danced on the sublight control buttons. The voice of Raoul Penard was howling his battle-song again:

> . . . When you come drive de beeg saw log,
> You got to jump jus' lak de frog!
> De foreman come, he say go sak!
> You got in de watair all over your back!

"Check Ten!" shouted Jim. "All ships check Ten. Transmit in three seconds. Three. Two——"

No Laggi ships in the telltale sphere. . . .

Suddenly the *Fourth Mary* bucked and slammed. Flame flickered for a fraction of a second through the cabin. The telltale was alive with green lights, closing fast.

Fifteen of them or more. . . . Directly ahead of the *Fourth Mary* were three of them in formation, closing on her alone. In Jim's ears rang the wild voice of Penard:

> *P'raps you work on drive, tree-four day—*
> *You find dat drive dat she don' pay.*

"Gunner!" cried Jim, seeing the green lights almost on top of him. It was as desperate as a cry for help. In a moment——

Two of the green lights flared suddenly and disappeared. The third flashed and veered off.

"Bodysnatcher!" yelped Jim, suddenly drunk on battle delight. "You're a gunner! A real gunner!"

"More to the left and up—Sector Ten—" said a thick voice he could hardly recognize as Walt's, in his ear. He veered, saw two more green lights. Saw one flare and vanish—saw suddenly one of his own white lights flare and vanish as the scream of torn metal sounded from one of the screens below him. Glancing at the screens, he saw for the moment the one picturing *Andfriend's* cabin, showing the cabin split open, emptied and flattened for a second before the screen went dark and blank.

Grief tore at him. And rage.

"Transmit at will!" he howled at the other ships. "Check Ten! Check Ten——"

He slapped a magnetic on the battered cone shape that fled by a miracle still beside him and punched for the jump——

Disorientation. Nausea. And——

The stars of the Frontier. Jim stared into his screens. They floated in empty space, three gray-white dart shapes and the ravaged cone of *La Chasse Gallerie. Lela* rode level with Jim's ship, but *Swallow* was slowly turning sideways like a dying fish drifting in the ocean currents. Jim stared into the small screen showing the *Swallow's* interior. The two suited figures sat in a blackened cabin, unmoving.

"*Swallow!*" said Jim, hoarsely. "Are you all right? Acknowledge. Acknowledge!"

But there was no answer from the two figures, and the *Swallow* continued to drift, turning, as if she was sliding off some invisible slope into the endless depths of the universe. Jim shook with a cold, inner sickness like a chill. They're just unconscious, he thought. They have to be just unconscious. Otherwise they wouldn't have been able to make the jump to here.

". . . *Brigadier!*" the voice of Penard was singing with strange softness . . .

> . . . *repondit Pandore*
> *Brigadier! vous avez raison,*
> *Brigadier! respondit Pandore*
> *Brigadier! vous avez raison!*

Jim turned slowly to look in to the screen showing *La Chasse Gallerie*. He stared at what he saw. If the old ship had been badly slashed before, she was a ruin now. Nothing could be alive in such a wreck. Nothing. But the voice of Penard sang on.

"No . . ." muttered Jim out loud, unbelievingly. "Not even a semianimate control center could come through that. It couldn't——"

"Identify yourself!" crackled a voice suddenly on Jim's ears. "Identify yourself! This is Picket Six. B Sector, Frontier area."

"Wander Section . . ." muttered Jim, automatically thumbing the communications control, still staring at the tattered cone shape of *La Chasse Gallerie*. Once more he remembered the original legend about the return of the dead voyageurs in their ghost canoes, and a shiver went down his back. "Wander Section, returning from deep probe and rescue mission into Laggi territory. Five ships with two lost and one sent wide and home, separately. Wander Leader speaking."

"Wander Leader!" crackled the voice from Picket Six. "Alert has been passed all along the Frontier for you and your ships and orders issued for your return. Congratulations, Wander Section, and welcome back."

"Thanks, Picket Six," said Jim, wearily. "It's good to be back, safe on this side of the Frontier. We had half the Laggi forces breathing down our——"

A siren howled from the control board, cutting him off. Unbelieving, Jim jerked his head about to stare at the telltale sphere. It was filled with the white lights of the ships of Picket Six in formation spread out over a half light-year of distance. But, as he watched, green lights began to wink into existence all about his own battered Section. By sixes, by dozens, they were jumping into the area of Picket Six on the human side of the Frontier.

"Formation B! Formation B!" Jim found himself shouting at the *Lela* and the *Swallow*. But only the *Lela* responded. The *Swallow*, lost to ordinary vision, was still on its long, drowning fall into nothingness still. "Cancel that. *Lela*, follow me. Help me carry *La Chasse*——"

His voice was all but drowned out by transmissions from Picket Six.

"Alert General. Alert General! All Pickets, all Sectors!" Picket Six was calling. "Full fleet Laggi attack. Three wings enemy forces already in this area. We are overmatched! Repeat. We are overmatched! Alert General——"

At maximum normal acceleration, the *Fourth Mary* and *Lela*, with *La Chasse Gallerie* caught in a magnetic grip between them, were running from the enemy ships, while Jim computed frantically for a jump to any safe area, his fingers dancing on the black buttons.

"Alert General! All ships Picket Six hold until relieved! All ships hold! Under fire here at Picket Six. We are under——" the voice of Picket Six went dead. There was a moment's silence and then a new voice broke in.

"——This is Picket Five. Acknowledge, Picket Six. Acknowledge!" Another moment of silence, then the new voice went on. "All ships Picket Six. This is Picket Five taking over. Picket Five taking over. Our ships are on the way to you now, and the ships from other Sectors. Hold until relieved! Hold until relieved——"

Jim fought the black buttons, too busy even to swear.

"Wander Section! Wander Section!" shouted the voice of Picket Five. "Acknowledge!"

"Wander Section. Acknowledging!" grunted Jim.

"Wander Section! Jump for home. Wander Leader, key for data. Key to receive data, and Check Ten. Check Ten."

"Acknowledged!" snapped Jim, dropping his own slow computing. He keyed for data, saw the data light flash and knew he had received into his computing center the information for the jump back to Earth. "Hang on *Lela*!" he shouted. "Here we go. . . ."

He punched for jump——

Disorientation. Nausea. And . . .

Peace.

The *Fourth Mary* lay without moving under the landing lights of a concrete pad in the open, under the nighttime sky and the stars of Earth. The daylight hours had passed while Wander Section had been gone. Next to the *Fourth Mary* lay the dark, torn shape of *La Chasse Gallerie,* and beyond the ancient ship lay *Lela.* Three hundred light-years away the Frontier battle would still be raging. Laggi and men were out there dying, and they would go on dying until the Laggi realized that Wander Section had finally made good its escape. Then the Laggi ships would withdraw from an assault against a Frontier line that two hundred and more years of fighting had taught was unbreachable by either combatant. But how many, thought Jim with a dry and bitter bleakness, would die before the withdrawal was made?

He punched the button to open the port of the *Fourth Mary*, and got clumsily to his feet in the bulky suit. During the hours just past he had forgotten he was wearing it. Now, it was like being swaddled in a mattress. He was as thoroughly wet with sweat as if he had been in swimming with his clothes on.

There was no sound coming from *La Chasse Gallerie.* Had the voice of Raoul Penard finally been silenced? Sodden with weariness, Jim could not summon up the energy even to wonder about it. He turned clumsily around and stumbled back through the ship four steps and out the open port, vaguely hearing Walt Trey rising and following behind him.

He stumped heavy-footed across the concrete toward the lights of the Receiving Section, lifting like an ocean liner out of a sea of night. It seemed to him that he was a long time reaching the door of the Section, but he kept on stolidly, and at last he passed through and into a desuiting room. Then attendants were helping him off with his suit.

In a sort of dream he stripped off his soaked clothing and showered, and put on a fresh jumper suit. The cloth felt strange and harsh against his arms and legs as if his body as well as what was inside him had been rubbed raw by what he had just been through. He walked heavily on into the debriefing room, and dropped heavily into one of the lounge chairs.

A debriefing officer came up to him and sat down in a chair opposite, turning on the little black recorder pickup he wore at his belt. The debriefing officer began asking questions in the safe, quiet monotone that had been found least likely to trigger off emotional outbursts in the returned pilots. Jim answered slowly, too drained for emotion.

". . . No," he said at last. "I didn't see *Swallow* again.

She didn't acknowledge when I called for Formation B, and I had to go on without her. No, she never answered after we reached the Frontier.''

"Thank you, Major." The debriefing officer got to his feet, clicking off his recorder pickup, and went off. An enlisted man came around with a tray of glasses half filled with brownish whisky. He offered it first to the pilot and the gunner of the *Lela*, who were standing together on the other side of the room with a debriefing officer. The two men took their glasses absent-mindedly and drank from them without reaction, as if the straight liquor had been water. The enlisted man brought his tray over to where Jim sat.

Jim shook his head. The enlisted man hesitated.

"You're supposed to drink it, sir," he said. "Surgeon's orders.''

Jim shook his head again. The enlisted man went away. A moment later he came back followed by a major with the caduceus of the Medical Corps on his jacket lapel.

"Here, Major," he said to Jim, taking a glass from the tray and holding it out to Jim. "Down the hatch.''

Jim shook his head, rolling the back of it against the top of the chair he sat in.

"It's no good," he said. "It doesn't do any good.''

The Medical Corps major put the glass back on the tray and leaned forward. He put his thumb gently under Jim's right eye and lifted the lid with his forefinger. He looked for a second, then let go and turned to the enlisted man.

"That's all right," he said. "You can go on.''

The enlisted man took his tray of glasses away. The doctor reached into the inside pocket of his uniform jacket and took out a small silver tube with a button on its side. He rolled up Jim's right sleeve, put the end of the tube against it and pressed the button.

Jim felt what seemed like a cooling spray against the skin of his arm. And something woke in him, after all.

"What're you doing?" he shouted, struggling to his feet. "You can't knock me out now! I've got two ships not in yet. The *Fair Maid* and the *Swallow*——" The room began to tilt around him. "You can't—" his tongue thickened into unintelligibility. The room swung grandly around him and he felt the medical major's arms catching him. And unconsciousness closed upon him like a trap of darkness.

He slept, evidently for a long time, and when he woke he was not in the bed of his own quarters but in the bed of a hospital room. Nor did they let him leave it for the better part of a week, and when he did, it was to go on sixty days' leave. Nonetheless, he had had time, lying there in the peaceful, uneventful hospital bed, to come to an understanding with himself. When he got out he went looking for Walt Trey.

He located the geriatrics man finally on the secret site where *La Chasse Gallerie* was being probed and examined by the Geriatrics Bureau. Walt was at work with the crew that was doing this, and for some little time word could not be gotten to him; and without his authorization, Jim could not be let in to see him.

Jim waited patiently in a shiny, sunlit lounge until a young man came to guide him into the interior of a vast building where *La Chasse Gallerie* lay dwarfed by her surroundings and surrounded by complicated items of equipment. It was apparently a break period for most of the people working on the old ship, for only one or two figures were to be seen doing things with this equipment outside the ship. The young man shouted in through the open port of *La Chasse Gallerie*, and left. Walt came out and shook hands with Jim.

There were dark circles under Walt's eyes and he seemed thinner under the loose shirt and slacks he wore.

"Sorry to hear about *Swallow*," he said.

"Yes," said Jim, a little bleakly, "they think she must have drifted back into Laggi territory. The unmanned probes couldn't locate her, and the Laggi may have taken her in. That's what chews on you, of course, not knowing if her pilot and gunner were dead or not. If they were, then there's nothing to think about. But if they weren't . . . we'll never know what becomes of them—" He broke off that train of thought with a strong effort of will. "*Fair Maid* made it in, safely. Anyway, it wasn't about the Section I came to see you."

"No," Walt looked at him sympathetically. "It was about Raoul Penard you came, wasn't it?"

"I couldn't find out anything. Is it—is he, alive?"

"Yes," said Walt. "He's alive."

"Can you get through to him? What came to me," said Jim quickly, "while I was resting up in the hospital, was that I finally began to understand the reason behind all his poetry-quoting, and such. It struck me that he must have started all that deliberately. To remind himself of where he was trying to get back to. To make it sharp and clear in his mind so he couldn't forget it.''

"Yes," said Walt nodding. "You're right. He wanted insurance against quitting, against giving up.''

"I thought so. You were right—bodysnatcher," Jim grinned with slight grimness at the other man. "I'd been trying to quit myself. Or find something that could quit me. You were right all the way down the line. I am a dragon-slayer. I was born that way, I'm stuck with it and I can't change it. I want to go through the Laggi, or around them and end this damn murderous stalemate. But I can't live long enough. None of us can. And so I wanted to give up.''

"And you aren't now?''

"No," said Jim, slowly. "It's still no use, but I'm going to keep hoping—for a miracle.''

"Miracles are a matter of time," said Walt. "To make yourself a millionaire in two minutes is just about impossible. To make it in two hundred years is practically a certainty. That's what we're after in the Bureau. If we could all live as long as Penard, all sorts of things would become possible.''

"And he's alive!" said Jim, shaking his head slowly. "He's really alive! I didn't even want to believe it, it was so far-fetched—" Jim broke off. "Is he . . .''

"Sane? No," said Walt. "And I don't think we'll ever be able to make him so. But maybe I'm wrong. As I say, with time, most near-impossibilities become practicabilities.'' He stepped back from the open port of *La Chasse Gallerie*, and gestured to the interior. "Want to come in?''

Jim hesitated.

"I don't have a Secret clearance for this project—" he began.

"Don't worry about it," interrupted Walt. "That's just to keep the news people off our necks until we decide how to handle this. Come on.''

He led the way inside. Jim followed him. Within, the ancient metal corridor leading to the pilot's compartment seemed swept clean and dusted shiny, like some exhibit in a museum. The interior had been hung with magnetic lights, but the gaps and tears made by Laggi weapons let almost as much light in. The pilot's compartment was a shambles that had been tidied and cleaned. The instruments and control panel were all but obliterated and the pilot's chair half gone. A black box stood in the center of the floor, an incongruous piece of modern equipment, connected by a thick gray cable to a bulkhead behind it.

"I wasn't wrong, then," said Jim, looking around him. "No human body could have lived through this. It was the semianimate control center that was running the ship as Penard's alterego, then, wasn't it? The man isn't really alive?"

"Yes," said Walt, "and no. You were right about the control center somehow absorbing the living personality of Penard. But look again. Could a control center like that, centered in living tissue floating and growing in a nutrient solution with no human hands to care for it—could something like that have survived this, either?"

Jim looked around at the slashed and ruined interior. A coldness crept into him and he thought once more of the legend of the long ghost cargo canoes sailing through the snow-filled skies with their dead crews, home to the New Year's feast of the living.

"No . . ." he said slowly, through stiff lips. "Then . . . where is he?"

"Here!" said Walt, reaching out with his fist to strike the metal bulkhead to which the gray cable was attached. The dull boom of the struck metal reverberated on Jim's ears. Walt looked penetratingly at Jim.

"You were right," said Walt, "when you said that the control center had become Penard—that it *was* Penard, after the man died. Not just a recordful of memories, but something holding the vital, decision-making spark of the living man himself. But that was only half the miracle. Because the tissue living in the heart of the control center had to die, too, and just as the original Penard knew he would die, long before he could get home, the tissue-Penard knew it, too. But their determination, Penard's determination, to do something, solved the problem."

He stopped and stood staring at Jim, as if waiting for some sign that he had been understood.

"Go on," said Jim.

"The control system," said Walt, "was connected to the controls of the ship itself through an intermediate solid-stage element which was the grandfather of the wholly inanimate solid-state computing centers in the ships you drive nowadays. The link was from living tissue through the area of solid-state physics to gross electronic and mechanical controls."

"I know that," said Jim. "Part of our training——"

"The living spark of Raoul Penard, driven by his absolute determination to get home, passed from him into the living tissue of the semianimate controls system," went on Walt, as if Jim had not spoken. "From there it bridged the gap by a sort of neurobiotaxis into the flow of impulse taking place in the solid-state elements. Once there, below all gross levels, there was nothing to stop it infusing every connected solid part of the ship."

Walt swept his hand around the ruined pilot's compartment.

"This,' he said, "is Raoul Penard. And this!" Once more he struck the bulkhead above the black box. "The human body died. The tissue activating the control center died. But Raoul came home just as he had been determined to do!"

Walt stopped talking. His voice seemed to echo away into the silence of the compartment.

"And doing it," said Walt, more quietly, "he brought home the key we've been hunting for in the Bureau for over two hundred years. It's pulled the plug on a dam behind which there's been piling up a flood of theory and research. What we needed to know was that the living human essence could exist independent of the normal human biochemical machinery. Now, we know it. It'll take a little time, but soon it won't be necessary for the vital element in anyone of us to admit extinction."

But Jim was only half listening. Something else had occurred to him, something so poignant it contracted his throat painfully.

"Does he know?" Jim asked. "You said he's insane. But does he know he finally got here? Does he know he made it—home?"

"Yes," said Walt. "We're sure he does. Listen. . . ."

He reached down and turned a control on the black box. And softly the voice of Raoul Penard came out of it, as if the man was talking to himself. But it was a quieter, happier talking to himself than Jim had heard before. Raoul was quoting another of the poems of William Henry Drummond. But this time it was a poem entirely in English and there was no trace of accent in the words at all:

O, Spirit of the mountain that speaks to us to-night,
Your voice is sad, yet still recalls past visions of delight,
When 'mid the grand old Laurentides, old when the earth
    was new,

With flying feet we followed the moose and caribou.
And backward rush sweet memories, like fragments of a
  dream,
We hear the dip of paddles. . . .

Raoul's voice went on, almost whispering contentedly to itself. Jim looked up from listening, and saw Walt's eyes fixed on him with a strange, hard look he had not seen before.

"You didn't seem to follow me, just now," said Walt. "You didn't seem to understand what I meant. You're one of our most valuable lives, the true white knight that all of us dream of being at one time or another, but only one in billions actually succeeds in being born to be."

Jim stared back at him.

"I told you," he said. "I can't help it."

"That's not what I'm talking about," said Walt. "You wanted to go out and fight the dragons, but life was too short. But what about now?"

"Now?" echoed Jim, staring at him. "You mean—me?"

"Yes," said Walt. His face was strange and intense, with the intensity of a crusader, and his voice seemed to float on the soft river of words flowing from the black box. "I mean you. What are you going to be doing—a thousand years from today?"

CITY OF YESTERDAY

by Terry Carr

"Wake up," said Charles, and J-1001011 instantly sat up. The couch sat up with him, jackknifing to form his pilot's seat. J-1001011 noted that the seat was in combat position, raised high enough to give him an unobstructed vision on all sides of the planetflier.

"We're in orbit around our objective," said Charles. "Breakout and attack in seven minutes. Eat. Eliminate."

J-1001011 obediently withdrew the red-winking tube from the panel before him and put it between his lips. Warm, mealy liquid fed into his mouth, and he swallowed at a regular rate. When the nourishment tube stopped, he removed it from his mouth and let it slide back into the panel.

The peristalsis stimulators began, and he asked, "Is there any news of my parents?"

"Personal questions are always answered freely," said Charles, "but only when military necessities have been completed. Your briefing for this mission takes precedence." A screen lit up on the flier's control panel, showing a 3-4 contour map of the planet they were orbiting.

J-1001011 sighed and turned his attention to the screen.

"The planet Rhinstruk," said Charles. "Oxygen 13.7%, nitro-

58

gen 82.4% plus inert gases. Full spacewear will be required for the high-altitude attack pattern in effect on this mission.''

The image on the screen zoomed in, selected one continent out of three he had seen revolving below, continued zooming down to near planet level. Charles said, ''Note that this is a totally enemy planet. Should I be shot down and you somehow survive, there will be no refuge. If that happens, destroy yourself.''

''The target?'' the pilot asked.

''The city you see below. It isn't fully automated, but its defenses will be formidable anyway.'' On the screen J-1001011 saw a towered city rising from a broad plain. The city was circular, and as the image sharpened with proximity he could make out individual streeets, parkways . . . and beam emplacements. The screen threw light-circles on seven of these in all.

''We will have nine fliers,'' said Charles. ''These beams will attempt to defend, but our mission will be simple destruction of the entire city, which presents a much larger target than any one of our fliers. We will lose between three and five of us, but we'll succeed. Attack pattern RO-1101 will be in effect; you'll take control of me at 30,000 feet. End of briefing.''

The pilot stretched in his chair, flexed muscles in his arms and hands. ''How long was I asleep?'' he asked.

''Eight months, seventeen days, plus,'' said Charles.

That long! A quarter-credit for sleep time, that would give him over two months on his term of service, leaving him . . . less than a year, Earth standard. J-1001011 felt his heart speed up momentarily, before Charles's nerve-implants detected and corrected it. The pilot had been in service for nearly seven subjective years. Adding objective sleep time, it came out to over nineteen years. The sleep periods, during Hardin Drive travel between star systems, ate up his service term easily for him . . . but then he remembered, as he always did, that the objective time was still the same, that his parents, whoever and wherever they were, would be getting older at objective time rate on some planet.

Nineteen years. They should still be alive, he thought. He remembered them from his childhood, on a planet where colors had been real rather than dyed or light-tinted, where winds had blown fresh and night had fallen with the regular revolution of the planet. He had had a name there not a binary number—Henry, or Hendrick, or Henried; he couldn't quite remember. When the Control machines had come for him he had been ten years old, old enough to know his own name, but they had erased it. They had had to clear his memory for the masses of minute data he'd need for service, so the machines had stored his personal memories in neat patterns of microenergy, waiting for his release.

Not all of them, though. The specific things, yes: his name, the name of his planet, its exact location, the thousand-and-one details that machines recognize as data. But not remembered sights, smells, tastes: flowerbursts of color amid green vegetation, the cold spray of rainbowed water as he stood beside a waterfall, the warmth of an animal held in the arms. He remembered what it was like to be Henry, or Hendrick or Henried, even though he couldn't remember the exact name of the person he had been.

And he remembered what his parents were like, though he had no memory at all of *their* names. His father: big and rangy, with bony hands and an awkward walk and a deep, distant voice, like thunder and rain on the other side of a mountain. His mother: soft and quiet, a quizzical face framed by dark hair, somehow smiling even when she was angry, as if she wasn't quite sure how to put together a stern expression.

By now they must be . . . fifty years old? Sixty? Or even a *hundred* sixty, he thought. He couldn't know; he had to trust what the machines told him, what Charles said. And they could be lying about the time he spent in sleep. But he had to assume they weren't.

"Breakout and attack in one minute," Charles said.

The voice startled him momentarily, but then he reached for his pressure helmet, sealed it in place with automatic movements, machine-trained muscle patterns. He heard the helmet's intercom click on.

"What about my parents?" he asked. "You have time to tell me before we break out. At least tell me if they're still alive."

"Breakout and attack in thirty seconds and counting," said Charles. "Twenty-eight, twenty-seven, twenty-six. . . ."

J-1001011, human pilot of a planetflier named Charles, shook his head in resignation and listened to the count, bracing himself for the coming shock of acceleration.

It hit him, as always, with more force than he had remembered, crushing him back into the chair as the planetflier rocketed out of the starship's hold along with its eight unit-mates. Charles had opaqued the pilot's bubble to prevent blinding him with sudden light, but the machine cleared it steadily as it drove downward toward the planet's surface, and soon the man could make out the other fliers around him. He recognized the flying formation, remembered the circular attack pattern they'd be using—a devastating ring of fliers equipped with pyrobombs. Charles was right. They'd lose some fliers, but the city would be destroyed.

He wondered about the city, the enemy. Was this another pacification mission, another planet feeling strong in its isolation from the rest of GalFed's far-flung worlds and trying to break away from central regulation? J-1001011 had been on dozens of such missions. But their attacks hadn't been destruct-patterns against whole cities, so this must be a different kind of problem. Maybe the city was really a military complex . . . even a stronghold of the Khallash. If they really existed.

When men had first made contact with an alien race a century and a half before, they had met with total enmity, almost mindlessly implacable hatred. War had flared immediately—a defensive war on the part of the humans, who hadn't been prepared for it. And in order to organize the loose-knit Galactic Federation efficiently, they'd computerized the central commands . . . and then the middle echelons . . . and finally, a little over a century ago, the whole of GelFed had been given to the machines to defend.

Or so he had been taught. There were rumors, of course, that there were no Khallash any longer, that they'd been destroyed or driven off long ago . . . or that they'd never existed in the first place, that the machines had invented them as an excuse for their own control of GelFed. J-1001011 didn't know. He'd never met the aliens in battle, but that proved nothing, considering the vastness of space and the many internal problems the machines had to cope with.

Yet perhaps he would meet them now . . . in the city below.

"30,000 feet," said Charles. "Attach your muscle contacts."

The pilot quickly drew from the walls of the compartment a network of small wires, one after the other, and touched each to magnetized terminals on his arms, hands, legs, shoulders. As he did so he felt the growing sensation of airflight: he was becoming one with the flier, a single unit of machine and man. Charles fed the sensory impressions into his nervous system through his regular nerve-implants, and as the muscle contacts were attached he could feel the flier's rockets, gyros, pyrolaunchers all coming under his control, responding instantly to movements of his body's muscles.

This was the part that he liked, that almost made his service term worth it. As the last contact snapped into place, he *became* the planetflier. His name was Charles, and he was a whole being once more. Air rushed past him, mottled fields tilted far below, he felt the strength of duralloy skin and the thrust of rockets; and he was not just a flesh-and-blood human wombed in his pilot's compartment, but a weapon of war swooping down for a kill.

The machines themselves don't appreciate this, he thought. *Charles and the rest have no emotions, no pleasures. But a human does . . . and we can even enjoy killing. Maybe that's why they need us—because we can love combat, so we're better at it than them.*

But he knew that wasn't true, only an emotional conceit. Human battle pilots were needed because their nervous systems were more efficient than any microminiaturized computer of the same size and mass; it was as simple as that. And human pilots were expendable where costly mechanization wouldn't be.

"Control is full now," he said; but Charles didn't answer. Charles didn't exist now. Only the computer aboard the orbiting starship remained to monitor the planetflier below.

In a moment the starship's voice came to him through Charles' receptors: "All human units are ready. Attack pattern RO-1101 will now begin."

The city was below him, looking just as it had on the contour map: wide streets, buildings thrusting up towards him, patches of green that must have been parks . . . or camouflage, he warned himself. The city was the enemy.

He banked into a spiral and knifed down through the planet's cold air. The other fliers fell into formation behind him, and as the starship cut in the intercommunications channels he heard the voices of the other pilots:

"Beautiful big target—we can't miss it. Anybody know if they're Khallash down there?"

"Only the machines would know that, and if they wanted to tell us, they'd have included it in the briefing."

"It looks like a human city to me. Must be another rebel planet."

"Maybe that's what the Khallash want us to think."

"It doesn't matter who they are," J-1001011 said. "They're

enemy; they're our mission. Complete enough missions and
we go home. Stop talking and start the attack; we're in range.''

As he spoke he lined his sights dead-center on the city and
fired three pyrobombs in quick succession. He peeled off and
slipped back into the flight circle as another flier banked into
firing trajectory. Three more bombs flared out and downward,
and the second flier rejoined the pattern.

Below, J-1001011's bombs hit. He saw the flashes, one,
two, three quick bursts, and a moment later red flames showed
where the bombs had hit. A bit off-center from where he had
aimed, but close enough. He could correct for it on the next pass.

More bombs burst below; more fires leapt and spread. The
fliers darted in, loosed their bombs and darted away. They
were in a complete ring around the city now, the pattern fully
established. It was all going according to plan.

Then the beams from the city began to fire.

The beams were almost invisible at a distance, just lightning-
quick lances of destructive energy cutting into the sky. Not
that it was important to see them—the fliers couldn't veer off
to evade them in time, wouldn't even be able to react before
a beam stuck.

But the planetfliers were small, and they stayed high. Any
beam hits would be as much luck as skill.

They rained fire and death on the city for an hour, each flier
banking inward just long enough to get off three or four bombs,
then veering out and up before he got too close. At the hour's
end the city below was dotted with fire. One of the planetfliers
had been hit; it had burst with an energy-release that buffeted
J-1001011 with its shock-wave, sending him momentarily off
course. But he had quickly righted himself, re-entered the pattern and returned to the attack.

As the destruction continued, he felt more and more the
oneness, the wholeness of machine and man. Charles the other-
thing was gone, merged into his own being, and now he was
the machine, the beautiful complex mass of metals and sensors,
relays and engines and weaponry. He was a destruction-
machine, a death-flier, a superefficient killer. It was like coming
out of the darkness of some prison, being freed to burst out with
all his pent-up hatreds and frustrations and destroy, destroy . . . .

It was the closest thing he had to being human again, to
being . . . what was the name he had back on that planet where

he'd been born? He couldn't remember now; there was no room
for even an echo of that name in his mind.

He was *Charles.*

He was a war-machine destroying a city—that and only that.
Flight and power occupied his whole being, and the screaming
release of hatred and fear within him was so intense it was
love. The attack pattern became, somehow, a ritual of courtship,
the pyrobombs and destruction and fire below a kind of
lovemaking whose insensitivity gripped him more and more
fiercely as the attack continued. It was a red hell, but it was
the only kind of real life he had known since the machines had
taken him.

When the battle was over, when the city was a flaming circle
of red and even the beams had stopped firing from below, he
was exhausted both physically and emotionally. He was able
to note dimly, with some back part of his brain or perhaps
through one of Charles' machine synapse-patterns, that they
had lost three of the fliers. But that didn't interest him; nothing
did.

When something clicked in him and Charles' voice said,
"Remove your muscle contacts now," he did so dully, uncar-
ing. And he became J-1001011 again.

Later, with the planetfliers back in the old of the starship and
awaiting the central computer's analysis of the mission's success, he remembered the battle like something in a dream. It
was a red, violent dream, a nightmare; and it was worse than
that, because it had been real.

He roused himself, licked dry lips, said, "You have time
now, Charles, to tell me about my parents. Are they alive?"

Charles said, "Your parents do not exist now. They've just
been destroyed."

There was a moment of incomprehension, then a dull shock
hit J-1001011 in the stomach. But it was almost as if he expected
to hear this—and Charles controlled his reaction instantly
through his nerve-implants.

"Then that was no Khallash city," he said.

"No," said Charles. "It was a human city, a rebel city."

The pilot searched vaguely through the fog of his memories
of home, trying to remember anything about a city such as
he'd destroyed today. But he could grasp nothing like that; his
memories were all of some smaller town, and of mountains,

not the open fields that had surrounded this city.

"My parents moved to the city after I was taken away," he said. "Is that right?"

"We have no way of knowing about that," said Charles. "Who your parents were, on what planet they lived—all this information has been destroyed in the city on Rhinstruk. It was the archives center of the Galactic Federation, storing all the memory-data of our service humans. Useless information, since none of it will ever be used again—and potentially harmful, because the humans assigned to guard it were engaged in a plot to broadcast data through official machine communications channels to the original holders of the memories. So it became necessary to destroy the city."

"You destroyed an entire city . . . just for that?"

"It was necessary. Humans perform up to minimum efficiency standards only when they're unhampered by pre-service memories; this is why all your memory-data was transferred from your mind when you were inducted. For a while it was expedient to keep the records on file, to be returned as humans terminated their service, and now we have great enough control in the Federation that it's no longer necessary. Therefore we're able to complete a major step toward totally efficient organization."

J-1001011 imagined fleetingly that he could feel the machine's nerve-implants moving within him to control some emotion that threatened to rise. Anger? Fear? Grief? He couldn't be sure just what was appropriate to this situation; all he actually felt was a dull, uncomprehending curiosity.

"But my parents . . . you said they were destroyed."

"They have been. There is no way of knowing where or who they were. They've become totally negligible factors, along with the rest of your pre-service existence. When we control all data in your mind, we then have proper control of the mind itself."

He remembered dark trees and a cushion of damp green leaves beneath them, where he had fallen asleep one afternoon. He heard the earthquake of his father's laughter once when he had drunk far too much, remembered how like a stranger his mother had seemed for weeks after she'd cut her hair short, tasted smoked meat and felt the heat of an open-hearth fire. . . .

The nerve-implants moved like ghosts inside him.

"The central computer's analysis is now complete," Charles

announced. "The city of Rhinstruk is totally destroyed; our mission was successful. So there's no more need for you to be awake; deactivation will now begin."

Immediately, Pilot J-1001011 felt his consciousness ebbing away. He said, more to himself than to Charles, "You can't erase the past like that. The mission was . . . unsuccessful." He felt a yawn coming, tried to fight it, couldn't. "Their names weren't . . . the important. . . ."

Then he couldn't talk any more; but there was no need for it. He drifted into sleep remembering the freedom of flight when he was Charles, the beauty and strength of destroying, of rage channeled through pyrobombs . . . of release.

For one last flickering moment he felt a stab of anger begin to rise, but then Charles' implants pushed it back inside. He slept.

Until his next awakening.

INDUSTRIAL ACCIDENT

by Lee Correy
(G. Harry Stine)

It was inevitable that it would happen someday.

And it did happen . . . and nobody will ever know why.

Perhaps an electron did not move from one crystal lattice to another because of a solar X-ray photon or a high-energy cosmic ray, in spite of shielding. Regardless of cause, the effect was known. The book-sized package of nucleide electronics of the autopilot and guidance system did not send the command signal to the fusion-powered pulsed plasma space drive. As a result, the space drive did not swivel, causing TriPlanet Transport's load SLZ-420 to perform the required end-over-end skew flip to begin deceleration for eventual Earth-orbit insertion. Instead, the glitch locked out the command receiver.

SLZ-420 had boosted away from the planetoid Pallas at a constant acceleration of one-tenth standard gravity. This doesn't sound like much acceleration. But, at the programmed turnover point, the SLZ-420 was moving at a sun-referenced velocity of more than six hundred kilometers per second.

Now, instead of starting to slow down on its journey to the space factories in orbit around the Earth, SLZ-420 kept on accelerating.

For centuries, people had been afraid of things falling on

them from the sky—early airplanes, meteors, comets and even small planetoids. The doomsday literature of the early space age was full of such scenarios because geological evidence pointed to the fact that large celestial bodies had collided with the Earth in the distant past. And there was abundant visible evidence of such celestial bombardment on the Moon, Mercury and Mars. Scientists and engineers pooh-poohed these fears as they learned that the solar system had swept itself clean of the debris of its birth.

Man-made meteors were rarely considered as one of the hazards of the Third Industrial Revolution.

SLZ-420 had become such a man-made meteor. It was nothing more than a solid cylinder of planetoid iron fifteen meters in diameter and twenty-three meters long, weighing a mere thirty-five thousand tons . . . a grain of celestial sand on the beach of the solar system.

The glitch in the electronic guidance system had not affected the instructions to "go to Earth" that had been implanted in its memory on Pallas. Faithfully, it continued to do its job . . . except for that one little program step. Faithfully, the reliable constant-boost space drive continued to work, adding one meter per second to the velocity every second . . . in the wrong direction. Toward Earth. Toward eight billion people aboard a giant spaceship living in an ecology that was vulnerable to the man-made meteor. Toward people who were ignorant of SLZ-420 and who did not understand the consequences of what could and would happen. But, also, toward people who had not ignored the possibility that it would indeed happen someday.

The House committee hearing room had not changed in nearly a hundred years. Established behind his elevated desk with the status symbols of the microphones before him sat a man who was almost indistinguishable from most of his predecessors. Representative Claypool Evans Perrin had served the people of his district for nearly a quarter of a century . . . or so they believed. However, he knew full well that politics was simply the interaction of various power groups . . . and thus he had remained in office through twelve election battles. He scorned implant lenses, preferring old rimless eyeglasses. He felt that they lent a distinctive touch to his craggy face topped by its famous shock of unruly hair, hair that was now pure white and worn long in the romantic fashion of the ancient seventies. Perrin believed it helped maintain his image as a young-thinking firebrand radical, the image that had served him well for all those years and all those elections.

He peered now through those spectacles and fixed his stare on the man behind the witness table below him. "Please let me get this absolutely clear in my mind, Mr. Armitage." He spoke in the measured cadence of his rasping voice. "The Control and Inspection Division of the Department of Space Commerce is requesting a budget line item of 4.7 billion dollars for something you term an 'emergency accident system.' If I understand this correctly, it's for the development and deployment of interceptor-type space vehicles based at L-5."

Chuck Armitage was quick to attempt a reply. "Yes, sir, we—"

But Perrin wasn't about to let the witness speak yet. "Under the terms of various United Nations treaties, some of them more than fifty years old, no nation is permitted to maintain any sort of deep-space military system beyond that necessary to police its own space operations . . . sort of the equivalent of the old Coast Guard, if you will. We've spent billions of dollars to ensure that the Space Watch can defend our national airspace up to a hundred kilometers, as we are permitted to do under international agreement." He paused and shook his long white hair out of his face. "Mr. Armitage, isn't the Department of Space Commerce asking Congress to let you build an armed force based in space and capable of carrying out offensive military acts against space facilities as well as against Earth?"

It was a loaded question, and Chuck Armitage knew it. Hunching forward over the witness table, he looked intently back at Congressman Perrin while he collected his thoughts and tried to choose his words very carefully. His thinking processes were quite rapid in this environment because he had fought his way through many congressional appropriations hearings in the past.

"Mr. Chairman, the department can't do what you are claiming, as Secretary Seton has said many times. The intent of the budget line item request is quite different, and this is why Secretary Seton has asked me to speak for it in her stead. As head of the Control and Inspection Division, I am the policeman of our space commerce activities and—"

"I have read your vitae, sir—" Perrin broke in, apparently

with impatience. It was, however, a technique that he used very effectively with witnesses. But it didn't work with Chuck Armitage.

"Then you know what sort of situation I am faced with on a daily basis," Armitage broke in himself. "In fact, for the past twenty-two years we have lived with the situation since the Whitney Drive was first used for constant-boost space-flight . . ."

"Ah, yes, but for those twenty-two years, there have been no problems that space crews have not been able to solve."

"Those were manned vehicles, Congressman," Armitage pointed out. The exchange was becoming rapid-fire as both men tried to gain and maintain control of the situation.

"What possible difference does that make?"

"Problems could be solved in transit. But things have changed. The majority of cargo vehicles today are unmanned because of various governmental restrictions—not in our department, by the way—that prevent the necessary capital accumulation required to finance manned ships."

"Well, such rules pertaining to the regulation of space commerce are not the province of this committee!"

"No, sir, but the unmanned cargo ship is a consequence that we must deal with here. The solar system is full of unmanned ships right this instant, some of them boosting at more than a standard g. I am responsible for the safe operation of those ships of United States registry. And I am especially worried about the unmanned, automated vehicles. There is a finite chance that something could go wrong with an unmanned ship . . . and we would be faced with the prospect of a very large mass coming at us with terminal velocity approaching a thousand kilometers per second . . . In effect, man-made meteors."

Perrin waved his hand. "That seems to be a rather remote possibility. Meteors have been hitting the Earth for millions of years. The government of the United States has never had to concern itself with any problems of protecting its citizens against falling meteors!" A titter of laughter ran around the hearing room. Perrin felt that he had counted coup on that one.

"We are not talking about natural meteors, Mr. Chairman! Most of the natural meteorite material out there is no bigger than a pebble . . . or somebody would be mining it right now! We are concerned with a recent man-made phenomenon: un-manned constant-boost cargo ships. There are more than a hundred of them boosting toward the Earth–Moon system right now. We need only one failure—*one failure*—to have a worldwide catastrophe on our hands.''

''Come, come! I have never known you to exaggerate in your testimony before, Mr. Armitage. Worldwide catastrophe? Really!''

''I wish it were not possible, Congressman. We estimate that the impact of a thirty-thousand-ton planetoid ore carrier at five hundred kilometers per second would produce an effect equivalent to several hundred megatons of TNT. But the scaling laws break down because we cannot extrapolate from the results of early thermonuclear warhead testing. The United States set off a ten-megaton thermonuclear device in 1952, and the Soviets blew off a fifty-megaton nuke shortly thereafter. We are not sure that—''

Perrin cut in again. ''We're not discussing military warheads, Mr. Armitage!''

''No, sir, but we are discussing the rapid release of large amounts of energy—and the only difference between a large nuke and a fast-moving rock is the lack of radiation from the rock impact. In addition, when a large unmanned ship hits, it will be moving many times faster than a natural meteor, and its kinetic energy increases as the square of—''

''Mr. Armitage, isn't your division responsible for seeing to it that a runaway spaceship could never occur? Aren't we discussing something so highly hypothetical as to be ridiculous? Aren't your people on top of the safety aspect?''

''Yes, sir, they are. Our specifications and technical directives must be followed by all manufacturers and users of equipment licensed or registered by the United States. By international agreements, all other spacefaring nations either adopt our rules or have rules that are compatible. Our field representatives inspect and sign-off all new equipment as it comes out of the factory door. They do the same for all routine maintenance, overhauls, and even for preboost checks.''

''Then what is it that could possibly go wrong, Mr. Armitage?''

''Mr. Chairman, no technology is ever perfect. We are not gods; we are people with a very incomplete understanding of the way the universe works. Sooner or later, no matter how diligent we are and no matter how exhaustive our tests, something will misbehave. Let me state categorically—and I'll back it up with numbers at a later time if you wish—that there is a statistically valid possibility that the Earth will be impacted by an unmanned multithousand-ton cargo ship within the next ten years. We *must* have an emergency system of long-range deep-space interceptors . . . a dozen is all that we are asking for. They would be based at our L-5 facility. They have to be because of the negligible gravity well there and because of the fact that it is easier to intercept a runaway ship as far out as possible . . . and not even very easy under those conditions.''

Perrin leaned back and made a steeple of his fingertips.

''Isn't the Space Watch prepared to take care of such matters?''

''Ask the Space Watch.''

''But I am asking you, Mr. Armitage.''

''The Space Watch interceptor force is Earth-based by treaty. The beam weapons at L-5 have limited power under the SWAP agreements with the Soviet Union, whose L-4 beam weapons are also limited. Ask the Space Watch, sir, because they are well equipped to handle defense against Earth-launched missiles or against anything the Soviets might try to do from L-4.''

''You haven't answered my question, have you?''

''I cannot answer it in open session, nor am I privileged to know all of the sensitive details of the Space Watch systems.'' Chuck Armitage *did* know these details. He wasn't supposed to. He wasn't cleared for that information, but he had his channels of information that were zealously protected. He had known for five years that the Space Watch did not have the capability to even deflect the course of an unmanned runaway. ''This is why I suggested, Mr. Chairman, that you might ask the Space Watch to . . .''

An aide leaned over Perrin's shoulder and whispered something into the congressman's right ear. Perrin nodded and glanced at his old-fashioned digital wristwatch. He turned his attention again to Armitage. ''We have an important roll-call vote coming up in a few minutes. So we'll not have time to discuss this further today. We may have a duplication of effort conflict arising between DSC and the Space Watch. The fine line of division between military and civilian utilization of space has been a major problem for nearly sixty years, and I doubt that we will find the solution to it today.'' Perrin decided that he would mention the matter to the presidents of TriPlanet

Spaceways and TransWorld Transit at dinner that evening to find out if there was any support for this program from the space transportation lobby.

The session adjourned for the day. Armitage inwardly chewed his fingernails as he gathered up his papers and stalked out of the hearing room with his deputy, George Bonnieul.

"Wait until some nonsked Zaire registry load slams into his constituency!" Chuck growled so that only George could hear.

"No reason to be upset, Chuck," Bonnieul remarked smoothly. "Perrin was Perrin today, as usual but more so. He's up for reelection and he's got some hot young competition. He wants political advantage out of this." He looked over at Armitage.

"Too damned many things in space operations have been determined by political compromise rather than by technical or economic realities," Armitage continued to mutter. "I once thought that when private enterprise became involved, it would be the end of the political football game . . . but they just started playing again with new rules . . ."

"So what else is new?" George wanted to know. "Let's say to hell with it. You-know-who called from Singapore this morning. Says the offer is still open for all of us."

"And turn the division over to The Slob?" Chuck was referring to the civil service hack who would most probably be promoted into Chuck's position from a nonoperating division of the department because there just wasn't anybody to take it if Chuck and his colleagues left. If the deal had just been for Chuck alone, he might have given it more consideration because George would have then been in line for division chief.

"You have a disturbing habit of bringing up unsavory matters," George told him as they descended the long stairway to reach the elevators going to the roof. Only in a government building would one have to walk down stairs to get an elevator going up. The two men were quiet in the elevator because there were others present, although they were the only ones going all the way to the roof.

An agency aircar was waiting for them, manned and running.

Chuck sensed that something was wrong. "Didn't you park that heap in the transient area over there?"

George nodded.

The two of them walked normally over to the waiting aircar. If there was something wrong somewhere, this was not the place to indicate it by unusual action because there were, as always, news media crews standing by on the roof to interview important witnesses and newsworthy congressmen.

Immediately the door was closed, the driver put the air to the Coanda wings and went straight up to transition altitude. Only then did Chuck remark, "Howdy, Jed. How did you get here?"

The wiry little pilot, another of Armitage's assistants, replied without turning his head. "Pete brought me over and dropped me off. We didn't dare call you out of the hearing, and we wanted to make sure that you got back to the center as quickly as possible once it was over." He paused, listened to the radio loudspeaker, replied into a microphone, then continued his monologue, "Thirty minutes ago, we got the data that cargo load SLZ-420 out of Pallas at one-tenth g missed turnover a little over three hours ago."

There was not a trace of emotion on the faces or in the actions of either man, but this belied the inner feelings that each of them had at the moment. But they were professionals in a high-tech area and were trained not to display their emotions. George took out his pocket computer, pulled out the antenna, and put it near the south window of the aircar so that it could communicate with the geosynchronous data transfer satellite that was linked to the computers at the center and with the internationally maintained master unit at Singapore. "A little more than sixty-six hours to arrival here," George announced.

"Any telemetry indication of the malfunction?" Chuck then asked the driver.

"I've told you all I know. I left the center just after the alert sounded," Jed remarked. "Please let me handle this rush hour traffic so that I can get you to center as quickly as possible without arousing interest."

"The sheer coincidence of this amazes me," George said in deliberate understatement, looking at Chuck.

"History is a record of coincidental happenings and the people who managed to take opportune advantage of them," Armitage observed quietly. "I will not relish what I will have to do in the next few hours."

The traffic room of the Control and Inspection Center was large. It was quiet, but it was busy. The several dozen people hardly moved, but the data presentations on the walls were active. Chuck Armitage slumped in a chair behind one of the supervisory desks in the glassed-off gallery. He contemplated the data on the CRT display before him and on the walls of the traffic room. It had been a very busy several hours since he had walked in. Several telephone calls had been made. Hot lines between national traffic control centers had been activated on a permanent basis. Tacit agreements had been reached with Chuck's counterparts around the world. Some traffic in the Earth–Moon system had been rerouted or rescheduled; the department's public affairs people kept their cool and announced that the traffic changes were probably caused by the detection of a close-approach planetoid that might be moving near the Earth–Moon system. Traffic centers were normally closed to the news media, and they remained sealed off. Some of the news media were enraged; others decided to play it cool and wait for the inevitable leaks or further developments. However, news of wars, revolutions, murders, looting, rapes, invasions, famines and other commonplace, everyday happenings around the planet continued to occupy the major news slots; after all, those stories were about people, and very few media persons could get very excited about a rock in space.

Chuck Armitage had a decision to make, and he waited until the very last moment to make it. In one smooth motion, he reached out and picked a telephone handset out of its cradle. When he punched the call buttons, his motions were sharp, rapid and almost vicious. "Tom, Chuck Armitage. It's a 'go' situation, my friend. Let me know whether you or Kim decide to be number one. . . . Yes, it will be messy . . . I'll take care of that. . . . Good luck, Tom . . . and *arigato*." He put the handset back in its cradle softly. For minutes, he stared straight ahead at nothing.

The telephone blinked at him. He lifted it from its cradle again. "Armitage here. . . . Good, bring them up, George. . . . Yes, everything's going as planned. . . . Well, I'm glad you were able to find him. When will he get here? . . . Too bad. No latecomers, George. He'll just have to read about it later." After hanging up, he rose and walked slowly to the rear of the room where the bar and the buffet were stocked and ready. He couldn't eat; he didn't have any appetite just then. He wanted a drink, but he didn't dare. He didn't even want the stimulant of coffee.

Over the next thirty minutes, his guests arrived. Some were

indignant. Some were quizzical. Some were somber. None of them knew the full story, some of them had snatches of data that they had agreed would not be discussed until Chuck had given them a full briefing, but almost all of them sensed that there was an aura of quiet, controlled, constrained terror in the air.

It had taken the full power of the president's office plus that of Secretary Seton to convene every one of the people who arrived. Chuck could not make small talk with any of them; it was impossible for him to do so. He fretted inwardly until the final group of three people came in. The youngest of the three came up and shook hands with Chuck.

"Good to see you, Senator," Chuck remarked. "I'm glad you were able to locate Congressman Perrin and bring him with you."

"It wasn't easy," Senator Davidoff replied. "Thanks to Tri-Planet, I located Clay with Jeremiah at the Cosmos Club."

Chuck greeted Jeremiah Morris, the scarecrowlike ruler of TriPlanet Spaceways, who said nothing in return. Jeremiah knew the score. A quick telephone call from the Cosmos Club to his operations office did it, and he had passed the information along to Perrin in the aircar en route to the center. He didn't need to say anything to Chuck at this time; later, when liability had been established, he might make a statement. In any event, a Lloyd's associate would do the sweating. Or so he thought.

"I'm sorry I interrupted your dinner, Congressman," Chuck tried to apologize to Perrin.

Perrin's reply was a growl from an important man who has had his arm twisted. "If it hadn't been for Senator Davidoff, I would have considered this whole matter as a grandstand play resulting from the hearings. I'm still not certain that I . . ."

"Chuck Armitage does not make grandstand plays," the young senator cut in. "I've know him too long to . . ."

"How do we know this isn't a dry run?" Perrin wanted to know.

"I wish to God it were a dry run," was Chuck's reply. Raising his voice above the conversational hubbub of the room, he announced, "Please take a seat, everyone. I want to tell everyone what's going on here."

Most of the people in the room knew one another . . . Star

Admiral Jacobs, top man of the Space Watch; Joseph Hirschfeld of TransWorld; Andrew Watermann of Terra-Luna Transport; Jeremiah Morris of TriPlanet; foreign liaison professionals from Europe, Japan and the Soviet Union; and Secretary Helen Seton, secretary of the Department of Space Commerce with the gleaming Distinguished Space Star pinned like a brooch to her high-necked tunic covering the scars and prosthetics from the power satellite accident.

"Ladies and gentlemen, you are here at the request of the president of the United States, who is fully aware of the crisis that now exists," Chuck began. "George, please get the rest of the teleconference on the line. Now, to anticipate some objections concerning national security, I wish to further tell you that I am acting with the full authority and approval of the president in establishing this hologram teleconference with our compatriots in Europe, Singapore and the Soviet Union. Please stand by until George completes the circuits."

The side wall of the room disappeared, revealing three more rooms similar to the one they were in. In each of the shimmering three rooms, the holographic projections from Europe, Singapore and the Soviet Union flickered into being as the circuits through the geosynchronous comsat platforms were given a final tuning. Brief greetings were exchanged, but they were short. The holographic participants seemed to know what the situation was, and they were all business.

"We have a crisis on our hands with worldwide implications," Chuck announced. "Our colleagues elsewhere must participate on a real-time basis. A space vehicle of United States' registry has become a runaway, and it may impact Earth . . ."

The room exploded with voices.

"Gospodin Armitage," the Soviet hologram spoke, causing the room to become quiet, "is it as bad as our information indicates to us?"

Chuck nodded. "Here are the full details. TriPlanet cargo load SLZ-420 running in from Pallas at thirty-five thousand tons gross weight did not execute turnover at 17:10 Universal Time today. Because of the distance involved, our tracking net did not learn about this for almost two hours. Neither we nor the people at TriPlanet know what is wrong. Telemetry indicated that everything aboard SLZ-420 is operating normally, but the autopilot will not acknowledge nor execute commands. This should not happen with triple-redundant circuits, but it has."

Luxemburg wanted to know, "What is the inspection history?"

"Our records and those of TriPlanet indicate that all systems have undergone periodic inspections as required and that all spaceworthiness directives have been complied with. Our Pallas field office gave clearance to boost based on an affirmative preboost check."

"Can we compare computer data?" the Soviet asked.

"Of course," Chuck said and noticed that Star Admiral Jacobs flinched slightly. "Call it up on our standard data transfer net. You can also get the graphic presentation we have on the walls here at center. At turnover, velocity was 612 kilometers per second, and it is still boosting toward us at one-tenth standard g. That doesn't sound like much, but it is adding one kilometer per second to its velocity every sixteen minutes and forty seconds."

A few people in the room were rapidly keying display consoles, calling up additional data. But most did not know how. They sat there, responsible for the use of the technology, but unable to manipulate it.

Senator Davidoff broke the silence. "But it doesn't seem to be boosting wild. According to the shape of the trajectories you're plotting on the walls out here, its guidance system seems to be working."

"Working perfectly and homing on Earth," Chuck told him.

"Have you alerted the Space Watch?" It was the first time Perrin had spoken since the briefing began. "Can they stop it?"

Chuck indicated the star admiral.

Jacobs was young, but he was both a competent engineer and an experienced leader. He first looked directly at the hologram of his Soviet counterpart. Then he turned to Perrin. "No," came the flat answer.

"But you've got an interceptor force!" Perrin complained.

Jacobs glanced at the Soviet hologram. "I am not free to discuss it."

Chuck picked up a telephone. "As Secretary Seton can verify, the president has authorized complete cooperation and the total lifting of security restrictions. Shall I call him to satisfy you?"

Jacobs hesitated.

"Since we began this teleconference, SLZ-420 has added one hundred fifty meters per second to its velocity, Admiral," Chuck pointed out, holding up the telephone. "Do you want me to get the president on the line for you, or are you willing to accept what I tell you?"

Jacobs looked at Secretary Seton. "I spoke with the president," she said quietly. "Speak freely, there is no security barrier."

"Our interceptors are Earth-based according to treaty. We've built some slight excess performance into them so that we could operate them de-rated," Jacobs rationalized. "With a very great deal of very good luck and everything working perfectly, we might intercept with a nuke at a range of three hundred kilometers from Earth. But at that point, the SLZ-420 is moving at eight hundred kilometers per second . . . and those rates are beyond . . . are beyond the capabilities of . . . of our intercept system."

"You have exceeded SWAP treaty limitations!" the Soviet hologram objected strongly.

"Gospodin!" Chuck snapped. "I would be very happy now if you had exceeded them to a greater extent!"

"Burn it with your beam weapons at L-5!" Perrin suggested.

"Congressman," Jacobs told him, "those beam weapons won't make a dent in thirty-five thousand tons of iron! By treaty, they're defocused beyond four hundred thousand kilometers. We can refocus them in about four days' time . . . which is several days faster than I know my Soviet counterpart can manage. But even if we could refocus, we haven't got enough time to input enough energy into the target. At the velocity it will be moving, it will take only seven minutes from time of crossing the lunar orbit until it impacts."

"Mein Herr, do you have an impact prediction yet?" was the question from Luxemburg Center.

Chuck paused to key a terminal. "Here's the latest update, Fritz. Barring any malfunction of the SLZ-420's guidance system, which is unlikely, the ship will impact near Genk, Belgium, in fifty-nine hours and approximately ten minutes from now. Entry velocity is estimated to be 867 kilometers per second, which means that the Earth's atmosphere will have negligible effect on its mass from ablation or on its impact velocity. The impact will release kinetic energy equivalent to a 284-megaton bomb . . . and we do not know what the effects will be. The atmosphere shock wave will rebound around the planet several times, and the ground shock will certainly go off the top end of the Richter Scale. Some of the thirty-five thousand tons of iron will vaporize on impact, and some of it will get tossed clear around the planet as secondaries . . . some of which may pose a problem to near-Earth orbital facilities. Other than the brief burst of hard X-rays from the atmospheric entry plasma sheath, there will be no radiation other than heat . . . and the fireball of impact will probably rise to the top of the stratosphere and squat there, radiating most of its heat to space. The meteor experts at Flagstaff couldn't even guess the effects on the planetary weather . . .''

"Is there any chance it may go into the Atlantic Ocean instead?" the hologram that was Fritz in Luxemburg asked.

"That just makes it worse," Chuck pointed out. "The impact might vaporize enough sea water to create a worldwide cloud layer . . . which in turn could raise the world temperatures by several degrees by virtue of greenhouse effect. . . . Look, all of you, I just don't know everything that could happen because we have never experienced anything like this in all recorded history! We can't even extrapolate from fairly recent strikes such as the Barringer Crater in Arizona . . . which was made by a small slowpoke in comparison to SLZ-420. . . .''

There was complete silence for moments as the full import of the information sunk in. It was Claypool Perrin who lost his cool. "We've got to start evacuation of the impact area!"

"Clay," Davidoff said, "an announcement would start a panic."

"But millions of people will die! How can you just sit here and let the sky literally fall on those millions in Europe without telling them?"

"Congressman, will you provide me with some guidelines on how to evacuate a *whole continent*?" Chuck said.

"But *you've got to do something*!" Perrin exploded. "How can you sit here and watch blinking lights and program computers and let the world come to an end? This is madness! *You've* got to do something!"

The people in the room, including the holographic projections, were now looking at one another, often with quick glances, sometimes with long eye contacts. Nobody said a word. Most were afraid to say anything.

Slowly and softly, Chuck broke the heavy silence. "I have already done something about it."

The room exploded again in voices. Chuck merely held up his hand, and the room fell silent again. Of all the powerful people in the room, Chuck Armitage was now the most powerful. He turned around and pointed to a screen in the traffic room. Two green triangles were now leaving a green trail on the near-Earth display. One of them appeared to be accelerating rapidly. The display had been up for several minutes, but only Chuck had noticed. The others had been far too engrossed in the problem or did not understand the display.

"Madame Secretary," Chuck addressed his boss who, because of her astronaut training, had maintained her cool consideration of the affair. "You know nothing of what I have done. I haven't told you about its planning. I initiated its implementation without your knowledge or approval. I utilized funds from several parts of the budget in such a way that the expenditures wouldn't be noticed until GAO audits us. I'm sorry that I had to do it this way, but I had to protect you and the department from the storm that is to follow. I accept full and complete responsibility."

"You still haven't told me what you've done, Chuck," Helen Seton pointed out with no trace of emotion.

"First off, here is my resignation, effective immediately." Chuck withdrew an envelope from his jacket pocket and proffered it to his boss.

"We'll discuss it at a later time when things are not so critical," she replied with a wave of her hand, refusing to accept the envelope. "What is going on now?" she asked quietly.

"My grandstand play. Senator Davidoff said a few minutes ago that I don't make them. That is not precisely true. I don't make them until it counts. If I had yelled and made a bloody nuisance of myself over the runaway possibility when I took over here seven years ago, I would not have remained in the position for more than six weeks . . ."

"That's a very astute observation, Chuck," Davidoff told him.

"I know. Jeremiah, your people, combined with those from TransWorld and Terra-Luna, would never live with any system that could reach into deep space. Neither would the League of Free Traders—"

"Don't try to put the blame for all of this on us, Armitage," Jeremiah Morris growled. "Because of your unreasonable regulations, we've had to put safety devices on the safety devices . . . and something was bound to go wrong sooner or—"

"Gentlemen!" Helen Seton's voice was still quiet, but it carried both leadership and authority in its tone. "Please! There will be ample time for bickering later . . . if we survive. Let Chuck explain what it is that he has done behind the scenes."

"Thank you. I did a bootleg engineering job that is something far less than perfect with high risk involved and exorbitant ultimate cost . . . hoping that I would never have to use it because others might be convinced to give us the means to do it right. Well, SLZ-420 forced the issue and pushed me into using my Plan B which is one-shot. We can never use it again, so we've got to get our heads together even while it is probably saving our necks . . . which is why the president acceded to my requests to bring you together here."

Perrin was on his feet, using his full-volumed House speaking voice. "I will not permit myself to be pressured in this manner. . . . Please excuse me!"

"You will have some trouble getting out of here," Chuck Armitage pointed out. "Madame Secretary, do I not have the authority to seal off the center in an emergency?"

"You do, and I will not countermand your order. But I would really like to know what you are doing, Chuck. All of this preamble obviously seems important, and it probably is. But SLZ-420 is coming down our throats, and that is Priority Number One. *Will everybody please be quiet and listen?*" When she raised her voice with emotion in it, the shock rippled through the room, which instantly became silent.

Chuck spun a chair around and literally fell into it. Fatigue was beginning to get to him, and there was a long time yet to go. "Those two green triangles boosting hard away from Earth are two of our deep-space inspection cutters from Hilo Base, Hawaii. They have been highly modified and each is manned only by a single pilot."

"Manned? Why manned?" Star Admiral Jacobs wanted to know.

"Because we had neither the time nor the money to develop the necessary long-range active guidance and homing systems that are required for an interceptor that can handle high closure rates at distances far beyond lunar orbit," Chuck explained.

"I had to use a guidance system that was already available: a human being. The first triangle represents the cutter *Toryu*, which is boosting at four standard g's, the limit of sustained human endurance, under the control of Tomio Hattori. The second triangle represents the *Shoki*, boosting at two standard g under the control of Kimsuki Kusabake. In approximately twenty-five hours, the *Toryu* will intercept the SLZ-420. If Tom Hattori does the kind of job I know he can do, the impact of that two-thousand-ton cutter will do one or both of two jobs: deflect the SLZ-420 from its present trajectory and/or disable its constant-boost drive. If Tom doesn't do the complete job, we have the *Shoki* following with Kim to finish it off . . . but that will be a tough one because of the increased closure rate . . ."

Again, it was Congressman Claypool Perrin, the reelected romantic of the let-it-all-hang-out seventies, who broke in almost hysterically. "Do you mean to tell us that you have deliberately sent at least one person to a certain death? How can you possibly do this . . . this *inhumane* thing?"

"I know of no other way to do it at this time with the tools that you have permitted me," Chuck fired back. "And spare me the outrage. Ain't nobody here but us chickens, fellas . . . and that is an American folk saying for the benefit of our teleconferencing guests. Every one of us in this room, including the teleconferencing guests, has contributed to this situation in his own unique way."

"Now, that certainly isn't true, Chuck! This should have been a Space Watch job—" Star Admiral Jacobs started to say.

"See what I mean?" Chuck said. "The Watch fought us tooth and nail when we instituted orbital sweeping for the thousands of dead satellites up there. No, they wanted high-power beam weapons installed in L-5 to do the job. . . . And I know that your intelligence people knew that, Dimitri!"

"That's not a fair assessment!" Jacobs tried to break in. "The State Department didn't—"

"I don't care who tries to put the blame on who!" Chuck said in exasperation. "Governments, private enterprise, everyone involved in space commerce is right here, right now! Reading it on the news tube wouldn't have helped toward a solution; you had to be here right in the middle of it living with the consequences of your actions. You had to see and experience it, and it is a very difficult thing to do. And please don't think that taking care of this industrial accident was an easy thing for me to do, either!" He sighed deeply and rubbed his eyes. "But it *will* be an easy thing for Tom and Kim."

"What do you mean, Chuck?" Senator Davidoff asked.

"Admiral Jacobs knows what I mean. There are always people who are willing to sacrifice themselves for the greater good. Some people seek self-destruction for a cause in order to give meaning to their lives. Our psychologists can spot them. And sometimes it is a cultural trait. . . ."

"Kamikazes," Jacob muttered.

"Over two thousand pilots of World War II, and several thousand from time to time since then in suicide missions in brushfire wars for a glorious cause greater than they believe themselves to be." Chuck noticed that Perrin was now shaking his head in total disbelief. "No, Congressman Perrin, this job isn't all technology. It deals with people because technical problems are rarely unsolved due to technical factors. In this case, I am giving two people the opportunity to fulfill themselves. Tom and Kim are out there by their own free choice. I have been the only one who did not have a real choice."

Most of the people present in the room sat aghast, with three exceptions—the hologram from Singapore whose Japanese features indicated full understanding, Secretary Helen Seton, whose own sacrifice on PowerSat One had made her life as a woman and mother impossible, and Star Admiral Jacobs, who nodded as though he had discovered in Chuck Armitage a man he could fully understand. "We have them in the Space Watch, too. No military establishment could exist without them," he said with pride.

It was now very quiet in the room again. Armitage looked around. "We have twenty-five hours before we know if Tom Hattori succeeds. In the meantime, we have placed the tightest possible worldwide news lid on this. There will be no leaks from Singapore or from the centers. Food and beverages will be available here, and there are secure rooms down the hall if anyone needs to rest. Your respective organizations have been notified that you are in a special international conference, which is no lie. We have all seen the consequences of our past activities. We now have the unique opportunity to work out an arrangement so that this sort of thing can never happen again. Madame Secretary, you are the logical one to chair this *ad hoc* conference. Would you care for some coffee?"

• • •

Tom Hattori and the *Toryu* did the job. The haggard group in the gallery of the center watched the displays as what was left careered around the Earth and plunged outward forever into deep space with a velocity that would take it to the stars. There were no cheers. The conference group was far too exhausted physically and emotionally. New agreements had been hammered out. A joint communiqué had been written and released to the news media.

Both in space and in the center, the solutions were compromises . . . but workable compromises.

Chuck Armitage was the first to leave the center.

He discovered Senator Davidoff and Secretary Seton walking on either side of him.

"Where are you going, Chuck?" Helen Seton asked.

"Home. To stay."

"Take a few days' rest. Then come and see me. There's work to be done . . . lots of work."

"Madame Secretary . . . Helen . . . my resignation holds. It has to."

"Chuck, you're a good man," Senator Davidoff put in. "We've always needed good men. Why do you think you're finished in your present position? With the new agreements, we need you more than ever. You were the spark plug that got it all together for us."

"Ah, my dear colleague from the good old days of the Shuttle missions!" Chuck Armitage replied. "Perhaps you and Helen can handle the political aspects of this and swing enough clout with GAO so that Justice does not indict me for misappropriation of funds . . ."

"But you saved the whole damned world!" Davidoff pointed out.

"Temporarily . . . until the next crisis in an era of crises."

"I can't be as dramatic as the senator," the petite secretary of space commerce remarked, "but he's right. We need you more than ever. When forced to make a decision, you didn't waffle . . . and it was a very tough decision. Both the senator and I know such a thing is rare among people today, but absolutely necessary in space. Chuck, your career and job are not in jeopardy. I'll stick by you, whatever happens . . ."

"And I will do the same," Davidoff added quickly, earnestly.

Chuck stopped walking so suddenly that his two companions went two steps beyond him, then turned to face where he stood. "No. For several reasons. You're on top of the hill, and I am down on a ridge. I see some things differently. I pushed around a lot of internationally powerful and influential people. I rubbed their noses in their own accumulated folly and made them admit to it by forcing them to come up with a new set of rules. I'll never be one of them and I'll no longer be able to work for them because I have proved that I am willing to rock the boat and make big waves. I am no longer to be trusted . . ."

"Nonsense!" Davidoff snorted.

"You know it isn't. I cannot ask you to risk your own careers. I've already sent one man to his willing destruction; I cannot ask anyone else to even risk it. In fact, my own personal values are making it very difficult for me to rationalize Tomio Hattori. In my own case, it doesn't count. When I spoke of people willing to sacrifice themselves for a greater cause, I knew exactly what I was talking about. . . . Now, please excuse me. I'm very tired . . ."

He turned and took a side path, walking away from them. In the star-specked evening, the ex-astronaut senator and the ex-astronaut minister watched him go. There wasn't anything either of them could say.

ENDER'S GAME

by Orson Scott Card

"Whatever your gravity is when you get to the door, re-member—the enemy's gate is *down*. If you step through your own door like you're out for a stroll, you're a big target and you deserve to get hit. With more than a flasher." Ender Wiggin paused and looked over the group. Most were just watching him nervously. A few understanding. A few sullen and resist-ing.

First day with this army, all fresh from the teacher squads, and Ender had forgotten how young new kids could be. He'd been in it for three years, they'd had six months—nobody over nine years old in the whole bunch. But they were his. At eleven, he was half a year early to be a commander. He'd had a toon of his own and knew a few tricks but there were forty in his new army. Green. All marksmen with a flasher, all in top shape, or they wouldn't be here—but they were all just as likely as not to get wiped out first time into battle.

"Remember," he went on, "they can't see you till you get through that door. But the second you're out, they'll be on you. So hit that door the way you want to be when they shoot at you. Legs up under you, going straight *down*." He pointed at a sullen kid who looked like he was only seven, the smallest of them all. "Which way is down, greenoh!"

"Toward the enemy door." The answer was quick. It was also surly, saying, "yeah, yeah, now get on with the important stuff."

"Name, kid?"

"Bean."

"Get that for size or for brains?"

Bean didn't answer. The rest laughed a little. Ender had chosen right. This kid *was* younger than the rest, must have been advanced because he was sharp. The others didn't like him much, they were happy to see him taken down a little. Like Ender's first commander had taken him down.

"Well, Bean, you're right onto things. Now I tell you this, nobody's gonna get through that door without a good chance of getting hit. A lot of you are going to be turned into cement somewhere. Make sure it's your legs. Right? If only your legs get hit, then only your legs get frozen, and in nullo that's no sweat." Ender turned to one of the dazed ones. "What're legs for? Hmmm?"

Blank stare. Confusion. Stammer.

"Forget it. Guess I'll have to ask Bean here."

"Legs are for pushing off walls." Still bored.

"Thanks, Bean. Get that, everybody?" They all got it, and didn't like getting it from Bean. "Right. You can't *see* with legs, you can't *shoot* with legs, and most of the time they just get in the way. If they get frozen sticking straight out you've turned yourself into a blimp. No way to hide. So how do legs go?"

A few answered this time, to prove that Bean wasn't the only one who knew anything. "Under you. Tucked up under."

"Right. A shield. You're kneeling on a shield, and the shield is your own legs. And there's a trick to the suits. Even when your legs are flashed you can *still* kick off. I've never seen anybody do it but me—but you're all gonna learn it."

Ender Wiggin turned on his flasher. It glowed faintly green in his hand. Then he let himself rise in the weightless workout room, pulled his legs under him as though he were kneeling, and flashed both of them. Immediately his suit stiffened at the knees and ankles, so that he couldn't bend at all.

"Okay, I'm frozen, see?"

He was floating a meter above them. They all looked up at him, puzzled. He leaned back and caught one of the handholds on the wall behind him, and pulled himself flush against the wall.

"I'm stuck at a wall. If I had legs, I'd use legs, and string myself out like a string *bean*, right?"

They laughed.

"But I don't have legs, and that's *better*, got it? Because of this." Ender jackknifed at the waist, then straightened out violently. He was across the workout room in only a moment. From the other side he called to them. "Got that? I didn't use hands, so I still had use of my flasher. *And* I didn't have my legs floating five feet behind me. Now watch it again."

He repeated the jackknife, and caught a handhold on the wall near them. "Now, I don't just want you to do that when they've flashed your legs. I want you to do that when you've still got legs, because it's better. And because they'll never be expecting it. All right now, everybody up in the air and kneeling."

Most were up in a few seconds. Ender flashed the stragglers, and they dangled, helplessly frozen, while the others laughed. "When I give an order, you move. Got it? When we're at a door and they clear it, I'll be giving you orders in two seconds, as soon as I see the setup. And when I give the order you better be out there, because whoever's out there first is going to win, unless he's a fool. I'm not. And you better not be, or I'll have you back in the teacher squads." He saw more than a few of them gulp, and the frozen ones looked at him with fear. "You guys who are hanging there. You watch. You'll thaw out in about fifteen minutes, and let's see if you can catch up to the others."

For the next half hour Ender had them jackknifing off walls. He called a stop when he saw that they all had the basic idea. They were a good group, maybe. They'd get better.

"Now you're warmed up," he said to them, "we'll start working."

Ender was the last one out after practice, since he stayed to help some of the slower ones improve on technique. They'd had good teachers, but like all armies they were uneven, and some of them could be a real drawback in battle. Their first battle might be weeks away. It might be tomorrow. A schedule was never printed. The commander just woke up and found a note by his bunk, giving him the time of his battle and the name of his opponent. So for the first while he was going to drive his boys until they were in top shape—all of them. Ready for anything, at any time. Strategy was nice, but it was worth nothing if the soldiers couldn't hold up under the strain.

He turned the corner into the residence wing and found himself face to face with Bean, the seven-year-old he had picked on all through practice that day. Problems. Ender didn't want problems right now.

"Ho, Bean."

"Ho, Ender."

Pause.

"Sir," Ender said softly.

"We're not on duty."

"In my army, Bean, we're always on duty." Ender brushed past him.

Bean's high voice piped up behind him. "I know what you're doing, Ender, sir, and I'm warning you."

Ender turned slowly and looked at him. "Warning me?"

"I'm the best man you've got. But I'd better be treated like it."

"Or what?" Ender smiled menacingly.

"Or I'll be the worst man you've got. One or the other."

"And what do you want? Love and kisses?" Ender was getting angry.

Bean was unworried. "I want a toon."

Ender walked back to him and stood looking down into his eyes. "I'll give a toon," he said, "to the boys who prove they're worth something. They've got to be good soldiers, they've got to know how to take orders, they've got to be able to think for themselves in a pinch, and they've got to be able to keep respect. That's how I got to be a commander. That's how you'll get to be a toon leader."

Bean smiled. "That's fair. *If* you actually work that way, I'll be a toon leader in a month."

Ender reached down and grabbed the front of his uniform and shoved him into the wall. "When I say I work a certain way, Bean, then that's the way I work."

Bean just smiled. Ender let go of him and walked away, and didn't look back. He was sure, without looking, that Bean was still watching, still smiling, still just a little contemptuous. He might make a good toon leader at that. Ender would keep an eye on him.

•　　•　　•

Captain Graff, six foot two and a little chubby, stroked his belly as he leaned back in his chair. Across his desk sat Lieutenant Anderson, who was earnestly pointing out high points on a chart.

"Here it is, Captain," Anderson said. "Ender's already got them doing a tactic that's going to throw off everyone who meets it. Doubled their speed."

Graff nodded.

"And you know his test scores. He thinks well, too."

Graff smiled. "All true, all true, Anderson, he's a fine student, shows real promise."

They waited.

Graff sighed. "So what do you want me to do?"

"Ender's the one. He's got to be."

"He'll never be ready in time, Lieutenant. He's eleven, for heaven's sake, man, what do you want, a miracle?"

"I want him into battles, every day starting tomorrow. I want him to have a year's worth of battles in a month."

Graff shook his head. "That would have his army in the hospital."

"No sir. He's getting them into form. And we need Ender."

"Correction, Lieutenant. We need somebody. You think it's Ender."

"All right, I think it's Ender. Which of the commanders if it isn't him?"

"I don't know, Lieutenant." Graff ran his hands over his slightly fuzzy bald head. "These are children, Anderson. Do you realize that? Ender's army is nine years old. Are we going to put them against the older kids? Are we going to put them through hell for a month like that?"

Lieutenant Anderson leaned even further over Graff's desk.

"Ender's test scores, Captain!"

"I've seen his bloody test scores! I've watched him in battle, I've listened to tapes of his training sessions, I've watched his sleep patterns, I've heard tapes of his conversations in the corridors and in the bathrooms, I'm more aware of Ender Wiggin than you could possibly imagine! And against all the arguments, against his obvious qualities, I'm weighing one thing. I have this picture of Ender a year from now, if you have your way. I see him completely useless, worn down, a failure, because he was pushed farther than he or any living person could go. But it doesn't weigh enough, does it, Lieutenant, because there's a war on, and our best talent is gone, and the biggest battles are ahead. So give Ender a battle every day this week. And then bring me a report.''

Anderson stood and saluted. ''Thank you sir.''

He had almost reached the door when Graff called his name. He turned and faced the captain.

''Anderson,'' Captain Graff said. ''Have you been outside, lately I mean?''

''Not since last leave, six months ago.''

''I didn't think so. Not that it makes any difference. But have you ever been to Beaman Park, there in the city? Hmm? Beautiful park. Trees. Grass. No nullo, no battles, no worries. Do you know what else there is in Beaman Park?''

''What sir?'' Lieutenant Anderson asked.

''Children,'' Graff answered.

''Of course children,'' said Anderson.

''I mean children. I mean kids who get up in the morning when their mothers call them and they go to school and then in the afternoons they go to Beaman Park and play. They're happy, they smile a lot, they laugh, they have fun. Hmmm?''

''I'm sure they do sir.''

''Is that all you can say, Anderson?''

Anderson cleared his throat. ''It's good for children to have fun, I think, sir. I know I did when I was a boy. But right now the world needs soldiers. And this is the way to get them.''

Graff nodded and closed his eyes. ''Oh, indeed, you're right, by statistical proof and by all the important theories, and dammit they work and the system is right but all the same Ender's older than I am. He's not a child. He's barely a person.''

''If that's true, sir, then at least we all know that Ender is making it possible for the others of his age to be playing in the park.''

''And Jesus died to save all men, of course.'' Graff sat up and looked at Anderson almost sadly. ''But we're the ones,'' Graff said, ''we're the ones who are driving in the nails.''

Ender Wiggin lay on his bed staring at the ceiling. He never slept more than five hours a night—but the lights went off at 2200 and didn't come on again until 0600. So he stared at the ceiling and thought. He'd had his army for three and a half weeks. Dragon Army. The name was assigned, and it wasn't a lucky one. Oh, the charts said that about nine years ago a Dragon Army had done fairly well. But for the next six years the name had been attached to inferior armies, and finally, because of the superstition that was beginning to play about the name, Dragon Army was retired. Until now. And now, Ender thought smiling, Dragon Army was going to take them by surprise.

The door opened softly. Ender did not turn his head. Someone stepped softly into his room, then left with the quiet sound of the door shutting. When soft steps died away Ender rolled over and saw a white slip of paper lying on the floor. He reached down and picked it up.

"Dragon Army against Rabbit Army, Ender Wiggin and Carn Carby, 0700."

The first battle. Ender got out of bed and quickly dressed. He went rapidly to the rooms of each of his toon leaders and told them to rouse their boys. In five minutes they were all gathered in the corridor, sleepy and slow. Ender spoke softly.

"First battle, 0700 against Rabbit Army. I've fought them twice before but they've got a new commander. Never heard of him. They're an older group, though, and I know a few of their old tricks. Now wake up. Run, doublefast, warmup in workroom three."

For an hour and a half they worked out, with three mockbattles and calisthenics in the corridor out of the nullo. Then for fifteen minutes they all lay up in the air, totally relaxing in the weightlessness. At 0650 Ender roused them and they hurried into the corridor. Ender led them down the corridor, running again, and occasionally leaping to touch a light panel on the ceiling. The boys all touched the same light panel. And at 0658 they reached their gate to the battleroom.

The members of Toons C and D grabbed the first eight handholds in the ceiling of the corridor. Toons A, B, and E crouched on the floor. Ender hooked his feet into two handholds in the middle of the ceiling, so he was out of everyone's way.

"Which way is the enemy's door?" he hissed.

"Down!" they whispered back, and laughed.

"Flashers on." The boxes in their hands glowed green. They waited for a few seconds more, and then the gray wall in front of them disappeared and the battleroom was visible.

Ender sized it up immediately. The familiar open grid of the most early games, like the monkey bars at the park, with seven or eight boxes scattered through the grid. They called the boxes *stars*. There were enough of them, and in forward enough

positions, that they were worth going for. Ender decided this
in a second, and he hissed, ''Spread to near stars. E hold!''

The four groups in the corners plunged through the forcefield
at the doorways and fell down into the battleroom. Before the
enemy even appeared through the opposite gate Ender's army
had spread from the door to the nearest stars.

Then the enemy soldiers came through the door. From their
stance Ender knew they had been in a different gravity, and
didn't know enough to disorient themselves from it. They came
through standing up, their entire bodies spread and defenseless.

''Kill em, E!'' Ender hissed, and threw himself out the door
knees first, with his flasher between his legs and firing. While
Ender's group flew across the room the rest of Dragon Army
lay down a protecting fire, so that E group reached a forward
position with only one boy frozen completely, though they had
all lost the use of their legs—which didn't impair them in the
least. There was a lull as Ender and his opponent, Carn Carby,
assessed their positions. Aside from Rabbit Army's losses at
the gate, there had been few casualties, and both armies were
near full strength. But Carn had no originality—he was in a
four-corner spread that any five-year-old in the teacher squads
might have thought of. And Ender knew how to defeat it.

He called out, loudly, ''E covers A, C down. B, D angle
east wall.'' Under E toon's cover, B and D toons lunged away
from their stars. While they were still exposed, A and C toons
left their stars and drifted toward the near wall. They reached
it together, and together jackknifed off the wall. At double the
normal speed they appeared behind the enemy's stars, and
opened fire. In a few seconds the battle was over, with the
enemy almost entirely frozen, including the commander, and
the rest scattered to the corners. For the next five minutes, in
squads of four, Dragon Army cleaned out the dark corners of
the battleroom and shepherded the enemy into the center, where
their bodies, frozen at impossible angles, jostled each other.
Then Ender took three of his boys to the enemy gate and went
through the formality of reversing the one-way field by simultaneously touching a Dragon Army helmet at each corner. Then
Ender assembled his army in vertical files near the knot of
frozen Rabbit Army soldiers.

Only three of Dragon Army's soldiers were immobile. Their
victory margin—38 to 0—was ridiculously high, and Ender
began to laugh. Dragon Army joined him, laughing long and

loud. They were still laughing when Lieutenant Anderson and Lieutenant Morris came in from the teachergate at the south end of the battleroom.

Lieutenant Anderson kept his face stiff and unsmiling, but Ender saw him wink as he held out his hand and offered the stiff, formal congratulations that were ritually given to the victor in the game.

Morris found Carn Carby and unfroze him, and the thirteen-year-old came and presented himself to Ender, who laughed without malice and held out his hand. Carn graciously took Ender's hand and bowed his head over it. It was that or be flashed again.

Lieutenant Anderson dismissed Dragon Army, and they silently left the battleroom through the enemy's door—again part of the ritual. A light was blinking on the north side of the square door, indicating where the gravity was in that corridor. Ender, leading his soldiers, changed his orientation and went through the forcefield and into gravity on his feet. His army followed him at a brisk run back to the workroom. When they got there they formed up into squads, and Ender hung in the air, watching them.

"Good first battle," he said, which was excuse enough for a cheer, which he quieted. "Dragon Army did all right against Rabbits. But the enemy isn't always going to be that bad. And if that had been a good army we would have been smashed. We still would have won, but we would have been smashed. Now let me see B and D toons out here. Your takeoff from the stars was way too slow. If Rabbit Army knew how to aim a flasher, you all would have been frozen solid before A and C even got to the wall."

They worked out for the rest of the day.

That night Ender went for the first time to the commanders' mess hall. No one was allowed there until he had won at least one battle, and Ender was the youngest commander ever to make it. There was no great stir when he came in. But when some of the other boys saw the Dragon on his breast pocket, they stared at him openly, and by the time he got his tray and sat at an empty table, the entire room was silent, with the other commanders watching him. Intensely self-conscious, Ender wondered how they all knew, and why they all looked so hostile.

Then he looked above the door he had just come through. There was a huge scoreboard across the entire wall. It showed the win/loss record for the commander of every army; that day's battles were lit in red. Only four of them. The other three winners had barely made it—the best of them had only two men whole and eleven mobile at the end of the game. Dragon Army's score of thirty-eight mobile was embarrassingly better.

Other new commanders had been admitted to the commanders' mess hall with cheers and congratulations. Other new commanders hadn't won thirty-eight to zero.

Ender looked for Rabbit Army on the scoreboard. He was surprised to find that Carn Carby's score to date was eight wins and three losses. Was he that good? Or had he only fought against inferior armies? Whichever, there was still a zero in Carn's mobile and whole columns, and Ender looked down from the scoreboard grinning. No one smiled back, and Ender knew that they were afraid of him, which meant that they would hate him, which meant that anyone who went into battle against Dragon Army would be scared and angry and incompetent. Ender looked for Carn Carby in the crowd, and found him not too far away. He stared at Carby until one of the other boys nudged the Rabbit commander and pointed to Ender. Ender smiled again and waved slightly. Carby turned red, and Ender, satisfied, leaned over his dinner and began to eat.

At the end of the week Dragon Army had fought seven battles in seven days. The score stood 7 wins and 0 losses. Ender had never had more than five boys frozen in any game. It was no longer possible for the other commanders to ignore Ender. A few of them sat with him and quietly conversed about game strategies that Ender's opponents had used. Other much larger groups were talking with the commanders that Ender had defeated, trying to find out what Ender had done to beat them.

In the middle of the meal the teacher door opened and the groups fell silent as Lieutenant Anderson stepped in and looked over the group. When he located Ender he strode quickly across the room and whispered in Ender's ear. Ender nodded, finished his glass of water, and left with the lieutenant. On the way out, Anderson handed a slip of paper to one of the older boys. The room became very noisy with conversation as Anderson and Ender left.

Ender was escorted down corridors he had never seen before. They didn't have the blue glow of the soldier corridors. Most were wood paneled, and the floors were carpeted. The doors were wood, with nameplates on them, and they stopped at one they said, "Captain Graff, Supervisor." Anderson knocked softly, and a low voice said, "Come in."

They went in. Captain Graff was seated behind a desk, his hands folded across his pot belly. He nodded, and Anderson sat. Ender also sat down. Graff cleared his throat and spoke.

"Seven days since your first battle, Ender."

Ender did not reply.

"Won seven battles, one every day."

Ender nodded.

"Scores unusually high, too."

Ender blinked.

"Why?" Graff asked him.

Ender glanced at Anderson, and then spoke to the captain behind the desk. "Two new tactics, sir. Legs doubled up as a shield, so that a flash doesn't immobilize. Jackknife takeoffs from the walls. Superior strategy, as Lieutenant Anderson taught, think places, not spaces. Five toons of eight instead of four of ten. Incompetent opponents. Excellent toon leaders, good soldiers."

Graff looked at Ender without expression. Waiting for what, Ender thought. Lieutenant Anderson spoke.

"Ender, what's the condition of your army?"

"A little tired, in peak condition, morale high, learning fast. Anxious for the next battle."

Anderson looked at Graff, and Graff shrugged slightly. Then he nodded, and Anderson smiled. Graff turned to Ender.

"Is there anything you want to know?"

Ender held his hands loosely in his lap. "When are you going to put us up against a good army?"

Anderson was surprised, and Graff laughed out loud. The laughter rang in the room, and when it stopped, Graff handed a piece of paper to Ender. "Now," the Captain said, and Ender read the paper.

"Dragon Army against Leopard Army. Ender Wiggin and Pol Slattery, 2000."

Ender looked up at Captain Graff. "That's ten minutes from now, sir."

Graff smiled. "Better hurry, then, boy."

As Ender left he realized Pol Slattery was the boy who had been handed his orders as Ender left the mess hall.

He got to his army five minutes later. Three toon leaders were already undressed and lying naked on their beds. He sent them all flying down the corridors to rouse their toons, and gathered up their suits himself. As all his boys were assembled in the corridor, most of them still getting dressed, Ender spoke to them.

"This one's hot and there's no time. We'll be late to the door, and the enemy'll be deployed right outside our gate. Ambush, and I've never heard of it happening before. So we'll take our time at the door. E toon, keep your belts loose, and give your flashers to the leaders and seconds of the other toons."

Puzzled, E toon complied. By then all were dressed, and Ender led them at a trot to the gate. When they reached it the forcefield was already on one-way, and some of his soldiers were panting. They had had one battle that day and a full workout. They were tired.

Ender stopped at the entrance and looked at the placement of the enemy soldiers. Most of them were grouped not more than twenty feet out from the gate. There was no grid, there were no stars. A big empty space. Where were the other enemy soldiers? There should have been ten more.

"They're flat against this wall," Ender said, "where we can't see them."

He thought for a moment, then took two of the toons and made them kneel, their hands on their hips. Then he flashed them, so that their bodies were frozen rigid.

"You're shields," Ender said, and then had boys from two other toons kneel on their legs, and hook both arms under the frozen boys' shoulders. Each boy was holding two flashers. Then Ender and the members of the last toon picked up the duos, three at a time, and threw them out the door.

Of course, the enemy opened fire immediately. But they only hit the boys who were already flashed, and in a few moments pandemonium broke out in the battleroom. All the soldiers of Leopard Army were easy targets as they lay pressed flat against the wall, and Ender's soldiers, armed with two flashers each, carved them up easily. Pol Slattery reacted quickly, ordering his men away from the wall, but not quickly enough—only a few were able to move, and they were flashed before they could get a quarter of the way across the battleroom.

When the battle was over Dragon Army had only twelve boys whole, the lowest score they had ever had. But Ender was satisfied. And during the ritual of surrender Pol Slattery broke form by shaking hands and asking, "Why did you wait so long getting out of the gate?"

Ender glanced at Anderson, who was floating nearby. "I was informed late," he said. "It was an ambush."

Slattery grinned, and gripped Ender's hand again. "Good game."

Ender didn't smile at Anderson this time. He knew that now the games would be arranged against him, to even up the odds. He didn't like it.

It was 2150, nearly time for lights out, when Ender knocked at the door of the room shared by Bean and three other soldiers. One of the others opened the door, then stepped back and held it wide. Ender stood for a moment, then asked if he could come in. They answered, of course, of course, come in, and he walked to the upper bunk, where Bean had set down his book and was leaning on one elbow to look at Ender.

"Bean, can you give me twenty minutes?"

"Near lights out," Bean answered.

"My room," Ender answered. "I'll cover for you." Bean sat up and slid off his bed. Together he and Ender padded silently down the corridor to Ender's room. Bean entered first, and Ender closed the door behind them.

"Sit down," Ender said, and they both sat on the edge of the bed, looking at each other.

"Remember four weeks ago, Bean? When you told me to make you a toon leader?"

"Yeah."

"I've made five toon leaders since then, haven't I? And none of them was you."

Bean looked at him calmly.

"Was I right?" Ender asked.

"Yes, sir," Bean answered.

Ender nodded. "How have you done in these battles?"

Bean cocked his head to one side. "I've never been immobilized, sir, and I've immobilized forty-three of the enemy. I've obeyed orders quickly, and I've commanded a squad in mop-up and never lost a soldier."

"Then you'll understand this." Ender paused, then decided to back up and say something else first.

"You know you're early, Bean, by a good half year. I was, too, and I've been made a commander six months early. Now they've put me into battles after only three weeks of training with my army. They've given me eight battles in seven days. I've already had more battles than boys who were made commander four months ago. I've won more battles than many who've been commanders for a year. And then tonight. You know what happened tonight.''

Bean nodded. ''They told you late.''

''I don't know what the teachers are doing. But my army is getting tired, and I'm getting tired, and now they're changing the rules of the game. You see, Bean, I've looked in the old charts. No one has ever destroyed so many enemies and kept so many of his own soldiers whole in the history of the game. I'm unique—and I'm getting unique treatment.''

Bean smiled. ''You're the best, Ender.''

Ender shook his head. ''Maybe. But it was no accident that I got the soldiers I got. My worst soldier could be a toon leader in another army. I've got the best. They've loaded things my way—but now they're loading it against me. I don't know why. But I know I have to be ready for it. I need your help.''

''Why mine?''

''Because even though there are some better soldiers than you in Dragon Army—not many, but some—there's nobody who can think better and faster than you.'' Bean said nothing. They both knew it was true.

Ender continued, ''I need to be ready, but I can't retrain the whole army. So I'm going to cut every toon down by one, including you—and you and four others will be a special squad under me. And you'll learn to do some new things. Most of the time you'll be in the regular toons just like you are now. But when I need you. See?''

Bean smiled and nodded. ''That's right, that's good, can I pick them myself?''

''One from each toon except your own, and you can't take any toon leaders.''

''What do you want us to do?''

''Bean, I don't know. I don't know what they'll throw at us. What would you do if suddenly our flashers didn't work, and the enemy's did? What would you do if we had to face two armies at once? The only thing I know is—we're not going for score anymore. We're going for the enemy's gate. That's when the battle is technically won—four helmets at the corners of the gate. I'm going for quick kills, battles ended even when we're outnumbered. Got it? You take them for two hours during regular workout. Then you and I and your soldiers, we'll work at night after dinner.''

''We'll get tired.''

"I have a feeling we don't know what tired is."

Ender reached out and took Bean's hand, and gripped it. "Even when it's rigged against us, Bean. We'll win."

Bean left in silence and padded down the corridor.

Dragon Army wasn't the only army working out after hours now. The other commanders finally realized they had some catching up to do. From early morning to lights out soldiers all over Training and Command Center, none of them over fourteen years old, were learning to jackknife off walls and use each other as living shields.

But while other commanders mastered the techniques that Ender had used to defeat them, Ender and Bean worked on solutions to problems that had never come up.

There were still battles every day, but for a while they were normal, with grids and stars and sudden plunges through the gate. And after the battles, Ender and Bean and four other soldiers would leave the main group and practice strange maneuvers. Attacks without flashers, using feet to physically disarm or disorient an enemy. Using four frozen soldiers to reverse the enemy's gate in less than two seconds. And one day Bean came to workout with a 300-meter cord.

"What's that for?"

"I don't know yet." Absently Bean spun one end of the cord. It wasn't more than an eighth of an inch thick, but it could have lifted ten adults without breaking.

"Where did you get it?"

"Commissary. They asked what for. I said to practice tying knots."

Bean tied a loop in the end of the rope and slid it over his shoulders.

"Here, you two, hang onto the wall here. Now don't let go of the rope. Give me about fifty yards of slack." They complied, and Bean moved about ten feet from them along the wall. As soon as he was sure they were ready, he jackknifed off the wall and flew straight out, fifty meters. Then the rope snapped taut. It was so fine that it was virtually invisible, but it was strong enough to force Bean to veer off at almost a right angle. It happened so suddenly that he had inscribed a perfect arc and hit the wall before most of the other soldiers knew what had happened. Bean did a perfect rebound and drifted quickly back where Ender and the others waited for him.

Many of the soldiers in the five regular squads hadn't noticed

the rope, and were demanding to know how it was done. It
was impossible to change direction that abruptly in nullo. Bean
just laughed.

"Wait till the next game without a grid! They'll never know
what hit them."

They never did. The next game was only two hours later,
but Bean and two others had become pretty good at aiming
and shooting while they flew at ridiculous speeds at the end of
the rope. The slip of paper was delivered, and Dragon Army
trotted off to the gate, to battle with Griffin Army. Bean coiled
the rope all the way.

When the gate opened, all they could see was a large brown
star only fifteen feet away, completely blocking their view of
the enemy's gate.

Ender didn't pause. "Bean, give yourself fifty feet of rope
and go around the star." Bean and his four soldiers dropped
through the gate and in a moment Bean was launched sideways
away from the star. The rope snapped taut, and Bean flew
forward. As the rope was stopped by each edge of the star in
turn, his arc became tighter and his speed greater, until when
he hit the wall only a few feet away from the gate he was
barely able to control his rebound to end up behind the star.
But he immediately moved all his arms and legs so that those
waiting inside the gate would know that the enemy hadn't
flashed him anywhere.

Ender dropped through the gate, and Bean quickly told him
how Griffin Army was situated. "They've got two squares of
stars, all the way around the gate. All their soldiers are under
cover, and there's no way to hit any of them until we're clear
to the bottom wall. Even with shields, we'd get there at half
strength and we wouldn't have a chance."

"They moving?" Ender asked.

"Do they need to?"

Ender thought for a moment. "This one's tough. We'll go
for the gate, Bean."

Griffin Army began to call out to them.

"Hey, is anybody there!"

"Wake up, there's a war on!"

"We wanna join the picnic!"

They were still calling when Ender's army came out from
behind their star with a shield of fourteen frozen soldiers. William Bee, Griffin Army's commander, waited patiently as the
screen approached, his men waiting at the fringes of their stars

for the moment when whatever was behind the screen became visible. About ten meters away the screen exploded as the soldiers behind it shoved the screen north. The momentum carried them south twice as fast, and at the same moment the rest of Dragon Army burst from behind their star at the opposite end of the room, firing rapidly.

William Bee's boys joined battle immediately, of course, but William Bee was far more interested in what had been left behind when the shield disappeared. A formation of four frozen Dragon Army soldiers was moving headfirst toward the Griffin Army gate, held together by another frozen soldier whose feet and hands were hooked through their belts. A sixth soldier hung to his wrist and trailed like the tail of a kite. Griffin Army was winning the battle easily, and William Bee concentrated on the formation as it approached the gate. Suddenly the soldier trailing in back moved—he wasn't frozen at all! And even though William Bee flashed him immediately, the damage was done. The formation drifted to the Griffin Army gate, and their helmets touched all four corners simultaneously. A buzzer sounded, the gate reversed, and the frozen soldier in the middle was carried by momentum right through the gate. All the flashers stopped working, and the game was over.

The teacher door opened and Lieutenant Anderson came in. Anderson stopped himself with a slight movement of his hands when he reached the center of the battleroom. "Ender," he called, breaking protocol. One of the frozen Dragon soldiers near the south wall tried to call through jaws that were clamped shut by the suit. Anderson drifted to him and unfroze him.

Ender was smiling.

"I beat you again, sir," Ender said. Anderson didn't smile.

"That's nonsense, Ender," Anderson said softly. "Your battle was with William Bee of Griffin Army."

Ender raised an eyebrow.

"After that maneuver," Anderson said, "the rules are being revised to require that all of the enemy's soldiers must be immobilized before the gate can be reversed."

"That's all right," Ender said. "It could only work once, anyway." Anderson nodded, and was turning away when Ender added, "Is there going to be a new rule that armies be given equal positions to fight from?"

Anderson turned back around. "If you're in one of the positions, Ender, you can hardly call them equal, whatever they are."

William Bee counted carefully and wondered how in the world he had lost when not one of his soldiers had been flashed, and only four of Ender's soldiers were even mobile.

And that night as Ender came into the commanders' mess hall, he was greeted with applause and cheers, and his table was crowded with respectful commanders, many of them two or three years older than he was. He was friendly, but while he ate he wondered what the teachers would do to him in his next battle. He didn't need to worry. His next two battles were easy victories, and after that he never saw the battleroom again.

It was 2100 and Ender was a little irritated to hear someone knock at his door. His army was exhausted, and he had ordered them all to be in bed after 2030. The last two days had been regular battles, and Ender was expecting the worst in the morning.

It was Bean. He came in sheepishly, and saluted.

Ender returned his salute and snapped, "Bean, I wanted everybody in bed."

Bean nodded but didn't leave. Ender considered ordering him out. But as he looked at Bean it occurred to him for the first time in weeks just how young Bean was. He had turned eight a week before, and he was still small and—no, Ender thought, he wasn't young. Nobody was young. Bean had been in battle, and with a whole army depending on him he had come through and won. And even though he was small, Ender could never think of him as young again.

Ender shrugged and Bean came over and sat on the edge of the bed. The younger boy looked at his hands for a while, and finally Ender grew impatient and asked, "Well, what is it?"

"I'm transferred. Got orders just a few minutes ago."

Ender closed his eyes for a moment. "I knew they'd pull something new. Now they're taking—where are you going?"

"Rabbit Army."

"How can they put you under an idiot like Carn Carby!"

"Carn was graduated. Support squads."

Ender looked up. "Well, who's commanding Rabbit then?"

Bean held his hands out helplessly.

"Me," he said.

Ender nodded, and then smiled, "Of course. After all, you're only four years younger than the regular age."

"It isn't funny," Bean said. "I don't know what's going on here. First all the changes in the game. And now this. I wasn't the only one transferred, either, Ender. Ren, Peder, Wins, Younger, Paul. All commanders now.''

Ender stood up angrily and strode to the wall. "Every damn toon leader I've got!" he said, and whirled to face Bean. "If they're going to break up my army, Bean, why did they bother making me a commander at all?''

Bean shook his head. "I don't know. You're the best, Ender. Nobody's ever done what you've done. Nineteen battles in fifteen days, sir, and you won every one of them, no matter what they did to you.''

"And now you and the others are commanders. You know every trick I've got, I trained you, and who am I supposed to replace you with? Are they going to stick me with six greenohs?''

"It stinks, Ender, but you know that if they gave you five crippled midgets and armed you with a roll of toilet paper you'd win.''

They both laughed, and then they noticed that the door was open.

Lieutenant Anderson stepped in. He was followed by Captain Graff.

"Ender Wiggin," Graff said, holding his hands across his stomach.

"Yes sir," Ender answered.

"Orders.''

Anderson extended a slip of paper. Ender read it quickly, then crumpled it, still looking at the air where the paper had been. After a few moments he asked, "Can I tell my army?''

"They'll find out," Graff answered. "It's better not to talk to them after orders. It makes it easier.''

"For you or for me?" Ender asked. He didn't wait for an answer. He turned to Bean, took his hand for a moment, and headed for the door.

"Wait," Bean said. "Where are you going? Tactical or Support School?''

"Command School," Ender answered, and then he was gone and Anderson closed the door.

Command School, Bean thought. Nobody went to Command School until they had gone through three years of Tactical. But then, nobody went to Tactical until they had been through at least five years of Battle School. Ender had only had three.

The system was breaking up. No doubt about it, Bean thought. Either somebody at the top was going crazy, or something was going wrong with the war—the real war, the one they were training to fight in. Why else would they break down the training system, advance somebody—even somebody as good as Ender—straight to Command School? Why else would they have an eight-year-old greenoh like Bean command an army?

Bean wondered about it for a long time, and then he finally lay down on Ender's bed and realized that he'd never see Ender again, probably. For some reason that made him want to cry. But he didn't cry, of course. Training in the preschools had taught him how to force down emotions like that. He remembered how his first teacher, when he was three, would have been upset to see his lip quivering and his eyes full of tears.

Bean went through the relaxing routine until he didn't feel like crying anymore. Then he drifted off to sleep. His hand was near his mouth. It lay on his pillow hesitantly, as if Bean couldn't decide whether to bite his nails or suck on his fingertips. His forehead was creased and furrowed. His breathing was quick and light. He was a soldier, and if anyone had asked him what he wanted to be when he grew up, he wouldn't have known what they meant.

There's a war on, they said, and that was excuse enough for all the hurry in the world. They said it like a password and flashed a little card at every ticket counter and customs check and guard station. It got them to the head of every line.

Ender Wiggin was rushed from place to place so quickly he had no time to examine anything. But he did see trees for the first time. He saw men who were not in uniform. He saw women. He saw strange animals that didn't speak, but that followed docilely behind women and small children. He saw suitcases and conveyor belts and signs that said words he had never heard of. He would have asked someone what the words meant, except that purpose and authority surrounded him in the persons of four very high officers who never spoke to each other and never spoke to him.

Ender Wiggin was a stranger to his world he was being trained to save. He did not remember ever leaving Battle School before. His earliest memories were of childish war games under the direction of a teacher, of meals with other boys in the gray and green uniforms of the armed forces of his world. He did not know that the gray represented the sky and the green represented the great forests of his planet. All he knew of the world was from vague references to "outside."

And before he could make any sense of the strange world he was seeing for the first time, they enclosed him again within the shell of the military, where nobody had to say there's a war on anymore because nobody in the shell of the military forgot it for a single instant in a single day.

They put him in a space ship and launched him to a large artificial satellite that circled the world.

This space station was called Command School. It held the ansible.

On his first day Ender Wiggin was taught about the ansible and what it meant to warfare. It meant that even though the starships of today's battles were launched a hundred years ago, the commanders of the starships were men of today, who used the ansible to send messages to the computers and the few men on each ship. The ansible sent words as they were spoken, orders as they were made. Battleplans as they were fought. Light was a pedestrian.

For two months Ender Wiggin didn't meet a single person. They came to him namelessly, taught him what they knew, and left him to other teachers. He had no time to miss his friends at Battle School. He only had time to learn how to operate the simulator, which flashed battle patterns around him as if he were in a starship at the center of the battle. How to command mock ships in mock battles by manipulating the keys on the simulator and speaking words into the ansible. How to recognize instantly every enemy ship and the weapons it carried by the pattern that the simulator showed. How to transfer all that he learned in the nullo battles at Battle School to the starship battles at Command School.

He had thought the game was taken seriously before. Here they hurried him through every step, were angry and worried beyond reason every time he forgot something or made a mistake. But he worked as he had always worked, and learned as he had always learned. After a while he didn't make any more mistakes. He used the simulator as if it were a part of himself. Then they stopped being worried and they gave him a teacher. The teacher was a person at last, and his name was Maezr Rackham.

Maezr Rackham was sitting cross-legged on the floor when Ender awoke. He said nothing as Ender got up and showered and dressed, and Ender did not bother to ask him anything. He had long since learned that when something unusual was going on, he would find out more information faster by waiting than by asking.

Maezr still hadn't spoken when Ender was ready and went to the door to leave the room. The door didn't open. Ender turned to face the man sitting on the floor. Maezr was at least forty, which made him the oldest man Ender had ever seen close up. He had a day's growth of black and white whiskers that grizzled his face only slightly less than his close-cut hair. His face sagged a little and his eyes were surrounded by creases and lines. He looked at Ender without interest.

Ender turned back to the door and tried again to open it. "All right," he said, giving up. "Why's the door locked?" Maezr continued to look at him blankly.

Ender became impatient. "I'm going to be late. If I'm not supposed to be there until later, then tell me so I can go back to bed." No answer. "Is it a guessing game?" Ender asked. No answer. Ender decided that maybe the man was trying to make him angry, so he went through a relaxing exercise as he leaned on the door, and soon he was calm again. Maezr didn't take his eyes off Ender.

For the next two hours the silence endured, Maezr watching Ender constantly, Ender trying to pretend he didn't notice the old man. The boy became more and more nervous, and finally ended up walking from one end of the room to the other in a sporadic pattern.

He walked by Maezr as he had several times before, and Maezr's hand shot out and pushed Ender's left leg into his right in the middle of a step. Ender fell flat on the floor.

He leaped to his feet immediately, furious. He found Maezr sitting calmly, cross-legged, as if he had never moved. Ender stood poised to fight. But the other's immobility made it impossible for Ender to attack, and he found himself wondering if he had only imagined the old man's hand tripping him up.

The pacing continued for another hour, with Ender Wiggin trying the door every now and then. At last he gave up and took off his uniform and walked to his bed.

As he leaned over to pull the covers back, he felt a hand jab roughly between his thighs and another hand grab his hair. In a moment he had been turned upside down. His face and shoulders were being pressed into the floor by the old man's knee, while his back was excruciatingly bent and his legs were pinioned by Maezr's arm. Ender was helpless to use his arms,

and he couldn't bend his back to gain slack so he could use
his legs. In less than two seconds the old man had completely
defeated Ender Wiggin.

"All right," Ender gasped. "You win."

Maezr's knee thrust painfully downward.

"Since when," Maezr asked in a soft, rasping voice, "do
you have to tell the enemy when he has won?"

Ender remained silent.

"I surprised you once, Ender Wiggin. Why didn't you destroy me immediately afterward? Just because I looked peaceful? You turned your back on me. Stupid. You have learned
nothing. You have never had a teacher."

Ender was angry now. "I've had too many damned teachers;
how was I supposed to know you'd turn out to be a—" Ender
hunted for a word. Maezr supplied one.

"An enemy, Ender Wiggin," Maezr whispered. "I am your
enemy, the first one you've ever had who was smarter than
you. There is no teacher but the enemy, Ender Wiggin. No
one but the enemy will ever tell you what the enemy is going
to do. No one but the enemy will ever teach you how to destroy
and conquer. I am your enemy, from now on. From now on I
am your teacher."

Then Maezr let Ender's legs fall to the floor. Because the
old man still held Ender's head to the floor, the boy couldn't
use his arms to compensate, and his legs hit the plastic surface
with a loud crack and a sickening pain that made Ender wince.
Then Maezr stood and let Ender rise.

Slowly the boy pulled his legs under him, with a faint groan
of pain, and he knelt on all fours for a moment, recovering.
Then his right arm flashed out. Maezr quickly danced back
and Ender's hand closed on air as his teacher's foot shot forward
to catch Ender on the chin.

Ender's chin wasn't there. He was lying on his back, spinning
on the floor, and during the moment that Maezr was off balance
from his kick Ender's feet smashed into Maezr's other leg. The
old man fell on the ground in a heap.

What seemed to be a heap was really a hornet's nest. Ender
couldn't find an arm or leg that held still long enough to be
grabbed, and in the meantime blows were landing on his back
and arms. Ender was smaller—he couldn't reach past the old
man's flailing limbs.

So he leaped back out of the way and stood poised near the
door.

The old man stopped thrashing about and sat up, cross-legged again, laughing. "Better, this time, boy. But slow. You will have to be better with a fleet than you are with your body or no one will be safe with you in command. Lesson learned?"

Ender nodded slowly.

Maezr smiled. "Good. Then we'll never have such a battle again. All the rest with the simulator. I will program your battles, I will devise the strategy of your enemy, and you will learn to be quick and discover what tricks the enemy has for you. Remember, boy. From now on the enemy is more clever than you. From now on the enemy is stronger than you. From now on you are always about to lose."

Then Maezr's face became serious again. "You will be about to lose, Ender, but you will win. You will learn to defeat the enemy. He will teach you how."

Maezr got up and walked toward the door. Ender stepped back out of the way. As the old man touched the handle of the door, Ender leaped into the air and kicked Maezr in the small of the back with both feet. He hit hard enough that he rebounded onto his feet, as Maezr cried out and collapsed on the floor.

Maezr got up slowly, holding onto the door handle, his face contorted with pain. He seemed disabled, but Ender didn't trust him. He waited warily. And yet in spite of his suspicion he was caught off guard by Maezr's speed. In a moment he found himself on the floor near the opposite wall, his nose and lip bleeding where his face had hit the bed. He was able to turn enough to see Maezr open the door and leave. The old man was limping and walking slowly.

Ender smiled in spite of the pain, then rolled over onto his back and laughed until his mouth filled with blood and he started to gag. Then he got up and painfully made his way to the bed. He lay down and in a few minutes a medic came and took care of his injuries.

As the drug had its effect and Ender drifted off to sleep he remembered the way Maezr limped out of his room and laughed again. He was still laughing softly as his mind went black and the medic pulled the blanket over him and snapped off the light. He slept until pain woke him in the morning. He dreamed of defeating Maezr.

The next day Ender went to the simulator room with his nose bandaged and his lip still puffy. Maezr was not there. Instead a captain who had worked with him before showed him an addition that had been made. The captain pointed to a tube with a loop at one end. "Radio. Primitive, I know, but it loops over your ear and we tuck the other end into your mouth with this piece here . . ."

"Watch it," Ender said as the captain pushed the end of the tube into his swollen lip.

"Sorry. Now you just talk."

"Good. Who to?"

The captain smiled. "Ask and see."

Ender shrugged and turned to the simulator. As he did a voice reverberated through his skull. It was too loud for him to understand, and he ripped the radio off his ear.

"What are you trying to do, make me deaf?"

The captain shook his head and turned a dial on a small box on a nearby table. Ender put the radio back on.

"Commander," the radio said in a familiar voice. Ender answered, "Yes."

"Instructions, sir?"

The voice was definitely familiar. "Bean?" Ender asked.

"Yes sir."

"Bean, this is Ender."

Silence. And then a burst of laughter from the other side. Then six or seven more voices laughing, and Ender waited for silence to return. When it did, he asked, "Who else?" A few voices spoke at once, but Bean drowned them out. "Me, I'm Bean, and Peder, Wins, Younger, Lee, and Vlad."

Ender thought for a moment. Then asked what the hell was going on. They laughed again.

"They can't break up the group," Bean said. "We were commanders for maybe two weeks, and here we are at Command School, training with the simulator, and all of sudden they told us we were going to form a fleet with a new commander. And that's you."

Ender smiled. "Are you boys any good?"

"If we aren't, you'll let us know."

Ender chuckled a little. "Might work out. A fleet."

For the next ten days Ender trained his toon leaders until they could maneuver their ships like precision dancers. It was like being back in the battleroom again, except that Ender could always see everything, and could speak to the toon leaders and change their orders at any time.

One day as Ender sat down at the control board and switched on the simulator, harsh green lights appeared in the space—the enemy.

"This is it," Ender said. "X, Y, bullet, C, D, reserve screen, E, south loop, Bean, angle north."

The enemy was grouped in a globe, and outnumbered Ender two to one. Half of Ender's force was grouped in a tight, bulletlike formation, with the rest in a flat circular screen—except for a tiny force under Bean that moved off the simulator, heading behind the enemy's formation. Ender quickly learned the enemy's strategy; whenever Ender's bullet formation came close, the enemy would give way, hoping to draw Ender inside the globe where he would be surrounded. So Ender obligingly fell into the trap, bringing his bullet to the center of the globe.

The enemy began to contract slowly, not wanting to come within range until all their weapons could be brought to bear at once. Then Ender began to work in earnest. His reserve screen approached the outside of the globe, and the enemy began to concentrate his force there. Then Bean's force appeared on the opposite side, and the enemy again deployed ships on that side.

Which left most of the globe only thinly defended. Ender's bullet attacked, and since at the point of attack it outnumbered the enemy overwhelmingly, he tore a hole in the formation. The enemy reacted to try to plug the gap, but in the confusion the reserve force and Bean's small force attacked simultaneously, while the bullet moved to another part of the globe. In a few minutes the formation was shattered, most of the enemy ships destroyed, and the few survivors rushing away as fast as they could go.

Ender switched the simulator off. All the lights faded. Maezr was standing beside Ender, his hands in his pockets, his body tense. Ender looked up at him.

"I thought you said the enemy would be smart," Ender said.

Maezr's face remained expressionless. "What did you learn?"

"I learned that a sphere only works when your enemy is a fool. He had his forces so spread out that I outnumbered him whenever I engaged him."

"And?"

"And," Ender said, "you can't stay committed to one pattern. It makes us too easy to predict."

"Is that all?" Maezr asked quietly.

Ender took off his radio. "The enemy could have defeated me by breaking the sphere earlier."

Maezr nodded. "You had an unfair advantage."

Ender looked up at him coldly. "I was outnumbered two to one."

Maezr shook his head. "You have the ansible. The enemy doesn't. We include that in the mock battles. Their messages travel at the speed of light."

Ender glanced toward the simulator. "Is there enough space to make a difference?"

"Don't you know?" Maezr asked. "None of the ships was ever closer than thirty thousand kilometers to another."

Ender tried to figure the size of the enemy's sphere. Astronomy was beyond him. But now his curiosity was stirred.

"What kind of weapons are on those ships? To be able to strike so fast and so far apart?"

Maezr shook his head. "The science is too much for you. You'd have to study many more years than you've lived to understand even the basics. All you need to know is that the weapons work."

"Why do we have to come so close to be in range?"

"The ships are all protected by force fields. A certain distance away the weapons are weaker, and we can't get through. Closer in the weapons are stronger than the shields. But the computers take care of all that. They're constantly firing in any direction that won't hurt one of our ships. The computers pick targets, aim, they do all the detail work. You just tell them when and get them in a position to win. All right?"

"No." Ender twisted the little tube of the radio around his fingers. "I have to know how the weapons work."

"I told you, it would take—"

"I can't command a fleet—not even on the simulator—unless I know." Ender waited a moment, then added, "Just the rough idea."

Maezr stood up and walked a few steps away. "All right, Ender. It won't make any sense, but I'll try. As simply as I can." He shoved his hands into his pockets. "It's this way, Ender. Everything is made up of atoms, little particles so small you can't see them with your eyes. These atoms, there are only a few different types, and they're all made up of even smaller particles that are pretty much the same. These atoms can be broken, so that they stop being atoms. So that this metal doesn't hold together anymore. Or the plastic floor. Or your body. Or even the air. They just seem to disappear, if you break the atoms. All that's left is the pieces. And they fly around and break more atoms. The weapons on the ships set up an area where it's impossible for atoms of anything to stay together. They all break down. So things in that area—they disappear.''

Ender nodded. "You're right, I don't understand it. Can it be blocked?"

"No. But it gets wider and weaker the farther it goes from the ship, so that after a while a force field will block it. Okay? And to make it strong at all, it has to be focused, so that a ship can only fire effectively in maybe three or four directions at once."

Ender nodded again. Maezr wondered if the boy really understood it at all.

"If the pieces of the broken atoms go breaking more atoms, why doesn't it just make everything disappear?"

"Space. Those thousands of kilometers between the ships, they're empty. Almost no atoms. The pieces don't hit anything, and when they finally do hit something, they're so spread out they can't do any harm.'' Maezr cocked his head quizzically. "Anything else. . .?"

Ender nodded. "Do the weapons on the ships—do they work against anything besides ships?"

Maezr moved in close to Ender and said firmly, "We only use them against ships. Never anything else. If we used them against anything else, the enemy would use them against us. Got it?"

Maezr walked away, and was nearly out the door when Ender called to him.

"I don't know your name yet," Ender said blandly.

"Maezr Rackham."

"Maezr Rackham," Ender said, "I defeated you."

Maezer laughed.

"Ender, you weren't fighting me today," he said. "You were fighting the stupidest computer in the Command School, set on a ten-year-old program. You don't think I'd use a sphere, do you?" He shook his head. "Ender, my dear little fellow, when you fight me you'll know it. Because you'll lose." And Maezr left the room.

Ender still practiced ten hours a day with his toon leaders. He never saw them, though, only heard their voices on the radio. Battles came every two or three days. The enemy had something new every time, something harder—but Ender coped with it. And won every time. And after every battle Maezr would point out mistakes and show Ender had really lost. Maezr only let

Ender finish so that he would learn to handle the end of the game.

Until finally Maezr came in and solemnly shook Ender's hand and said, "That, boy, was a good battle."

Because the praise was so long in coming, it pleased Ender more than praise had ever pleased him before. And because it was so condescending, he resented it.

"So from now on," Maezr said, "we can give you hard ones."

From then on Ender's life was a slow nervous breakdown.

He began fighting two battles a day, with problems that steadily grew more difficult. He had been trained in nothing but the game all his life—but now the game began to consume him. He woke in the morning with new strategies for the simulator, and went fitfully to sleep at night with the mistakes of the day preying on him. Sometimes he woke with his knuckles bloody from biting them. But every day he went impassively to the simulator and drilled his toon leaders until the battles, and drilled his toon leaders after the battles, and endured and studied the harsh criticism that Maezr Rackham piled on him. He noted that Rackham perversely criticized him more after his hardest battles. He noted that every time he thought of a new strategy the enemy was using it within a few days. And he noted that while his fleet always stayed the same size, the enemy increased in numbers every day.

He asked his teacher.

"We are showing you what it will be like when you really command. The ratios of enemy to us."

"Why does the enemy always outnumber us in these battles?"

Maezr bowed his gray head for a movement, as if deciding whether to answer. Finally he looked up and reached out his hand and touched Ender on the shoulder. "I will tell you, even though the information is secret. You see, the enemy attacked us first. He had good reason to attack us, but that is a matter for politicians, and whether the fault was ours or his, we could not let him win. So when the enemy came to our worlds, we fought back, hard, and spent the finest of our young men in the fleets. But we won, and the enemy retreated."

Maezr smiled ruefully. "But the enemy was not through, boy. The enemy would never be through. They came again, with more numbers, and it was harder to beat them. And another generation of young men was spent. Only a few survived. So we came up with a plan—the big men came up with the plan. We knew that we had to destroy the enemy once and for all, totally, eliminate his ability to make war against us. To do that we had to go to his home worlds—his home world, really, since the enemy's empire is all tied to his capital world."

"And so?" Ender asked.

"And so we made a fleet. We made more ships than the enemy ever had. We made a hundred ships for every ship he had sent against us. And we launched them against his twenty-eight worlds. They left a hundred years ago. And they carried on them the ansible, and only a few men. So that someday a commander could sit on a planet somewhere far from the battle and command the fleet. So that our best minds would not be destroyed by the enemy."

Ender's question had still not been answered.

"Why do they outnumber us?"

Maezr laughed. "Because it took a hundred years for our ships to get there. They've had a hundred years to prepare for us. They'd be fools, don't you think, boy, if they waited in old tugboats to defend their harbors. They have new ships, great ships, hundreds of ships. All we have is the ansible, that and the fact that they have to put a commander with every fleet, and when they lose—and they will lose—they lose one of their best minds every time."

Ender started to ask another question.

"No more, Ender Wiggin. I've told you more than you ought to know as it is."

Ender stood angrily and turned away. "I have a right to know. Do you think this can go on forever, pushing me through one school and another and never telling me what my life is for? You use me and the others as a tool, someday we'll command your ships, someday maybe we'll save your lives, but I'm not a computer, and I have to *know!*"

"Ask me a question, then, boy," Maezr said, "and if I can answer, I will."

"If you use your best minds to command the fleets, and you never lose any, then what do you need me for? Who am I replacing, if they're all still there?"

Maezr shook his head. "I can't tell you the answer to that, Ender. Be content that we will need you, soon. It's late. Go to bed. You have a battle in the morning."

Ender walked out of the simulator room. But when Maezr

left by the same door a few minutes later, the boy was waiting in the hall.

"All right, boy," Maezr said impatiently, "what is it? I don't have all night and you need to sleep."

Ender stayed silent, but Maezr waited. Finally the boy asked softly. "Do they live?"

"Does who live?"

"The other commanders. The ones now. And before me."

Maezr snorted. "Live. Of course they live. He wonders if they live." Still chuckling the old man walked off down the hall. Ender stood in the corridor for a while, but at last he was tired and he went off to bed. They live, he thought. They live, but he can't tell me what happens to them.

That night Ender didn't wake up crying. But he did wake up with blood on his hands.

Months wore on with battles every day, until at last Ender settled into the routine of the destruction of himself. He slept less every night, dreamed more, and he began to have terrible pains in his stomach. They put him on a very bland diet, but soon he didn't even have an appetite for that. "Eat," Maezr said, and Ender would mechanically put food in his mouth. But if nobody told him to eat he didn't eat.

One day as he was drilling his toon leaders the room went black and he woke up on the floor with his face bloody where he had hit the controls.

They put him to bed then, and for three days he was very ill. He remembered seeing faces in his dreams, but they weren't real faces, and he knew it even while he thought he saw them. He thought he saw Bean, sometimes, and sometimes he thought he saw Lieutenant Anderson and Captain Graff. And then he woke up and it was only his enemy, Maezr Rackham.

"I'm awake," he said to Maezr.

"So I see," Maezr answered. "Took you long enough. You have a battle today."

So Ender got up and fought the battle and he won it. But there was no second battle that day, and they let him go to bed earlier. His hands were shaking as he undressed.

During the night he thought he felt hands touching him gently, and he dreamed he heard voices, saying, "How long can he go on?"

"Long enough."

"So soon?"

"In a few days, then he's through."

"How will he do?"

"Fine. Even today, he was better than ever."

Ender recognized the last voice as Maezr Rackham's. He resented Rackham's intruding even in his sleep.

He woke up and fought another battle and won.

Then he went to bed.

He woke up and won again.

And the next day was his last day in Command School, though he didn't know it. He got up and went to the simulator for the battle.

Maezr was waiting for him. Ender walked slowly into the simulator room. His step was slightly shuffling, and he seemed tired and dull. Maezr frowned.

"Are you awake, boy?" If Ender had been alert, he would have noticed the concern in his teacher's voice. Instead, he simply went to the controls and sat down. Maezr spoke to him.

"Today's game needs a little explanation, Ender Wiggin. Please turn around and pay strict attention."

Ender turned around, and for the first time he noticed that there were people at the back of the room. He recognized Graff and Anderson from Battle School, and vaguely remembered a few of the men from Command School—teachers for a few hours at some time or another. But most of the people he didn't know at all.

"Who are they?"

Maezr shook his head and answered, "Observers. Every now and then we let observers come in to watch the battle. If you don't want them, we'll send them out."

Ender shrugged. Maezr began his explanation. "Today's game, boy, has a new element. We're staging this battle around a planet. This will complicate things in two ways. The planet isn't large, on the scale we're using, but the ansible can't detect anything on the other side of it—so there's a blind spot. Also, it's against the rules to use weapons against the planet itself. All right?"

"Why, don't the weapons work against planets?"

Maezr answered coldly, "There are rules of war, Ender, that apply even in training games."

Ender shook his head slowly. "Can the planet attack?"

Maezr looked nonplussed for a moment, then smiled. "I

guess you'll have to find that one out, boy. And one more thing. Today, Ender, your opponent isn't the computer. I am your enemy today, and today I won't be letting you off so easily. Today is a battle to the end. And I'll use any means I can to defeat you.''

Then Maezr was gone, and Ender expressionlessly led his toon leaders through maneuvers. Ender was doing well, of course, but several of the observers shook their heads, and Graff kept clasping and unclasping his hands, crossing and uncrossing his legs. Ender would be slow today, and today Ender couldn't afford to be slow.

A warning buzzer sounded, and Ender cleared the simulator board, waiting for today's game to appear. He felt muddled today, and wondered why people were there watching. Were they going to judge him today? Decide if he was good enough for something else? For another two years of grueling training, another two years of struggling to exceed his best? Ender was twelve. He felt very old. And as he waited for the game to appear, he wished he could simply lose it, lose the battle badly and completely so that they would remove him from the program, punish him however they wanted, he didn't care, just so he could sleep.

Then the enemy formation appeared, and Ender's weariness turned to desperation.

The enemy outnumbered him a thousand to one, the simulator glowed with them, and Ender knew that he couldn't win.

And the enemy was not stupid. There was no formation that Ender could study and attack. Instead the vast swarms of ships were constantly moving, constantly shifting from one momentary formation to another, so that a space that for one moment was empty was immediately filled with a formidable enemy force. And even though Ender's fleet was the largest he had ever had, there was no place he could deploy it where he could outnumber the enemy long enough to accomplish anything.

And behind the enemy was the planet. The planet, which Maezr had warned him about. What different did a planet make, when Ender couldn't hope to get near it? Ender waited, waited for the flash of insight that would tell him what to do, how to destroy the enemy. And as he waited, he heard the observers behind him begin to shift in their seats, wondering what Ender was doing, what plan he would follow. And finally it was obvious to everybody that Ender didn't know what to do, that there was nothing to do, and a few of the men at the back of the room made quiet little sounds in their throats.

Then Ender heard Bean's voice in his ear. Bean chuckled and said, "Remember, the enemy's gate is *down*." A few of the other leaders laughed, and Ender thought back to the simple games he had played and won in Battle School. They had put him against hopeless odds there, too. And he had beaten them. And he'd be damned if he'd let Maezr Rackham beat him with a cheap trick like outnumbering him a thousand to one. He had won a game in Battle School by going for something the enemy didn't expect, something against the rules—he had won by going against the enemy's gate.

And the enemy's gate was down.

Ender smiled, and realized that if he broke this rule they'd probably kick him out of school, and that way he'd win for sure: he would never have to play a game again.

He whispered into the microphone. His six commanders each took part of the fleet and launched themselves against the enemy. They pursued erratic courses, darting off in one direction and then another. The enemy immediately stopped his aimless maneuvering and began to group around Ender's six fleets.

Ender took off his microphone, leaned back in his chair, and watched. The observers murmured out loud, now. Ender was doing nothing—he had thrown the game away.

But a pattern began to emerge from the quick confrontations with the enemy. Ender's six groups lost ships constantly as they brushed with each enemy force—but they never stopped for a fight, even when for a moment they could have won a small tactical victory. Instead they continued on their erratic course that led, eventually, down. Toward the enemy planet.

And because of their seemingly random course the enemy didn't realize it until the same time that the observers did. By then it was too late, just as it had been too late for William Bee to stop Ender's soldiers from activating the gate. More of Ender's ships could be hit and destroyed, so that of six fleets only two were able to get to the planet, and those were decimated. But those tiny groups *did* get through, and they opened fire on the planet.

Ender leaned forward now, anxious to see if his guess would pay off. He half expected a buzzer to sound and the game to be stopped, because he had broken the rule. But he was betting on the accuracy of the simulator. If it could simulate a planet, it could simulate what would happen to a planet under attack.

It did.

The weapons that blew up little ships didn't blow up the entire planet at first. But they did cause terrible explosions. And on the planet there was no space to dissipate the chain reaction. On the planet the chain reaction found more and more fuel to feed it.

The planet's surface seemed to be moving back and forth, but soon the surface gave way in an immense explosion that sent light flashing in all directions. It swallowed up Ender's entire fleet. And then it reached the enemy ships.

The first simply vanished in the explosion. Then, as the explosion spread and became less bright, it was clear what happened to each ship. As the light reached them they flashed brightly for a moment and then disappeared. They were all fuel for the fire of the planet.

It took more than three minutes for the explosion to reach the limits of the simulator, and by then it was much fainter. All the ships were gone, and if any had escaped before the explosion reached them, they were few and not worth worrying about. Where the planet had been there was nothing. The simulator was empty.

Ender had destroyed the enemy by sacrificing his entire fleet and breaking the rule against destroying the planet. He wasn't sure whether to feel triumphant at his victory or defiant at the rebuke he was certain would come. So instead he felt nothing. He was tired. He wanted to go to bed and sleep.

He switched off the simulator, and finally heard the noise behind him.

There were no longer two rows of dignified military observers. Instead there was chaos. Some of them were slapping each other on the back, some of them were bowed with their head in their hands, others were openly weeping. Captain Graff detached himself from the group and came to Ender. Tears streamed down his face, but he was smiling. He reached out his arms, and to Ender's surprise he embraced the boy, held him tightly, and whispered, "Thank you, thank you, thank you, Ender."

Soon all the observers were gathered around the bewildered child, thanking him and cheering him and patting him on the shoulder and shaking his hand. Ender tried to make sense of what they were saying. He had passed the test after all? Why did it matter so much to them?

Then the crowd parted and Maezr Rackham walked through.

He came straight up to Ender Wiggin and held out his hand.

"You made the hard choice, boy. But heaven knows there was no other way you could have done it. Congratulations. You beat them, and it's all over."

All over. Beat them. "I beat *you*, Maezr Rackham."

Maezr laughed, a loud laugh that filled the room. "Ender Wiggin, you never played me. You never played a *game* since I was your teacher."

Ender didn't get the joke. He had played a great many games, at a terrible cost to himself. He began to get angry.

Maezr reached out and touched his shoulder. Ender shrugged him off. Maezr then grew serious and said, "Ender Wiggin, for the last months you have been the commander of our fleets. There were no games. The battles were real. Your only enemy was *the* enemy. You won every battle. And finally today you fought them at their home world, and you destroyed their world, their fleet, you destroyed them completely, and they'll never come against us again. You did it. You."

Real. Not a game. Ender's mind was too tired to cope with it all. He walked away from Maezr, walked silently through the crowd that still whispered thanks and congratulations to the boy, walked out of the simulator room and finally arrived in his bedroom and closed the door.

He was asleep when Graff and Maezr Rackham found him. They came in quietly and roused him. He woke slowly, and when he recognized them he turned away to go back to sleep.

"Ender," Graff said. "We need to talk to you."

Ender rolled back to face them. He said nothing.

Graff smiled. "It was a shock to you yesterday, I know. But it must make you feel good to know you won the war."

Ender nodded slowly.

"Maezr Rackham here, he never played against you. He only analyzed your battles to find out your weak spots, to help you improve. It worked, didn't it?"

Ender closed his eyes tightly. They waited. He said, "Why didn't you tell me?"

Maezr smiled. "A hundred years ago, Ender, we found out some things. That when a commander's life is in danger he becomes afraid, and fear slows down his thinking. When a commander knows that he's killing people, he becomes cautious or insane, and neither of those help him do well. And when he is mature, when he has responsibilities and an understanding of the world, he becomes cautious and sluggish and can't do his job. So we trained children, who didn't know anything but the game, and never knew when it would become real. That was the theory, and you proved that the theory worked.''

Graff reached out and touched Ender's shoulder. ''We launched the ships so that they would all arrive at their destination during these few months. We knew that we'd probably only have one good commander, if we were lucky. In history it's been very rare to have more than one genius in a war. So we planned on having a genius. We were gambling. And you came along and we won.''

Ender opened his eyes again and they realized he was angry. ''Yes, you won.''

Graff and Maezr Rackham looked at each other. ''He doesn't understand,'' Graff whispered.

''I understand,'' Ender said. ''You needed a weapon, and you got it, and it was me.''

''That's right,'' Maezr answered.

''So tell me,'' Ender went on, ''how many people lived on that planet that I destroyed.''

They didn't answer him. They waited a while in silence, and then Graff spoke. ''Weapons don't need to understand what they're pointed at, Ender. We did the pointing, and so we're responsible. You just did your job.''

Maezr smiled. ''Of course, Ender, you'll be taken care of. The government will never forget you. You served us all very well.''

Ender rolled over and faced the wall, and even though they tried to talk to him, he didn't answer them. Finally they left.

Ender lay in his bed for a long time before anyone disturbed him again. The door opened softly. Ender didn't turn to see who it was. Then a hand touched him softly.

''Ender, it's me, Bean.''

Ender turned over and looked at the little boy who was standing by his bed.

''Sit down,'' Ender said.

Bean sat. ''That last battle. I didn't know how you were going to get us out of it.''

Ender smiled. ''I didn't. I cheated. I thought they'd kick me out.''

''Can you believe it! We won the war. The whole war's over, and we thought we'd have to wait till we grew up to fight in it, and it was us fighting it all the time. I mean, Ender, we're little kids. I'm a little kid, anyway.'' Bean laughed and

Ender smiled. Then they were silent for a little while, Bean sitting on the edge of the bed, and Ender watching him out of half-closed eyes.

Finally Bean thought of something else to say.

"What will we do now that the war's over?" he said.

Ender closed his eyes and said, "I need some sleep, Bean."

Bean got up and left and Ender slept.

Graff and Anderson walked through the gates into the park. There was a breeze, but the sun was hot on their shoulders.

"Abba Technics? In the capital?" Graff asked.

"No, in Biggock County. Training division," Anderson replied. "They think my work with children is good preparation. And you?"

Graff smiled and shook his head. "No plans. I'll be here for a few more months. Reports, winding down. I've had offers. Personnel development for DCIA, executive vice-president for U and P, but I said no. Publisher wants me to do memoirs of the war. I don't know."

They sat on a bench and watched leaves shivering in the breeze. Children on the monkey bars were laughing and yelling, but the wind and the distance swallowed their words. "Look," Graff said, pointing. A little boy jumped from the bars and ran near the bench where the two men sat. Another boy followed him, and holding his hands like a gun he made an explosive sound. The child he was shooting at didn't stop. He fired again.

"I got you! Come back here!"

The other little boy ran on out of sight.

"Don't you know when you're dead?" The boy shoved his hands in his pockets and kicked a rock back to the monkey bars. Anderson smiled and shook his head. "Kids," he said. Then he and Graff stood up and walked on out of the park.

THE CLAW AND THE CLOCK

by Christopher Anvil

Iadrubel Vire glanced over the descriptive documents thoughtfully.

"A promising world. However, considering the extent of the Earthmen's possessions, and the size of their Space Force, one hesitates to start trouble."

Margash Grele bowed deferentially.

"Understood, Excellency. But there is a significant point that we have just discovered. We have always supposed this planet was a part of their Federation. It is not. It is *independent*."

Vire got his two hind ripping claws up onto their rest.

"Hm-m-m . . . How did we come by this information?"

"One of their merchant ships got off course, and Admiral Arvast Nade answered the distress signal." Grele gave a bone-popping sound, signifying wry humor. "Needless to say, the Earthmen were more distressed after the rescue than before."

Vire sat up.

"So, contrary to my specific instructions, Nade has given the Earthmen pretext to strike at us?"

"Excellency, restraint of the kill-instinct requires high moral development when dealing with something as helpless as these

Earthmen. Nade, himself, did not take part in the orgy, of course, but he was unable to restrain his men. It was the Earthlings' fault, because they were not armed. If they had been in full battle armor, with their tools of war—Well, who wants to crack his claws on a thing like that? But they presented themselves as defenseless offerings. The temptation was too great.''

"Were the Earthmen aware of the identity of the rescue craft?"

Grele looked uneasy.

"Admiral Nade feared some trap, and . . . ah . . . undertook to forestall treachery by using an Ursoid recognition signal."

Vire could feel the scales across his back twitch. This fool, Nade, had created out of nothing the possibility of war with both Earth *and* Ursa.

Vire said shortly, "Having given the Ursoid recognition signal, the Earthmen naturally would not be prepared. Therefore Nade would naturally be unable to restrain his men. So, what—"

Grele gave his bone-grinding chuckle, and suddenly Vire saw it as amusement at the ability of Nade to disobey Vire's orders, and get away with it.

Vire's right-hand battle-pincer came up off its rest, his manipulators popped behind his bony chest armor, three death-dealing stings snicked into position in his left-hand battle pincer—

Grele hurtled into a corner, all claws menacingly thrust out, but screaming, "Excellency, I meant no offense! Forgive my error! I mean only respect!"

"*Then get to the point!* Let's have the *facts!*"

Grele said in a rush, "Admiral Nade saved several Earthlings, to question them. They saw him as their protector, and were frank. It seems the Earthmen on this planet have a method for eliminating warlike traits from their race, and—"

"From their race *on this planet along?*"

"Yes. The planet was settled by very stern religionists, who believe in total peace unless attacked. They eliminate individuals who show irrepressible warlike traits."

Vire settled back in his seat. "They believe in 'Total peace, unless attacked.' *Then* what?"

"Apparently, they believe in self-defense. A little impractical, if proper precautions have not been made."

"Hm-m-m. How did the crewmen know about this?"

"They had made many delivery trips to the planet. It seems that the Earthmen call this planet, among themselves, 'Storehouse.' The code name is given in the documents there, and it is formally names 'Faith.' But to the Earthmen, it is 'Storehouse.' "

"Why?"

"These religious Earthlings have perfected means to preserve provisions with no loss whatever. Even live animals are in some way frozen, gassed, irradiated—or somehow treated—so they are just as good when they come out as when they went in. This is handy for shippers who have a surplus due to a temporary glut on the market, or because it's a bad year for the buyers. So, within practicable shipping distance, Storehouse does a thriving business, preserving goods from a time of surplus to a time of need."

Vire absently grated his ripping claws on their rests.

"Hm-m-m . . . And the basis of this process is not generally known?"

"No, sir. They have a monopoly. Moreover, they use their monopoly to enforce codes of conduct on the shippers. Shippers who employ practices they regard as immoral, or who deal in goods they disapprove of, have their storage quotas cut. Shippers they approve of get reduced rates. And they are incorruptible, since they are religious fanatics—like our Cult of the Sea, who resist the last molt, and stick to gills."

"Well, well, this *does* offer possibilities. But, would the Earthmen be willing to lose this valuable facility, even if it is not a member of their Federation? On the other hand—I wonder if these fanatics have antagonized the Earthmen as the cursed sea cult antagonizes us? That collection of righteous clams."

Grele nodded. "From what Admiral Nade learned, it certainly seems so. The crew of the distressed ship, for instance, had just had their quota cut because they had been caught 'shooting craps'—a form of gambling—while on their own ship waiting to unload."

"Yes, that sounds like it. Nade, I suppose, has his fleet in position?"

"Excellency, he chafes at the restraints."

"No doubt."

Vire balanced the possibilities.

"It is rumored that some who have attacked independent Earth-settled planets have not enjoyed the experience."

"The Earthlings would be bound to spread such rumors. But what can mere religious fanatics do against the guns of our men? The fanatics are skilled operators of a preserving plant; of what use is *that* in combat?"

Vire settled back. Either the Earthmen were truly unprepared, in which case he, Vire, would receive partial credit for a valuable acquisition; or else the Earthmen *were* prepared, and Nade would get such a dent in his shell that his reputation would never recover.

"All right," said Vire cheerfully, "but we must have a pretext—these religious fanatics must have delivered some insult that we want to avenge, and it must fit in with their known character. If possible, it must rouse sympathy, even, for us. Let's see . . ."

Elder Hugh Phillips eyed the message dourly.

"These lobsters have their gall. Look at this."

Deacon Bentley adjusted his penance shirt to make the bristles bite in better, and took the message. He read aloud in a dry methodical voice:

" 'Headquarters, the Imperial Hatchery, Khlaftschffran'—lot of heathenish gabble there, I'll skip all that. Let's see '. . . Pursuant to the blessings of the' . . . heh . . . 'fertility god Fflahvritschtsvri . . . Pursuant to the blessings of the fertility god What's-His-Name, the Royal Brood has exceeded expectations this season, all praise to So-and-So, et cetera, and exceeds the possibility of the Royal Hatchery to handle. We, therefore, favor you with the condescension of becoming for the next standard year an Auxiliary Royal Hatchery, consecrated according to the ritual of Fflahvrit . . . et cetera . . . and under due direction of the Imperial Priesthood, and appropriate Brood Masters, you to receive in addition to the honor your best standard payment for the service of maintaining the Royal Brood in good health, and returning same in time for the next season, undamaged by the delay, to make up the deficiency predicted by the Brood Masters. The fertility god, What's-His-Name, directs us through his Priesthood to command your immediate notice of compliance, as none of the precious Brood must be endangered by delay.' "

Deacon Bentley looked up.

"To make it short, we're supposed to store the royal lobsters for a year, is that it?"

"Evidently."

"There's no difficulty there." Bentley eyed the message coldly. "As for being consecrated according to the lobster's fertility god, *there* we part company."

Elder Phillips nodded.

"They *do* offer good pay, however."

"All worldly money is counterfeit. The only reward is in Heaven."

"Amen. But from their own heathen viewpoint, the offer is fair. Obviously, we can't accept it. But we must be fair in return, even to lobsters. We will take care of the Royal Brood, but as for their Priesthood"—he cleared his throat—"with due humility, we must decline that provision. Now, who writes the answer?"

"Brother Fry would be ideal for it."

"He's on a fast. How about Deacon Fenell?"

"No good. He went into a cell on Tuesday. Committed himself for a month."

"He did, eh? Able's boy, Wilder, would have been good at this. Too bad."

Phillips nodded.

"Unfortunately, not all can conquer their own nature. Some require grosser enemies." He sighed. "Let's see. How do we start the thing off?"

"Let's just say, 'We will put up your brood for so-and-so much per year. We decline the consecration.' That's the gist of the matter. Then we nail some diplomacy on both ends of it, dress it up a little, and there we are."

"I wish Brother Fry were here. This nonsense can eat up time. However, he's *not* here, so let's get at it."

Iadrubel Vire read the message over again intently:
From:
Central Contracting Office
Penitence City
Planet of Faith
To:
Headquarters
The Imperial Hatchery
Khlaftschiffranzitschopendischkla
Dear Sirs:

We are in receipt of your request of the 22nd instant that we put the excess of the Royal Brood in storage for a period approximating one standard year.

We agree to do this, in accord with our standard rate schedule "D" appended, suitable for nonpreferred live shipments. Kindly note that these rates apply from date of delivery to the storehouse entrance, to date of reshipment from the same point.

We regret that we must refuse your other terms, to wit:

a) Accompaniment of the shipment by priests and broodmasters.

b) Consecration to the fertility god, referred to in your communication.

In reference to a), no such accompaniment is necessary or allowed.

In reference to b), the said god, so-called, is, of course, nonexistent.

In view of the fact that your race is known to be heathen, these requests will not be held against you in determining the rate schedule, beyond placing you in the nonpreferred status.

We express our appreciation for this order, and trust that our service will be found satisfactory in every respect.

Truly yours,
Hugh Bentley
Chief Assistant
Central Contracting Office

Vire sat back, absently scratched his ripping claws on their rest, reached out with a manipulator, and punched a call-button.

A door popped open, and Margash Grele stepped in and bowed.

"Excellency?"

"Read this."

Grele read it, and looked up.

"These people are, as I told you, sir, like our sea cult—only worse."

"They certainly take an independent line for an isolated planet dealing with an interstellar empire—and on a sensitive subject, at that."

"Not so, Excellency. It is independent from *our* viewpoint. If you read between the lines, you can see that, for *them,* they are bent over backwards."

Vire absently squeaked the sharp tips of his right-hand battle claw together.

"Maybe. In any case, I don't think we would be quite justified by this reply in doing anything drastic. However, I think we can improve on this. Tell Nade to get his claws sharpened up, and we'll see what happens with the next message."

Hugh Phillips handed the message to Deacon Bentley.

"There seems to have been something wrong with our answer to these crabs."

"What, did we lose the order? Let's see."

Bentley's eyebrows raised.

"Hm-m-m . . . 'Due to your maligning the religious precepts of our Race, we must demand a full retraction and immediate apology . . .' When did we do that?"

"There was something about that part where we said they were heathens."

"They *are* heathens."

"I know."

"Truth is Truth."

"That is so. Nevertheless—well, Brother Fry would know how to handle this."

"Unfortunately, he is not here. Well, what to do about this?" Phillips looked at it.

"What is there to do?"

Bentley's look of perplexity cleared away.

"True. We can't have lobsters giving us religious instruction." He looked wary. "On the other hand, we mustn't fall into the sin of pride, either."

"Here, let's have a pen." Phillips wrote rapidly, frowned, then glanced at Bentley. "How is your sister's son coming along? Her next-to-eldest?"

Bentley shook his head.

"I fear he is not meant for righteousness. He has refused to do his penances."

Phillips shook his head, then looked at what he had written. After a moment, he glanced up.

"If the truth were told, some of us shaved by pretty close, ourselves. I suppose it's to be expected. The first settlers were certainly descended from a rough lot." He cleared his throat. "I am not so sure my eldest is going to make it."

Bentley caught his breath.

"Perhaps you judge too harshly?"

"No. As a boy, he did not *play* marbles. He lined them up in ranks, and studied the formations. We would find him with his mother's pie plate and a pencil, holding them to observe how a space fleet in disk might destroy in one column. I have tried to . . .'' Phillips cleared his throat. ''Here, read this. See if you can improve it. We must be strictly honest, and we must not truckle to these heathens. It would be bad for them as well as us.''

''Amen, Elder. Let's see, now—''

Iadrubel Vire straightened up in his seat, reread the message, and summoned Margash Grele.

Margash bowed deferentially.

''Excellency?''

''This is incredible. Read this.''

Grele read aloud:

'' 'Sirs: We acknowledge receipt of yours of the 28th instant, and are constrained, in all truth, to reply that you are heathen; that your so-called fertility god is no god at all; that your priests are at best misled, and at worst representatives of the devil; and that we can on no account tolerate priests of heathen religions on this planet. As these are plain facts, there can be no retraction and no apology, as there is no insult, but only a plain statement of truth. As a gesture of compromise, and to prove good will, we will allow one (1) broodmaster to accompany the shipment, provided he is not a priest of any godless 'religion,' so-called. We will not revise the schedule of charges on this occasion, but warn you plainly that this is our final offer. Truly yours . . .' ''

Grele looked up blankly.

Vire said, ''There is a tone to this, my dear Grele, that does not appear consistent with pacifism. Not with pacifism as *I* understand the word.''

''I certainly see what you mean, sir. Nevertheless, they *are* pacifists. We have carefully checked our information.''

''And we are *certain* they are not members of the Federation?''

''Absolutely certain.''

''Well, there is *something* here that we do not understand. This message could not be better planned if it were a bait to draw us to the attack.''

''It is certainly an insulting message, but one well suited to our purpose.''

"That, too, is suspicious. Events rarely fall into line so easily."

"Excellency, they are religious fanatics. There is the explanation."

"Nevertheless, we must draw the net tighter before we attempt to take them. Such utter fearlessness usually implies either a formidable weapon, or a formidable protector. We must be certain the Federation does not have some informal agreement with this planet."

"Excellency, Admiral Nade grows impatient."

Vire's right-hand battle claw quivered. "We will give him the chance to do the job, once we have done ours. We must make certain we do not send our troops straight into the jaws of a trap. There is a strong Space Force fleet so situated that it *might* intervene."

General Larssen, of the Space Force, looked up from copies of the message. "The only place in this end of space where we can store supplies with *no* spoilage, and they have to wind up in a fight with the lobsters over royal lobster eggs. And we aren't allowed to do anything about it."

"Well, sir," said Larssen's aide, "they *were* pretty insulting about it. And they've had every chance to join the Federation. It's hard to see why the Federation should take on all Crustax for them now."

" 'All Crustax,' nuts. The lobsters would back down if we'd ram a stiff note down their throat. Do we have any reply from the . . . . er . . . . 'court of last resort' on this?"

"No, sir, they haven't replied yet."

"Much as I dislike them, they don't pussyfoot around, anyway. Let's hope—"

There was a quiet rap, and Larssen looked up.

"Come in!"

The communications officer stepped in, looking serious.

"I wanted to bring you this myself, sir. The Interstellar Patrol declines to intervene, because it feels that the locals can take care of themselves."

Larssen stared. "They're a bunch of pacifists! All *they're* strong at is fighting off temptation!"

"Yes, sir. We made that point. All we got back was, 'Wait and see.' "

"Well, we tried, at least. Now we've got a ringside seat for the slaughter."

Admiral Nade was in his bunk when the top priority message came in. His aide entered the room, approached the bunk, and hesitated. Nade was completely covered up, out of sight.

The aide looked around nervously. The chief was a trifle peevish when roused out of a sound sleep.

The aide put the message on the admiral's cloak of rank on the nightstand near the bunk, retraced his steps to the hatch, opened it wide, then returned to the bunk. Hopefully, he waited, but Nade didn't stir.

The aide spoke hesitantly: "Ah . . . a message, sir." Nothing happened. He tried again.

Nade didn't move.

The aide climbed over the raised lip of the catch tray, took hold of the edge of the bunk, dug several claws into the wood in his nervousness, and cautiously scratched back a little of the fine white sand. The admiral was in there *somewhere*. He scratched a little more urgently. A few smooth pebbles rattled into the tray.

Just then, he bumped into something.

Claws shot up. Sand flew in all directions.

The aide fell over the edge of the tray, scrabbled violently, and hurled himself through the doorway.

The admiral bellowed, "WHO DARES—"

The aide rounded corners, and shot down cross-corridors as the admiral grabbed his cloak of rank, then spotted the message.

Nade seized the message, stripped off various seals the message machine had plastered on it, growled: "The fool probably wants *more* delay." Then he tore open the lightproof envelope that guaranteed no one would see it but him, unfolded the message itself, and snarled, " '. . . received your message #4e67t3fs . . . While I agree—' Bah! ' . . . extreme caution is advised . . .' That clawless wonder! Let's see, what's this? '. . . Provided due consideration is given to these precautions, you are hereby authorized to carry out the seizure by force of the aforesaid planet, its occupation, its annexation, and whatever ancillary measures may appear necessary or desirable. You are, however, warned on no account to engage forces of the Federation in battle, the operation to be strictly limited to the seizure, et cetera, of the aforesaid planet. If possible, minimum damage is to be done to the planet's storage equipment, as possession of this equipment should prove extremely valuable . . .' Well, he's a hard-shell, after all! Let's see . . . 'Security against surprise by Federation forces will be employed without however endangering success of the operation by undue dividing of the attacking force . . .' *That* doesn't hurt anything. Now, the quicker we take them, the better!''

He whipped his cloak of rank around him, tied it with a few quick jerks of his manipulators, strode into the corridor, and headed for the bridge, composing an ultimatum as he went.

Elder Phillips examined the message, and cleared his throat. ''We appear to have a war on our hands.''

Deacon Bentley made a clucking noise. ''Let's see.''

Phillips handed him the message. Bentley sat back.

''Ha-hm-m-m. 'Due to your deliberately insulting references to our religion, to your slandering of our gods, and to your refusal to withdraw the insult, we are compelled to extend claws in battle to defend our honor. I hereby authorize the Fleet of Crustax to engage in lawful combat, and have notified Federation authorities as the contiguous independent power in this region that a state of war exists. Signed, Iadrubel Vire, Chief Commander of the Forces.' Well, it appears, Elder, that our message was not quite up to Brother Fry's level. Hm-m-m, there's more to this. Did this all come in at once?''

''It did, Deacon. The first part apparently authorizes the second part.''

''Quite a different style, this. 'I, Arvast Nade, Commander Battle Fleet IV, hereby demand your immediate surrender. Failure to comply within one hour, your time, following receipt of this ultimatum, as determined by my communications center, will open your planet to pillage by my troops. Any attempt at resistance will be crushed without mercy, and your population decimated in retaliation. Any damage, or attempted damage, by you to goods and facilities of value on the planet will be avenged by execution of leading citizens selected at my command. By my fiat as conqueror, your status, retroactive to the moment of transmission of this ultimatum, is that of bond-sleg to the conquering race. Any lack of instantaneous obedience will be dealt with accordingly. Signed, Arvast Nade, Battle Fleet Commander.' ''

Deacon Bentley looked up.

"What do we do with this?"

"I see no alternative to activating War Preventive Measures, as described in Chapter XXXVIII of the Lesser Works."

"I was afraid of that. Well . . . so be it."

"We can't have a war here. As soon as we saw a few of these heathen loose on the planet, we'd all revert to type. You know what *that* is."

"Well, let's waste no time. You take care of that, and I'll answer this ultimatum. Common courtesy requires that we answer it, I suppose."

Arvast Nade got the last of his battle armor on, and tested the joints.

"There's a squeak somewhere."

"Sir?" said his aide blankly.

"There's a squeak. Listen."

It could be heard plainly:

Squeak, squeak, squeak, squeak, squeak.

The aide got the oil can. "Work your claws one at a time, sir . . . Let's see . . . Again. *There* it is!"

"Ah, good," said Nade, working everything soundlessly. "That's what comes of too long a peace. And this stuff is supposed to be rustproof!"

There was a polite rap at the door. The aide leaned outside, and came back with a message. "For you, sir. It's from the Storehousers."

"Good. Wait till I get a hand out through this . . . uh . . . the thing is stiff. There, let's have it."

Reaching out with a manipulator through a kind of opened trapdoor in the armor, and almost knocking loose a hand-weapon clamped to the inside, Nade took hold of the message, which was without seals or embellishments, as befitted the mouthings of slegs.

Behind the clear visor, Nade's gaze grew fixed as he read:

From:
Central Contracting Office
Penitence City
Planet of Faith
To:
Arvast Nade
Commander

Battle Fleet IV
Crustax

Dear Sir:
We regret to inform you that we must decline the conditions mentioned in your message of the 2nd instant. As
you may be aware, the planetary government of the planet
Faith does not recognize war, and can permit no war to
be waged on, or in the vicinity of, this planet. Our decision on this matter is final, and is not open to discussion.

> Truly yours,
> Hugh Bentley
> Chief Assistant
> Central Contracting Office

Nade dazedly handed the message to his aide.
"And just how," he demanded, "are they going to enforce
that?"

Elder Phillips's hand trembled slightly as he reached out to
accept the proferred hand of the robed figure.
"Judge Archer Goodwin," said the dignitary politely.
"Elder, I bring you tidings of your eldest son, and I fear you
will not find them happy tidings."
Phillips kept his voice level.
"I suspected as much, Judge."
"With due allowance for the fallibility of human judgment,
Lance appears unsuited to a life of peace. Study bores him.
Conflict and its techniques fascinate him. He is pugnacious,
independent. He sees life in terms of conflict. He is himself
authoritative, though subject to subordination to a superior authority. He is not dull. The acquisition of useful skills, and
even a quite deep knowledge, are well within his grasp, potentially. However, his basic bent is in another direction. On a
different planet, we might expect him to shine in some limited
but strategically placed field, using it as a springboard to power
and rank. Here, to allow him to pass into the populace would
require us, out of fairness, to allow others to do the same. But
the proportions of such traits are already so high that our way
of living could not endure the shock. You see, he not only
possesses these traits, plus a lust to put them in action, but *he
sees nothing wrong with this*. Accordingly, he will not attempt

to control his natural tendencies. Others of even greater combativeness have entered our population, but have recognized the sin of allowing such tendencies sway, unless the provocation is indeed serious. Then—" Judge Goodwin's face for an instant bent into a chilling smile, which he at once blinked away. He cleared his throat. "I am sorry to have to bring you this news."

Elder Phillips bowed his head. Somehow, somewhere, he had failed in proper discipline, in stern council. But, defiant, the boy always—He put down the thoughts with an effort. Others took their place. People would talk. He would never live this down, would never know if a word, or a tone of voice, was a sly reference.

His fists clenched. For an instant, everything vanished in rage. Sin of sins, in a blur of mental pictures, he saw himself seek similarly afflicted parents—the planet teemed with them—rouse them to revolt, saw himself outwit the guards, seize an armory, arm the disaffected, and *put this unholy law to the test of battle!*

So real was the illusion that for an instant he felt the sword in his hand, saw the Council spring to their feet as he stepped over the bodies of the guards; his followers, armed to the teeth, were right behind him as he entered—

With a sob, he dropped to his knees.

The judge's hand gripped his shoulder. "Be steadfast. With the aid of the Almighty, you will conquer this. You can do it. Or you would not be here."

Arvast Nade studied the green and blue sphere swimming in the viewscreen.

"Just as I thought. They lack even a patrol ship."

"Sir," said the aide, "another message from the Storehousers."

Nade popped open his hatch, and reached out.

Gaze riveted to the page, he read:

From:
Office of the Chief
War Prevention Department
Level VI
Penitence City
Planet of Faith

To:
Arvast Nade
Commander
Battle Fleet IV
Crustax

Sir:
   We hereby deliver final warning to you that this Department will not hesitate to use all measures necessary to
bar the development of war on this planet or in its contiguous regions.
   You are warned to signify peaceful intent by immediately altering course away from our planet. If this
is impossible, signal the reason at once.
        Hiram Wingate
        Chief
        War Prevention Dept.

Nade lowered the message. He took another look at the screen.
He looked back at the message, then glanced at his aide.
   "You've read this?"
   "Certainly, sir. Communications from slegs have no right
of privacy."
   "How did it seem to you?"
   The aide hesitated. "If I did not know they were disarmed
pacifists, who destroy every warlike son born to them—well,
then I would be worried, sir."
   "There is certainly a very hard note to this message. There
is even a tone of command that can be heard in it. I find it
difficult to believe this could have been written by one unfamil-
iar with and unequipped for war."
   Nade hesitated, then activated his armored-suit communicator.
   "Alter course ten girids solaxially outward of the planet
Storehouse."
   Nade's aide looked shocked.
   The admiral said, "War is not unlimited heroics, my boy.
We lose nothing from this maneuver but an air of omnipotence
that has a poor effect on tactics, anyway. Conceivably, there
are warships on the far side of that planet. But if these soft
shells are just putting up a smudge with no claws behind it,
we will gobble them up, and I will add an additional two *skrads*

free pillage to what they have already earned. The Storehouse regions being off-limits, off course.''

The aide beamed, and clashed his claws in anticipation.

Admiral Nade adjusted the screen to a larger magnification.

Elder Phillips formally shook hands with his son, Lance, who was dressed in battle armor, with sword and pistol, and a repeater slung across his back.

''Sorry, Dad,'' said the younger Phillips, ''I couldn't take this mush-mouthed hypocrisy, that's all. It's a trap, and the fact that you and the rest of your generation let themselves get caught in it is no reason why *I* should.''

Tight-lipped, the elder said nothing.

His son's lip curled. Then he shrugged. ''Wish me luck, at least, Dad.''

''Good luck, son.'' The elder began to say more, but caught himself.

A harsh voice boomed over the gathering.

''Those who have been found unsuitable for life on this planet, do now seperate from those who will remain, and step forward to face each other in armed combat. Those who will do battle on the physical level, assemble by the sign of the sword. Those who will give battle on the level of tactics, assemble by the stacked arms. Those who will give battle on the plane of high strategy, assemble by the open book. You will now be matched one with another until but one champion remains in each group. Those champions will have earned the right to life, but must still prove themselves against an enemy of the race or of the Holy Word. In any case, settlement shall not be here amongst the scenes of your childhood. Let any who now have second thoughts speak out. Though a—''

A shrill voice interrupted. ''Overthrow them! We have the guns!''

There was an instantaneous *crack!* One of the armored figures collapsed.

The harsh voice went on, a little lower-pitched:

''Anyone else who wants to defy regulations is free to try. The punishment is instantaneous death. I was about to say that anyone who has second thoughts should speak out, though a courage test will be required to rejoin your family, and you must again submit to judgment later. The purpose of the Law is not to raise a race of cowards, but a race capable of controlling its warlike instincts. Naturally, anyone who backs out of *this*, and fails the courage test, will be summarily killed. Does anyone on mature consideration regret the stand he has taken?''

There was a silence.

The armored figures, their faces through the raised visors expressing surprise, glanced at the outstretched rebel, then at each other.

Edler Phillips's son turned, and his gaze sought out his father. He grinned and raised the naked sword in salute. The elder, startled, raised his hand. Now, what was that about?

''Very well,'' said the harsh voice. ''Take your positions by your respective emblems.''

Elder Phillips, watching, saw his son hesitate, and then walk toward the open book. The elder was surprised; after all, some fool might think him cowardly, not realizing the type of courage the test would involve.

The voice said, ''After a brief prayer, we will begin . . .''

Arvast Nade glanced at the ranked screens in the master control room.

''There is no hidden force off that planet. It was a bluff.'' He activated his armored-suit communicator, and spoke briefly: ''Turn the Fleet by divisions, and land in the preselected zones.''

Hiram Wingate, Chief, War Prevention Department, watched the maneuver on the screen, turned to a slanting console bearing ranks of numbered levers and redly glowing lights, and methodically pulled down levers. The red lights winked off, to be replaced by green. On a second console, a corresponding number of blue lights went out, to be replaced by red.

Near the storage plant, huge camouflaged gates swung wide. An eager voice shouted over the communicator. ''Men! Squadron A strikes the first blow! Follow me!''

Arvast Nade, just turning from the screen, jerked back to take another look.

Between his fleet and the planet, a swarm of blurs had materialized.

The things were visibly growing large on the screen, testifying to an incredible velocity.

Abruptly the blurred effect vanished, and he could see what

appeared to be medium-sized scout ships, all bearing some kind of angular symbol that apparently served as a unit identification.

Now again they blurred.

Nade activated his suit communicator.

"Secondary batteries open fi—"

The deck jumped underfoot. A siren howled, changed pitch, then faded out. Across the control room, a pressure-monitor needle wound down around its dial, then the plastic cover of the instrument blew off.

The whole ship jumped.

A tinny voice spoke in Nade's ear. "Admiral, we are being attacked by small ships of the Storehousers!"

"Fire back!" shouted Nade.

"They're too fast, sir! Fire control can't keep up with them! *Look out!* HERE COMES—"

Nade raised his battle pincers.

Before him, the whole scene burst into one white-hot incandescence.

General Larssen, watching on the long-range pickup, sat in shock as glare from the viewer lit his face.

"And they don't believe in war! Look at *that!*"

"Sir," said a dazed subordinate, "that *isn't* war."

"It isn't? What do *you* call it?"

"Extermination, sir. Pest control. War assumes some degree of equality between opponents."

Lance Phillips, feeling dazed and drained, but with a small warm sense of achievement, straightened from the battle computer.

"I didn't do too badly?"

"Best of the lot," said the examiner cheerfully. "Your understanding of the geometrical aspects of space strategy is outstanding."

"I had a sense of drag—as if I couldn't get the most out of my forces."

"You didn't. You aren't dealing with pure abstract force, but with human beings. You made no allowance for that."

"But I did well enough to survive?"

"You did."

"What about the others?"

"They had their opportunity. Those who conquered will be saved. Any really outstanding fighters who lost because of bad luck, or superb opposition, will also be saved."

"We get a chance to do battle later?"

"Correct."

"We fight for our own planet?"

"That's right."

"But—how long since the planet was attacked?"

"Yesterday, when this trial began. Prior to that, not for about a hundred years."

"*Yesterday!* What are we doing here? We should—"

The examiner shook his head.

"The attack never amounted to anything. Just a fleet of lobsters wiped out in fifteen minutes."

Lance Phillips looked quite dizzy.

"I thought we didn't believe in war!"

"Of course not," said the examiner. "War, of the usual kind, has a brutalizing effect. As likely as not, the best are sent to slaughter each other, so at least the physical level of the race is lowered. The conquered are plundered of the fruits of their labor, which is wrong, while the conquerors learn to expect progress by pilllage instead of by work; they become a burden on everyone around them; *that* leads to a desire to exterminate them. The passions aroused do not end with the conflict, but go on to make more conflict. We *don't* believe in war. Unfortunately, not everyone is equally enlightened. Should we, because we reconginze the truth, be at the mercy of every sword-rattler and egomaniac? Of course not. But how are we to avoid it? By simultaneously understanding the evils of war, and being prepared to wage it defensively on the greatest scale."

"But that's a contradiction! You can't distinguish between offensive and defensive weapons! And we have too small a planet to support a large-scale war!"

The examiner looked him over coolly.

"With due respect to your logic, your understanding is puny. Now, we have something here we call 'discipline.' Think carefully before you tell me again to my face that I am a fool, or a liar. I repeat, 'How do we avoid war? By simultaneously understanding the evils of war, and being prepared to wage it defensively on the greatest scale.' "

Lance Phillips felt the objections well up, felt the overpowering certainty, the determination to brush aside nonsense.

Simultaneously, he felt something else.

He opened his mouth. No words came out.

Could this be fear?

Not exactly.

What was it?

Suddenly he recognized it.

Caution.

Warily, he said, "In that case . . . ah . . . *how—*"

Iadrubel Vire scanned the fragmentary reports, and looked at Margash Grele. Grele's normally iridescent integument was a muddy gray.

"This is all?" said Vire.

"Yes, sir."

"No survivors?"

"Not one, so far as we know. It was a slaughter."

Vire sat back dazed. A whole battle fleet wiped out—just like that. This would alter the balance of force all along the frontier.

"What word from the Storehousers?"

"Nothing, sir."

"No demands?"

"Not a word."

"After a victory like this, they could—" He paused, frowning. They were *pacifists, who believed in self-defense.*

That sounded fine, in principle, but—how had they reduced it to practice? After all, they were only one planet. Their productive capacity and manpower did not begin to approach that of Crustax and—

Vire cut off that line of thought. *This* loss, with enough patience and craft, could be overcome. Two or three more like it would be the finish. There was just not enough potential gain to risk further attempts on that one little planet. He had probed the murk with a claw, and drawn back a stub. Best to avoid trouble while that grew back, and just keep away from the place in the future.

"Release the announcement," said Vire slowly, "that Fleet IV, on maneuvers, has been caught in a meteor storm of unparalleled intensity. Communications have been temporarily cut off, and there is concern at headquarters over the fate of the fleet. It will be some time before we will know with certainty what has happened, but it is feared that a serious disaster may have occurred. As this fleet is merely a reserve fleet on maneuvers in the region of the border with the Federation, with which we have friendly relations, this, of course, in no way imperils our defenses, but . . . h'm-m-m . . . we are deeply concerned for the crewmen and their loved ones.''

Grele made swift notes, and looked up.

"Excellency, might it not be wise to let this information out by stages? First, the word of the meteor shower—but our experts doubt the accuracy of the report. Next, a substantiating report has come in. Then—''

"No, because in the event of a real meteor shower, we would make no immediate public announcements. We have to be liars in this, but let's keep it to the minimum.''

Grele bowed respectfully, and went out.

"Damned gravitor," said Squadron A's 2nd-Flight leader over the communicator, "cut off just as we finished off the lobster fleet. I was signaling for assembly on my ship, and aimed to cut a little swath through crab-land before going home. Instead, we've been streaking off on our own for the last week, and provisions are slim on these little boats, I'll tell you that! *What* outfit did you say you are?''

The strange, roughly minnow-shaped ship, not a great deal bigger than the scout, answered promptly:

"Interstellar Patrol. We have a few openings for recruits who can qualify. Plenty of chance for adventure, special training, top-grade weapons, good food, the pay's O.K., no bureaucrats to tangle things up. If you can qualify, it's a good outfit.''

"Interstellar Patrol, huh? Never heard of it. I was thinking of the Space Force.''

"Well, you *could* come in that way. We get quite a few men from the Space Force. It's a fair outfit, but they have to kowtow to Planetary Development. Their weapons aren't up to ours; but, their training isn't so tough, either. They'd be *sure* to let you in, where we're a little more selective. You've got a point, all right. It would be a lot easier—if you want things easy.''

"Well, I didn't mean—''

"We could shoot you supplies to last a couple of weeks, and *maybe* a Space Force ship will pick you up. If not, we could help—if we're still in the region. Of course, if not—''

The flight leader began to perspire.

"Listen, tell me a little more about this Interstellar Patrol."

Lance Phillips stared at rank on rank of mirrorlike glittering forms stretching off into the distance, and divided into sections by massive pillars that buttressed the ceiling.

"*This* is part of the storage plant?"

"It is. Naturally, foreigners know nothing of this, and our own people have little cause to learn the details. You say a small planet can't afford a large striking force. It can, *if* the force is accumulated slowly, and requires no maintenance whatever. Bear in mind, we make our living by *storing* goods, with no loss. How can there be *no* loss? Obviously, if, from the viewpoint of the observer, *no time passes for the stored object*."

"How could that be unless the object were moving at near the velocity of light?"

"How does an object increase its speed to near the velocity of light?"

"It *accelerates*."

The examiner nodded. "When you see much of this, you have a tendency to speculate. Now, we regularly add to our stock of fighting men and ships, and our ability to control the effects of time enables us to operate, from the observer's viewpoint, either very slowly, or very fast. *How* is not in my department, and this knowledge is not handed out to satisfy curiosity. But—it's natural to speculate. The only way we know to slow time, from the observer's viewpoint, is to accelerate, and increase velocity to near the speed of light. A great ancient named Einstein said there is no way, without outside references, to distinguish the *force of gravity* from acceleration. So, I think some wizardry with gravitors is behind this." He looked thoughtfully at Lance Phillips. "The main thing is, you see what you have to know to be one of our apprentice strategists. We accumulate strength slowly, take the toughest, most generally uncivilizable of each generation, provided they have certain redeeming qualities. *These* are our fighting men. We take a few standard types of ships, improve them as time goes on, and when we are attacked, we accelerate our response, to strike with such speed that the enemy cannot react. We obliterate him. He, mortified, blames the defeat on something else. His fleet was caught in a nova, the gravitors got in reasonating synchrony, *something* happened, but it didn't have anything to do with *us*. Nevertheless, he leaves us alone.''

''Why not use our process to put his whole fleet in stasis, and use it as a warning?''

''*That* would be an insult he would have to respond to, and we are opposed to war. In the second place, we agreed to give you an opportunity to fight for the planet, and then live your life elsewhere. There has to be some outlet somewhere. We can't just keep stacking ships and warriors in here indefinitely.''

''After we get out—*then* what happens?''

''It depends on circumstances. However, fighting men are in demand. If, say, a properly keyed signal cut power to the engines, and after some days of drifting, the warrior were offered the opportunity to enlist in some outfit that meets our standards—''

''Yes, that fits.'' He hesitated, then thrust out his jaw. ''I know I'm not supposed to even think about this, but—''

The examiner looked wary: ''Go ahead.''

''With what we have here, we could rival the whole works—Federation, Crustax Empire—the lot. Well—why not? We could be the terror of all our opponents!''

The examiner shook his head in disgust.

''After what you've experienced, you can still ask *that*. Let's go at it from another direction. Consider what you know about the warlike character of our populace, and what we have to do to restrain it. Now, just ask yourself: What could such a stock as this be descended *from?*''

A great light seemed to dawn on Lance Phillips.

''You see,'' said the examiner, ''we've already *done* that. We had to try something a little tougher.''

TIME PIECE

by Joe Haldeman

They say you've got a fifty-fifty chance every time you go out. That makes it one chance in eight that you'll live to see your third furlough; the one I'm on now.

Somehow the odds don't keep people from trying to join. Even though not one in a thousand gets through the years of training and examination, there's no shortage of cannon fodder. And that's what we are. The most expensive, best trained cannon fodder in the history of warfare. Human history, anyhow; who can speak for the enemy?

I don't even call them snails anymore. And the thought of them doesn't trigger that instant flash of revulsion, hate, kill-fever—the psyconditioning wore off years ago, and they didn't renew it. They've stopped doing it to new recruits; no percentage in berserkers. I was a wild one the first couple of trips, though.

Strange world I've come back to. Gets stranger every time, of course. Even sitting here in a bogus twenty-first century bar, where everyone speaks Basic and there's real wood on the walls and peaceful holograms instead of plugins and music made by men . . .

But it leaks through. I don't pay by card, let alone by coin.

The credit register monitors my alpha waves and communicates with the bank every time I order a drink. And, in case I've become addicted to more modern vices, there's a feelie matrix (modified to look like an old-fashioned visiphone booth) where I can have my brain stimulated directly. Thanks but no, thanks—always get this picture of dirty hands inside my skull, kneading, rubbing. Like when you get too close to the enemy and they open a hole in your mind and you go spinning down and down and never reach the bottom till you die. I almost got too close last time.

We were on a three-man reconnaissance patrol, bound for a hellish little planet circling the red giant Antares. Now red giant stars don't form planets in the natural course of things, so we had ignored Antares; we control most of the space around it, so why waste time in idle exploration? But the enemy had detected this little planet—God knows how—and about ten years after they landed there, we monitored their presence (gravity waves from the ships' braking) and my team was assigned the reconnaissance. Three men against many, many of the enemy—but we weren't supposed to fight if we could help it; just take a look around, record what we saw, and leave a message beacon on our way back, about a light-year out from Antares. Theoretically, the troopship following us by a month will pick up the information and use it to put together a battle plan. Actually, three more recon patrols precede the troop ship at one-week intervals; insurance against the high probability that any one patrol will be caught and destroyed. As the first team in, we have a pretty good chance of success, but the ones to follow would be in trouble if we didn't get back out. We'd be past caring, of course: the enemy doesn't take prisoners.

We came out of lightspeed close to Antares, so the bulk of the star would mask our braking disturbance, and inserted the ship in a hyperbolic orbit that would get us to the planet—Anomaly, we were calling it—in about twenty hours.

"Anomaly must be tropical over most of its surface." Fred Sykes, nominally the navigator, was talking to himself and at the two of us while he analyzed the observational data rolling out of the ship's computer. "No axial tilt to speak of. Looks like they've got a big outpost near the equator, lots of electromagnetic noise there. Figures . . . the goddamn snails like it hot. We requisitioned hot-weather gear, didn't we, Pancho?''

Pancho, that's me. ''No, Fred, all we got's parkas and snow-shoes.'' My full name is Francisco Jesus Mario Juan-José Hugo de Naranja, and I outrank Fred, so he should at least call me Francisco. But I've never pressed the point. Pancho it is. Fred looked up from his figure and the rookie, Paul Spiegel, almost dropped the pistol he was cleaning.

''But why . . .'' Paul was staring. ''We knew the planet was probably Earthlike if the enemy wanted it. Are we gonna have to go tromping around in spacesuits?''

''No, Paul, our esteemed leader and supply clerk is being sarcastic again.'' He turned back to his computer. ''Explain, Pancho.''

''No, that's all right.'' Paul reddened a bit and also went back to his job. ''I remember you complaining about having to take the standard survival issue.''

''Well, I was right then and I'm doubly right now. We've *got* parkas back there, and snowshoes, and a complete terranorm environment recirculator, and everything else we could possibly need to walk around in comfort on every planet known to man—*Dios!* That issue masses over a metric ton, more than a giga-watt laser. A laser we could use, but crampons and pith helmets and elephant guns . . .''

Paul looked up again. ''Elephant guns?'' He was kind of a freak about weapons.

''Yeah.''

''That's a gun that shoots elephants?''

''Right. An elephant gun shoots elephants.''

''Is that some new kind of ammunition?''

I sighed, I really sighed. You'd think I'd get used to this after twelve years—or four hundred—in the service. ''No, kid, elephants were animals, big gray wrinkled animals with horns. You used an elephant gun to shoot *at* them.

''When I was a kid in Rioplex, back in the twenty-first, we had an elephant in the zoo; used to go down in the summer and feed him synthos through the bars. He had a long nose like a fat tail, he ate with that.''

''What planet were they from?''

It went on like that for a while. It was Paul's first trip out, and he hadn't yet gotten used to the idea that most of his compatriots were genuine antiques, preserved by the natural process of relativity. At lightspeed you age imperceptibly, while the universe's calendar adds a year for every light-year you travel. Seems like cheating. But it catches up with you eventually.

We hit the atmosphere of Anomaly at an oblique angle and came in passive, like a natural meteor, until we got to a position where we were reasonably safe from detection (just above the south polar sea), then blasted briefly to slow down and splash. Then we spent a few hours in slow flight at sea level, sneaking up on their settlement.

It appeared to be the only enemy camp on the whole planet, which was typical. Strange for a spacefaring, aggressive race to be so incurious about planetary environments, but they always seemed to settle in one place and simply expand radially. And they do expand; their reproduction rate makes rabbits look sick. Starting from one colony, they can fill a world in two hundred years. After that, they control their population by infantiphage and stellar migration.

We landed about a hundred kilometers from the edge of their colony, around local midnight. While we were outside setting up the espionage monitors, the ship camouflaged itself to match the surrounding jungle optically, thermally, magnetically, etc.—we were careful not to get too far from the ship; it can be a bit hard to find even when you know where to look.

The monitors were to be fed information from flea-sized flying robots, each with a special purpose, and it would take several hours for them to wing into the city. We posted a one-man guard, one-hour shifts; the other two inside the ship until the monitors started clicking. But they never started.

Being senior, I took the first watch. A spooky hour, the jungle making dark little noises all around, but nothing happened. Then Fred stood the next hour, while I put on the deepsleep helmet. Figured I'd need the sleep—once data started coming in, I'd have to be alert for about forty hours. We could all sleep for a week once we got off Anomaly and hit lightspeed.

Getting yanked out of deepsleep is like an ice-water douche to the brain. The black nothing dissolved and there was Fred a foot away from my face, yelling my name over and over. As soon as he saw my eyes open, he ran for the open lock, priming his laser on the way (definitely against regulations, could hole the hull that way; I started to say something but couldn't form the words). Anyhow, what were we doing in free fall? And how could Fred run across the deck like that while we were in free fall?

Then my mind started coming back into focus and I could analyze the sinking, spinning sensation—not free-fall vertigo at all, but what we used to call snail-fever. The enemy was very near. Crackling combat sounds drifted in from outdoors.

I sat up on the cot and tried to sort everything out and get going. After long seconds my arms and legs got the idea, I struggled up and staggered to the weapons cabinet. Both the lasers were gone, and the only heavy weapon left was a grenade launcher. I lifted it from the rack and made my way to the lock.

Had I been thinking straight, I would've just sealed the lock and blasted—the presence in my mind was so strong that I should have known there were too many of the enemy, too close, for us to stand and fight. But no one can think while their brain is being curdled that way. I fought the urge to just let go and fall down that hole in my mind, and slid along the wall to the airlock. By the time I got there my teeth were chattering uncontrollably and my face was wet with tears.

Looking out, I saw a smoldering gray lump that must have been Paul, and Fred screaming like a madman, fanning the laser on full over a 180-degree arc. There couldn't have been anything alive in front of him; the jungle was a lurid curtain of fire, but a bolt lanced in from behind and Fred dissolved in a pink spray of blood and flesh.

I saw them then, moving fast for snails, shambling in over thick brush toward the ship. Through the swirling fog in my brain I realized that all they could see was the light pouring through the open lock, and me silhouetted in front. I tried to raise the launcher but couldn't—there were too many, less than a hundred meters away, and the inky whirlpool in my mind just got bigger and bigger and I could feel myself slipping into it.

The first bolt missed me; hit the ship and it shuddered, ringing like a huge cathedral bell. The second one didn't miss, taking off my left hand just above the wrist, roasting what remained of my left arm. In a spastic lurch I jerked up the launcher and yanked the trigger, holding it down while dozens of micro-ton grenades popped out and danced their blinding way up to and across the enemy's ragged line. Dazzled blind, I stepped back and stumbled over the med-robot, which had smelled blood and was eager to do its duty. On top of the

machine was a switch that some clown had labeled EMERGENCY
EXIT; I slapped it, and as the lock clanged shut the atomic
engines muttered — growled — screamed into life and a ten-grav-
ity hand slid me across the blood-slick deck and slammed me
back against the rear-wall padding. I felt ribs crack and something in my neck snapped. As the world squeezed away, I knew
I was a dead man but it was better to die in a bed of pain than
to just fall and fall.

I woke up to the less-than-tender ministrations of the med-robot,
who had bound the stump of my left arm and was wrapping
my chest in plastiseal. My body from forehead to shins ached
from radiation burns, earned by facing the grenades' bursts,
and the nonexistent hand seemed to writhe in painful, impossible contortions. But numbing anesthetic kept the pain at a
bearable distance, and there was an empty space in my mind
where the snail-fever had been, and the gentle hum told me
we were at lightspeed; things could have been one flaming hell
of a lot worse. Fred and Paul were gone but that just moved
them from the small roster of live friends to the long list of
dead ones.

A warning light on the control panel was blinking stroboscop-
ically. We were getting near the hole — excuse me, "relativistic
discontinuity" — and the computer had to know where I wanted
to go. You go in one hole at light-speed and you'll come out
of some other hole; *which* hole you pop out of depends on your
angle of approach. Since they say that only about one percent
of the holes are charted, if you go in at any old angle you're
liable to wind up in Podunk, on the other side of the galaxy,
with no ticket back.

I just let the light blink, though. If it doesn't get any response
from the crew, the ship programs itself automatically to go to
Heaven, the hospital world, which was fine with me. They
cure what ails you and then set you loose with a compatible
soldier of the opposite sex, for an extended vacation on that
beautiful world. Someone once told me there were over a
hundred worlds named Hell, but there's only one Heaven.
Clean and pretty from the tropical seas to the Northern pine
forests. Like Earth used to be, before we strangled it.

A bell had been ringing all the time I'd been conscious, but
I didn't notice it until it stopped. That meant that the information
capsule had been jettisoned, for what little it was worth. Planet-

ary information, very few espionage-type data; just a tape of the battle. Be rough for the next recon patrol.

I fell asleep knowing I'd wake up on the other side of the hole, bound for Heaven.

I pick up my drink—an old-fashioned old-fashioned—with my new left hand and the glass should feel right, slick but slightly tacky with the cold-water sweat, fine ridges molded into the plastic. But there's something missing, hard to describe, a memory stored in your fingertips that a new growth has to learn all over again. It's a strange feeling, but in a way seems to fit with this crazy Earth, where I sit in my alcoholic time capsule and, if I squint with my mind, can almost believe I'm back in the twenty-first.

I pay for the nostalgia—wood and natural food, human bartender and waitress who are also linguists, it all comes dear—but I can afford it, if anyone can. Compound interest, of course. Over four centuries have passed on Earth since I first went off to the war, and my salary's been deposited at the Chase Manhattan Credit Union ever since. They're glad to do it; when I die, they keep the interest and the principal reverts to the government. Heirs? I had one illegitimate son (conceived on my first furlough) and when I last saw his gravestone, the words on it had washed away to barely legible dimples.

But I'm still a young man (at lightspeed you age imperceptibly while the universe winds down outside) and the time you spend going from hole to hole is almost incalculably small. I've spent most of the past half millenium at lightspeed, the rest of the time usually convalescing from battle. My records show that I've logged a trifle under one year in actual combat. Not bad for 438 years' pay. Since I first lifted off I've aged twelve years by my biological calendar. Complicated, isn't it—next month I'll be thirty, 456 years after my date of birth.

But one week before my birthday I've got to decide whether to try my luck for a fourth trip out or just collect my money and retire. No choice, really. I've got to go back.

It's something they didn't emphasize when I joined up, back in 2088—maybe it wasn't so obvious back then, the war only decades old—but they can't hide it nowadays. Too many old vets wandering around, like animated museum pieces.

I could cash in my chips and live in luxury for another

hundred years. But it would get mighty lonely. Can't talk to anybody on Earth but other vets and people who've gone to the trouble to learn Basic.

Everyone in space speaks Basic. You can't lift off until you've become fluent. Otherwise, how could you take orders from a fellow who should have been food for worms centuries before your grandfather was born? Especially since language melted down into one Language.

I'm tone-deaf. Can't speak or understand Language, where one word has ten or fifteen different meanings, depending on pitch. To me it sounds like puppydogs yapping. Same words over and over; no sense.

Of course, when I first lived on Earth, there were all sorts of languages, not just one Language. I spoke Spanish (still do when I can find some other old codger who remembers) and learned English—that was before they called it Basic—in military training. Learned it damned well, too. If I weren't tone-deaf I'd crack Language and maybe I'd settle down.

Maybe not. The people are so strange, and it's not just the Language. Mindplugs and homosex and voluntary suicide. Walking around with nothing on but paint and powder. We had Fullerdomes when I was a kid; but you didn't *have* to live under one. Now if you take a walk out in the country for a breath of fresh air, you'll drop over dead before you can exhale.

My mind keeps dragging me back to Heaven. I'd retire in a minute if I could spend my remaining century there. Can't, of course; only soldiers allowed in space. And the only way a soldier gets to Heaven is the hard way.

I've been there three times; once more and I'll set a record. That's motivation of a sort, I suppose. Also, in the unlikely event that I should live another five years, I'll get a commission, and a desk job if I live through my term as a field officer. Doesn't happen too often—but there aren't too many desk jobs that people can handle better than cyborgs.

That's another alternative. If my body gets too garbaged for regeneration, and they can save enough of my brain, I could spend the rest of eternity hooked up to a computer, as a cyborg. The only one I've ever talked to seemed to be happy.

I once had an African partner named N'gai. He taught me how to play O'wari, a game older than Monopoly or even chess. We sat in this very bar (or the identical one that was in

its place two hundred years ago) and he tried to impress on my
non-Zen-oriented mind just how significant this game was to
men in our positon.

You start out with forty-eight smooth little pebbles, four in
each one of the twelve depressions that make up the game
board. Then you take turns, scooping the pebbles out of one
hole and distributing them one at a time in holes to the left. If
you dropped your last pebble in a hole where your opponent
had only one or two, why, you got to take those pebbles off
the board. Sounds exciting, doesn't it?

But N'gai sat there in a cloud of bhang-smoke and mumbled
about the game and how it was just like the big game we were
playing, and everytime he took a pebble off the board, he called
it by name. And some of the names I didn't know, but a lot
of them were on my long list.

And he talked about how we were like the pieces in this
simple game; how some went off the board after the first couple
of moves, and some hopped from place to place all through
the game and came out unscathed, and some just sat in one
place all the time until they got zapped from out of nowhere. . . .

After a while I started hitting the bhang myself, and we
abandoned the metaphor in a spirit of mutual intoxication.

And I've been thinking about that night for six years, or two
hundred, and I think that N'gai—his soul find Buddha—was
wrong. The game isn't all that complex.

Because in O'wari, either person can win.

The snails populate ten planets for every one we destroy.

Solitaire, anyone?

MEDAL
OF HONOR

by Mack Reynolds

Don Mathers snapped to attention, snapped a crisp salute to his superior, said, "Sub-lieutenant Donal Mathers reporting, sir."

The Commodore looked up at him, returned the salute, looked down at the report on the desk. He murmured, "Mathers, One Man Scout V-102. Sector A22-K223."

"Yes, sir," Don said.

The Commodore looked up at him again. "You've been out only five days, Lieutenant."

"Yes, sir, on the third day I seemed to be developing trouble in my fuel injectors. I stuck it out for a couple of days, but then decided I'd better come in for a check." Don Mathers added, "As per instructions, sir."

"Ummm, of course. In a Scout you can hardly make repairs in space. If you have any doubts at all about your craft, orders are to return to base. It happens to every pilot at one time or another."

"Yes, sir."

"However, Lieutenant, it has happened to you four times out of your last six patrols."

Don Mathers said nothing. His face remained expressionless.

157

"The mechanics report that they could find nothing wrong with your engines, Lieutenant."

"Sometimes, sir, whatever is wrong fixes itself. Possibly a spot of bad fuel. It finally burns out and you're back on good fuel again. But by that time you're also back to the base."

The Commodore said impatiently, "I don't need a lesson in the shortcomings of the One Man Scout, Lieutenant. I piloted one for nearly five years. I know their shortcomings—and those of their pilots."

"I don't understand, sir."

The Commodore looked down at the ball of his thumb. "You're out in space for anywhere from two weeks to a month. All alone. You're looking for Kraden ships, which practically never turn up. In military history the only remotely similar situation I can think of were the pilots of World War One pursuit planes, in the early years of the war, when they still flew singly, not in formation. But even they were up there alone for only a couple of hours or so."

"Yes, sir," Don said meaninglessly.

The Commodore said, "We, here at command, figure on you fellows getting a touch of space cafard once in a while and, ah, *imagining* something wrong in the engines and coming in. But," here the Commodore cleared his throat, "four times out of six? Are you sure you don't need a psych, Lieutenant?"

Don Mathers flushed. "No, sir, I don't think so."

The Commodore's voice went militarily expressionless. "Very well, Lieutenant. You'll have the customary three weeks leave before going out again. Dismissed."

Don saluted snappily, wheeled and marched from the office.

Outside, in the corridor, he muttered a curse. What did that chairborne brass hat know about space cafard? About the depthless blackness, the wretchedness of free fall, the tides of primitive terror that swept you when the animal realization hit that you were away, away, away from the environment that gave you birth. That you were alone, alone, *alone*. A million, a million-million miles from your nearest fellow human. Space cafard, in a craft little larger than a good-sized closet! What did the Commodore know about it?

Don Mathers had conveniently forgotten the other's claim to five years service in the Scouts.

•　　•　　•

He made his way from Space Command Headquarters, Third Division, to Harry's Neuvo Mexico Bar. He found the place empty at this time of the day and climbed onto a stool.

Harry said, "Hi, Lootenant, thought you were due back for patrol. How come you're back so soon?"

Don said coldly, "You prying into security subjects, Harry?"

"Well, gee, no Lootenant. You know me. I know all the boys. I was just making conversation."

"Look, how about some more credit, Harry? I don't have any pay coming up for a week."

"Why, sure. I got a boy on the light cruiser *New Taos*. Any spaceman's credit is good with me. What'll it be?"

"Tequila."

Tequila was the only concession the Neuvo Mexico Bar made to its name. Otherwise, it looked like every other bar has looked in every other land and in every era. Harry poured, put out lemon and salt.

Harry said, "You hear the news this morning?"

"No, I just got in."

"Colin Casey died." Harry shook his head. "Only man in the system that held the Galactic Medal of Honor. Presidential proclamation, everybody in the system is to hold five minutes of silence for him at two o'clock, Sol Time. You know how many times that medal's been awarded, Lootenant?" Before waiting for an answer, Harry added, "Just thirty-six times."

Don added dryly, "Twenty-eight of them posthumously."

"Yeah." Harry, leaning on the bar before his sole customer, added in wonder, "But imagine. The Galactic Medal of Honor, the bearer of which can do no wrong. Imagine. You come to some town, walk into the biggest jewelry store, pick up a diamond bracelet, and walk out. And what happens?"

Don growled, "The jewelry store owner would be over-reimbursed by popular subscription. And probably the mayor of the town would write you a letter thanking you for honoring his fair city by deigning to notice one of the products of its shops. Just like that."

"Yeah." Harry shook his head in continued awe. "And, imagine, if you shoot somebody you don't like, you wouldn't spend even a single night in the Nick."

Don said, "If you held the Medal of Honor, you wouldn't have to shoot anybody. Look, Harry, mind if I use the phone?"

"Go right ahead, Lootenant."

Dian Fuller was obviously in the process of packing when the screen summoned her. She looked into his face and said, surprised, "Why, Don, I thought you were on patrol."

"Yeah, I was. However, something came up."

She looked at him, a slight frown on her broad, fine forehead. "Again?"

He said impatiently, "Look, I called you to ask for a date. You're leaving for Callisto tomorrow. It's our last chance to be together. There's something in particular I wanted to ask you, Di."

She said, a touch irritated, "I'm packing, Don. I simply don't have time to see you again. I thought we said our goodbyes five days ago."

"This is important, Di."

She tossed the two sweaters she was holding into a chair, or something, off-screen, and faced him, her hands on her hips.

"No it isn't, Don. Not to me, at least. We've been all over this. Why keep torturing yourself? You're not ready for marriage, Don. I don't want to hurt you, but you simply aren't. Look me up, Don, in a few years."

"Di, just a couple of hours this afternoon."

Dian looked him full in the face and said, "Colin Casey finally died of his wounds this morning. The President has asked for five minutes of silence at two o'clock. Don, I plan to spend that time here alone in my apartment, possibly crying a few tears for a man who died for me and the rest of the human species under such extreme conditions of gallantry that he was awarded the highest honor of which man has ever conceived. I wouldn't want to spend that five minutes while on a date with another member of my race's armed forces who had deserted his post of duty."

Don Mathers turned, after the screen had gone blank, and walked stiffly to a booth. He sank into a chair and called flatly to Harry, "Another tequila. A double tequila. And don't bother with that lemon and salt routine."

An hour or so later a voice said, "You Sub-lieutenant Donal Mathers?"

Don looked up and snarled. "So what? Go away."

There were two of them. Twins, or could have been. Empty of expression, heavy of build. The kind of men fated to be ordered around at the pleasure of those with money, or brains, none of which they had or would ever have.

The one who had spoken said, "The boss want to see you."

"Who the hell is the boss?"

"Maybe he'll tell you when he sees you," the other said, patiently and reasonably.

"Well, go tell the boss he can go to the . . . "

The second of the two had been standing silently, his hands in his greatcoat pockets. Now he brought his left hand out and placed a bill before Don Mathers. "The boss said to give you this."

It was a thousand unit note. Don Mathers had never seen a bill of that denomination before, nor one of half that.

He pursed his lips, picked it up and looked at it carefully. Counterfeiting was a long lost art. It didn't even occur to him that it might be false.

"All right," Don said, coming to his feet. "Let's go see the boss, I haven't anything else to do and his calling card intrigues me."

At the curb, one of them summoned a cruising cab with his wrist screen and the three of them climbed into it. The one who had given Don the large denomination bill, dialed the address and they settled back.

"So what does the boss want with me?" Don said.

They didn't bother to answer.

The Interplanetary Lines building was evidently their destination. The car whisked them up to the penthouse which topped it, and they landed on the terrace.

Seated in beach chairs, an autobar between them, were two men. They were both in their middle years. The impossibly corpulent one, Don Mathers vaguely recognized. From a newscast? From a magazine article? The other could have passed for a video stereotype villain, complete to the built-in sneer. Few men, in actuality, either look like or sound like the conventionalized villain. This was an exception, Don decided.

He scowled at them. "I suppose one of you is the boss," he said.

"That's right," the fat one grunted. He looked at Don's two escorts. "Scotty, you and Rogers take off."

They got back into the car and left.

The vicious-faced one said, "This is Mr. Lawrence Demming. I am his secretary."

Demming puffed, "Sit down, Lieutenant. What'll you have

to drink? My secretary's name is Rostoff. Max Rostoff. Now we all know each other's names. That is, assuming you're Sub-Lieutenant Donal Mathers.''

Don said, ''Tequila.''

Max Rostoff dialed the drink for him and, without being asked, another cordial for his employer.

Don placed Demming now. Lawrence Demming, billionaire. Robber baron, he might have been branded in an earlier age. Transportation baron of the solar system. Had he been a pig he would have been butchered a long time ago, he was going unhealthily to grease.

Rostoff said, ''You have identification?''

Don Mathers fingered through his wallet, brought forth his I.D. card. Rostoff handed him his tequila, took the card and examined it carefully, front and back.

Demming huffed and said, ''Your collar insignia tells me you pilot a Scout. What sector do you patrol, Lieutenant?''

Don sipped at the fiery Mexican drink, looked at the fat man over the glass. ''That's military information, Mr. Demming.''

Demming made a move with his plump lips. ''Did Scotty give you a thousand unit note?'' He didn't wait for an answer. ''You took it. Either give it back or tell me what sector you patrol, Lieutenant.''

Don Mathers was aware of the fact that a man of Demming's position wouldn't have to go to overmuch effort to acquire such information, anyway. It wasn't of particular importance.

He shrugged and said, ''A22-K223. I fly the V-102.''

Max Rostoff handed back the I.D. card to Don and picked up a Solar System sector chart from the short-legged table that sat between the two of them and checked it. He said, ''Your information was correct, Mr. Demming. He's the man.''

Demming shifted his great bulk in his beach chair, sipped some of his cordial and said, ''Very well. How would you like to hold the Galactic Medal of Honor, Lieutenant?''

Don Mathers laughed. ''How would you?'' he said.

Demming scowled. ''I am not jesting, Lieutenant Mathers. I never jest. Obviously, I am not of the military. It would be quite impossible for me to gain such an award. But you are the pilot of a Scout.''

''And I've got just about as much chance of winning the

Medal of Honor as I have of giving birth to triplets.''

The transportation magnate wiggled a disgustingly fat finger at him. ''I'll arrange for that part of it.''

Don Mathers goggled him. He blurted finally, ''Like hell you will. There's not enough money in the system to fiddle with the awarding of the Medal of Honor. There comes a point, Demming, where even *your* dough can't carry the load.''

Demming settled back in his chair, closed his eyes and grunted, ''Tell him.''

Max Rostoff took up the ball. ''A few days ago, Mr. Demming and I flew in from Io on one of the Interplanetary Lines freighters. As you probably know, they are completely automated. We were alone in the craft.''

''So?'' Without invitation, Don Mathers leaned forward and dialed himself another tequila. He made it a double this time. A feeling of excitement was growing within him, and the drinks he'd had earlier had worn away. Something very big, very, very big, was developing. He hadn't the vaguest idea what.

''Lieutenant, how would you like to capture a Kraden light cruiser? If I'm not incorrect, probably Miro class.''

Don laughed nervously, not knowing what the other was at but still feeling the growing excitement. He said, ''In all the history of the war between our species, we've never captured a Kraden ship intact. It'd help a lot if we could.''

''This one isn't exactly intact, but nearly so.''

Don looked from Rostoff to Demming, and then back. ''What in the hell are you talking about?''

''In your sector,'' Rostoff said, ''we ran into a derelict Miro class cruiser. The crew—repulsive creatures—were all dead. Some thirty of them. Mr. Demming and I assumed that the craft had been hit during one of the actions between our fleet and theirs and that somehow both sides had failed to recover the wreckage. At any rate, today it is floating, abandoned of all life, in your sector.'' Rostoff added softly, ''One has to approach quite close before any signs of battle are evident. The ship looks intact.''

Demming opened his eyes again and said, ''And you're going to capture it.''

Don Mathers bolted his tequila, licked a final drop from the edge of the lip. ''And why should that rate the most difficult decoration to achieve that we've ever instituted?''

''Because,'' Rostoff told him, his tone grating mockery,

"you're going to radio in reporting a Miro class Kraden cruiser. We assume your superiors will order you to stand off, that help is coming, that your tiny scout isn't large enough to do anything more than to keep the enemy under observation until a squadron arrives. But you will radio that you plan to attack. When your reinforcments arrive, Lieutenant, you will have conquered the Kraden, single-handed, against odds of—what would you say, fifty to one?"

Don Mathers' mouth was dry, his palms moist. He said, "A One Man Scout against a Miro class cruiser? At least fifty to one, Mr. Rostoff. At least."

Demming grunted. "There would be little doubt of you getting the Galactic Medal of Honor, Lieutenant, especially since Colin Casey is dead and there isn't a living bearer of the award. Max, another drink for the Lieutenant."

Don said, "Look. Why? I think you might be right about getting the award. But why, and why me, and what's your percentage?"

Demming muttered, "Now we get to the point." He settled back in his chair again and closed his eyes while his secretary took over.

Max Rostoff leaned forward, his wolfish face very serious. "Lieutenant, the exploitation of the Jupiter satellites is in its earliest stages. There is every reason to believe that the new sources of radioactives on Callisto alone may mean the needed power edge that can give us the victory over the Kradens. Whether or not that is so, someone is going to make literally billions out of this new frontier."

"I still don't see . . ."

"Lieutenant Mathers," Rostoff said patiently, "the bearer of the Galactic Medal of Honor is above law. He carries with him an unalienable prestige of such magnitude that . . . Well, let me use an example. Suppose a bearer of the Medal of Honor formed a stock corporation to exploit the pitchblende of Callisto. How difficult would it be for him to dispose of the stock?"

Demming grunted. "And suppose there were a few, ah, crossed wires in the manipulation of the corporation's business?" He sighed deeply. "Believe me, Lieutenant Mathers, there are an incredible number of laws which have accumulated down through the centuries to hamper the businessman. It is a continual fight to be able to carry on at all. The ability to do no legal wrong would be priceless in the development of a new frontier." He sighed again, so deeply as to make his bulk quiver. "Priceless."

Rostoff laid it on the line, his face a leer. "We are offering you a three-way partnership, Mathers. You, with your Medal of Honor, are our front man. Mr. Demming supplies the initial capital to get underway. And I . . . ." He twisted his mouth with evil self-satisfaction. "I was present when the Kraden ship was discovered, so I'll have to be cut in. I'll supply the brains."

Demming grunted his disgust, but added nothing.

Don Mathers said slowly, looking down at the empty glass he was twirling in his fingers. "Look, we're up to our necks in a war to the death with the Kradens. In the long run it's either us or them. At a time like this you're suggesting that we fake an action that will eventually enable us to milk the new satellites to the tune of billions."

Demming grunted meaninglessly.

Don said, "The theory is that all men, all of us, ought to have our shoulders to the wheel. This project sounds to me like throwing rocks under it."

Demming closed his eyes.

Rostoff said, "Lieutenant, it's a dog eat dog society. If we eventually lick the Kradens, one of the very reasons will be because we're a dog eat dog society. Every man for himself and the devil take the hindmost. Our apologists dream up some beautiful gobbledygook phrases for it, such as free enterprise, but actually it's a dog eat dog. Surprisingly enough, it works, or at least has so far. Right now, the human race needs the radioactives of the Jupiter satellites. In acquiring them, somebody is going to make a tremendous amount of money. Why shouldn't it be us?"

"Why not, if you—or we—can do it honestly?"

Demming's grunt was nearer a snort this time.

Rostoff said sourly, "Don't be naive, Lieutenant. Whoever does it is going to need little integrity. You don't win in a sharper's card game by playing your cards honestly. The biggest sharper wins. We've just found a joker somebody dropped on the floor; if we don't use it, we're suckers."

Demming opened his pig eyes and said, "All this is on the academic side. We checked your background thoroughly before approaching you, Mathers. We know your record, even before you entered the Space Service. Just between the three of us, wouldn't you like out? There are a full billion men and women in our armed forces, you can be spared. Let's say you've already done your share. Can't you see the potentialities in spending the rest of your life with the Galactic Medal of Honor in your pocket?''

It was there all right, drifting slowly. Had he done a more thorough job of his patrol last time, he should have stumbled upon it himself.

If he had, there was no doubt that he would have at first reported it as an active enemy cruiser. Demming and Rostoff had been right. The Kraden ship looked untouched by battle.

That is, if you approached it from the starboard and slightly abaft the beam. From that angle, in particular, it looked untouched.

It had taken several circlings of the craft to come to that conclusion. Don Mathers was playing it very safe. This thing wasn't quite so simple as the others had thought. He wanted no slip-ups. His hand went to a food compartment and emerged with a space thermo which should have contained fruit juice, but didn't. He took a long pull at it.

Finally he dropped back into the position he'd decided upon, and flicked the switch of his screen.

A base lieutenant's face illuminated it. He yawned and looked questioningly at Don Mathers.

Don said, allowing a touch of excitement in his voice. ''Mathers, Scout V-102, Sector A22-K223.''

''Yeah, yeah . . .'' the other began, still yawning.

''I've spotted a Kraden curiser. Miro class, I think.''

The lieutenant flashed into movement. He slapped a button before him, the screen blinked, to be lit immediately again.

A gray-haired Fleet Admiral looked up from papers on his desk.

''Yes?''

Don Mathers rapped, ''Miro class Kraden in sector A22-K223, sir. I'm lying about fifty miles off. Undetected thus far—I think. He hasn't fired on me yet, at least.''

The Admiral was already doing things with his hands. Two subalterns came within range of the screen, took orders, dashed off. The Admiral was rapidly firing orders into two other screens. After a moment, he looked up at Don Mathers again.

"Hang on, Lieutenant. Keep him under observation as long as you can. What're your exact coordinates?"

Don gave them to him and waited.

A few minutes later the Admiral returned to him. "Let's take a look at it, Lieutenant."

Don Mathers adjusted the screen to relay the Kraden cruiser. His palms were moist now, but everything was going to plan. He wished that he could take another drink.

The Admiral said, "Miro class, all right. Don't get too close, Lieutenant. They'll blast you to hell and gone. We've got a task force within an hour of you. Just hang on."

"Yes, sir," Don said. An hour. He was glad to know that. He didn't have much time in which to operate.

He let it go another five minutes, then he said, "Sir, they're increasing speed."

"Damn," the Admiral said, then rapid-fired some more into his other screens, barking one order after another.

Don said, letting his voice go very flat, "I'm going in, sir. They're putting on speed. In another five minutes they'll be underway to the point where I won't be able to follow. They'll get completely clear."

The Admiral looked up, startled. "Don't be a fool."

"They'll get away, sir." Knowing that the other could see his every motion, Don Mathers hit the cocking lever of his flakflak gun with the heel of his right hand.

The Admiral snapped, "Let it go, you fool. You won't last a second." Then, his voice higher, "That's an order, Lieutenant!"

Don Mathers flicked off his screen. He grimaced sourly and then descended on the Kraden ship, his flakflak gun beaming it. He was going to have to expend every erg of energy in his Scout to burn the other ship to the point where his attack would look authentic, and to eliminate all signs of previous action.

The awarding of the Galactic Medal of Honor, as always, was done in the simplest of ceremonies.

Only the President and Captain Donal Mathers himself were present in the former's office in the Presidential Palace.

However, as they both knew, every screen in the Solar System was tuned into the ceremony.

Don Mathers saluted and stood to attention.

The President read the citation. It was very short, as Medal of Honor citations were always.

. . . *for conspicuous gallantry far and beyond the call of duty, in which you singlehandedly, and against unbelievable odds, attacked and destroyed an enemy cruiser while flying a Scout armed with only a short beam flakflak gun* . . .

He pinned a small bit of ribbon and metal to Don Mather's tunic. It was an inconspicuous, inordinarily ordinary medal, the Galactic Medal of Honor.

Don said hoarsely, "Thank you, sir."

The President shook hands with him and said, "I am President of the United Solar System, Captain Mathers, supposedly the highest rank to which a man can attain." He added simply, "I wish I were you."

Afterwards, alone in New Washington, and wanting to remain alone, Don Mathers strolled the streets for a time, bothered only occasionally when someone recognized his face and people would stop and applaud.

He grinned inwardly.

He had a suspicion already that after a time he'd get used to it and weary to death of it, but right now it was still new and fun. Who was the flyer, way back in history, the one who first flew over the Alantic in a propeller-driven aircraft? His popularity must have been something like this.

He went into O'Donnell's at lunchtime and as he entered the orchestra broke off the popular tune they were playing and struck up the Interplanetary Anthem. The manager himself escorted him to his table and made suggestions as to the specialties and the wine.

When he first sat down the other occupants of the restaurant, men and women, had stood and faced him and applauded. Don flushed. There could be too much of a good thing.

After the meal, a fantastic production, Don finished his cigar and asked the head waiter for his bill, reaching for his wallet.

The other smiled. "Captain, I am afraid your money is of no value in O'Donnell's, not just for this luncheon but whenever you honor us." The head waiter paused and added, "In fact, Captain, I doubt if there is a restaurant in the Solar System where your money holds value. Or that there will ever be."

Don Mathers was taken aback. He was only beginning to

realize the ramifications of his holding his Galactic Medal of
Honor.

At Space Command Headquarters, Third Division, Don came
to attention before the Commodore's desk and tossed the other
a salute.

The Commodore returned it snappily and leaned back in his
chair. "Take a seat, Captain. Nice to see you again." He added
pleasantly, "Where in the world have you been?"

Don Mathers slumped in a chair, said wearily, "On a bust.
The bust to end all busts."

The Commodore chuckled. "Don't blame you," he said.

"It was quite a bust," Don said.

"Well," the Commodore chuckled again, "I don't suppose
we can throw you in the guardhouse for being A.W.O.L. Not
in view of your recent decoration."

There was nothing to say to that.

"By the way," the Commodore said, "I haven't had the opportunity to congratulate you on your Kraden. That was quite
a feat, Captain."

"Thank you, sir," Don added, modestly, "rather foolish of
me, I suppose."

"Very much so. On such foolishness are heroic deeds based,
Captain." The Commodore looked at him questioningly. "You
must have had incredible luck. The only way we've been able
to figure it was that his detectors were on the blink. That may
be what happened."

"Yes, sir," Don nodded quickly. "That's the way I figure
it. And my first blast must have disrupted his fire control or
something."

The Commodore said, "He didn't get in any return fire at
all?"

"A few blasts. But by that time I was in too close and
moving too fast. Fact of the matter is, sir, I don't think they
ever recovered from my first beaming of them."

"No, I suppose not," the Commodore said musingly. "It's
a shame you had to burn them so badly. We've never recovered
a Kraden ship in good enough shape to give our techs something
to work on. It might make a basic difference in the war, particularly if there was something aboard that'd give us some indication of where they were coming from. We've been fighting
this war in our backyard for a full century. It would help if we

could get into *their* backyard for a change. It's problematical
how long we'll be able to hold them off, at this rate."

Don Mathers said uncomfortably, "Well, it's not as bad as
all that, sir. We've held them this far."

His superior grunted. "We've held them this far because
we've been able to keep out enough patrol ships to give us
ample warning when one of their task forces come in. Do you
know how much fuel that consumes, Captain?"

"Well, I know it's a lot."

"So much so that Earth's industry is switching back to pe-
troleum and coal. Every ounce of radioactives is needed by the
Fleet. Even so, it's just a matter of time."

Don Mathers pursed his lips. "I didn't know it was that bad."

The Commodore smiled sourly at him. "I'm afraid I'm being
a wet blanket thrown over your big bust of a celebration, Captain. Tell me, how does it feel to hold the system's highest
award?"

Don shook his head, marveling. "Fantastic, sir. Of course,
like any member of the services I've always known of the
Medal of Honor, but . . . well, nobody ever expects to get
it." He added wryly, "Certainly not while he's still alive and
in health. Why, sir, do you realize that I haven't been able to
spend one unit of money since?" There was an element of awe
in his voice. "Sir, do you realize that not even a beggar will
take currency from me?"

The Commodore nodded in appreciation. "You must understand the position you occupy, Captain. Your feat was inspiring
enough, but that's not all of it. In a way you combine a popular
hero with an *Unknown Soldier* element. Awarding you the
Galactic Medal of Honor makes a symbol of you. A symbol
representing all the millions of unsung heroes and heroines who
have died fighting for the human species. It's not a light burden
to carry on your shoulders, Captain Mathers. I would imagine
it a very humbling honor."

"Well, yes, sir," Don said.

The Commodore switched his tone of voice. "That brings
me to the present, and what your next assignment is to be.
Obviously, it wouldn't do for you to continue in a Scout. Big
brass seems to be in favor of using you for morale and . . ."

Don Mathers cleared his throat and interrupted. "Sir, I've
decided to drop out of the Space Service."

"Drop out!" The other stared at Mathers uncomprehending.
"We're at war, Captain!"

Don nodded seriously. "Yes, sir. And what you just said is
true. I couldn't be used any longer in a Scout. I'd wind up
selling bonds and giving talks to old ladies' clubs."

"Well, hardly that, Captain."

"No, sir, I think I'd really be of more use out of the services.
I'm tendering my resignation and making arrangements to help
in the developing of Callisto and the other Jupiter satellites."

The Commodore said nothing. His lips seemed whiter than
before.

Don Mathers said doggedly, "Perhaps my prestige will help
bring volunteers to work the new mines out there. If they see
me, well, sacrificing, putting up with the hardships . . ."

The Commodore said evenly, "Mr. Mathers, I doubt if you
will ever have to put up with hardships again, no matter where
you make your abode. However, good luck. You deserve it."

Outside headquarters, Don Mathers summoned a cab and dialed
his hotel. On the way over, he congratulated himself. It had
gone easier than he had expected, really. Although, come to
think of it, there wasn't a damn thing that the brass could do.

He had to laugh to himself.

Imagine if he'd walked in on the Commodore a month ago
and announced that he was going to *drop out* of the Space
Service. He would have been dropped all right, all right. Right
into the lap of a squadron of psycho experts.

At the hotel he shucked his uniform, an action which gave
him considerable gratification, and dressed in one of the score
of civilian costumes that filled his closets to overflowing. He
took pleasure in estimating what this clothing would have cost
in terms of months of Space Service pay for a Sub-lieutenant
or even a Captain. *Years, my boy, years.*

He looked at himself in the dressing room mirror with satisfaction, then turned to the autobar and dialed himself a stone-
age-old Metaxa. He'd lost his taste for the plebian tequila in
the last few days.

He held the old Greek brandy to the light and wondered
pleasurably what the stuff cost, per pony glass. Happily, he'd
never have to find out.

He tossed the drink down and, whistling, took his private

elevator to the garages in the second level of the hotel's basement floors. He selected a limousine and dialed the Interplanetary Lines building.

He left the car at the curb before the main entrance, ignoring all traffic regulations and entered the building, still whistling softly and happily to himself. He grinned when a small crowd gathered outside and smiled and clapped their hands. He grinned and waved to them.

A receptionist hurried to him and he told her he wanted to see either Mr. Demming or Mr. Rostoff, and then when she offered to escort him personally he noticed her pixie-like cuteness and said, "What're you doing tonight, Miss?"

Her face went pale. "Oh, anything, sir," she said weakly.

He grinned at her. "Maybe I'll take you up on that if I'm not too busy."

He had never seen anyone so taken aback. She said, all flustered, "I'm Toni. Toni Fitzgerald. You can just call this building and ask for me. Any time."

"Maybe I'll do that," he smiled. "But now, let's see Old Man Demming."

That took her back too. Aside from being asked for a date—if asked could be the term—by the system's greatest celebrity, she was hearing for the first time the interplanetary tycoon being called *Old Man Demming.*

She said, "Oh, right this way, Captain Mathers."

Don said, "Mr. Mathers now, I'm afraid. I have new duties."

She looked up into his face. "You'll always be Captain Mathers to me, sir." She added, softly and irrelevantly, "My two brothers were lost on the *Minerva* in that action last year off Pluto." She took a deep breath, which only stressed her figure. "I've applied six times for Space Service, but they won't take me."

They were in an elevator now. Don said, "That's too bad, Toni. However, the Space Service isn't as romantic as you might think."

"Yes, sir," Toni Fitzgerald said, her soul in her eyes. "You ought to know, sir."

Don was somehow irritated. He said nothing further until they reached the upper stories of the gigantic office building. He thanked her after she'd turned him over to another receptionist.

Don Mathers' spirits had been restored by the time he was

brought to the door of Max Rostoff's office. His new guide evidently hadn't even bothered to check on the man's availability before ushering Mathers into the other's presence.

Max Rostoff looked up from his desk, wolfishly aggressive looking as ever. "Why, Captain," he said. "How fine to see you again. Come right in. Martha, that will be all."

Martha gave the interplanetary hero one more long look and then turned and left.

As soon as the door closed behind her, Max Rostoff turned and snarled, "Where have you been, you rummy?"

He couldn't have shocked Don Mathers more if he'd suddenly sprouted a unicorn's horn.

"We've been looking for you for a week," Rostoff snapped. "Out of one bar, into another, our men couldn't catch up with you. Dammit, don't you realize we've got to get going? We've got a dozen documents for you to sign. We've got to get this thing underway, before somebody else does."

Don blurted, "You can't talk to me that way."

It was the other's turn to stare. Max Rostoff said, low and dangerously, "No? Why can't I?"

Don glared at him.

Max Rostoff said, low and dangerously, "Let's get this straight, Mathers. To everybody else, but Demming and me, you might be the biggest hero in the Solar System. But you know what you are to us?"

Don felt his indignation seeping from him.

"To us," Max Rostoff said flatly, "you're just another demi-buttocked incompetent on the make." He added definitely, "And make no mistake, Mathers, you'll continue to have a good thing out of this only so long as we can use you."

A voice from behind them said, "Let me add to that, period, end of paragraph."

It was Lawrence Demming, who'd just entered from an inner office.

He said, even his voice seeming fat, "And now that's settled, I'm going to call in some lawyers. While they're around, we conduct ourselves as though we're three equal partners. On paper, we will be."

"Wait a minute, now," Don blurted. "What do you think you're pulling? The agreement was we split this whole thing three ways."

Demming's jaw wobbled as he nodded. "That's right. And

your share of the loot is your Galactic Medal of Honor. That and the dubious privilege of having the whole thing in your name. You'll keep your medal, and we'll keep you share.'' He growled heavily, ''You don't think you're getting the short end of the stick, do you?''

Max Rostoff said, "Let's knock this off and get the law boys in. We've got enough paper work to keep us busy for the rest of the week." He sat down again at his desk and looked up at Don. "Then we'll all be taking off for Callisto, to get things underway. With any luck, in six months we'll have every ounce of pitchblende left in the system sewed up."

There was a crowd awaiting his ship at the Callisto Spaceport. A crowd modest by Earth standards but representing a large percentage of the small population of Jupiter's moon.

On the way out, a staff of the system's best speech writers and two top professional actors had been working with him.

Don Mathers gave a short preliminary talk at the spaceport, and then the important one, the one that was broadcast throughout the system, that night from his suite at the hotel. He'd been well rehearsed, and they'd kept him from the bottle except for two or three quick ones immediately before going on.

The project at hand is to extract the newly discovered deposits of pitchblende on these satellites of Jupiter.

He paused impressively before continuing.

It's a job that cannot be done in slipshod, haphazard manner. The system's need for radioactives cannot be overstressed.

In short, fellow humans, we must allow nothing to stand in the way of all-out, unified effort to do this job quickly and efficiently. My associates and I have formed a corporation to manage this crash program. We invite all to participate by purchasing stock. I will not speak of profits, fellow humans, because in this emergency we all scorn them. However, as I say, you are invited to participate.

Some of the preliminary mining concessions are at present in the hands of individuals or small corporations. It will be necessary that these turn over their holdings to our single all-embracing organization for the sake of efficiency. Our experts will evaluate such holdings and recompense the owners.

Don Mathers paused again for emphasis.

This is no time for quibbling. All must come in. If there are those who put private gain before the needs of the system, then pressures must be found to be exerted against them.

We will need thousands and tens of thousands of trained workers to operate our mines, our mills, our refineries. In the past, skilled labor here on the satellites was used to double or even triple the wage rates on Earth and the settled planets and satellites. I need only repeat, this is no time for personal gain and quibbling. The corporation announces proudly that it will pay only prevailing Earth rates. We will not insult our employees by "bribing" them to patriotism through higher wages.

There was more, along the same lines.

It was all taken very well. Indeed, with enthusiasm.

On the third day, at an office conference, Don waited for an opening to say, "Look, somewhere here on Callisto is a young woman named Dian Fuller. After we get me established in an office, I'd like her to be my secretary."

Demming looked up from some reports he was scanning. He grunted to Max Rostoff, "Tell him," and went back to the papers.

Max Rostoff settled back into his chair. He said to the two bodyguards, stationed at the door, "Scotty, Rogers, go and make the arrangements to bring that damned prospector into line."

When they were gone, Rostoff turned back to Don Mathers. "You don't need a secretary, Mathers. All you need is to go back to your bottles. Just don't belt it so hard that you can't sign papers every time we need a signature."

Don flushed angrily. "Look, don't push me, you two. You need me. Plenty. In fact, from what I can see, this corporation needs me more than it does you." He looked scornfully at Demming. "Originally, the idea was that you put up the money. What money? We have fifty-one percent of the stock in my name, but all the credit units needed are coming from sales of stock." He turned to Rostoff. "You were supposed to put up the brains. What brains? We hired the best mining engineers, the best technicians, to do their end, the best corporation executives to handle that end. You're not needed."

Demming grunted amusement at the short speech, but didn't bother to look up from his perusal.

Max Rostoff's face had grown wolfishly thin in his anger. "Look, bottle-baby," he sneered, "you're the only one that's vulnerable in this set-up. There's not a single thing that Dem-

ming and I can be held to account for. You have no beefs
coming, for that matter. You're getting everything you ever
wanted. You've got the best suite in the best hotel on Callisto.
You eat the best food the Solar System provides. And, most
important of all to a rummy, you drink the best booze and as
much of it as you want. What's more, unless either Demming
or I go to the bother, you'll never be exposed. You'll live your
life out being the biggest hero in the system.''

It was Don Mathers' turn to sneer. ''Wha do you mean, I'm
the only one vulnerable? There's no evidence against me, Rostoff, and you know it. Who'd listen to you if you sounded off?
I burned that Kraden cruiser until there wasn't a sign to be
found that would indicate it wasn't in operational condition
when I first spotted it.''

Demming grunted his amusement again.

Max Rostoff laughed sourly. ''Don't be an ass, Mathers.
We took a series of photos of that derelict when we stumbled
on it. Not only can we prove you didn't knock it out, we can
prove that it was in good shape before you worked it over. I
imagine the Fleet technician would have loved to have seen
the inner workings of that Kraden cruiser—before you loused
it up.''

Demming chuckled flatly. ''I wonder what kind of court
martial they give a hero who turns out to be a saboteur.''

He ran into her, finally, after he'd been on Callisto for nearly
eight months. Actually, he didn't remember the circumstances
of their meeting. He was in an alcoholic daze and the fog rolled
out, and there she was across the table from him.

Don shook his head, and looked about the room. They were
in some sort of night spot. He didn't recognize it.

He licked his lips, scowled at the taste of stale vomit.

He slurred, ''Hello, Di.''

Dian Fuller said, ''Hi, Don.''

He said, ''I must've blanked out. Guess I've been hitting it
too hard.''

She laughed at him. ''You mean you don't remember all the
things you've been telling me the past two hours?'' She was
obviously quite sober. Dian never had been much for the sauce.

Don looked at her narrowly. ''What've I been telling you
for the past two hours?''

''Mostly about how it was when you were a little boy. About

fishing, and your first .22 rifle. And the time you shot the squirrel, and then felt so sorry."

"Oh," Don said. He ran his right hand over his mouth.

There was a champagne bucket beside him, but the bottle in it was empty. He looked about the room for a waiter.

Dian said gently, "Do you really think you need any more, Don?"

He looked across the table at her. She was as beautiful as ever. No, that wasn't right. She was pretty, but not beautiful. She was just a damn pretty girl, not one of these glamour items.

Don said, "Look, I can't remember. Did we get married?"

Her laugh tinkled. "Married! I only ran into you two or three hours ago." She hesitated before saying further, "I had assumed that you were deliberately avoiding me. Callisto isn't that big."

Don Mathers said slowly, "Well, if we're not married, let me decide when I want another bottle of the grape, eh?"

Dian flushed. "Sorry, Don."

The headwaiter approached bearing another magnum of vintage wine. He beamed at Don Mathers. "Having a good time, sir?"

"Okay," Don said shortly. When the other was gone he downed a full glass, felt the fumes almost immediately.

He said to Dian, "I haven't been avoiding you, Di. We just haven't met. The way I remember, the last time we saw each other, back on Earth, you gave me quite a slap in the face. The way I remember, you didn't think I was hero enough for you." He poured another glass of the champagne.

Di's face was still flushed. She said, her voice low, "I misunderstood you, Don. Even after your brilliant defeat of that Kraden cruiser, I still, I admit, think I basically misunderstood you. I told myself that it could have been done by any pilot of a Scout, given that one in a million break. It just happened to be you, who made that suicide drive attack that succeeded. A thousand other pilots might also have taken the million to one suicide chance rather than let the Kraden escape."

"Yeah," Don said. Even in his alcohol, he was surprised at her words. He said gruffly, "Sure anybody might've done it. Pure luck. But why'd you change your mind about me, then? How come the switch of heart?"

"Because of what you've done since, darling."

He closed one eye, the better to focus.

"Since?"

He recognized the expression in her eyes. A touch of star gleam. That little girl back on Earth, the receptionist at the Interplanetary Lines building, she'd had it. In fact, in the past few months Don had seen it in many feminine faces. And all for him.

Dian said, "Instead of cashing in on your prestige, you've been devoting yourself to something even more necessary to the fight than bringing down individual Kraden cruisers."

Don looked at her. He could feel a nervous tic beginning in his left eyebrow. Finally, he reached for the champagne again and filled his glass. He said, "You really go for this hero stuff, don't you?"

She said nothing, but the star shine was still in her eyes.

He made his voice deliberately sour. "Look, suppose I asked you to come back to my apartment with me tonight?"

"Yes," she said softly.

"And told you to bring your overnight bag along," he added brutally.

Dian looked into his face. "Why are you twisting yourself, your inner-self, so hard, Don? Of course I'd come—if that's what you wanted."

"And then," he said flatly, "suppose I kicked you out in the morning?"

Dian winced, but she kept her eyes even with his, her own moist now. "You forget," she whispered. "You have been awarded the Galactic Medal of Honor, the bearer of which can do no wrong."

"Oh, God," Don muttered. He filled his glass, still again, motioned to a nearby waiter.

"Yes, sir," the waiter said.

Don said, "Look, in about five minutes I'm going to pass out. See that I get back to my hotel, will you? And that this young lady gets to her home. And, waiter, just send my bill to the hotel too."

The other bowed. "The owner's instructions, sir, are that Captain Mathers must never see a bill in this establishment."

Dian said, *"Don!"*

He didn't look at her. He raised his glass to his mouth and shortly afterward the fog rolled in again.

When it rolled out, the unfamiliar taste of black coffee was in his mouth. He shook his head for clarity.

He seemed to be in some working-class restaurant. Next to him, in a booth, was a fresh-faced Sub-lieutenant of the—Don squinted at the collar tabs—yes, of the Space Service. A Scout pilot.

Don stuttered, "What's . . . goin' . . . on?"

The pilot said apologetically, "Sub-lieutenant Pierpont, sir. You seemed so far under the weather, I took over."

"Oh, you did, eh?"

"Well, yes, sir. You were, well, reclining in the gutter, sir. In spite of your, well, appearance, your condition, I recognized you, sir."

"Oh." His stomach was an objecting turmoil.

The Lieutenant said, "Want to try some more of this coffee now, sir? Or maybe some soup or a sandwich?"

Don groaned. "No. No, thanks. Don't think I could hold it down."

The pilot grinned. "You must've thrown a classic, sir."

"I guess so. What time is it? No, that doesn't make any difference. What's the date?"

Pierpont told him.

It was hard to believe. The last he could remember he'd been with Di. With Di in some nightclub. He wondered how long ago that had been.

He fumbled in his clothes for a smoke and couldn't find one. He didn't want it anyway.

He growled at the Lieutenant, "Well, how go the One Man Scouts?"

Pierpont grinned back at him. "Glad to be out of them, sir?"

"Usually."

Pierpont looked at him strangely. "I don't blame you, I suppose. But it isn't as bad these days as it used to be while you were still in the Space Service, sir."

Don grunted. "How come? Two weeks to a month, all by yourself, watching the symptoms of space cafard progress. Then three weeks of leave, to get drunk in, and then another stretch in space."

The pilot snorted deprecation. "That's the way it used to be." He fingered the spoon of his coffee cup. "That's the way it still should be, of course. But it isn't. They're spreading the duty around now and I spend less than one week out of four on patrol."

Don hadn't been listening too closely, but now he looked up. "What'd'ya mean?"

Pierpont said, "I mean, sir, I suppose this isn't bridging security, seeing who you are, but fuel stocks are so low that we can't maintain full patrols any more."

There was a cold emptiness in Don Mathers's stomach.

He said, "Look, I'm still woozy. Say that again, Lieutenant."

The Lieutenant told him again.

Don Mathers rubbed the back of his hand over his mouth and tried to think.

He said finally, "Look, Lieutenant. First let's get another cup of coffee into me, and maybe that sandwich you were talking about. Then would you help me to get back to my hotel?"

By the fourth day, his hands weren't trembling any longer. He ate a good breakfast, dressed carefully, then took a hotel limousine down to the offices of the Mathers, Demming and Rostoff Corporation.

At the entrance of the inner sanctum the heavyset Scotty looked up at his approach. He said, "The boss has been looking for you, Mr. Mathers, but right now you ain't got no appointment, have you? Him and Mr. Rostoff is having a big conference. He says to keep everybody out."

"That doesn't apply to me, Scotty," Don snapped. "Get out of my way."

Scotty stood up, reluctantly, but barred the way. "He said it applied to everybody, Mr. Mathers."

Don put his full weight into a blow that started at his waist, dug deep into the other's middle. Scotty doubled forward, his eyes bugging. Don Mathers gripped his hands together into a double fist and brought them upward in a vicious uppercut.

Scotty fell forward and to the floor.

Don stood above him momentarily, watchful for movement which didn't develop. The hefty bodyguard must have been doing some easy living himself. He wasn't as tough as he looked.

Don knelt and fished from under the other's arm a vicious looking short-barrelled scrambler. He tucked it under his own jacket into his belt and entered the supposedly barred office.

Demming and Rostoff looked up from their work across a double desk.

Both scowled. Rostoff opened his mouth to say something and Don Mathers rapped, "Shut up."

Rostoff blinked at him. Demming leaned back in his swivel chair. "You're sober for a change," he wheezed, almost accusingly.

Don Mathers pulled up a stenographer's chair and straddled it, leaning his arms on the back. He said coldly, "Comes a point when even the lowest worm turns. I've been checking on a few things."

Demming grunted amusement.

Don said, "Space patrols have been cut far below the danger point."

Rostoff snorted. "Is that supposed to interest us? That's the problem of the military—and the government."

"Oh, it interests us, all right," Don growled. "Currently, Mathers, Demming and Rostoff control probably three-quarters of the system's radioactives."

Demming said in greasy satisfaction, "More like four-fifths."

"Why?" Don said bluntly. "Why are we doing what we're doing?"

They both scowled, but another element was present in their expression too. They thought the question unintelligent.

Demming closed his eyes in his porcine manner and grunted, "Tell him."

Rostoff said, "Look, Mathers, don't be stupid. Remember when we told you, during that first interview, that we wanted your name in the corporation, among other reasons, because we could use a man who was above the law? That a maze of ridiculously binding ordinances have been laid on business down through the centuries?"

"I remember," Don said bitterly.

"Well, it goes both ways. Government today is also bound, very strongly, and even in great emergency, not to interfere in business. These complicated laws balance each other, you might say. Our whole legal system is based upon them. Right now, we've got government right where we want it. This is free enterprise, Mathers, at its pinnacle. Did you ever hear of Jim Fisk and his attempt to corner gold in 1869, the so-called Black Friday affair? Well, Jim Fisk was a peanut peddler compared to us."

"What's this got to do with the Fleet having insufficient fuel to . . ." Don Mathers stopped as comprehension hit him. "You're holding our radioactives off the market, pressuring the government for a price rise which it can't afford."

Demming opened his eyes and said fatly, "For triple the price, Mathers. Before we're through, we'll corner half the wealth of the system."

Don said, "But . . . but the species is . . . at . . . *war.*"

Rostoff sneered, "You seem to be getting noble rather late in the game, Mathers. Business is business."

Don Mathers was shaking his head. "We immediately begin selling our radioactives at cost of production. I might remind you gentlemen that although we're supposedly a three-way partnership, actually, everything's in my name. You thought you had me under your thumb so securely that it was safe—and you probably didn't trust each other. Well, I'm blowing the whistle."

Surprisingly fast for such a fat man, Lawrence Demming's hand flitted into a desk drawer to emerge with a twin of the scrambler tucked in Don's belt.

Don Mathers grinned at him, even as he pushed his jacket back to reveal the butt of his weapon. He made no attempt to draw it, however.

He said softly, "Shoot me, Demming, and you've killed the most popular man in the Solar System. You'd never escape the gas chamber, no matter how much money you have. On the other hand, if I shoot you . . ."

He put a hand into his pocket and it emerged with a small, inordinately ordinary bit of ribbon and metal. He displayed it on his palm.

The fat man's face whitened at the ramifications and his hand relaxed to let the gun drop to the desk. "Listen, Don," he broke out. "We've been unrealistic with you. We'll reverse ourselves and split, honestly—split three ways."

Don Mathers laughed at him. "Trying to bribe me with money, Demming? Why, don't you realize that I'm the only man in existence who has no need for money, who can't spend money? That my fellow men—whom I've done such a good job of betraying—have honored me to a point where money is meaningless?"

Rostoff snatched up the fallen gun, snarling, "I'm calling your bluff, you gutless rummy."

Don Mathers said, "Okay, Rostoff. There's just two other things I want to say first. One—I don't care if I die or not. Two—you're only twenty feet or so away, but you know what? I think you're probably a lousy shot. I don't think you've had much practice. I think I can get my scrambler out and cut you down before you can finish me." He grinned thinly. "Wanta try?"

Max Rostoff snarled a curse and his finger whitened on the trigger.

Don Mathers fell sideward, his hand streaking for his weapon. Without thought there came back to him the long hours of training in hand weapons, in judo, in hand to hand combat. He went into action with cool confidence.

At the spaceport he took a cab to the Presidential Palace. It was an auto-cab, of course, and at the Palace gates he found he had no money on him. He snorted wearily. It was the first time in almost a year that he'd had to pay for anything.

Four sentries were standing at attention. He said, "Do one of you boys have some coins to feed into this slot? I'm fresh out."

A sergeant grinned, approached, and did the necessary.

Don Mathers said wearily, "I don't know how you go about this. I don't have an appointment, but I want to see the President."

"We can turn you over to one of the assistant secretaries, Captain Mathers," the sergeant said. "We can't go any further than that. While we're waiting, what's the chances of getting your autograph, sir? I gotta kid . . ."

It wasn't nearly as complicated as he'd thought it was going to be. In half an hour he was seated in the office where he'd received his decoration only—how long ago was it, really less than a year?

He told the story briefly, making no effort to spare himself. At the end he stood up long enough to put a paper in front of the other, then sat down again.

"I'm turning the whole corporation over to the government . . ."

The President said, "Wait a minute. My administration does not advocate State ownership of industry."

"I know. When the State controls the industry you only put

the whole mess off one step, the question then becomes, who controls the State? However, I'm not arguing political economy with you, sir. You didn't let me finish. I was going to say, I'm turning it over to the government to untangle, even while making use of the inventories of radioactives. There's going to be a lot of untangling to do. Reimbursing the prospectors and small operators who were blackjacked out of their holdings by our super-corporation. Reimbursing of the miners and other laborers who were talked into accepting low pay in the name of patriotism.'' Don Mathers cut it short. "Oh, it's quite a mess.''

"Yes," the President said. "And you say Max Rostoff is dead?''

"That's right. And Demming is off his rocker. I think he always was a little unbalanced and the prospect of losing all that money, the greatest fortune ever conceived of, tipped the scales.''

The President said, "And what about you, Donal Mathers?''

Don took a deep breath. "I wish I was back in the Space Services, frankly. Back where I was when all this started. However, I suppose that after my court martial, there won't be . . .''

The President interrupted gently. "You seem to forget, Captain Mathers. You carry the Galactic Medal of Honor, the bearer of which can do no wrong.''

Don Mathers gaped at him.

The President smiled at him, albeit a bit sourly. "It would hardly do for human morale to find out our supreme symbol of heroism was a phoney, Captain. There will be no trial, and you will retain your decoration.''

"But I don't want it!''

"I'm afraid that is the cross you'll have to bear for the rest of your life, Captain Mathers. I don't suppose it will be an easy one.''

His eyes went to a far corner of the room, but unseeingly. He said after a long moment, "However, I am not so very sure about your not deserving your award, Captain.''

WINGS OUT OF SHADOW

by Fred Saberhagen

In Malori's first and only combat mission the berserker came to him in the image of a priest of the sect into which Malori had been born on the planet Yaty. In a dreamlike vision that was the analogue of a very real combat he saw a robed figure standing tall in a deformed pulpit, eyes flaming with malevolence, lowering arms winglike with the robes they stretched. With their lowering, the lights of the universe were dimming outside the windows of stained glass and Malori was being damned.

Even with his heart pounding under damnation's terror Malori retained sufficient consciousness to remember the real nature of himself and of his adversary and that he was not powerless against him. His dream-feet walked him timelessly toward the pulpit and its demon-priest while all around him the stained glass windows burst, showering him with fragments of sick fear. He walked a crooked path, avoiding the places in the smooth floor where, with quick gestures, the priest created snarling, snapping stone mouths full of teeth. Malori seemed to have unlimited time to decide where to put his feet. *Weapon*, he thought, a surgeon instructing some invisible aide. *Here—in my right hand.*

185

From those who had survived similar battles he had heard how the inhuman enemy appeared to each in different form, how each human must live the combat through in terms of a unique nightmare. To some a berserker came as a ravening beast, to others as devil or god or man. To still others it was some essence of terror that could never be faced or even seen. The combat was a nightmare experienced while the subconscious ruled, while the waking mind was suppressed by careful electrical pressures on the brain. Eyes and ears were padded shut so that the conscious mind might be more easily suppressed, the mouth plugged to save the tongue from being bitten, the nude body held immobile by the defensive fields that kept it whole against the thousands of gravities that came with each movement of the one-man ship while in combat mode. It was a nightmare from which mere terror could never wake one; waking came only when the fight was over, came only with death or victory or disengagement.

Into Malori's dream-hand there now came a meat cleaver keen as a razor, massive as a guillotine blade. So huge it was that had it been what it seemed it would have been far too cumbersome to even lift. His uncle's butcher shop on Yaty was gone, with all other human works of that planet. But the cleaver came back to him now, magnified, perfected to suit his need.

He gripped it hard in both hands and advanced. As he drew near the pulpit towered higher. The carved dragon on its front, which should have been an angel, came alive, blasting him with rosy fire. With a shield that came from nowhere he parried the splashing flames.

Outside the remnants of the stained glass windows the lights of the universe were almost dead now. Standing at the base of the pulpit, Malori drew back his cleaver as if to strike overhand at the priest who towered above his reach. Then, without any forethought at all, he switched his aim at the top of his backswing and laid the blow crashing against the pulpit's stem. It shook, but resisted stoutly. Damnation came.

Before the devils reached him, though, the energy was draining from the dream. In less than a second of real time it was no more than a fading visual image, a few seconds after that a dying memory. Malori, coming back to consciousness with eyes and ears still sealed, floated in a soothing limbo. Before post-combat fatigue and sensory deprivation could combine to send him into psychosis, attachments on his scalp began to feed his brain with bursts of pins-and-needles noise. It was the safest signal to administer to a brain that might be on the verge of any of a dozen different kinds of madness. The noise made a whitish roaring scattering of light and sound that seemed to fill his head and at the same time somehow outlined for him the positions of his limbs.

His first fully conscious thought: he had just fought a berserker and survived. He had won—or had at least achieved a stand-off—or he would not be here. It was no mean achievement.

Berserkers were like no other foe that Earth-descended human beings had ever faced. They had cunning and intelligence and yet were not alive. Relics of some interstellar war over long ages since, automated machines, warships for the most part, they carried as their basic programming the command to destroy all life wherever it could be found. Yaty was only the latest of many Earth-colonized planets to suffer a berserker attack, and it was among the luckiest; nearly all its people had been successfully evacuated. Malori and other now fought in deep space to protect the *Hope,* one of the enormous evacuation ships. The *Hope* was a sphere several kilometers in diameter, large enough to contain a good proportion of the planet's population stored tier on tier in defense-field stasis. A trickle-relaxation of the fields allowed them to breathe and live with slowed metabolism.

The voyage to a safe sector of the galaxy was going to take several months because most of it, in terms of time spent, was going to be occupied in traversing an outlying arm of the great Taynarus nebula. Here gas and dust were much too thick to let a ship duck out of normal space and travel faster than light. Here even the speeds attainable in normal space were greatly restricted. At thousands of kilometers per second, manned ship or berserker machine could alike be smashed flat against a wisp of gas far more tenuous than human breath.

Taynarus was a wilderness of uncharted plumes and tendrils of dispersed matter, laced through by corridors of relatively empty space. Much of the wilderness was completely shaded by interstellar dust from the light of all the suns outside. Through dark shoals and swamps and tides of nebula the *Hope* and her escort *Judith* fled, and a berserker pack pursued. Some berserkers were even larger than the *Hope,* but those that had taken up this chase were much smaller. In regions of space so thick with matter, a race went to the small as well as to the swift; as the impact cross-section of a ship increased, its maximum practical speed went inexorably down.

The *Hope*, ill-adapted for this chase (in the rush to evacuate, there had been no better choice available) could not expect to outrun the smaller and more maneuverable enemy. Hence the escort carrier *Judith*, trying always to keep herself between *Hope* and the pursuing pack. *Judith* mothered the little fighting ships, spawning them out whenever the enemy came too near, welcoming survivors back when the threat had once again been beaten off. There had been fifteen of the one-man ships when the chase began. Now there were nine.

The noise injections from Malori's life support equipment slowed down, then stopped. His conscious mind once more sat steady on its throne. The gradual relaxation of his defense fields he knew to be a certain sign that he would soon rejoin the world of waking men.

As soon as his fighter, Number Four, had docked itself inside the *Judith* Malori hastened to disconnect himself from the tiny ship's systems. He pulled on a loose coverall and let himself out of the cramped space. A thin man with knobby joints and an awkward step, he hurried along a catwalk through the echoing hangar-like chamber, noting that three or four fighters besides his had already returned and were resting in their cradles. The artificial gravity was quite steady, but Malori stumbled and almost fell in his haste to get down the short ladder to the operations deck.

Petrovich, commander of the *Judith*, a bulky, iron-faced man of middle height, was on the deck apparently waiting for him.

"Did—did I make my kill?" Malori stuttered eagerly as he came hurrying up. The forms of military address were little observed aboard the *Judith*, as a rule, and Malori was really a civilian anyway. That he had been allowed to take out a fighter at all was a mark of the commander's desperation.

Scowling, Petrovich answered bluntly. "Malori, you're a disaster in one of these ships. Haven't the mind for it at all."

The world turned a little gray in front of Malori. He hadn't understood until this moment just how important to him certain dreams of glory were. He could find only weak and awkward words. "But . . . I thought I did all right." He tried to recall his combat-nightmare. Something about a church.

"Two people had to divert their ships from their original combat objectives to rescue you. I've already seen their gun-camera tapes. You had Number Four just sparring around with that berserker as if you had no intention of doing it any damage at all." Petrovich looked at him more closely, shrugged, and softened his voice somewhat. "I'm not trying to chew you out, you weren't even aware of what was happening, of course. I'm just stating facts. Thank probability the *Hope* is twenty AU deep in a formaldehyde cloud up ahead. If she'd been in an exposed position just now they would have got her."

"But—" Malori tried to begin an argument but the com-mander simply walked away. More fighters were coming in. Locks sighed and cradles clanged, and Petrovich had plenty of more important things to do than stand here arguing with him. Malori stood there alone for a few moments, feeling deflated and defeated and diminished. Involuntarily he cast a yearning glance back at Number Four. It was a short, windowless cylin-der, not much more than a man's height in diameter, resting in its metal cradle while technicians worked about it. The stubby main laser nozzle, still hot from firing, was sending up a wisp of smoke now that it was back in atmosphere. There was his two-handed cleaver.

No man could direct a ship or a weapon with anything like the competence of a good machine. The creeping slowness of human nerve impulses and of conscious thought disqualified humans from maintaining direct control of their ships in any space fight against berserkers. But the human subconscious was not so limited. Certain of its processes could not be corre-lated with any specific synaptic activity within the brain, and some theorists held that these processes took place outside of time. Most physicists stood aghast at this view—but for space combat it made a useful working hypothesis.

In combat, the berserker computers were coupled with sophisticated randoming devices, to provide the flair, the unpre-dictability that gained an advantage over an opponent who simply and consistently chose the maneuver statistically most likely to bring success. Men also used computers to drive their ships, but had now gained an edge over the best randomizers by relying once more on their own brains, parts of which were evidently freed of hurry and dwelt outside of time, where even speeding light must be as motionless as carved ice.

There were drawbacks. Some people (including Malori, it

now appeared) were simply not suitable for the job, their subconscious minds seemingly uninterested in such temporal matters as life or death. And even in suitable minds the subconscious was subject to great stress. Connection to external computers loaded the mind in some way not yet understood. One after another, human pilots returning from combat were removed from their ships in states of catatonia or hysterical excitement. Sanity might be restored, but the man or woman was worthless thereafter as a combat-computer's teammate. The system was so new that the importance of these drawbacks was just coming to light aboard the *Judith* now. The trained operators of the fighting ships had been used up, and so had their replacements. Thus it was that Ian Malori, historian, and others were sent out, untrained, to fight. But using their minds had bought a little extra time.

From the operations deck Malori went to his small single cabin. He had not eaten for some time, but he was not hungry. He changed clothes and sat in a chair looking at his bunk, looking at his books and tapes and violin, but he did not try to rest or to occupy himself. He expected that he would promptly get a call from Petrovich. Because Petrovich now had nowhere else to turn.

He almost smiled when the communicator chimed, bringing a summons to meet with the commander and other officers at once. Malori acknowledged and set out, taking with him a brown leather-like case about the size of a briefcase but differently shaped, which he selected from several hundred similar cases in a small room adjacent to his cabin. The case he carried was labeled: CRAZY HORSE.

Petrovich looked up as Malori entered the small planning room in which the handful of ship's officers were already gathered around a table. The commander glanced at the case Malori was carrying, and nodded. "It seems we have no choice, historian. We are running out of people, and we are going to have to use your pseudopersonalities. Fortunately we now have the necessary adapters installed in all the fighting ships."

"I think the chances of success are excellent." Malori spoke mildly as he took the seat left vacant for him and set his case out in the middle of the table. "These of course have no real subconscious minds, but as we agreed in our earlier discussions, they will provide more sophisticated randoming devices than are available otherwise. Each has a unique, if artificial, personality.''

One of the other officers leaned forward. "Most of us missed these earlier discussions you speak of. Could you fill us in a little?"

"Certainly." Malori cleared his throat. "These personae, as we usually call them, are used in the computer simulation of historical problems. I was able to bring several hundred of them with me from Yaty. Many are models of military men." He put his hand on the case before him. "This is a reconstruction of the personality of one of the most able cavalry leaders on ancient Earth. It's not one of the group we have selected to try first in combat. I just brought it along to demonstrate the interior structure and design for any of you who are interested. Each persona contains about four million sheets of two-dimensional matter."

Another officer raised a hand, "How can you accurately reconstruct the personality of someone who must have died long before any kind of direct recording techniques were available?"

"We can't be positive of accuracy, of course. We have only historical records to go by, and what we deduce from computer simulations of the era. These are only models. But they should perform in combat as in the historical studies for which they were made. Their choices should reflect basic aggressiveness, determination—"

The totally unexpected sound of an explosion brought the assembled officers as one body to their feet. Petrovich, reacting very fast, still had time only to get clear of his chair before a second and much louder blast resounded through the ship. Malori himself was almost at the door, heading for his battle station, when the third explosion came. It sounded like the end of the galaxy, and he was aware that furniture was flying, that the bulkheads around the meeting room were caving in. Malori had one clear, calm thought about the unfairness of his coming death, and then for a time he ceased to think at all.

Coming back was a slow unpleasant progress. He knew *Judith* was not totally wrecked for he still breathed, and the artificial gravity still held him sprawled out against the deck. It might have been pleasing to find the gravity gone, for his body was one vast, throbbing ache, a pattern of radiated pain from a

center somewhere inside his skull. He did not want to pin down
the source any more closely than that. To even imagine touching
his own head was painful.

At last the urgency of finding out what was going on over-
came the fear of pain and he raised his head and probed it.
There was a large lump just above his forehead, and smaller
injuries about his face where blood had dried. He must have
been out for some time.

The meeting room was ruined, shattered, littered with debris.
There was a crumpled body that must be dead, and there
another, and another, mixed in with the furniture. Was he the
only survivor? One bulkhead had been torn wide open, and the
planning table was demolished. And what was that large, unfamiliar piece of machinery standing at the other end of the
room? Big as a tall filing cabinet, but far more intricate. There
was something peculiar about its legs, as if they might be
movable . . .

Malori froze in abject terror, because the thing did move,
swiveling a complex of turrets and lenses at him, and he understood that he was seeing and being seen by a functional berserker
machine. It was one of the small ones, used for boarding and
operating captured human ships.

"Come here," the machine said. It had a squeaky, ludicrous
parody of a human voice, recorded syllables of captives' voices
stuck together electronically and played back. "The badlife
has awakened."

Malori in his great fear thought that the words were directed
at him but he could not move. Then, stepping through the hole
in the bulkhead, came a man Malori had never seen before—a
shaggy and filthy man wearing a grimy coverall that might
once have been part of some military uniform.

"I see he has, sir," the man said to the machine. He spoke
the standard interstellar language in a ragged voice that bore
traces of a cultivated accent. He took a step closer to Malori.
"Can you understand me, there?"

Malori grunted something, tried to nod, pulled himself up
slowly into an awkward sitting position.

"The question is," the man continued, coming a little closer
still, "how d'you want it later, easy or hard? When it comes
to your finishing up, I mean. I decided a long time ago that I
want mine quick and easy, and not too soon. Also that I still
want to have some fun here and there along the way."

Despite the fierce pain in his head, Malori was thinking now, and beginning to understand. There was a name for humans like the man before him, who went along more or less willingly with the berserker machines. A word coined by the machines themselves. But at the moment Malori was not going to speak that name.

"I want it easy," was all he said, and blinked his eyes and tried to rub his neck against the pain.

The man looked him over in silence a little longer. "All right," he said then. Turning back to the machine, he added in a different, humble voice: "I can easily dominate this injured badlife. There will be no problems if you leave us here alone."

The machine turned one metal-cased lens toward its servant. "Remember," it vocalized, "the auxiliaries must be made ready. Time grows short. Failure will bring unpleasant stimuli."

"I will remember, sir." The man was humble and sincere. The machine looked at both of them a few moments longer and then departed, metal legs flowing suddenly into a precise and almost graceful walk. Shortly after, Malori heard the familiar sound of an airlock cycling.

"We're alone now," the man said, looking down at him. "If you want a name for me you can call me Greenleaf. Want to try to fight me? If so, let's get it over with." He was not much bigger than Malori but his hands were huge and he looked hard and very capable despite his ragged filthiness. "All right, that's a smart choice. You know, you're actually a lucky man, though you don't realize it yet. Berserkers aren't like the other masters that men have—not like the governments and parties and corporations and causes that use you up and then just let you drop and drag away. No, when the machines run out of uses for you they'll finish you off quickly and cleanly—if you've served well. I know, I've seen 'em do it that way with other humans. No reason why they shouldn't. All they want is for us to die, not suffer."

Malori said nothing. He thought perhaps he would be able to stand up soon.

Greenleaf (the name seemed so inappropriate that Malori thought it probably real) made some adjustment on a small device that he had taken from a pocket and was holding almost concealed in one large hand. He asked: "How many escort carriers besides this one are trying to protect the *Hope?*''

"I don't know," Malori lied. There had been only the *Judith*.

"What is your name?" The bigger man was still looking at the device in his hand.

"Ian Malori."

Greenleaf nodded, and without showing any particular emotion in his face took two steps forward and kicked Malori in the belly, precisely and with brutal power.

"That was for trying to lie to me, Ian Malori," said his captor's voice, heard dimly from somewhere above as Malori groveled on the deck, trying to breathe again. "Understand that I am infallibly able to tell when you are lying. Now, how many escort carriers are there?"

In time Malori could sit up again, and choke out words. "Only this one." Whether Greenleaf had a real lie detector, or was only trying to make it appear so by asking questions whose answers he already knew, Malori decided that from now on he would speak the literal truth as scrupulously as possible. A few more kicks like that and he would be helpless and useless and the machines would kill him. He discovered that he was by no means ready to abandon his life.

"What was your position on the crew, Malori?"

"I'm a civilian."

"What sort?"

"An historian."

"And why are you here?"

Malori started to try to get to his feet, then decided there was nothing to be gained by the struggle and stayed sitting on the deck. If he ever let himself dwell on his situation for a moment he would be too hideously afraid to think coherently. "There was a project . . . you see. I brought with me from Yaty a number of what we call historical models—blocks of programmed responses we use in historical research."

"I remember hearing about some such things. What was the project you mentioned?"

"Trying to use the persona of military men as randomizers for the combat computers on the one-man ships."

"Aha." Greenleaf squatted, supple and poised for all his raunchy look. "How do they work in combat? Better than a live pilot's subconscious mind? The machines know all about *that*."

"We never had a chance to try. Are the rest of the crew here all dead?"

Greenleaf nodded casually. "It wasn't a hard boarding. There must have been a failure in your automatic defenses. I'm glad to find one man alive and smart enough to cooperate. It'll help me in my career." He glanced at an expensive chronometer strapped to his dirty wrist. "Stand up, Ian Malori. There's work to do."

Malori got up and followed the other toward the operations deck.

"The machines and I have been looking around, Malori. These nine little fighting ships you still have on board are just too good to be wasted. The machines are sure of catching the *Hope* now, but she'll have automatic defenses, probably a lot tougher than this tub's were. The machines have taken a lot of casualties on this chase so they mean to use these nine little ships as auxiliary troops—no doubt you have some knowledge of military history?"

"Some." The answer was perhaps an understatement, but it seemed to pass as truth. The lie detector, if it was one, had been put away. But Malori would still take no more chances than he must.

"Then you probably know how some of the generals on old Earth used their auxiliaries. Drove them on ahead of the main force of trusted troops, where they could be killed if they tried to retreat, and were also the first to be used up against the enemy."

Arriving on the operations deck, Malori saw few signs of damage. Nine tough little ships waited in their launching cradles, re-armed and returned and refueled for combat. All that would have been taken care of within minutes of their return from their last mission.

"Malori, from looking at these ships' controls while you were unconscious, I gather that there's no fully automatic mode in which they can be operated."

"Right. There has to be some controlling mind, or randomizer, connected on board."

"You and I are going to get them out as berserker auxiliaries, Ian Malori." Greenleaf glanced at his timepiece again. "We have less than an hour to think of a good way and only a few hours more to complete the job. The faster the better. If we delay we are going to be made to suffer for it." He seemed almost to relish the thought. "What do you suggest we do?"

Malori opened his mouth as if to speak, and then did not.

Greenleaf said: "Installing any of your military personae is of course out of the question, as they might not submit well to being driven forward like mere cannon-fodder. I assume they are leaders of some kind. But have you perhaps any of these personae from different fields, of a more docile nature?"

Malori, sagging against the operations officer's empty combat chair, forced himself to think very carefully before he spoke. "As it happens, there are some personae aboard in which I have a special personal interest. Come."

With the other following closely, Malori led the way to his small bachelor cabin. Somehow it was astonishing that nothing had been changed inside. There on the bunk was his violin, and on the table were his music tapes and a few books. And here, stacked neatly in their leather-like curved cases, were some of the personae that he liked best to study.

Malori lifted the top case from the stack. "This man was a violinist, as I like to think I am. His name would probably mean nothing to you."

"Musicology was never my field. But tell me more."

"He was an Earthman, who lived in the twentieth century CE—quite a religious man, too, as I understand. We can plug the persona in and ask it what it thinks of fighting, if you are suspicious."

"We had better do that." When Malori had shown him the proper receptacle beside the cabin's small computer console, Greenleaf snapped the connections together himself. "How does one communicate with it?"

"Just talk."

Greenleaf spoke sharply toward the leather-like case. "Your name?"

"Albert Ball." The voice that answered from the console speaker sounded more human by far than the berserker's had.

"How does the thought of getting into a fight strike you, Albert?"

"A detestable idea."

"Will you play the violin for us?"

"Gladly." But no music followed.

Malori put in: "More connections are necessary if you want actual music."

"I don't think we'll need that." Greenleaf unplugged the Albert Ball unit and began to look through the stack of others, frowning at unfamiliar names. There were twelve or fifteen cases in all. "Who are these?"

"Albert Ball's contemporaries. Performers who shared his profession." Malori let himself sink down on the bunk for a few moments' rest. He was not far from fainting. Then he went to stand with Greenleaf beside the stack of personae. "This is a model of Edward Mannock, who was blind in one eye and could never have passed the physical examination necessary to serve in any military force of his time." He pointed to another. "This man served briefly in the cavalry, as I recall, but he kept getting thrown from his horse and was soon relegated to gathering supplies. And this one was a frail, tubercular youth who died at twenty-three standard years of age."

Greenleaf gave up looking at the cases and turned to size up Malori once again. Malori could feel his battered stomach muscles trying to contract, anticipating another violent impact. It would be too much, it was going to kill him if it came like that again . . .

"All right." Greenleaf was frowning, checking his chronometer yet again. Then he looked up with a little smile. Oddly, the smile made him look like the hell of a good fellow. "All right! Musicians, I suppose, are the antithesis of the military. If the machines approve, we'll install them and get the ships sent out. Ian Malori, I may just raise your pay." His pleasant smile broadened. "We may just have bought ourselves another standard year of life if this works out as well as I think it might."

When the machine came aboard again a few minutes later, Greenleaf bowing before it explained the essence of the plan, while Malori in the background, in an agony of terror, found himself bowing too.

"Proceed, then," the machine approved. "If you are not, the ship infected with life may find concealment in the storms that rise ahead of us." Then it went away again quickly. Probably it had repairs and refitting to accomplish on its own robotic ship.

With two men working, installation went very fast. It was only a matter of opening a fighting ship's cabin, inserting an uncased persona in the installed adapter, snapping together standard connectors and clamps, and closing the cabin hatch again. Since haste was vital to the berserkers' plans, testing was restricted to listening for a live response from each persona as it was activated inside a ship. Most of the responses were utter banalities about nonexistent weather or ancient food or drink, or curious phrases that Malori knew were only phatic social remarks.

All seemed to be going well, but Greenleaf was having some last minute misgivings. "I hope these sensitive gentlemen will stand up under the strain of finding out their true situation. They will be able to grasp that, won't they? The machines won't expect them to fight well, but we don't want them going catatonic, either."

Malori, close to exhaustion, was tugging at the hatch of Number Eight, and nearly fell off the curved hull when it came open suddenly. "They will apprehend their situation within a minute after launching, I should say. At least in a general way. I don't suppose they'll understand it's interstellar space around them. You have been a military man, I suppose. If they should be reluctant to fight—I leave to you the question of how to deal with recalcitrant auxiliaries."

When they plugged the persona into ship Number Eight, its test response was: "I wish my craft to be painted red."

"At once, sir," said Malori quickly, and slammed down the ship's hatch and started to move on to Number Nine.

"What was that all about?" Greenleaf frowned, but looked at his timepiece and moved along.

"I suppose the maestro is already aware that he is about to embark in some kind of a vehicle. As to why he might like it painted red . . ." Malori grunted, trying to open up Number Nine, and let his answer trail away.

At last all the ships were ready. With his finger on the launching switch, Greenleaf paused. For one last time his eyes probed Malori's. "We've done very well, timewise. We're in for a reward, as long as this idea works at least moderately well." He was speaking now in a solemn near-whisper. "It had better work. Have you ever watched a man being skinned alive?"

Malori was gripping a stanchion to keep erect. "I have done all I can."

Greenleaf operated the launching switch. There was a polyphonic whisper of airlocks. The nine ships were gone, and simultaneously a holographic display came alive above the

operations officer's console. In the center of the display the
Judith showed as a fat green symbol, with nine smaller green
dots moving slowly and uncertainly nearby. Farther off, a steady
formation of red dots represented what was left of the berserker
pack that had so long and so relentlessly pursued the *Hope* and
her escort. There were at least fifteen red berserker dots, Malori
noted gloomily.

"The trick," Greenleaf said as if to himself, "is to make
them more afraid of their own leaders than they are of the
enemy." He keyed the panel switches that would send his voice
out to the ships. "Attention, units One through Nine!" he
barked. "You are under the guns of a vastly superior force,
and any attempt at disobedience or escape will be severely
punished . . ."

He went on browbeating them for a minute, while Malori observed in the screen that the dirty weather the berserker had
mentioned was coming on. A sleet of atomic particles was
driving through this section of the nebula, across the path of
the *Judith* and the odd hybrid fleet that moved with her. The
Hope, not in view on this range scale, might be able to take
advantage of the storm to get away entirely unless the berserker
pursuit was swift.

Visibility on the operations display was failing fast and
Greenleaf cut off his speech as it became apparent that contact
was being lost. Orders in the berserkers' unnatural voices,
directed at auxiliary ships One through Nine, came in fragmen-
tarily before the curtain of noise became an opaque white-out.
The pursuit of the *Hope* had not yet been resumed.

For a while all was silent on the operations desk, except for
an occasional crackle of noise from the display. All around
them the empty launching cradles waited.

"That's that," Greenleaf said at length. "Nothing to do now
but worry." He gave his little transforming smile again, and
seemed to be almost enjoying the situation.

Malori was looking at him curiously. "How do you—manage
to cope so well?"

"Why not?" Greenleaf stretched and got up from the now-
useless console. "You know, once a man gives up his old
ways, badlife ways, admits he's really dead to them, the new
ways aren't so bad. There are even women available from time
to time, when the machines take prisoners."

"Goodlife," said Malori. Now he had spoken the obscene, provoking epithet. But at the moment he was not afraid.

"Goodlife yourself, little man." Greenleaf was still smiling. "You know, I think you still look down on me. You're in as deep as I am now, remember?"

"I think I pity you."

Greenleaf let out a little snort of laughter, and shook his own head pityingly. "You know, I may have ahead of me a longer and more pain-free life than most of humanity has ever enjoyed—you said one of the models for the personae died at twenty-three. Was that a common age of death in those days?"

Malori, still clinging to his stanchion, began to wear a strange, grim little smile. "Well, in his generation, in the continent of Europe, it was. The First World War was raging at the time."

"But he died of some disease, you said."

"No. I said he *had* a disease, tuberculosis. Doubtless it would have killed him eventually. But he died in battle, in 1917 CE, in a place called Belgium. His body was never found, as I recall, an artillery barrage having destroyed it and his aircraft entirely."

Greenleaf was standing very still. "Aircraft! What are you saying?"

Malori pulled himself erect, somewhat painfully, and let go of his support. "I tell you now that Georges Guynemer—that was his name—shot down fifty-three enemy aircraft before he was killed. Wait!" Malori's voice was suddenly loud and firm, and Greenleaf halted his menacing advance in sheer surprise. "Before you begin to do anything violent to me, you should perhaps consider whether your side or mine is likely to win the fight outside."

"The fight . . ."

"It will be nine ships against fifteen or more machines, but I don't feel too pessimistic. The personae we have sent out are not going to be meekly slaughtered."

Greenleaf stared at him for a moment longer, then spun around and lunged for the operations console. The display was still blank white with noise and there was nothing to be done. He slowly sank into the padded chair. "What have you done to me?" he whispered. "That collection of invalid musicians—you couldn't have been lying about them all."

"Oh, every word I spoke was true. Not all World War One fighter pilots were invalids, of course. Some were in perfect health, indeed fanatical about staying that way. And I did not say they were all musicians, though I certainly meant you to think so. Ball had the most musical ability among the aces, but was still only an amateur. He always said he loathed his real profession."

Greenleaf, slumped in the chair now, seemed to be aging visibly. "But one was blind . . . it isn't possible."

"So his enemies thought, when they released him from an internment camp early in the war. Edward Mannock, blind in one eye. He had to trick an examiner to get into the army. Of course the tragedy of these superb men is that they spent themselves killing one another. In those days they had no berserkers to fight, at least none that could be attacked dashingly, with an aircraft and a machine gun. I suppose men have always faced berserkers of some kind."

"Let me make sure I understand." Greenleaf's voice was almost pleading. "We have sent out the personae of nine fighter pilots?"

"Nine of the best. I suppose their total of claimed aerial victories is more than five hundred. Such claims were usually exaggerated, but still . . ."

There was silence again. Greenleaf slowly turned his chair back to face the operations display. After a time the storm of atomic noise began to abate. Malori, who had sat down on the deck to rest, got up again, this time more quickly. In the hologram a single glowing symbol was emerging from the noise, fast approaching the position of the *Judith*.

The approaching symbol was bright red.

"So there we are," said Greenleaf, getting to his feet. From a pocket he produced a stubby little handgun. At first he pointed it toward the shrinking Malori, but then he smiled his nice smile and shook his head. "No, let the machines have you. That will be much worse."

When they heard the airlock begin to cycle, Greenleaf raised the weapon to point at his own skull. Malori could not tear his eyes away. The inner door clicked and Greenleaf fired.

Malori bounded across the intervening space and pulled the gun from Greenleaf's dead hand almost before the body had completed its fall. He turned to aim the weapon at the airlock as its inner door sighed open. The berserker standing there was the one he had seen earlier, or the same type at least. But it had just been through violent alterations. One metal arm was cut short in a bright bubbly scar, from which the ends of truncated cables flapped. The whole metal body was riddled with small holes, and around its top there played a halo of electrical discharge.

Malori fired, but the machine ignored the impact of the forcepacket. They would not have let Greenleaf keep a gun with which they could be hurt. The battered machine ignored Malori too, for the moment, and lurched forward to bend over Greenleaf's nearly decapitated body.

"Tra-tra-tra-treason," the berserker squeaked. "Ultimate unpleasant ultimate unpleasant stum-stum-stimuli. Badlife bad-life bad—"

By then Malori had moved up close behind it and thrust the muzzle of the gun into one of the still-hot holes where Albert Ball or perhaps Frank Luke or Werner Voss or one of the others had already used a laser to good effect. Two forcepackets beneath its armor and the berserker went down, as still as the man who lay beneath it. The halo of electricity died.

Malori backed off, looking at them both, then spun around to scan the operations display again. The red dot was drifting away from the *Judith*, the vessel it represented now evidently no more than inert machinery.

Out of the receding atomic storm a single green dot was approaching. A minute later, Number Eight came in alone, bumping to a gentle stop against its cradle pads. The laser nozzle at once began smoking heavily in atmosphere. The craft was scarred in several places by enemy fire.

"I claim four more victories," the persona said as soon as Malori opened the hatch. "Today I was given fine support by my wingmen, who made great sacrifices for the Fatherland. Although the enemy outnumbered us by two to one, I think that not a single one of them escaped. But I must protest bitterly that my aircraft still has not been painted red."

"I will see to it at once, *meinherr*," murmured Malori, as he began to disconnect the persona from the fighting ship. He felt a little foolish for trying to reassure a piece of hardware. Still, he handled the persona gently as he carried it to where the little formation of empty cases were waiting on the operations deck, their labels showing plainly:

ALBERT BALL;
WILLIAM AVERY BISHOP;
RENE PAUL FONCK;
GEORGES MARIE GUYNEMER;
FRANK LUKE;
EDWARD MANNOCK;
CHARLES NUNGESSER;
MANFRED VON RICHTHOFEN;
WERNER VOSS.

They were English, American, German, French. They were Jew, violinist, invalid, Prussian, rebel, hater, bon vivant, Christian. Among the nine of them they were many other things besides. Maybe there was only the one word—man—which could include them all.

Right now the nearest living humans were many millions of kilometers away, but still Malori did not feel quite alone. He put the persona back into its case gently, even knowing that it would be undamaged by ten thousand more gravities than his hands could exert. Maybe it would fit into the cabin of Number Eight with him, when he made his try to reach the *Hope*.

"Looks like it's just you and me now, Red Baron." The human being from which it had been modeled had been not quite twenty-six when he was killed over France, after less than eighteen months of success and fame. Before that, in the cavalry, his horse had thrown him again and again.

GAMBLER'S WAR

by Eric Vinicoff
and Marcia Martin

With the development of the tachyon FTL drive humanity discovered that the stellar-planet creation theory was true—virtually all the nearby suns the starships could reach had planets.
Since humanity's primary concerns were finding worlds to colonize and familiar life, they sought Earthlike worlds. These
they found in abundance—suitable worlds too young for any
intelligent life, and older worlds with races at levels of advance-
ment short of Earth's. But none more advanced—just a handful
of worlds burned bare of all life by forces only imaginable to
humanity's science. Humanity wasn't the smartest race
spawned in the region. Just the luckiest in somehow avoiding
self-destruction.

Of course the other planets in these systems were cursorily
examined. And life of bizarre types was found in bizarre environments. Some races were intelligent, and a few even tech-
nologically advanced. But there was so much to do on the
Earthlike worlds. These incomprehensible races, relatively
backward and oblivious to events beyond their worlds, could
wait.

Then the exploration ship Tau Zero, conducting such a probe
of the Jovan-type world Epsilon Eridani VI, named Moulay,
was fired upon and severely damaged by the dominant race of
that world.

• • •

Captain Kerry strode toward the briefing room confidently despite the ravages of an all-nighter in the "morale wing" bars and red light rooms. The stim pills he had downed before breakfast were doing their deceptive work, as were the premission awareness and courage enhancers. He was walking on clouds, ready to go.

Outside the room's door several officers were milling about, chatting and smoking away their last few minutes before the briefing.

Lieutenant Orloff came rumbling down the corridor toward the door, glaring lasers, his usual mood. Kerry gestured, and he came over.

"Should have come with me last night," Kerry said. "If you don't ease up, you're going to blow your hull."

"This whole crazy war is blowing my hull."

Kerry sighed. "Still on that, huh. Why don't you leave strategic planning to the Admiralty."

"What makes you think they—or even U.N. Command— know one damned thing more than us?"

"Will you for God's sake please get your mind on today's mission."

"Today's game."

"Keep thinking that way and we'll end up like AFX-47, in the deep soup."

Before Orloff could fire off a reply, a firm voice intervened. "Come with me, please, gentlemen." Colonel Foster had materialized beside them.

"What about the briefing, sir?" Kerry asked.

"Special orders, Captain. Come on."

Mildly curious about the deviation from SOP, they followed him into a bounce capsule. Down it went to the squadron cradles. Kerry felt the strong tension between him and Orloff, but as always under tight mutual control. Philosophical differences festered in the stress and uncertainty, but they were a team. They needed each other to survive.

The cradles were anthills of activity as men and machines readied the Third Squadron for battle. Eight gleaming white flattened-cigar shapes, seventy meters in length. Douglas F-72BX's. Years of intensive development had gone into adapting the standard F-72 suborbital fighter for dense atmosphere work. Twin Korchnoi C-455F ion thrusters supplied the necessary acceleration to operate deep in Moulay's gravity well.

Cruiser-rated laser fusion MHD generators were required to power them. Gone was the regulation panoply of ordnance—not even lasers could punch through Moulay's soup for any range. In their place was a single fixed-forward proton accelerator tube.

They walked halfway down the long, brilliantly lit hangar and climbed into the tiny cabin of AFX-37.

"What the hell are you doing!" Orloff exclaimed. A young man in an ill-fitting flight suit was wiring a new unit into the com board.

The man turned languidly. "Hooking in my equipment."

"You foul up that board and we'll never find our way back out of the soup!"

"I'm not disrupting anything. Just enabling my computer to use your in-soup radio."

The man pointed to the observer's seat, which was folded out from the bulkhead, and smiled.

"This is a *military vessel!*" Orloff jumped into the brief silence. "You hired brains get pushier every wake period!"

"Dog it down, Lieutenant," the Colonel snapped. Orloff reluctantly bit off further comment.

The Colonel went on. "Doctor Chan will observe this mission, and test some new equipment."

Orloff shrugged pointedly and went over to inspect Doctor Chan's work. "*The* Doctor Chan?" Kerry asked.

"You've heard of me," Doctor Chan said without looking up.

"When a scientist of your prominence joins the research teams, it's wardroom scuttlebutt for days. The word is that Secretary General Aidala personally asked you to take the job. Have you figured out what the polyps are all about yet?"

"Doctor Chan is a brilliant cryptographer and philologist," Colonel Foster put in. "His work on the polyp language holds great promise. Which is why you will cooperate fully with him."

"I've heard some other things about you, Doctor," Kerry said. "You were a world-class chess-master, weren't you?"

"The dalliances of youth."

"So you moved on to more adult pursuits. You're rather legendary, you know—we Rangers bet on everything. Is it true you've been banned from every casino in Sol System?"

Doctor Chan nodded. "Very shortsighted of them—the

promotional value far outweighed my actual winnings. But there are more exciting games. Much more exciting.''

Colonel Foster handed Kerry a black tape disk. "Your copy of the mission briefing. Scan it and get tight. The other crews will be scrambling in six minutes." He ducked out after an exchange of salutes.

The hatch sealed with a clang.

"I'm done," Doctor Chan announced, and began bolting the panel back in place. Orloff was watching unhappily, but not closely enough to spot him attaching a small gray metal capsule under the engineering console in the process.

Kerry fed the disk to the flight computer, then he and Orloff scanned it. A typical scout probe of a new landmass discovered in the southern hemisphere. "Strap in, folks," he said sharply.

As they did so he went on. "Doctor, do your testing, but remember this is a combat mission. Don't get in our way."

The officers activated their boards, and watched the ready lights for the rest of the squadron go from red to green.

"Squadron Three—green go for launch," droned Tower through the com to the pilots.

Kerry waited his turn, then barked, "Three-Seven, roger," into his throat mike. His hands moved over the piloting board, locking in the program. Orloff sat back and fidgeted. His job would come later.

Status lights indicated that the hangar was evacuated of people and atmosphere. The deck rolled back, and in its turn AFX-37 was slung by its cradle into space.

Shipboard pseudograv immediately replaced Orbital Base's. In the stern camera screen Kerry saw the great white globe dwindle. Twenty-nine months ago a star freighter had disgorged a machine into orbit around Moulay. Drones had broken up a tiny moon and fed the chunks into its maw. The machine grew. In less than a month it became Orbital Base. More ships brought personnel, supplies, equipment and the F-72BX's.

"Squadron Leader to Seven, do you copy?" came another voice from the comset speaker.

"Seven here," Kerry replied. "We copy you. Over."

"Hear you onloaded a green sparrow. Any complications?"

"Negative."

"As you say. Out."

In the STADEX tank Kerry could see the eight white dots in a tight V formation, arcing down toward Moulay.

Kerry leaned back and sighed. So far, routine. The computer was doing most of the work. Once in the soup, though, that would change.

"Four point one minutes to atmosphere," Kerry said to Orloff. "Time to unlimber the gun."

"Roger." Orloff brought his proton gun status lights to green. "Ready to blast."

The soft cough startled Kerry—he had almost forgotten about Doctor Chan. Before he could say anything Orloff demanded, "What do you want?"

"To be informed of our situation."

"We're about to make a scout run," Orloff grated. "An hour from now we could be dead. Did you think about that before butting in?"

"Quite a bit, I assure you. But the probabilities are favorable, and I must monitor the polyp radio transmissions at close range."

"What's wrong with the beams they keep throwing at Base?"

"Too limited in nature and intent."

"You know their intent?" Kerry cut in sharply.

Doctor Chan merely smiled. His position in the rear of the cabin was such that he could lean forward and manipulate his newly installed computer. He did so, checking it over.

On the forward camera screen a chord of Moulay grew against the starry mat. Awesomely large it was, and coiled around with fuzzy bands of yellow and brown. Tints of deep blue stood out at the pole. Paler zones were barely visible, small spots moving slowly beneath the outer atmosphere layers.

"We make war on a race we know virtually nothing about," Doctor Chan mused.

"They make war on us," Kerry corrected. "We're just trying to find out why. We can't have a hostile unknown here while we colonize Two. That's the official line."

"You don't agree?"

Orloff snorted—this argument was as old as their team. Kerry went on. "I hate to see all this money, ability and effort wasted on a planet that poses no real military threat."

"But your comrades die in this war," Doctor Chan said.

"Because we're forcing ourselves on them. First our survey probe, now these scout missions. They're too primitive to bother us in space. And we have so much more valuable work to do on worlds and with races we can understand."

"Yet you pilot scout missions?"

"I do my duty."

"Some duty." Orloff swiveled in his seat. "Playing target drone."

"I beg your pardon?"

"We dive into the soup, as close to a landmass as possible. Our scanners record data for you hired brains. The polyps jump us in their planes. We fight. Or seem to."

"Seem to fight?"

"Come on, Doc. Even you must know what's going on. They always come at us. But only to disable, not to kill. We can almost always rescue downed fighters—they don't interfere. They don't try to hurt us enough to keep us from coming back. Why? It doesn't make sense."

"There are many theories."

"Including one of yours?" Kerry drove home sharply.

"What would you propose to replace our present course of action?" Doctor Chan asked Orloff.

"Lithium fusion nukes. Destroy every landmass. Blow them back into their version of a stone age."

"Isn't that a rather drastic way to deal with such a backward race?"

"We're too damned cocky about that. We can't be *sure* they aren't a threat, or won't become one, because we know nothing about them."

Doctor Chan eyed the officers speculatively. "There are many who agree with each of you. Fortunately the power of decision lies with moderates supporting the present compromise."

"You would say that," Orloff rasped. "Mysteries to unravel, and big research budgets."

Doctor Chan showed no reaction.

"All units, tighten up," the Squadron Leader's com voice ended the conversation. "One minute to atmosphere. Stand by."

In the STADEX the V formation shrank slightly.

Kerry switched to manual override mode just in case. Moulay had swollen to fill almost all the forward screen.

They drove into the discernable atmosphere. Drag grabbed the hull, and it began to heat up. The heavens gradually turned from black to a yellow glow.

They plowed through the increasingly syrupy cloud cover,

at this level mostly droplets of frozen ammonia. The fighter bucked as it entered thick turbulence. Alkali-metal shaded fogs oozed across the screens.

The pressure grew. And grew. Gas became denser and denser, forming a medium unlike any known to humanity. The fighter crawled through it at a mere handful of hundreds of KPH. Radar range fell off drastically, and sonar took over. The screens showed undulating tan murk, leaving the STADEX computer simulation the only visual scanner.

Down, and further down they drove. "No contact yet," the Squadron Leader reported. "But they should have us on their scopes. Stand by."

Far below the STADEX showed an irregular mass several hundred kilometers in the least dimension. It was landmass S1364, discovered in a recent scout mission. Experts disagreed on their origin; either remnants of asteroids sucked in by the enormous gravity pull, or bits of the solid core thrown up by seismic activity. They drifted at this level in density equilibrium with the atmosphere.

Upon the thousands of them the polyps had built their material culture, weird structures mostly buried beneath the surface and armored against insanely ferocious storms. Polyps were occasionally seen swimming in the soup as they hunted the "plankton" which also drifted there. They were armorphous creatures, the size of small groundcars and reminiscent of Earthly coelenterates. Liquid ammonia was their water. A few had been captured and studied, but none had reached Orbital Base alive.

"Bandits coming up at four o'clock," the Squadron Leader's voice announced tersely. "At least twelve, maybe more. Defense mode R-for-Robert. Out."

Orloff fired a test burst, grinning. Kerry switched to full manual. A century of progress had evolved back to World War II-style dogfighting. Low speeds. Awkward weapons. Insufficient communications and target tracking. Computers couldn't fight with such fragmentary data, so they gave way to intuition.

Kerry sent AFX-37 slanting down and starboard, covering 39. Its team was green sparrows, and he wanted to see them through their roughening period.

Both sides put out jamming frequencies. Communication was out. Training and experience took over.

"Battle systems in," Kerry rapped as his hands flew. 39 was a kilometer ahead, diving at a polyp plane—a slender dart powered by a fission jet and armed with a fixed-forward electrostatic cannon, primitive but dangerous at close range. The other fighters of the Third Squadron were also diving.

"Get out of my way!" Orloff shouted at the unhearing STADEX dot representing 39, locked in its attack run between 37 and the polyp.

39 was firing, but the polyp, apparently a vet, swerved easily. Orloff got his target. "Taking the helm!" he said as his board overrode Kerry's and brought 37 around. The cabin lurched as the proton gun discharged.

Kerry took it back and banked hard to port, hitting emergency thrust to avoid another polyp's attack. "Missed!" Orloff reported as he eyed his targeting STADEX.

But 39, coming up on the first polyp's stern, didn't. The latter's STADEX dot vanished. Seconds later a shudder wracked the cabin. "Damned beginner's luck," Orloff muttered.

"Target opportunity at eight o'clock," Kerry cut in urgently. A polyp was slicing at them almost dead-on, already firing but missing 37's foreshortened hull.

"My turn, creep!" Orloff took the helm, lined up the shot, touched the black-rimmed switch, and was rewarded with a near-miss that sent the plane retreating at reduced speed toward the landmass.

Then 37 went through a violent set of evasive maneuvers as another polyp hung on its tail, firing. "Somebody get on this bastard," Kerry whispered.

But the rest of the squadron were having their own troubles. 32 and 36 were damaged and limping home, while the other fighters were heavily engaged. The scout mission was a total bust. Somehow the polyps had guessed it—they were damned good guessers—and brought in a crack intercepter group.

The more immediate problem was survival. "Get me a shot!" Orloff pleaded.

Kerry was sweating, and running out of maneuvers. Doctor Chan was sweating too, but his expression was one of fascination and excitement. He was on some kind of private high.

The polyp was closing. Any second now it would put a shot into a thruster. And there wasn't a bloody thing he could do. No *deus ex machina*. No brilliant tactic. No secret weapon. Nothing but—

BOOOOOM!

Heat and noise battered the three men. Smoke poured from

the engineering board. Alarms whooped. Circulators and emergency lights switched on. The throbbing of the thrusters was gone.

When things settled down, the first datum they noticed was that they were still alive. "Jeez," Orloff said.

Kerry shunted E-power to the STADEX, and bypassed the engineering board. Remarkably, it glowed.

"What's the scan?" Orloff demanded stridently.

"The good guys seem to be in retreat. The Squadron Leader must have fired the withdrawal bomb. The polyps are breaking off too, heading home," Kerry's voice held firm.

Orloff asked the question. "Any chance of our making Base?"

Kerry studied the mostly dark piloting board. "The thruster circuitry is shredded, including the backup and ES bypass. We aren't going anywhere except inside a rescue ship."

His earphone told him the jamming was off, so he triggered the E-beacon. Or tried to. The light that should have turned green began to flash red. The breath in his lungs turned to hydrogen ice. Orloff saw it too, and sagged back, cheeks pale beneath whisker stubble.

"What does that light mean?" Doctor Chan asked calmly.

Orloff turned to glare at him. "It means we're going to die down here, you damned Jonah!"

"Back off," Kerry said softly. "It's bad, but we still have a chance. Base will send a rescue ship. Without the E-beacon, it'll have to find us on STADEX. But the range is so limited down here, it'll practically have to trip over us. And this is a big world."

"How long can we survive unrescued?" Doctor Chan asked.

"Who knows? Air, water and pseudograv seem to be no immediate problem. The hull is rated for two days at this depth, with a safety margin. But we've taken a hard knock. The external stress monitors are out. If the hull weakens . . . we'll never know we died."

Humming equipment sounds became a discordant symphony in the silence.

"All we can do is sit tight."

Orloff unstrapped and went over to the ruined console. "I don't get it. Looked like an internal blast. How could a shot do that?"

Kerry only half-heard him, and didn't answer. He didn't want to think about anything. Orloff drew strength from agitation; he sought calm. It could be a long wait.

Doctor Chan leaned forward and activated his computer. "Good. It still seems to be functioning."

"Are you crazy?" Orloff exclaimed. "We could be breathing soup any second, and you want to expand the horizons of science!"

"We'll be here for some time, if we're lucky. It won't harm our chances for survival, and it may prove useful. Captain?"

Kerry shrugged. "Go ahead."

Orloff returned to his seat, visibly dissatisfied with what he had seen at the console, and lapsed into his own bleak thoughts.

Doctor Chan tended to his computer. He began typing on the keyboard. Putting an earphone in the appropriate orifice, he listened. Then he typed again.

Curiosity roused Kerry slightly. "What are you up to?"

"Communicating with the polyps," he replied.

That roused him the rest of the way. "You're kidding, right?"

"I don't joke. I've compiled a 'dictionary' which is programmed into this unit."

"But the best brains the U.N. could buy have been chewing at that wall for years. You just walked in and fell over the answer?"

"Hardly. I built on their efforts. And added a vital element— my own imagination."

"I like a modest man."

Doctor Chan ignored the comment. "Since philologists have been communicating with alien races, we've learned that many 'incomprehensible' concepts can be understood by recalling that language grows from heredity and environment."

"But we hardly know a damned thing about either here."

"We know enough. For example, we recently discovered that polyps have a multi-tonal speech system."

"You mean those bird choruses they're always beaming at us are voices?" Kerry said increduously.

"Yes. Those transmissions, by the way, are picture-and-word primers aimed at teaching us one of their languages. With the multi-tonal clue, I was able to use the Base computers to translate much of it."

"You mean to tell me you understanding what they're saying?"

Doctor Chan listened to his earphone for long seconds, then talked as he typed. "Not everything. Some of their concepts are very difficult. But enough to communicate. Here, listen—''

He touched a button. From a small speaker in the computer came a tinny chirp with two or three softer chirps and buzzes over it. Then a pseudovoice said, ''Discover (verb) (first person plural) (present active imperative). We must discover.'' He touched it again.

''The primary tone is the base word. The subsidiary overlays modify it—person, gender, tense, case and so on.''

Kerry's mind wandered. He wished there was some repair work he could do. But to do anything useful he would have needed the facilities of a Base repair dock. And EVA here was definitely out. The hull would hold, or it wouldn't. Rescue would come in time, or it wouldn't.

Doctor Chan looked very happy with what he was learning through the earphone. He resumed typing.

''Why come down here to communicate?'' Kerry asked. ''Base could punch through a signal if it had a good reason.''

''To do that I would first have had to report my discovery to your superiors.''

Orloff was listening, a queer expression on his face. Kerry felt queer too. He didn't like what he was thinking a damned bit. He watched out of the corner of his eyes as Orloff returned to the engineering console remains and began giving them another, more careful examination.

''You haven't told them?'' Kerry asked.

''Of course not. They would have taken over the communication process, and there were questions I had to ask,'' the doctor replied coolly.

''Like what?''

''As you suggested earlier, I have a theory concerning this odd war. It is based on another recently discovered fact of polyp biology.''

Kerry felt like he had stepped into a duster's delirium. Some of the awesome pressure beyond the hull gripped him. Here he was, at the bottom of a well, chatting with a madman. ''Care to elaborate?''

Doctor Chan paused much longer this time to listen. Inside the computer a tape cartridge turned. Then: ''From polyp corpses we have learned that they reproduce by fission. Like some anemones. They reach maturity at about age thirty Earth years. At any time during the next four decades they can divide if they wish. Or not. If they don't, their life span approximately equals ours. If they do, two things can occur. Both new polyps

may have new brains—in which case the old polyp 'dies.' Or
one of the new polyps may possess the old brain, rejuvenated
somewhat—in which case the old polyp lives for another generation. The odds are affected by innumerable factors, but
remain primarily random.''

He stopped. Kerry stared. ''Is that supposed to mean something to me?''

With an inarticulate scream of rage Orloff shot up from the
console like an angry kangaroo, and reached Doctor Chan in
one long stride. Drawing his Walther XX, he smashed the butt
through the computer's plastic case, shattering it. Doctor Chan
watched the destruction calmly. ''Don't damage the tape,
please—Secretary General Aidala will want to hear it.''

''What the hell?'' Kerry demanded.

Orloff aimed the stubby laser at Doctor Chan's stomach.
''Don't move,'' he snarled. Then he held up a bit of twisted
metal so Kerry could see it. ''Shell casing from a K-16 hotshot! This traitor snuck it into the console!''

Kerry turned back to Doctor Chan. ''Why?''

''I had questions to ask. I needed the time.''

''You may have killed us all—yourself included.''

''I weighed the probabilities carefully, you can be sure.''

Kerry drew his own laser and held it casually. ''Sit down,
Orloff.'' The officer complied, but kept his gun on the scientist.

''Doctor.'' Kerry's voice had a very hard edge. ''You've
sabotaged a military vessel of the U.N. That's treason. A capital
crime. I want to know what's so important it's worth our lives.''

''He's conspiring with the enemy! What else do you need
to know!''

''Shut up. Now, Doctor, how about beginning with why you
couldn't report your discovery and go through channels?''

''My theory of the reason for this war was such that I had
to personally confirm it before revealing my work. Lieutenant
Orloff's views are shared by too many of your superiors. I
didn't want to be responsible for the genocide of an intelligent race.''

''You know our policy is to make peace if possible.''

''Policies change. And the reason behind the polyps' aggres-
sion is, ah, difficult to comprehend in the human matrix.
Wrongly understood, it could lead to stepped-up hostilities.''

''So, you are going to explain it to us ignorant military
types?'' Orloff cut in abruptly.

''Since you insist. I partially understand the polyps because of a certain affinity between our natures. I will be able to convey that understanding to the Secretary General and other leaders with the moderate viewpoint. But I doubt you will believe me.''

To Kerry, it sounded like Doctor Chan had been sniffing vacuum. "Get on with it. What did they tell you?''

"The polyps are like us in many ways. They are curious. Their astronomy is naturally primitive, but they share our hunger for the space frontier. They hunger for the knowledge and ideas of our advanced race.''

Kerry wasn't slow. "And they saw a chance for both in our survey ship.''

"Yes. But it quickly became clear that the unique opportunity was going to slip through their allegorical fingers. The survey ship held high aloft and made no effort to communicate. Finally it began to depart. Can you imagine the magnitude of their loss, their desperation?''

Kerry breathed fear. A failure of the hull, the pseudograv, the air or any of a dozen other systems would end his own personal universe. If no rescue ship came, it would be a race between deaths. But those were familiar dangers, mulled over for many months. The worst fear was being sucked into troubles too big for him. "So they attacked.''

"Of course. To attract our attention. The survey ship was obviously just observing. They couldn't take a chance on our lack of interest, our never making contact. How could they insure our interest? By posing a potential threat to our security requiring further investigation. They gambled that certain basics applied to both races. Correctly, as it turns out.''

Kerry shook his head. "Start a war with a superior race, risk destruction on a gamble? I don't buy it.''

"They knew they were walking a tightrope. But they couldn't be a serious threat in any case, being relatively backward and planetbound. Moreover, to avoid what you suggest, they kept up the pretense of war while avoiding actual death and destruction as much as possible.''

"Still, how could they take such a chance?''

"Because they are the greatest natural gamblers we have yet met in the galaxy. The prize was fabulous, the odds were favorable, so they went ahead. Their biology, their very lives are based on a calculated risk—they may bet extended life against life or death, or not. The philosophy of probabilities permeates every facet of their culture.''

Kerry split his attention between Doctor Chan and Orloff. The officer was flush with anger, his eyes slitted. Kerry prayed Orloff wouldn't push him into making a judgment. All he wanted to do was come out of this alive and dump Chan in Base's lap. But his pragmatism doubted happy endings. His grip on his laser tightened menacingly.

"They want to be our friends," Doctor Chan assured.

"If they aren't a threat," Kerry said, "we can end this farce of a war and go home."

"That too would be wrong! They have things to teach us, and trade us. A whole new world of possibilities. We can communicate—mutual profit will follow if we let it. We *must* learn to associate with non-humanoid races—someday we will meet one more advanced than us, one we won't be able to ignore."

"But how can we trust them?"

"Communication will bring understanding. If that is coupled to good will, trust will also come. In time. In time."

Kerry shook his head again. "You're right about one thing. This could start a real war. That they killed people just to flag us down won't sit well with some folks. It doesn't sit well with me, dammit!"

"Many more of them have died. They are willing to make any amends they can. Is brutal vengeance more desirable?"

"Logically, no. But logic is a sometime thing with us. I wonder if the polyps figured that in their probability calculations."

"They will now. Before Lieutenant Orloff damaged my computer, I explained somewhat about humanity's differing reactions to them."

"Why did you do that?"

"So they can enter the period of negotiation ahead with open eyes—figuratively speaking."

"You told them a large faction wants to destroy them?" Kerry felt a new fear looming.

"Of course."

"You don't think a diplomatic lie might have been in order?"

"That's the kind of thinking which made what I did necessary. We must have mutual understanding."

Orloff caught on. "You suicidal idiot! If they have any smarts at all, they'll figure out that their reason for starting this war is going to be as popular as a cyanide airtank back home! And you told them we're on the edge of smashing them as is!"

Doctor Chan looked puzzled. "So?"

"So they've only explained their reason to you so far! They must know from combat experience we can't come beyond the soup! Don't you see! Even if that fairy tale they told you is true, their chances for racial survival go way up if we never get home!" He began tinkering frantically with his fire control board.

"You're wrong," Doctor Chan said. "You can't understand their motivations. The basic nature of their gamble hasn't changed."

"But odds do," Kerry cut in, "and that can change bets. Fortunately the polyps will have as hard a time finding us as the rescue ship, what with the lousy scanning conditions and the incredible amount of planet to be lost in. It looks like we're way off in the boonies."

Doctor Chan coughed. "I gave them our location. They might have been able to triangulate it anyway, but I didn't want to take the risk. They are on their way now."

Orloff screamed and lunged at Doctor Chan, but Kerry got between them in time and flung the latter back in his seat. "Later for that. Can you do anything with the gun?"

"I was just checking! Looks like I can shunt around the engineering console! But on E-power it won't have much punch!"

"If we have to use it, we'll try for close range."

Orloff resumed work on his board. Kerry spun to face Doctor Chan. "I don't know which is worse, Orloff's paranoia or your naivety. That was an amazingly stupid thing to do."

"I think not. They are going to rescue us before the hull collapses, lift us to the upper atmosphere so we can call a rescue ship."

Kerry wiped sweat from his forehead. "So they say. If we can believe them. Of course your message told them we're drifting down here helplessly. So they could be coming to silence us—thanks to you."

"Trust has to begin somewhere."

"Something on STADEX!" Orloff exclaimed.

Kerry slid back into his seat. "Strap in, Orloff, Doctor." He followed his own order, then studied his tank. A large blip was closing in slowly.

"The gun is green go!" Orloff shouted. "Give me a target!"

Kerry touched several buttons. "I'm goosing us around on

gyros, very slowly. Don't want to be obvious about it.''

The blip was fifty kilometers away. It was much larger than a fighter. It could have been a special vehicle for moving heavy objects—or a mammoth warplane.

The sighting grid in the tank swung toward the blip.

"Don't do this," Doctor Chan pleaded. "You'll ruin everything. It's sheer murder."

Kerry's mouth was dry. He wished he was far, far away. He didn't want to die. But if Doctor Chan was right . . .

"Twenty-five kilometers and closing!" Orloff announced. "Effective firing range in twenty seconds!"

The sighting grid centered on the blip, and stopped.

What was the polyp commander of that monster thinking? Did he have definite orders, or was indecision tearing at him too? Did he fear?

And, assuming the polyps hadn't lied to Doctor Chan, how were they playing their gamble now; still in for the pot, or folding and cutting their losses?

"Entering firing range!"

"They aren't firing," Doctor Chan inserted. "Please don't fire first."

Orloff's hand poised over the black-rimmed button.

Kerry stared at the biggest hand he had ever been dealt. When you couldn't size up the player, you sized up his game. The polyps were real plungers. They liked the big stakes. He couldn't picture them bailing out. "Hold fire unless they fire first."

"It's a trick! Let them get any closer, and they can take us out before we can fire back."

"I said hold fire!"

Orloff snarled and started to stab at the button.

Kerry brought his laser around and burned a deep trench in the fire control board. Orloff jerked his hand back. "What the hell!" The gun remained silent.

"Sit still, shut up and pray," Kerry muttered.

"We're a big, fat sitting duck!"

Kerry ignored him, and concentrated on the tank. The big blip was about to swallow the central dot. Maybe they wanted to take prisoners, he thought belatedly. Or specimens.

Something bumped against the bottom of the hull. Orloff grunted as though hit, then retreated into wary silence. Doctor Chan was riding his excited high again. Kerry wiped again at the sweat above his eyebrows.

One of the surviving displays on the piloting board flickered with new data. "We're rising!" Kerry shouted.

Kerry watched in the tank as the reassuring blip of the rescue ship homed in on his com signal. The mysterious polyp vehicle had disengaged seconds ago and dropped away beyond range. The fighter was falling, but slowly so the ship would have no trouble retrieving it.

He turned to Orloff and Doctor Chan. The latter was under control again, and Orloff had let the fact that he would survive mellow his mood to mere sullenness. "Who was that masked man?" Kerry asked, giddy with relief.

"I beg your pardon?" Doctor Chan asked politely.

"Just part of an ancient legend. We're going home. Pickup in thirty seconds." He sobered. "When we get back to Base, Doctor, there's the matter of your sabotage. It'll be in my mission report." Unlike Orloff's itchy trigger finger—they were still a team.

"Surely you aren't so politically naive as to think I will be punished."

"*The* Doctor Chan? Of course not."

"I'm sorry you feel hostile. What I did was necessary, and turned out tremendously well."

Kerry raised an eyebrow. "You think this one act of polyp goodwill is going to convince everyone that they want peace? On top of their screwy reason? Who's being naive now?"

"True, it will be a long, cautious trail, but eventually the polyps will join the humanoid races in the community of worlds. Thanks to your decision."

Kerry turned back to his board so he didn't have to look at Doctor Chan. "No wonder you were able to figure out the polyps. You're like them. They gambled their race for a prize they could only imagine. You did the same with our three lives. You're as inhuman as they are."

"Am I? Do you really know why I did what I did?"

"I think that's pretty obvious."

"Don't bet on it, Captain."

SAFE TO SEA

by David Drake

Even in the first instants they knew that something had gone wrong. The transit that should have jumped them a quarter light year had hung the thirty-four of them as a ragged constellation among totally unfamiliar stars.

"Hey, my drive's going out!"

"Where the cop are we and how—"

"Johnnie, hang on. Perk and I'll get you out but you gotta hold your spin—"

Individually they were forty-foot daggers, maneuvered by solid-fuel rockets but flung between stars by the transit element amidships. Half each vessel's length was a weapons bay, its only reason for existence. They were neither armored nor fitted with damper fields to choke off incoming nuclear weapons, and while their hulls were studded and meshed with a score of sensor inputs that gave them the airflow of a cookie cutter, the sheeting was utterly opaque and left the pilots blind if the power failed. But nobody had ever pretended that an attack ship could last long in an engagement; only that it could last long enough.

A little sun flared as Corcoran's radiation-poisoned star drive failed catastrophically. The chatter ended, frozen by cold-voiced orders and replies as Attack Squadron 18 sorted itself

out. Three of the tiny warships snatched at the tumbling one
with their docking tractors, killing all motion relative to the
sun below. The ship's medicomp went to work on Calvados,
the pilot, his senses junked by the wild centrifuging.

Bernstein, Captain in Command—and the thought of how
far his command now reached ate at the edges of his mind—lay
rigidly suited in the center of his instruments and display
screens. He could move his body six inches at most in any
direction. His arms had a nearly full sweep, but each centimeter
of their circuit took them to control switches of invisible but
memorized significance.

"Heavy in IR," Lacie's voice was rumbling, "but visible
spectrum too. The planet itself has fairly regular contours, but
we'd want the high ground, the low spot's muck, pure muck.
Haven't got the trace readout yet, but we oughta be fine with
just breathers."

"Not after you redpill the field," Bernstein stated flatly.

"Aw. . . ." Lacie was six-four, a hugely fat man who began
to itch the moment he suited up.

"Sorry, Corporal, but we've got major maintenance to pull
and I don't want things creeping up on us while we pull it.
Slag it."

"Roger." The commo transmitted the clunk of a fusion
weapon leaving the scout ship's bay. "No sign of chicks, sir.
No sign of people either, of course, just a lot of jungle."

Individually in section order, most of AS 18 dropped toward
the mesa on the pale blue rods of their belly jets. Calvados
was an exception, still unconscious and laid down by the strain-
ing motors of the ships that had caught his. Herb Wester's craft
had been spiked by shrapnel in the instant of transit.

"Look, I can bring her in alone."

"Not until your metering controls get patched up, and we
can't do that till you're down."

"Look, sir, it's one hellova lot safer for me to go in alone
than with you and the el-tee locked—"

"Shut it off, Wester, I'm through talking about it. You're
going in between Lt. Hsi-men and myself and that's all."

Damaged craft locked between the two officers, the trio
began dropping toward the surface. Fog or yellow clouds boiled
about them. Visibility in the optical ranges was generally nil,
but occasional serpents of turbulance gaped unexpectedly. At
8300 meters, Wester's jets surged. All three ships tumbled.

Bernstein failed to hit his own motors swiftly enough and the
tractor snapped. The jowly captain fought his controls to stasis
before tracking the green dots of Hsi-men and Wester on his
volume display.

"Cut me, Chen!"

"No no, we'll get you—"

"Goddam slanteye I can't fight this bitch and you! Cut me!"

The dots separated.

Wester dropped his ship alone with the two officers parallel-
ing him at a thousand meters. When an asymetric surge rippled
the damaged vessel, Wester expertly brought it back with a
short burst from all motors, then freefell nearly two kays. As
the craft dropped below 3400, its green dot blipped out on the
other screens. The shock wave of the exploding craft reached
Bernstein and Hsi-men a few seconds later. They followed the
remainder of the squadron down to the landing site.

"I don't say we're out of the woods yet," the CinC's voice
rasped through the suit commo. "At the moment, none of us
know where we are."

Jobbins stood on the perimeter, cradling a fat-nosed missile
from his ship's defensive cluster; and a damn poor weapon it
was for a man on foot. Even if the cannibalized power supply
kicked off the motor, the backblast would probably fry him
alive; and the high explosive charge in the nose was contact
fuzed, making it suicide just to drop the coppy thing. Then for
back-up, all he had was a meter's length of chrome-van tubing
cut from Calvados' ship. Calvados' two 15cm power guns had
been dismounted onto jury-rigged tripods as well, but only his.
With available tools you had to butcher a ship to disarm it, so
only the hopeless wreck was being stripped. Besides, the guns
were designed for use in vacuum; fired in the thick, scattering
atmosphere of this planet they weren't going to last a dozen
shots.

"But we have a good chance—a damned good chance—to
find out. It'll take another jump. That means more time in
suits, I know."

Jobbins' suit made him ache all over, trying to walk in it.
Coppy things weren't made for gravity use. But who the hell
thought the chicks could slip an intruder into the center of the
1st Fleet undetected? The squadron was lucky at that. If their
tender had been going to boost them an instant later instead of

precisely when it vaporized, AS 18 wouldn't be around to wonder where the incredible surge of energy had flung them.

"We're picking up heavy diffusion in transit space from a location with ninety minutes hop of here. Lt. Reikart and I are working together to calibrate for it, and by the time AS 18 is set to move, we'll have a location to move to."

Jobbins fingered the tube. Both ends had been severed at 45°, and he wasn't sure whether he was meant to use it as a spear or a club. Clumsy either way. But even through his IR converters, there was nothing to be seen here but glass and pressure cracks spreading out from ground zero.

"We'll all move together. The signal source may be hostile, may be the chicks themselves. No one stays behind here, and every ship has to be as close to battle-ready as we can make it without shipyards."

Or even the tender's half-assed support, Jobbins thought without humor. Sudden realization of their position hit him, black gut-level knowledge that they would never get back. Nobody even knew they were spending their lives wandering out here instead of already being a gas cloud in space off Rigel XII.

There was movement in the shadowy fringes of Jobbins' vision. Dust devils or the like? But the ground was shaking. "Movement," he called in excitedly. "Ah, Jobbins, position, ah, two-seventy degrees."

"What sort of movement, flyer?"

"Second section, stand by."

"Jeez, it's big. Oh Jesus God my rocket won't fire! This coppy rocket won't fire! Get me some support!"

"Three-sixty, move toward him. Face out, everybody, we'll need—"

"Captain, my volume display's got it, it's like a mountain. . . . Get aloft, for God's sake, it's coming in!"

With the panicked flyer's voice echoing in his mind, Jobbins backed two steps. His left arm clamped the missile, dangerous to himself if not the intruder. His converters weren't running right, he couldn't see anything but a huge blur in front of him. Something snaked out of the fog and rippled past. He jabbed with the tube, feeling tough muscle rip under the point. The power guns opened up simultaneously, on infrared a blinking crisscross aimed high in the air.

The member he had stabbed lashed toward Jobbins cat swift,

coiled around his waist and flung him upwards. Even through the suit's rigidity, he felt his ribs groan. The tubing skittered through a separate trajectory as Jobbins fell toward the circular blur. It was too large to possibly be alive. The impact shook him. It didn't shake him so badly that he couldn't see the ring above him like a crater's mouth, feel the fleshy wavelets that washed him farther downward.

"Cop!" he shouted angrily as he aimed his missile down the maw and jabbed in vain at the jerry-built igniter. Still screaming meaninglessly, Jobbins grabbed the base of the missile with both hands and leaped.

Fluids and bits of flesh rained down on the squadron for several minutes. Nothing was ever recovered of Jobbins' body.

They were in communication, at least. Of a sort. Rodenhizer spoke a pretty fair grade of Interspeech, and the beings running the trading station dirtside knew a little of it. Or, filtered through a thousand tongues, a score of races, two languages linked by a few hundred words in common were being spoken.

So far as Rodenhizer could tell, the traders knew nothing about either other humans or the chicks.

"Well," Bernstein said to his officers on the command channel, "I don't see there's any choice. They must have some sort of charts down there. Star atlases look pretty much the same whoever draws them."

The lock channels didn't carry visuals, but there was no mistaking Lt. Reikart's quick tenor blurting, "Kyle, we've got three other sources now—"

"We can't—"

"No no no—"

"We can't hop around to every goddam transit user in the goddam universe!" Hsi-men snarled. "We need charts, and this is the nearest place to get a look at some."

"Well, it's dangerous to split up the force."

"Only for me, Mr. Reikart," the CinC said heavily.

"Look, take Murray down too. He's got some Interspeech, and with him and Juan sardined into one ship. . . ."

Murray dropped his ship in first. Nobody said it, but there was a good chance that with Calvados lying on top of him he'd miss a call. No point in having another ship beneath his then. AS 18 hadn't left anything behind on the nameless fog-world except two irreparably damaged vessels and Jobbins' thinly scattered remains. Murray hadn't complained about the passenger.

The CinC's craft shrieked in beside Murray's seconds later. The field was rammed earth, partly vitrified by something with less tendency to gouge and spatter than the Terran belly jets. About the field rose the massive walls of the compound, built more like a circular fortress than a warehouse. Maybe it was a fortress—the world had to be inhabited to have a trading station. At any rate, the structure had been easy to locate from space.

Murray and Calvados were already unsuiting when Bernstein locked back his hatch. He said nothing. The worst environmental threat was the high air temperature and a sky full of actinics from the blue-white sun. As for the fact resuiting in a crunch would mean several minutes' delay—well, the men knew that. The CinC kept his own armor on, even the faceplate.

"A vehicle's picked them up," Lacie reported from orbit, his high-resolution sensors trained on the landing field.

"Captain?" Reikart requested. "Captain?" switching frequencies up and down the scale. "Coppy thing's shielded, we've got no contact."

"So they shield trucks in the landing—"

"Lieutenant! The towers're opening. They've got missile batteries there, three and. . . . eighteen unmasked!"

Liquid Interspeech rustled on the commo.

"Ransom," Rodenhizer translated. "Somebody's supposed to land . . . they'll hostile—they'll kill, attack—"

"Lacie, where'd the vehicle go?" Hsi-men demanded.

"North tower, just before—"

"Kranski, put an R-60 into the south tower. Combat pass."

"Hey, hold up!"

"Lieutenant, shut your face. I'm senior and I'm giving orders until we get the CinC back. And that's just what—"

Hsi-men paused as the atmosphere lit up with the attack ship's passage in its star drive envelope. The effect of the penetrator missile that Kranski's computer spat out during a microsecond phase break was shrouded by the flaring pyrotechnics of its delivery. The southern quarter of the huge compound bulged, then crumbled at the explosion within it. All six missiles streaked from the eastern tower. They exploded barely their own length over the launching troughs.

"Bozeman, take out the west tower."

"Air car leaving the north tower, big, it's—"

"They're gabbling, they've dropped Inter—"

The second explosion was easily visible.

"You coppy son of a bitch, I didn't tell you to nuke it!"

"Crater radius one-three-ought-ought, depth at—"

"Oh, Jesus, the captain, oh Jesus I didn't—"

"Car is down, bearing two-two-ought from crater center, range— "

Kranski, perhaps unaware that he was speaking aloud, said it for all of them. "Well, they wasn't chicks. Not with no better dee-fense'n that."

There were forty-one bodies in the shock-flattened wreckage of the air car. None of them were human. The aliens' ropy limbs belied their endoskeletons, though only Doc Bordway, the ex-zoologist, cared much about that. Or the fact that most of the bodies were female and young. One of the few adult males found was clutching a blue case packed with documents. With no one left to translate the multi-colored squiggles, they were valueless to the squadron.

Eighty percent of the horizon was a hell of glass in a thousand dazzling forms: needles and vast, smooth clearings, iridescence and inkiness, sheets smeared vertically when a nearby pair of weapons had detonated simultaneously and conspired to create while destroying.

The three iron-gray towers dwarfed the attack ships huddled in their shadow.

"What're they doing here?" Ceriani asked, bending down to touch helmets with Hsi-men. "Broadcasting like this on all bands, transit space and normal; shut in behind a screen that's only open in the visible and that at damned low intensity—something's going on in there."

The stocky officer, suited against the vacuum and expected radiation—ground sensors showed the surface count was well below that of Colorado soil, but visual evidence to the contrary was all around—stared up the full length of a tower without answering. He had seen more impressive objects in his life, the coruscating ball of this world hanging in space among them; but the towers had a grim majesty he found unsettling.

"Somebody built to last," he said, helmet to helmet. All radio was drowned by the city's enormous output. "That isn't proof they lasted."

"But the signals—"

"Listen to the damn things, listen to them. A nine-word group, over and over, the same on every channel. You don't have to translate a bit of it to know exactly what it's asking. And if these poor damned machines were getting an answer, well, they'd say something else, wouldn't they?"

He snapped off a shard projecting from the ground, hurled it toward the nearest tower. The glass shattered a foot from his hand. "Something got through to them. Maybe age did. It's sure as death that AS 18 isn't going to, though. There's nothing here for us, nothing for men."

"I wish I knew one thing," the gangling, brown-eyed sergeant said morosely.

"Umm?"

"I wish I knew that whoever was fighting them back then was gone too."

Ignoring the hairless "squirrels," Roland turned over to set the sores on his back to the muted sunlight. There could be no true bedsores in freefall, but the constant abrasion by suit irregularities had welted every man in AS 18 during the seventy-nine days since they had suited up on their tender.

Seventy-nine days.

"Could've stayed where the CinC bought it," Lacie muttered from his nearby leaf pallet. "Wasn't so bad there. This jumping from one coppy place to another, before we can take our suits off. . . ."

A breeze riffled the overhanging leaves, a little too yellow for a Terran summer but close enough for men who had shipped on three years in the past. Little beads like scarlet oak galls spattered a number of the prominent veins, brightening the dappled shade.

"What's the matter with here?" Then, "Wish I had a place this nice back home. It's worth waiting for."

"Hellova long drag."

"There were gooks the other place. Here there ain't. Everything here but women. . . ."

That night, Lacie began screaming. Roland used a damp wad of cushion to try to bring his friend around and lower his fever. It wasn't until Bordway wandered over, curious as usual, that anybody realized Lacie was dying.

"Suit up—everybody suit up and get under your medi-comps," Bordway ordered. As he spoke, he was dragging Lacie's armor over the big man's swollen limbs. Part of the diagnostic and injection apparatus was built into the suits, since normally at least the tender's medical facilities would be available any time a flyer was out of his armor.

"What's the matter, Doc?" Hsi-men, squat and unperturbed, held the scout's leg without being asked.

"We're in trouble. Lacie's caught something here."

"Hey, even I know that's cop. You can't catch sick from a non-Earth disease. Everybody—"

"Not everybody's stupid enough to believe that," Bordway snapped. "A protein's a protein, and this place has raised one that's pretty damned compatible with ours. . . ."

Lacie screamed in delirium. Hsi-men pinioned his arms. "He caught a virus from the squirrels? God."

"Not the squirrels." Bordway gestured, his crooked index finger circling one of the abrasion sores on Lacie's chest. Ringing it now were a score of tiny scarlet beads. "The leaves."

He paused a moment, ran a hand through black hair months unshorn and glistening with natural oil. In the glare of the landing light rigged on a convex reflector for illumination, Hsi-men could see the wen on Bordway's elbow was beaded too.

Bordway was the second of the seven victims to die in space as Terran anti-virals proved worthless and supportive treatment insufficient.

Lacie. Bordway. Roland, who screamed to everyone around him as they scrambled into their suits, saying that Lacie was fine, he just had nightmares, that was all. Hamid. Jones, a thin, short man from somewhere in Britain, one of the few in AS 18 who liked the thought of killing. He had never been happier than the day at the Meadows of Altair when he had ripped open three Ch'koto transports with bursts from his power guns. Reikart took three days to die. There was no cut-off on the command channels, and Hsi-men's fingers crept to the weapons delivery console a dozen times during the hours of uninterrupted raving. Volomir.

The foliage below was bluer than the seas and starred with crystalline cities. There was no sign of highways—or aircraft, for that matter. But words crackled from the commo, loud and static-free: " 'Peace, welcome.' "

"You can get it clear, Rodie?"

"Yeah, this is pretty good. Hey, maybe we're back into the trade sphere?"

"Cop, I can't get any of the stars. Wish that little prick Reikart hadn't died just before he was good for something."

Slowly, tentatively, negotiations went on. The flat-faced Chinese officer was no diplomat, but he knew enough Interspeech to keep Rodenhizer from overmodifying his replies.

"We are distressed beings searching for our home."

"All beings are one in peace. Land, remain until your home is in peace."

"Rodie! They must know us if they know about the war. Baby, we're on the way!"

"Can you direct us to our home? We ask nothing but your instruction."

It was very hard to tell from the alien tones and syntax, but Rodenhizer suspected that after a brief pause a new voice came on. It blurred the labials of Interspeech slightly, but carried, even in its strangeness, a surprising dignity. "We here are beings of peace. We would have you wait with us in peace. While your home is at war, we cannot guide you to war."

Rodenhizer didn't have a command set. When he translated the statement on an open channel, the whole squadron exploded.

"What sorta cop is that? Look—"

"Wait a minute, wait, he can't have—"

Hsi-men let them run for a minute or more. Then he hit the override and ordered, "That's enough. Shut it off." They could hear his breathing alone for the next several seconds. Then, "Tell them we're going home now. We don't mean to hurt them, but they're not going to keep us away from home."

The ex-trader fitted his tongue to the syllables carefully. The answer was liquid, vibrant; uncompromising.

"Sir, he says they won't help us fight the chicks. We can stay or go our own way, but they won't guide us back to the war."

"Tell 'em they can start giving us the data we need right now, or I'll give 'em a war right here in their backyard."

"Sir, we can't! They've got all sorts of knowledge here, just incredible to have even heard of us and the chicks. We can't just smash them up because they got morals."

"Wanna bet? This is AS 18 and it's going home. You just tell them what I said."

"El-tee—"

"Tell'em or by God I'll blast a couple cities without it! Tell them!"

The answer was even shorter than the demand. Hsi-men didn't wait for the translation that was stuck in Rodenhizer's throat. "Kranski, pick yourself one of those cities and slag it." He knew the men pretty well. Kranski had already programmed his computer, hoping against hope, and his index finger was poised over the execute switch. A few milliseconds later the fireball bloomed through the false aurora of passage. A crystal glitter rode the edge of the shock wave like palings before a tsunami.

"Say it again, Rodie," Hsi-men thundered. "I've got bombs for a hundred more like that if they've got the cities."

"Dear God how could you do it? They'll guide . . . they'll guide us away, just give some time to match computer language. The whole city—we could have talked, have convinced them, maybe. . . ."

As the data was piped into the navigation units, Mizelle spoke his first words since they had lifted from the fog-world. That was the day Juan Calvados chose to share Murray's ship instead of Mizelle's. "They may be sending us into the center of a star," he said. If there was an emotion in his voice, it was not fear.

"Then they got better guidance systems than us by a long ways. My readout says we'll be jumping for about the next three days, and I'll sure be surprised if we hit anything as small as a star. . . ."

"And if we don't," Kranski purred in a husky whisper, "we know the way back."

On the battleship *Rahab*, the crews felt cramped by the enormous commo and guidance requirements of the flagship of the 3d Fleet; but the *Rahab* held only eight hundred men in a volume seven thousand times that of an attack ship. Vice-Admiral Ceriani stepped with a martinet's precision down the double row of monitors, each an expert overseeing the fraction of the ship's commo load routed to him. Only in the rarest of circumstances would a human override the computer's automatic response. Even more rarely, the datum or question would be forwarded directly to an officer.

As the admiral watched, his third monitor in the righthand

section threw the knife switch on top of his panel, setting the
ship on battle alert and clearing a circuit to every officer of
staff rank in the fleet. Rather than take the replay, the admiral
cut in on the monitor line.

"—main fleet. There's forty-eight blips of thirty kilotonne
or over, assorted light craft. And their dampers are down, all
down. If those mealy-mouthed peace-lovers hadn't dropped us
damn near on top of the chicks, it can't be three minutes, we'd
never have known there were any in twelve hours time. God
they run clean! But they've got the damper screens down too,
so they're wide open to nukes."

"Lieutenant," the Grand Marshal's labored voice queried,
"what is your strength?"

"Umm, eighteen Omega-class attack ships, one Epsilon-
class command," replied the other voice. They must be nearly
at the limits of intelligible transmission, one hell of a long way
still. More than far enough for the Ch'koto to catch the broad
wake of the oncoming 3d Fleet and activate their dampers for
a knock-down, drag-out fight. By now they could afford to
lose surprise once. "Mizelle hit his destruct as we came out
of transit, I swear to God, and that pansy bastard Rodenhizer
took himself off the pattern the second day out, so he's gone
too. . . ."

"Lieutenant?"

"God! Sir, I'm sorry; I'm—what do you want us to do?"

"Lieutenant, we are advancing on your plot." The admiral
could feel the truth of that, he realized, from the deck's squir-
reliness; the *Rahab* must be transiting at minimum interval,
less than ten seconds. "We need—we *must* have a strike within
the next fourteen minutes, before we enter the chicks' detection
range."

"Sir, we . . . sir, we have no support."

"Neither do we, Lieutenant. Since last Saturday, we are the
only fleet the Terran Federation has in space or is able to put
there. Do you understand?"

"Roger. Will do."

Nineteen slivers of electronics and thin alloy, the admiral
thought, razoring along some three minutes from destruction.
Don't think about the men, there were twenty-one thousand of
those in the 3d Fleet and nine billion more on Earth if you had
that kind of mind. "Get me into the intership channels for AS
18," he ordered brusquely into his right lapel.

"Sir, we'll have to squelch pretty tight above and below the orals, and there'll still be a lot of background."

"Don't talk—do it."

Hissing sharpened abruptly into words: "—appear on your screens in red."

"Roger."

"Roger."

"Team Nine; Kael, Ceriani, lead and backup. Your four targets appear on your screens in red."

"Roger."

"Roger."

"And they thought one nuke was enough for a command ship. Well, that big mother in the center may not be their flag, but it's sure worth a redpill. Last questions?"

"Sir, we don't have a reserve."

"Hell, we don't have forty-eight battlewagons, either. Bobby, we don't knock'em down on the first time through, you can write off any reserve along with the rest of us.

"OK, boys, let's take them out."

Hissing silence stalked the battle-lit commo room of the *Rahab.* "Kranski, not so short. Slide in at a flat angle or you'll blow us all."

"Two ready."

"Seven ready."

"El-tee, this is five. We're blocked from our targets unless we do a one-twenty around the whole coppy fleet. Got some alternates?"

"Roger, watch your screens. Clear?"

"Roger, that's fine."

"El-tee, I can zap the others with penetraters. Just run my pass on through—"

"Shut it off, Kranski. You'll reform with the rest of us after your pass. If you're lucky."

Seen in plane, the Ch'koto fleet was a roughly flattened zig-zag. The chicks were as disorderly in maneuver as they seemed to be as technicians, draping the gangways of their warships with festoons of wire and bare ranks of printed circuitry. But their sloppy formations reacted like bear traps in an engagement, and chick ships had cleaner drivers and better detection gear than the Terran Federation's.

Their only technical problem, near enough, was their noisy,

clumsy nuclear damper that took upwards of four minutes to
build from zero to a level that would squelch a 50-KT bomb.

The volume display danced with beads of four colors: white
for the enemy, red for the four targets spotted to Team Three,
Womack and Bozeman; green for the rest of AS 18, brilliant
sapphire for Womack's own ship as it slid toward a tight knot
of red beads and white. At present closing velocity, the chicks
were a minute and a quarter away. At maximum thrust—

"Go!"

Womack's stubby right forefinger smashed down. His vision
blurred with a rush of sweat from his forehead before the suit
dried him with a blast of hot air. Thirty-five seconds at full
thrust. And the chicks weren't going to miss nineteen rooster-
tails in transit space.

"Six, Chen; we're getting an IFF signal from a destroyer-
leader—orange tracer."

"Give'em a random return, Cooper pop them if—"

Womack's volume display overloaded in a blue flare as bolts
from the quad 80.3 turret of a chick battleship ripped past his
vessel. The chicks were too tightly formed to spray seeker
missiles, but big power guns wouldn't leave much if they hit.
Womack was screamingly blind for second on second, knowing
somewhere nearby an enemy computer was feeding corrections
to the guns—

With a treble thump, the redpills unloaded from his weapons
bay.

Still blind but able now to react, Womack hurled his ship
into a tight helix away from his delivery approach. The display
flickered wanly. The sapphire and its trailing green companion
winked suddenly into view, diving toward a single red-coded
hostile. Another near miss and the cube sagged and crackled
in the blue flame.

"Coppy bastards!" the flyer shouted. Without hesitation, he
tapped pre-eject, stripping off two square meters of hull above
him. He was so close that the battleship hung above him bright
as the sun seen from Jupiter. "Boze!" Womack called, "for
God's sake get the bastard!!"

The Ch'koto flashed again. Womack's body strained in the
salvo's viscous drag. "Bozeman!"

"Oh Jesus Captain oh Jesus I didn't—"

The next salvo hit both ships of Team Three squarely.

•   •   •

"Team Seven?"

"Farloe, but I've been pushing max too long."

"Team Eight?" Silence. "Nobody? Team Nine?"

"Kael bought it, I'm OK. Lost some sheeting's all."

"El-tee, those bastards're coming up on us and my drive, she just *won't* hang together much longer."

"OK, on the count we all come around. This isn't over yet."

"Sir, there's seven of us! We can't—"

"We can't take out a dozen chick wagons with HE? Well, we sure as death can't run away from'em in the shape these boats are. On the count, boys. Three, two, one, *hit'em*!"

A wash of static laced the channel. Then, very faintly, "Follow me home, you silly mothers, this squadron's going home."

In the red-lighted commo room of the *Rahab*, a monitor glanced sidelong from under his helmet. You didn't often get to see an admiral cry.

EMPIRE DREAMS

by Ian McDonald

She can smell the sickness everywhere. Her nostrils are not duped by the desperate odor of antiseptic; there is a peculiar stench to sickness that nothing will conceal, a stench mixed in with the thick glossy utility paint which, through the years of overpainting, overpainting, has built up into layer upon layer of ingrained despair. From these hopeless strata sickness leaks into the air. There is no concealing the smell of a hospital, it squeezes out of the floortiles every time a trolley rolls over them and under the slight pressure of a nurse's single footstep.

As she sits in the chair by the bed she breathes in the sickness and is surprised to find how cold it is. It is not the cold of the snow falling outside the window, the snow that softens and conceals the outlines of the Royal Victoria Hospital like white antiseptic. It is the cold which encircles death, the cold of the boy on the bed, which draws the living heat out of her; cold and sickness.

She does not know what the machines are for. The doctors have explained, more than once, but there must be more to her son's life than the white lines on the oscilloscopes. A person's life is not measure by lines, for if that is all a life is, which are the lines for love and the lines for devotion, which is the pulsebeat of happiness or the steady drone of pain? She does

236

not want to see those lines. Catherine Semple is a God-fearing woman who has heard the steady drone of pain more than anyone should have to in any lifetime, but she will not hear it whisper any blasphemous rumors. Joy and pain she accepts from the fingers of the same God, she may question but she never backbites. Her son lies in a coma, head shaved, wires trickling current into his brain, tubes down his nose, throat, arms, thighs. He has not moved for sixteen hours, no sign of life save the white measurements of the machines. But Catherine Semple will sit by that bed until she sees. At about midnight a nurse will bring coffee and some new used women's maga- zines; Nurse Hannon, the kindly, scared one from County Monaghan. By that time anything might have happened.

"Major Tom, Major Tom," booms out the huge voice of Cap- tain Zarkon, "Major Tom to fighter bay, Major Tom to fighter bay. Zygon battlefleet on long-range sensors, repeat, Zygon battlefleet on long-range sensors. Go get 'em, Tom, you're the Empire's last hope." And down in the hangar bay under dome under dome under dome (the high curved roof of the bay, the plasmoglass blister of the ship, the decaled bubble of your helmet) you scrunch down in the rear astrogator's seat of the X15 Astrofighter and mouth the fabulous words, "You're the Empire's last hope." Of course, you are not the Major Tom whose name thunders round the immense fighter bay, you are Thomas Junior, The Kid, less than fifty percent of the Galaxy's most famed (and feared, all the way from Centralis to Alphazar 3) fighting duo, but it is nice to sit there and close your eyes and think they are talking about you.

Here he comes, Major Tom; the last Great Starfighter, Space Ace, Astroblaster, Valiant Defender, thrice decorated by the Emperor Geoffrey himself with the Galaxian Medal and Bar, striding across the hangar deck magnificent in tight-fitting iridescent combat-suit, and, cradled beneath his arm, the helmet with the famous Flash of Lightning logo and the name "Major Tom" stenciled in bold black letters. The canopy rises to admit him and the hero snakily wiggles into the forward command- seat.

"Hi, Wee Tom."

"Hi, Big Tom."

Space-armored technicians are running ponderously to cover as the fighter deck is evacuated. The canopy seals, internal pressurization takes over and makes your ears pop, despite the gum you are looping round your back molars; the space door irises open and your fighter moves onto the launch catapult. What is beyond the space door? Vacuum, stars, Zygons. Not necessarily in that order. Tactical display lights blink green, little animated Imperial Astrofighters flash on half a dozen computer screens. You park your gum in the corner of the weapons status display board.

"Primary ignition sequence?"

"Green."

"Energy banks at full charge?"

"Check."

"All thrust and maneuvering systems, astrogation, and communication channels?"

"Okay, Wee Tom. Let's go get 'em. We're the Empire's Last Hope."

A blast of acceleration stuffs your teeth down your throat, flattens your eyeballs to fifty-pence pieces, and grips the back of your neck with an irresistible iron hand as the catapult seizes Astrofighter Orange Leader and shies it at the space door. The wind whistles out of you; everything goes red as the space door hurtles up at you. Then you are through, and, before the redness has faded from your eyes and the air filled your lungs once more, Major Tom has looped your X15 up and over the semi-eclipsed bulk of the miles-and-miles-and-miles-long *Excalibur*, throneship of Geoffrey I, Emperor of Space, Lord of the Shogon Marches, Defender of Altair, Liege of the Orion Arm, Master of the Dark Nebula.

"Astrogation check."

"Enemy force targeted in Sector Green 14 Delta J. Accelerating to attack speed. . . ."

"Good work, Wee Tom. Orange Leader to Force Orange, sign off. . . ."

One by one they climb away from the *Excalibur*, the valiant pilots of Force Orange: Big Ian, The Prince, John-Paul (J.P. to comrades only), Captain "Kit" Carson, Black Morrisey: nicknames known and respected (and in some places, dreaded) right across the sparkling spiral of the Galaxy. Such is these men's fame that it brings a lump to your throat to see the starlight catch on their polished wing-fairings and transform their battlescarred fighters into chariots of fire.

"Force Orange reported in, Orange One through Orange Five, Orange Leader," you say.

"Okay," says Major Tom with that resolute tightness in his voice you love to hear so much. He waggles his fighter's wings in the attack signal and Force Orange closes up into a deadly arrowhead behind him.

"Let's go get 'em. We've got a job to do."

PRESS CONFERENCE: 11:35 A.M. JANUARY 16, 1987

Yes, the original diagnosis was leukemia, but, as the disease was not responding to conventional treatment, Dr. Blair classified it as a psychologically dependent case . . . no, sorry, not psychosomatic, psychologically dependent is Dr. Montgomery's expression, the one Dr. Blair would like used. Put simply, the conventional chemotherapy was ineffective as long as the psychological block to its effectiveness remained. Yes, the leukemia has gone into complete remission. How long ago? About twelve days.

Gentleman at the back . . . sir. This is the thirty-eighth day of the coma, counting from the time when the growth of the cancer was first arrested, as opposed to the complete remission. The patient had been in the orthohealing state for some twenty-six days prior to that while the chemotherapy was administered and found to be effective. Yes sir, the chemotherapy was effective only while the patient was in the orthohealing state. It was discontinued after thirty days.

Gentleman from the Irish News . . . The boy is perfectly healthy—now, don't quote me on this, this is strictly off the record, there is no medical reason why Thomas Semple shouldn't get out of his bed and walk right out of this hospital. Our only conclusion is that there is some psychological imbalance that is keeping him, or, more likely, that is making him keep himself, in Montgomery/Blair suspension.

Sir, by the door . . . no, the project will not now be discontinued, it has been found to be medically very effective and the psychological bases of the process have been demonstrated to be valid. International medical interest in the process is high. I might add that more than one university across the water, as well as those here in Ireland, have sent representatives to observe the development of the case, and there is widescale commercial interest in the computer-assisted technology for the sensory-deprivation dream-simulation systems. In fact, Dr. Montgomery is attending an international conference in The Hague at which he is delivering his paper on the principles of orthohealing. Yes, sir, I can confirm that Dr. Montgomery is returning early from the Conference, and I wish I knew where you get your information from, but this is not due to any deterioration in Thomas Semple's condition. He is stable, but comatose, in the orthohealing state. Okay? Next question.

Sir, from the Guardian, isn't it? May I have your question. Yes, Mrs. Semple is in attendance by the bedside, we have a room set aside for her on the hospital premises, she is able to see her son at any time and spends most of her time in the ward with him. She will permit photographs, but under no circumstances will consent to be interviewed, so don't bother wasting your time trying. Yes, it was her idea, but we agree with her decision fully. I'm sure you must all appreciate, gentlemen, the strain she is under, after the tragic death of her husband, her only child developing leukemia, and now with the baffling nature of this coma. Next question. I.R.N.?

We have no evidence to cause us to believe that he has drifted away from the programmed orthohealing dream, this would be unlikely as the dream was designed specifically with his ideal fantasies in mind. We believe he is still mentally living out this *Star Wars* fantasy, what we call the Space Raiders simulation program. To explain a little, we have over a dozen archetype programs specifically engineered for typical psychological profiles. Thomas Semple Junior's is a kind of wish-fulfillment arcade-game, only with an infinite number of credits, if you'll pardon me stretching the analogy. The cancerous cells are represented as alien invaders to be destroyed, he himself is cast in the role of Luke Skywalker, the hero. I believe it was the gentleman from the Irish Times who coined the expression "Luke Skywalker Case," wasn't it?

Okay . . . any further questions? No? Good. There's a pile of press releases by the door, if you could pick one up as you leave it'd make it worth the trouble of having them printed. Afraid you won't find anything in them you haven't heard from me. Thank you, gentlemen, for being so patient and for coming on such a foul day. Thank you all, good morning.

(SHUTTLE FLIGHT BA4503 LONDON HEATHROW TO BELFAST: AFTER THE COFFEE, BEFORE THE DRINKS)

Mrs. MacNeill: I couldn't help noticing your briefcase, are you a doctor, Mr. Montgomery?

Dr. Montgomery: Well, a doctor, yes, but not an M.D., I'm afraid. Doctor of psychology.

Mrs. MacNeill: Oh. Have to be careful what I say then.

Dr. Montgomery: Ah, they all say that. Don't worry, I'm not a psychiatrist, I'm a research psychologist, clinical psychology. I'm attached to the R.V.H. team working on orthohealing, you know, the Luke Skywalker thing?

Mrs. MacNeill: I've heard about that, it was on the News at Ten, wasn't it, and it was on Tomorrow's World a couple of weeks back. That's the thing about getting people to dream themselves into getting better, isn't it?

Dr. Montgomery: That's it in a nutshell, Mrs. . . .

Mrs. MacNeill: Oh, sorry, there's me rabbiting on and never thought to tell you my name. Mrs. MacNeill, Violet MacNeill, of 32 Beechmount Park, Finaghy.

Dr. Montgomery: Well, you already guessed who I am, Mrs. MacNeill. Might I ask what takes you over the water?

Mrs. MacNeill: Ach, I was seeing my son, that's Michael, he's teaching English in a technical college in Dortmund in Germany, and he's always inviting me to come over and see him, so I thought, well now I've got the money, I might as well, because it could be the last time I'll see him.

Dr. Montgomery: Oh? How so? Is he moving even further afield?

Mrs. MacNeill: Oh no. But you could say I am. (LAUGHS, COUGHS) You see Dr. Montgomery, well, I haven't got long. I'm a person who believes in calling a spade a spade. I'm dying. It's this cancer thing, you know? You can't even talk about it these days, people don't like you to mention the word when they're around, but I don't care. I believe in calling a spade a spade, that's what I say. I tell who I like because it won't go away if you don't talk about it, it's stupid to try to hide from it, don't you think? You're a medical man, you should know.

Dr. Montgomery: Psychological, Mrs. MacNeill.

Mrs. MacNeill: You see? The very man to talk to. The trained ear. They picked it up about eight months ago, stomach cancer, well on its way, and they said I only had about a year at the most. I reckon longer than that, but I'm under no illusions it'll get better. My daughter, Christine, she wanted to put me in that hospice, you know, the place for the terminally ill, but I said, away out of that, all you do there is sit around all day and think about dying and they call that a positive attitude. 'Dying with dignity' they said, but if you ask me, I say you just live a bit less and die a little bit more every day until finally no one can tell the difference. Me, I intend to keep on living until the moment I drop. Away out of your hospices, I says to Christine, rather than waste good money on that abattoir give it me in my hand and I'll spend it doing all the things I've always wanted to do and never had the time for. And do you know what, Dr. Montgomery, she gave it to me and I took a little bit out of my savings and I've been having the time of my life.

Dr. Montgomery: Now that's what I call a positive attitude, Mrs. MacNeill.

Mrs. MacNeill: You see? That's the difference between a medical man; ach, I know you're a psychologist, but to me it's all the same, and an ordinary man. You can talk about these things, you can come out and say, 'That's what I call a positive attitude, Violet Mac-Neill' while anyone else would have only thought that and been afraid to say it in case they offended me or something. But I wouldn't mind, wouldn't mind a bit, what offends me is people not saying what's on their minds. But I tell you this, there's just one thing bothers me and won't give my head peace.

Dr. Montgomery: What's that?

Mrs. MacNeill: It's not me, nothing to do with me, why, I'm having the best time, I've been to Majorca on one of those winter breaks, and to London to see the shows, you know, that

Tim Rice and Andrew Lloyd-Webber thing, and I've a cousin in Toronto to see, and I have to get to Paris, I've always wanted to see Paris, in the spring, like that song. I'd love it any time of year, I've got to hang on 'til I've seen Paris. And then there was this joyride to Germany. Which brings me back to what I was talking to you about, don't I ramble on something dreadful? It's the kids I worry about, Michael and Christine and wee Richard, I say wee, but he's a full time R.U.C. man; it's them worries me. Now, I don't care much for dying, but it has to happen and at least I'm not bothering to let it ruin my life, but I worry about what I'm leaving behind. Will the kids ever forgive me?

Dr. Montgomery: That's a very good question, Mrs. MacNeill. Do you feel guilty about dying?

Mrs. MacNeill: See? Asked like a true psychologist. It's all right, never worry dear. In a way, it's stupid to feel guilty about dying; I mean to say, I'm not going to care, am I? But then again, I do feel bad in a sort of way because it's like I'm betraying them. I'm like the top layer between them and their own ends, and when I go they move up and become the top layer. Do you understand that?

Dr. Montgomery: I do. Would you care for a drink? Trolley's coming up the aisle.

Mrs. MacNeill: Oh please. Gin and bitter lemon for me. Should cut it out but I reckon when you add up the harm it does and good it's six of one and half a dozen of the other. Now, what was I saying? Oh yes, do you think children ever forgive their parents for dying? When you're wee, your parents are like God; I remember mine, God love 'em, they could do nothing wrong, they were as solid as the Rock of Gibraltar and always would be, but they both died in the bombing in '41 and you know, doctor, but I don't know if I ever forgave them? They'd built my life, they'd

given me everything, and then it was as if
they'd abandoned me, and I'm wondering
if my Michael and Christine and wee Richard
will think the same about me. Will they think
I've betrayed them, or will I have given
them that kick up the backside into being
mature? What do you think, Dr. Montgomery? Do children ever forgive their parents
for being human?

Dr. Montgomery: Mrs. MacNeill, I don't know. I just don't
know.

(THE DRINKS TROLLEY ARRIVES AT SEATS 28C & D
AT THE SAME INSTANT AS THE BOEING 757 MAKES
THE SUBTLE CHANGE OF ATTITUDE THAT MARKS
THE COMMENCEMENT OF ITS DESCENT TO SNOW-
BOUND NORTHERN IRELAND.)

She had wished upon a star, the star around which her son
orbits, a shooting star, fast and low and bright, diving down
behind Divis Mountain. When you wish upon a star, doesn't
matter who you are, everything your heart desires will come
to you, a cricket had sung to her once upon a rainy Saturday
afternoon in the sixties somewhen, but what if that star is a
satellite or an Army helicopter, does that invalidate the wish,
does that fold the heart's desire back on itself and leave it
staring at its reflection in the night-mirrored window? The night
outside fills the reflection's cheeks with shadows, and, in the
desperate warmth of the hospital room heavy with the scent of
sickness, she hugs herself and knows that she is the reflection
and it the object. Every night the hollows fill up again with
shadows from the shadowland outside where Army Saracens
roar through the night and joyriders hotwire Fords to cruise the
wee small hours away round the neat gravel paths of the City
Cemetery or stake their lives running the checkpoints manned
by weary police reservists watching from the backs of steel-grey
Landrovers with loaded rifles.

Stick them in neutral, he'd told her once, we do that sometimes, stick the Landrovers in neutral and cruise for a couple
of hundred yards, then shove them into second and when they
backfire it sounds like gunshots. Gets them ringing up the
Station—shots heard, Tennant Street, 1:15 A.M. Some of them
make it sound like Custer's Last Stand, he'd said. It had made
her laugh, once. Last Stand in Shadowland.

Somewhere in the room is the soul of a twelve-year-old boy,
somewhere among the piles of junk Dr. Montgomery had
suggested might trigger some response from him. Sometimes
she thinks she sees it, the hiding soul, like an imp, or like one
of the Brownies her mother had convinced her had lived behind
the dresser in the farmhouse's kitchen: an imp, darting from
under his American football helmet to hide behind his U2
poster, concealed like a lost chord in the strings of his guitar
or looping endlessly through his computer like the ghost of an
abandoned program. There are his favorite U2 albums, and the
cassettes recorded specially for him by John Cleese to try and
raise a smile on his face, there is the photograph of Horace,
half-collie, half Borzoi, wall-eyed and wild-willed; there is the
photograph of Tom Senior.

Tom Senior, who knew all about backfiring police Landrovers, and the room in the station with the ghetto-blaster turned
up loud outside it where they used to take the skinheads, and
the twelve different routes to work each day. Tom who had
always been just Dad to him. No, the soul of a twelve-year-old
boy, whatever its color, whatever its shape, is not something
that can be captured by computer-assisted machinery or lured
back to ground and trapped like a limed song-bird by a junk-shop
of emotional relics, not when it is out there in the night flying
loops around Andromeda.

As many as the stars in the sky or snowflakes in a blizzard or
grains of sand upon a beach, that is how many the Zygon fleet
is, wave upon wave of fighters and destroyers and scouts and
cruisers and battleships and dreadnoughts and mobile battlesta-
tions and there at the heart of it, like the black aniseed at the
center of a gobstopper: the Zygon flagship. The enemy is so
huge that it takes your breath away, and there is a beat of fear
in your heart, for the Imperial Throneship *Excalibur* is but
one ship and Major Tom is only one man. Major Tom points
his fighter's nose dead into the densest part of the pack and
leads Force Orange into the attack.

Is he totally without fear? you ask yourself, sweating under
your helmet as the sudden acceleration pushes you deep into
your padded seat, stamps all over your ribs, and stands forward
on its head to become up.

"Where do they all come from?" you whisper to give your
fear a name you can hold it by. Major Tom hears you, for
privacy is not a thing a fighting team with a Galaxy-wide

reputation can be bothered with, and answers.

"Survivors of the Empire's destruction of their capital world,
Carcinoma. Must have got the Zygon Prime Intelligence off
before we blasted Carcinoma, and now they're here, grouping
for another murderous attack on the peaceful planets of the
Empire. And we've got to stop them before they destroy the
entire universe. A battlefleet could fight for a hundred years
and still be no nearer the flagship of the Prime Intelligence,
but a small force of two-man fighters might, just might, be
able to slip past their defenses and attack the flagship with
pulsar torpedoes." And now he says into the relay channels
you have open for him,

"Orange Leader to Orange One through Five, accelerate to
combat speed. Let's go get 'em boys. The destiny of the Empire
is ours today."

How you wish you could make up lines like that, words to
inspire men and send them into battle, words that wave the
star-spangled banner of the Galactic Empire, words that make
the hair prickle under your helmet and proud tears leak from
the corners of rough-tough space-marines' eyes. You think that
it might not be such a terrible thing to die with words like that
ringing in your ears.

Your targeting computer has located the cluster of Zygon
dreadnoughts and fighters protecting the flagship of the Prime
Intelligence. The first photon blasts from the battleships' long-
range zappers rock your X15 as the enemy fighters peel out of
formation to intercept. Opaque spots appear on your visor to
screen out the searing light of the photon blasts.

"Orange Leader to Force Orange," says Major Tom, "I'm
going in."

"Tactical computer available," you say.

"Forget it, son, Major Tom does his own shooting." Your
thumbs twitch on imaginary triggers as Major Tom locks a
Zygon fighter in his sights and blasts it with his laser-zappers.
The black alien spacecraft unfolds into a beautiful blossom of
white flame. Already Major Tom has another in his sights.
Swooping up and away from the nuclear fireball, he rolls the
X15 and downs another. And another, and another, and an-
other . . .

On your tactical display a green grid square flashes red.

"Big Tom, one on your tail!"

"I mark him. Orange Leader to Orange Two, Big Ian, I've
a bogie on my tail. I'm going for the big one, the flagship."

He throws his fighter into a rapid series of bounce-about evasive maneuvers. A sudden flare of fusion-light throws your shadow before you onto the astrogational equipment as the Zygon pursuit ship explodes into a billion billion sparkling fragments. Orange Two thunders in to parallel your course. The daring star-pilots exchange greeting signals, and Orange Two rolls effortlessly away into a billion billion cubic light-years of space. Ahead, the Zygon flagship is sowing fighters like demon seed and now its heavy-duty laser turrets are swinging to bear on you. Photon-blasts fill the air like thistledown on a summer's day.

"Hold on to your seat, kid, this calls for some tight flying," shouts the voice of Major Tom in your helmet radio earphones, and he twists, turns, spins, loops, somersaults, and handstands the X15 past the criss-crossing Zygon fighters and the laser-fire from the flagship. The immense metal bulk of the enemy ship swells up before you, so close that you can see the space-armored gun-crews at their batteries.

"Arm pulsar torpedoes smart systems."

Click switch, press button; green lights reflect in your visor.

"Pulsar torpedoes armed." The infinitesimal white X15 Astrofighter hurtles over a crazy metal landscape bursting with laser-fire. Before you loom the engine ports, ponderous as mountain ranges, vulnerable as free-range eggs. Your mouth is dry, your hands are wet, your eyeballs are as dessicated as two round pebbles. Red lights . . .

"Squadron coming in behind us, fast." The metal landscape blurs beneath you: this alien vessel is so huge. . . .

"Damn. Orange Leader to Force Orange, what happened to the cover? Mark three bogies on my tail, take care of 'em, I'm going for the engine ducts . . . five . . ." The iron mountains open like jaws—"four." On your rear screen three evil black Zygon pursuit ships slip into tight cover . . . "three . . ." You veer down a sudden valley in the huge geography of the Flagship's drive section . . . "two . . ." ahead is the white doomsday glow of the stardrives . . . "one . . . Fire." Orange Leader climbs away from the engine pods. The pursuit ships come after you, never seeing the tiny blob of light detach itself from your fighter at count zero and steer itself down the engine tubes into the miles-distant bowels of the enemy flagship. Major Tom loops twelve thousand miles high above the doomed starship and declares, "detonation!"

At first there is nothing, as if it had taken time for Major

Tom's voice to travel across space and the torpedo to hear him, but then, as if by his express command, the Zygon Flagship silently expands into a rainbow of glowing particles. The afterblast paints the cockpit pink, a beautiful bathroom pink. The glow takes a long time to fade, a man-made sunset.

"Yahoo!" you shout, "Yahoo! We got him!"

"We sure did," says Major Tom, "son, we sure did."

"What now?" you ask, "take care of those pursuit ships and then back to *Excaliber?*

"Not yet," says Major Tom and there is a strange note in his voice that reminds you of something you have purposefully forgotten. "We're pressing on, continuing the attack on our own, because there's a planet out there beyond the lines of Zygon ships, a planet hidden for a million years away from Galactic knowledge, and we, and we alone, must go there to destroy Zygon power for ever."

PRESS RELEASE: DECEMBER 22, 1986 (Extracts)

. . . the concept of the "Mind Box," the baggage of beliefs and values which determines the individual's reactions to the events of his life. Research into depression has shown the relationship between psychosomatic symptoms and the state of the individual's "Mind Box." Dr. Montgomery hypothesised in his doctoral thesis that this Mind Box concept might account for many of the more severe medical cases which are never diagnosed as psychosomatic but which otherwise have no medical reasons for their lack of response to conventional treatment.

. . . developed "deep dreaming" from Luzerski and Baum's work on lucid dreams, dreams in which the dreamer exerts conscious control over the content of his dream. It is a highly refined version of Luzerski and Baum's dream techniques whereby the individual enters a state of interactive dreaming through a hypnotically and chemically induced process and effects the necessary repairs to his damaged Mind Box, thus relieving the psychological pressures that have led to his deteriorating medical condition. It could be said that he literally dreams himself into a state of self-healing. Dr. Blair has related this effect to the Nobel prizewinning Stoppard/Lowe theories of molecular iso-informational field-zones of order generated by individual protein molecules which stabilize genetic material against interference and mutation from eletromagnetic and gravitic fields. He argues the analogy of deep dreaming: "returning" the body's iso-informational fields to a state of biological and psychological metastasis, or "Harmony," which renders the patent—at the cellular level at least—responsive to conventional treatment.

Thomas Semple, Jr. is the process's pilot case. The patient, a twelve-year-old boy, contracted leukemia shortly after the death of his father, a police sergeant. He was admitted to hospital but did not respond to conventional chemotherapy.

. . . Doctors Montgomery and Blair have created a deep-dream scenario for young Thomas analogous to the computer games of which he is fond. In this dream simulation he plays the hero of a space-war arcade game shooting down invaders which are representations of the cancerous cells within him. He spends fifteen hours per day in this deep-dream suspension during which normal chemotherapy is administered. His dream state is constantly monitored by state-of-the-art computer technology which also maintains his illusion of deep-dreaming by direct stimulation (in sensory deprivation) of the neurons, both chemically and electrically. . . .

. . . During his waking periods he talks constantly about how exciting the space-war dream is and Doctors Montgomery and Blair are confident that their first case using this orthohealing process will be a complete success.

(THE FRONT SEATS OF A VAUXHALL CAVALIER REGISTRATION GXI 1293, SOMEWHERE ON THE MOTORWAY BETWEEN BELFAST AIRPORT AND THE ROYAL VICTORIA HOSPITAL. SCENERY: RAPIDLY MOVING PANORAMA OF SNOW-COVERED FIELDS AND MOTORWAY EXIT SIGNS. SETTING: TABLEAU FOR TWO CHARACTERS.)

Dr. Montgomery: How was the press conference then?

MacKenzie: Don't ask.

Dr. Montgomery: That bad? Oh come on, things haven't gotten any worse, the kid's stable, there's no cause for media panic, is there? Never was.

MacKenzie: If you really want to know, they're trying a human interest angle on the mother—you know, tragically widowed policeman's wife, her son struck down by you-know-what, can't mention cancer in the tabloids, hurts circulation; well, now to compound her suffering, this ancy-fancy untested medical experiment goes sour on her. That's what they were trying to get me to say at the press conference. Never again. Do your own next time.

Dr. Montgomery: Bastards. I take it you didn't—say anything, that is.

MacKenzie: Not a word.

Dr. Montgomery: Good girl yourself. Which papers?

MacKenzie: As I said, the tabloids: Mirror, Sun, Star, Mail, Express.

Dr. Montgomery: Bastards.

MacKenzie: Mrs. Semple's keeping them all at bay at the moment, but it's only a question of how long it is before some hack cons his way past the nurses and waves a checkbook under her nose.

Dr. Montgomery: Damn. Why all the sudden interest?

MacKenzie: Don't know. Some local must have picked up on the story and now the crusaders are waiting to take you apart the moment you get back there, Saladin. Gave me a rough enough time of it.

Dr. Montgomery: And drag the hospital's name through the mire. You didn't . . .

MacKenzie: Let them know I was in charge of simulation software and the computer systems? Think I'm stupid? Not a breath.

Dr. Montgomery: Thank God. (LOOKS AT THE SNOW AND IS SILENT FOR A WHILE) Roz, tell me, do you think children ever forgive their parents for dying?

MacKenzie: Wouldn't know. Mine are both disgustingly healthy. Better shape than I am.

Dr. Montgomery: You tell me what you think of this then. I'll review some facts about the case and you say what you think. One. Thomas Semple Junior's leukemia is cured but he still remains in the orthohealing coma which cured him. We assume he's still deep-dreaming because there's been no change in his vital signs between the two situations.

MacKenzie: Fair enough assumption. Two.

Dr. Montgomery: Two: in such a state of lucid dreaming, he can be anything he wants to be, anytime, anywhere — subjectively speaking — he exists in his own private universe where everything is exactly as he wishes it to be.

MacKenzie: Within the program parameters.

Dr. Montgomery: Well, that's your field of competence, not mine. Three: his father, a sergeant in the Royal Ulster Constabulary, was killed before his eyes by a bomb planted under his car.

MacKenzie: Deduced by yourself to be the neuro-psychological basis of the leukemia.

Dr. Montgomery: And his lack of response to conventional therapy, yes. Hell, twelve-year-olds shouldn't have death wishes, should they?

MacKenzie: You were the one who thought it was displaced punishment behavior.

Dr. Montgomery: Every other Tuesday I think the moon is made of green cheese and life is worth living after all. Listen to this: I think we have given Thomas Semple Junior the perfect environment to recreate his father. Now he does not have to die to join him, he has him all the time, all to himself in that dream-world of his. The kid can't face a world where his father was blown to bits by an I.N.L.A. bomb, he can't face the reality of his father's death, and now he doesn't have to when he can be with his father, his perfect idealized father, forever in the deep dream state.

MacKenzie: That's spooky.

Dr. Montgomery: That's all there is. What do you think?

MacKenzie: Did you think all this up on the plane over?

Dr. Montgomery: I got into conversation with the woman next to me — talk about strange bedfellows, airline booking computers lead the field — she had cancer, one of those six-months-to-live cases and she was a talker, you know how some are, it makes it easier for them if they can talk about it; well anyway, in the middle of this conversation she mentioned that she feared that her children would never forgive her for dying and leaving them alone in the world. Paranoid maybe, but it started me thinking.

MacKenzie: It fits. It all fits beautifully.
Dr. Montgomery: Doesn't it? I reckon if we go through the
                      print-outs on the dream-monitors we'll find
                      Thomas Semple Senior in there large as life
                      and twice as handsome, because his or-
                      phaned son is punishing him over and over
                      and over again.
MacKenzie: And what then? You going to exorcise his
                      ghost?
Dr. Montgomery: Yes, I am.
(OVERHEAD GANTRIES BEARING SIGNS READING M1,
CITY CENTRE, M5, CARRICKFERGUS, NEWTONAB-
BEY, BANGOR, LISBURN, APPEAR ABOVE THE CAR.
MACKENZIE SLIDES THE VAUXHALL CAVALIER INTO
THE LANE MARKED CITY CENTRE.)

She wishes they would go. She resents their noisy feet, their
busy bustle, their muted conversations over rustling sheets of
computer printout, their polite-polite ''Mrs. Semple excuse me
buts'' and ''Mrs. Semple, do you know ifs'' and ''Mrs. Semple,
could you tell us whethers.'' What are they doing that is so
important that they must stamp around in their noisy shoes and
remind her of the world beyond the swinging ward doors? She
does not like them near her son, though the man is the doctor
who invented the process and the woman is the one who developed the computers to which her son is wired from skull
eyes ears throat. It worries her to see their hands near the
machines, she fears that they might press buttons and throw
switches and she would never know why they had done so.
She hates not understanding and there is so much she does not
understand.

   They are talking now, excited about something on a computer
screen. She can see what it is that has excited them, though
she cannot understand why. Who is this ''Major Tom?'' The
empty coincidence of names does not fool her. Major Tom,
Major Tom . . . she remembers a song she had once heard
about Major Tom, the space man who never came down. Wasn't
that it, Major Tom, the space man, still orbiting round and
round and round the world in his tin-can? She never knew
Major Tom. But she knew Sergeant Tom, Sergeant Tom tall
and lovely in his bottle-green uniform, Sergeant Tom photo-
graphed in his swimming trucks on a Spanish beach, brown
and smiling, with that little Tom Selleck moustache, Sergeant

Tom sitting at the breakfast table in his shirt-sleeves, shoulder holster and police boots waiting for the phone call which would tell today's safe pick-up point, Sergeant Tom putting on his jacket, kissing her on the lips and telling Wee Tom to have a good day at school and take care with his head-sums. Sergeant Tom walking out to the Ford Sierra, Sergeant Tom turning the key in the ignition. . . .

"Mrs. Semple, Mrs. Semple."

Faces loom before her, changing size and distance as her eyes focus.

"Yes, Dr. Montgomery?"

"We'd like your permission to try something we think will bring your son out of his coma."

"What is it you want to do?" The weariness in her voice surprises her.

"Adapt the program parameters slightly. Ms. MacKenzie wants to inject new material into the dream simulation."

"You've tried that before. You tried switching off the machines altogether."

"I know, Mrs. Semple. It didn't work." The young doctor (how can anyone as young as he have the experience to mold people's lives?) completes her thoughts for her. He is clever but naïve. She envies him that. "Thomas merely maintained the dream-coma by exercise of his own imagination. No, what we want to do is inject something into the dream so unacceptable that his only escape is to come out of the deep-dream coma."

"And what is that something?"

"I'd rather not say at the moment, Mrs. Semple, in case it doesn't work."

"And if it doesn't work?"

"Then you and he are no worse off than you are now."

"And if it succeeds?"

"Do I really have to answer that question, Mrs. Semple?"

"Of course not. All right then. You have my permission, and my blessing."

"Thank you, Mrs. Semple. O.K. Roz."

What long fingers the girl has! She cannot get over those long, slender fingers as she types on the computer keypad. They are more like tentacles than fingers. Her attention is torn between the dancing fingers and the white words that float up on the green screen.

• • •

PROGRAM "LUKE SKYWALKER": INTERRUPTIVE
MODE CHANGE: IRRAY 70432 GOTO 70863:
READ: KILL MAJOR TOM
KILL MAJOR TOM

At the peak of the entry, when the X15 bucked and bounced like a bad dream from which you cannot waken and every bolt and rivet shuddered and your teeth shook loose in your head, the deflector shields glowed a violent blue and the fighter's ionization trail plumed out behind you like a shooting star on an autumn night. There had been a moment (just a moment) when the fear had won, when your trust in Major Tom's skill had not been its equal and you had seen your ship burst open like a drop-kicked egg and you hurled screaming and burning into three hundred miles of sky. The shriek had built in your chest and rattled the bars of your teeth and your brain had pounded pounded pounded against the dome of your helmet. Then you had come out and the air was smooth and the deflectors glowed a dull cherry red and your trusty fighter was dipping down through the miles of airspace to the carpet of woolen piled clouds.

Now there is fear again, not the fear of disintegration in the ionosphere, for that is only death and to die is to leave the self and join the others, but the fear of what waits for you below the cloud cover, for that is more terrible than death, for it denies the other and leaves you alone with only yourself.

"Big Tom, we must go back! *Excalibur* has been calling and calling, Captain Zarkon, even the Emperor Geoffrey himself, have been ordering you to turn back. It's too dangerous, you are forbidden to go any further alone!"

Major Tom says nothing but thrusts your X15 Astrofighter lower, lower, lower. Clouds shred like tissue-paper on your wing-tips, the fog swirls and thins patchily, then you are out of the cloud-base and below you is the surface. The Montgomery/Blair engines thunder as Major Tom throttles back; he is coming in for a landing and your stomach, now gripped firmly by six billion billion billion tons worth of gravity, is doing flip-flops, a sicky-lurchy feeling that overcomes you as he throws the X15 into a left-hand bank.

The ground is tip-of-the-nose close beyond the canopy, a forbidden planet standing on edge in mid-bank; red-brick neo-Georgian bungalows in fifteen hundred square feet of white-chained garden, trailers in the drive, boats and run-about second cars parked outside, rose beds flowering, children on BMX's, stopping, pointing, gaping.

"Commence landing sequence."

You do not want to. You cannot go down there. To go down there is dying and worse. A billion billion billion miles away *Excaliber*, the Imperial Throneship, hangs poised on the lip of jumpspace but its stupendous bulk is as insubstantial as a cloud compared to the painful truth of this place, so pin-sharp that you can even read the street name: Clifden Road. Suddenly you are no longer Wee Major Tom, half of the greatest fighting team the galaxy has ever known. Suddenly you are a small boy who is twelve years old and more frightened than he has ever been before.

"Commence landing sequence," orders Major Tom.

"No!" you wail wanting beyond want to hear the words which will make it all right, the words which would make men glad to die in the hollowness of space. "I want to go back! Take me back!"

"Commence landing sequence," says Major Tom again and there is nothing in his voice but determination and command.

"Landing sequence initiated," you sob, touching heavy fingers to cold control panels. Landing shocks slide from their fairings and lock with a thump. The engine noise rises to a scream. Major Tom brings the X15 Astrofighter in low above the rooftops like Santa Claus on his sled and stops it dead in the air over the turning circle at the end of the street. Housewives' morning coffees grow cold as their imbibers stand in their picture windows, babies in arms, to view the spectacle of the Astrofighter touching down. Whipped into tiny tornadoes, dust eddies chase down the street away from the downdraught. There is a gentle touch, as soft as a mother's finger upon a nightmared cheek: touchdown.

"Power down," says Major Tom, but before the noise of the engines has whispered away to nothing his canopy is open, his harness unbuckled and he is running down the street to a house with number 32 on the gatepose and a lovely white-and-tan hearth-rug dog lying on the front step. Behind the picture window, too, there is a woman, with a coffeecup in one hand and the head of a small boy of about twelve under the other.

Then the world folds up on itself like one of those paper fortune-tellers you used to make in school. Major Tom's shiny

uniform rips and shreds as he runs and the wind whips the
scraps away to reveal a new uniform beneath, dark green with
silver buttons. An X15 Astrofighter lifts into the air above
Clifden Road on a pillar of light, canopy open and climbs away
into forever. Your uniform is gone, and the gentle pressure on
your head is not the pressure of a helmet but the pressure of a
small, slender hand and you realize that you are the boy in the
window as the X15 dwindles into a shining dot and winks out.
You are held, you are trapped under the gentle hand, marooned
on the Planet of Nightmares.

Now Major Tom is at the car and he waves at you and all
you can do is wave back at him for the words you want to
shout, the warnings you want to scream, rattle round and round
and round your head like pebbles in a wave and will not be
cast out. Now he has the door open. Now he is in the car. Door
shut, belt on, key in ignition. . . .

This time you know the blast for what it is. This time you
are prepared and can appreciate its every vital moment in dreadful action-replay.

The ball of light fills the interior of the Ford Sierra. An
instant after, still twilit by the killing light, the roof swells up
like a balloon and the doors bulge on their hinges. Another
instant later the windows shatter into white sugar and then the
picture window before you flies into shards, a gale of whirling
knives carried on a white wind that blasts you from your feet
and blows you across the room in a whirling jumble of glass
and smashes you into the sofa. The skin of the car shatters and
the pieces take flight. The hood follows through the window
to join you on the sofa. The roof has blown clean away and is
flying up to heaven, up to join God. The car roars into flames
and within the car, behind the flames, a black puppet thing
gibbers and dances for a few endless moments before it falls
into crisp black ashes.

A red rain has spattered the wall-paper. There is not a window
intact on Clifden Road. Your mother is lying at a crazy angle
at the door, her dressing-gown hitched around her waist. Out
in the drive the pyre roars and trickles of burning fuel melt the
tarmac. Smoke plumes into the sky, black oily smoke, and
there at the place where your eyes wander, the place where the
smoke can no longer be seen, there is a bird-bright white dot:
an Imperial X15 Astrofighter coming in from space, and you
know that now it must happen all over again, the landing, the

running Major Tom, the strange transformations, the man in
the green uniform stepping into his car, the explosion, the
burning, the Astrofighter coming in for a landing, the changes,
the blast, the burning, landing blast burning, blast burning blast
burning blast burning over and over and over.

"Major Tom!" you cry, "Major Tom, don't leave me!
Daddy! Daddy!"

When the alarms had sounded, when the flashing lights had
thrown their thin red flickering shadows across the floor, she
had said to herself: He's dead, they have lost him, and though
the world had ended she found she could not bear any hatred
in her heart for those who had killed her son. They had acted
in good faith. She had consented. All responsibility was hers.
She could forgive them, but never herself. God might forgive
Catherine Semple, but she never would. Gone, she had thought,
and had risen from her chair to leave. Empty coffee cups and
women's magazines covered the table. She would slip away
quietly while the alarms were still ringing and the lights still
flashing. Nurses' running footsteps had come crashing down
the corridors, but at the door the sudden, terrifying quiet had
stopped her like ice in her heart. Then after the storm came
the still small voice, pitifully frail and poignant.

"Major Tom! Major Tom! Don't leave me! Daddy! Daddy!"

"I won't," she had whispered. "I won't leave you," and
everything had stopped then. It was as if the whole city had
fallen silent to hear the cries of the new nativity, and then with
a shudder the world had restarted. Lines had danced and chased
across oscilloscopes, rubber bladders had breathed their ersatz
breaths, valves had hissed and the electronic blip of the
pulsebeat had counted out time. But even she had known the
difference. The red lights which had been red so long she could
not remember them being any other color were now defiantly
green, and though she could not read the traces she had known
they were the normal signs of a twelve-year-old boy waking
gently from a troubled, healthy sleep. She could feel the warmth
from his bed upon her skin and smell the smell that was not
the reek of sickness but the smell of sickness purged, disease
healed.

She remembers all of this, she remembers the nurses, she
remembers the handshakes and the hugs and the hankies, she
remembers Dr. Montgomery's lips moving but the words escape

her, for time has been jumbled up and nurses, reporters, doctors, photographers, are all stacked next to each other without meaningful order, like a box of antique photographs found in an attic. She remembers flashguns and journalists, video cameramen trailing leads and sound engineers, television news reporters; she remembers their questions but none of her answers.

Now she sits by the bedside. There is a cold cup of coffee on the arm of her chair which the friendly nurse from County Monaghan had brought her. Dr. Montgomery and the MacKenzie woman, the one with the look of computers behind her eyes, answer questions. She does not pretend to understand what they have done, but she knows what it might have been. Ignored for a while she can sit and watch her son watch her back. Unseen by any cameras, eyes meet and smile. There has been pain, there will be pain again, but now, here, there is goodness.

Outside it seems to have stopped snowing but by the cast of the darkening sky she knows it will not be for long. The lights of an Army Lynx helicopter pass high over West Belfast, and if she squeezes her eyes half shut she can make herself believe that they are not the lights of a helicopter at all but the rocket trail of Major Tom, flying home from Andromeda.

STARS, WON'T YOU HIDE ME?

by Ben Bova

O sinner-man, where are you going to run to?
O sinner-man, where are you going to run to?
O sinner-man, where are you going to run
All on that day?

The ship was hurt, and Holman could feel its pain. He lay fetal-like in the contoured couch, his silvery uniform spider-webbed by dozens of contact and probe wires connecting him to the ship so thoroughly that it was hard to tell where his own nervous system ended and the electronic networks of the ship began.

Holman felt the throb of the ship's mighty engines as his own pulse, and the gaping wounds in the generator section, where the enemy beams had struck, were searing his flesh. Breathing was difficult, labored, even though the ship was working hard to repair itself.

They were fleeing, he and the ship; hurtling through the star lanes to a refuge. But where?

The main computer flashed its lights to get his attention. Holman rubbed his eyes wearily and said:

"Okay, what is it?"

YOU HAVE NOT SELECTED A COURSE, the computer said aloud, while printing the words on its viewscreen at the same time.

Holman stared at the screen. "Just away from here," he said at last. "Anyplace, as long as it's far away."

The computer blinked thoughtfully for a moment. SPECIFIC COURSE INSTRUCTION IS REQUIRED.

"What difference does it make?" Holman snapped. "It's over. Everything finished. Leave me alone."

IN LIEU OF SPECIFIC INSTRUCTIONS, IT IS NECESSARY TO TAP SUBCONSCIOUS SOURCES.

"Tap away."

The computer did just that. And if it could have been surprised, it would have been at the wishes buried deep in Holman's inner mind. But instead, it merely correlated those wishes to its singleminded purpose of the moment, and relayed a set of navigational instructions to the ship's guidance system.

> Run to the moon: O Moon, won't you hide me?
> The Lord said: O sinner-man, the moon'll be a-bleeding
> All on that day.

The Final Battle had been lost. On a million million planets across the galaxy-studded universe, mankind had been blasted into defeat and annihilation. The Others had returned from across the edge of the observable world, just as man had always feared. They had returned and ruthlessly exterminated the race from Earth.

It had taken eons, but time twisted strangely in a civilization of light-speed ships. Holman himself, barely thirty years old subjectively, had seen both the beginning of the ultimate war and its tragic end. He had gone from school into the military. And fighting inside a ship that could span the known universe in a few decades while he slept in cryogenic suspension, he had aged only ten years during the billions of years that the universe had ticked off in its stately, objective time-flow.

The Final Battle, from which Holman was fleeing, had been fought near an exploded galaxy billions of light-years from the Milky Way and Earth. There, with the ghastly bluish glare of uncountable shattered stars as a backdrop, the once-mighty fleets of mankind had been arrayed. Mortals and Immortals alike, men drew themselves up to face the implacable Others.

The enemy won. Not easily, but completely. Mankind was crushed, totally. A few fleeing men in a few battered ships was all that remained. Even the Immortals, Holman thought wryly, had not escaped. The Others had taken special care to make certain that they were definitely killed.

So it was over.

Holman's mind pictured the blood-soaked planets he had seen during his brief, ageless lifetime of violence. His thoughts drifted back to his own homeworld, his own family: gone long, long centuries ago. Crumbled into dust by geological time or blasted suddenly by the overpowering Others. Either way, the remorseless flow of time had covered them over completely, obliterated them, in the span of a few of Holman's heartbeats.

All gone now. All the people he knew, all the planets he had seen through the ship's electroptical eyes, all of mankind . . . extinct.

He could feel the drowsiness settling upon him. The ship was accelerating to lightspeed, and the cryogenic sleep was coming. But he didn't want to fall into slumber with those thoughts of blood and terror and loss before him.

With a conscious effort, Holman focused his thoughts on the only other available subject: the outside world, the universe of galaxies. An infinitely black sky studded with islands of stars. Glowing shapes of light, spiral, ovoid, elliptical. Little smears of warmth in the hollow unending darkness; drabs of red and blue standing against the engulfing night.

One of them, he knew, was the Milky Way. Man's original home. From this distance it looked the same. Unchanged by little annoyances like the annihilation of an intelligent race of star-roamers.

He drowsed.

The ship bore onward, preceded by an invisible net of force, thousands of kilometers in radius, that scooped in the rare atoms of hydrogen drifting between the galaxies and fed them into the ship's wounded, aching generators.

Something . . . a thought. Holman stirred in the couch. A consciousness—vague, distant, alien—brushed his mind.

He opened his eyes and looked at the computer viewscreen. Blank.

"Who is it?" he asked.

A thought skittered away from him. He got the impression

of other minds: simple, open, almost childish. Innocent and curious.

It's a ship.

Where is it . . . oh, yes. I can sense it now. A beautiful ship.

Holman squinted with concentration.

It's very far away. I can barely reach it.

And inside of the ship . . .

It's a man. A human!

He's afraid.

He makes me feel afraid!

Holman called out, "Where are you?"

He's trying to speak.

Don't answer!

But . . .

He makes me afraid. Don't answer him: We've heard about humans!

Holman asked, "Help me."

Don't answer him and he'll go away. He's already so far off that I can barely hear him.

But he asks for help.

Yes, because he knows what is following him. Don't answer. Don't answer!

Their thoughts slid away from his mind. Holman automatically focused the outside viewscreens, but here in the emptiness between galaxies he could find neither ship nor planet anywhere in sight. He listened again, so hard that his head started to ache. But no more voices. He was alone again, alone in the metal womb of the ship.

He knows what is following him. Their words echoed in his brain. Are the Others following me? Have they picked up my trail? They must have. They must be right behind me.

He could feel the cold perspiration start to trickle over him.

"But they can't catch me as long as I keep moving," he muttered. "Right?"

CORRECT, said the computer, flashing lights at him. AT A RELATIVISTIC VELOCITY, WITHIN LESS THAN ONE PERCENT OF LIGHTSPEED, IT IS IMPOSSIBLE FOR THIS SHIP TO BE OVERTAKEN.

"Nothing can catch me as long as I keep running."

But his mind conjured up a thought of the Immortals. Nothing could kill them . . . except the Others.

Despite himself, Holman dropped into deepsleep. His body

temperature plummeted to near-zero. His heartbeat nearly stopped. And as the ship streaked at almost lightspeed, a hardly visible blur to anyone looking for it, the outside world continued to live at its own pace. Stars coalesced from gas clouds, matured, and died in explosions that fed new clouds for newer stars. Planets formed and grew mantles of air. Life took root and multiplied, evolved, built myriad civilizations in just as many different forms, decayed and died away.

All while Holman slept.

Run to the sea: O sea, won't you hide me?
The Lord said: O sinner-man, the sea'll be a-sinking
All on that day.

The computer woke him gently with a series of soft chimes.

APPROACHING THE SOLAR SYSTEM AND PLANET EARTH, AS INDICATED BY YOUR SUBCONSCIOUS COURSE INSTRUCTIONS.

Planet Earth, man's original homeworld. Holman nodded. Yes, this was where he had wanted to go. He had never seen the Earth, never been on this side of the Milky Way galaxy. Now he would visit the teeming nucleus of man's doomed civilization. He would bring the news of the awful defeat, and be on the site of mankind's birth when the inexorable tide of extinction washed over the Earth.

He noticed, as he adjusted the outside viewscreen, that the pain had gone.

"The generators have repaired themselves," he said.

WHILE YOU SLEPT. POWER GENERATOR SYSTEM NOW OPERATING NORMALLY.

Holman smiled. But the smile faded as the ship swooped closer to the solar system. He turned from the outside viewscreens to the computer once again. "Are the 'scopes working all right?"

The computer hummed briefly, then replied. SUBSYSTEMS CHECK SATISFACTORY, COMPONENT CHECK SATISFACTORY. INTEGRATED EQUIPMENT CHECK POSITIVE. VIEWING EQUIPMENT FUNCTIONING NORMALLY.

Holman looked again. The sun was rushing up to meet his gaze, but something was wrong about it. He knew deep within him, even without having ever seen the sun this close before, that something was wrong. The sun was whitish and somehow stunted looked, not the full yellow orb he had seen in film-tapes. And the Earth . . .

The ship took up a parking orbit around a planet scoured clean of life: a blackened ball of rock, airless, waterless. Hovering over the empty, charred ground, Holman stared at the devastation with tears in his eyes. Nothing was left. Not a brick, not a blade of grass, not a drop of water.

"The Others," he whispered. "They got here first."

NEGATIVE, the computer replied. CHECK OF STELLAR POSITIONS FROM EARTH REFERENCE SHOWS THAT SEVEN BILLION YEARS HAVE ELAPSED SINCE THE FINAL BATTLE.

"Seven billion . . ."

LOGIC CIRCUITS INDICATE THE SUN HAS GONE THROUGH A NOVA PHASE. A COMPLETELY NATURAL PHENOMENON UNRELATED TO ENEMY ACTION.

Holman pounded a fist on the unflinching armrest of his couch. "Why did I come here? I wasn't born on Earth. I never saw Earth before . . ."

YOUR SUBCONSCIOUS INDICATES A SUBJECTIVE IMPULSE STIRRED BY . . .

"To hell with my subconscious!" He stared out at the dead world again. "All those people . . . the cities, all the millions of years of evolution, of life. Even the oceans are gone. I never saw an ocean. Did you know that? I've traveled over half the universe and never saw an ocean."

OCEANS ARE A COMPARATIVELY RARE PHENOMENON EXISTING ON ONLY ONE OUT OF APPROXIMATELY THREE THOUSAND PLANETS.

The ship drifted outward from Earth, past a blackened Mars, a shrunken Jupiter, a ringless Saturn.

"Where do I go now?" Holman asked.

The computer stayed silent.

> Run to the Lord: O Lord, won't you hide me?
> The Lord said: O sinner-man, you ought to be a-praying
> All on that day.

Holman sat blankly while the ship swung out past the orbit of Pluto and into the comet belt at the outermost reaches of the sun's domain.

He was suddenly aware of someone watching him.

No cause for fear. I am not of the Others.

It was an utterly calm, placid voice speaking in his mind: almost gentle, except that it was completely devoid of emotion.

"Who are you?"

An observer. Nothing more.

"What are you doing out here? Where are you, I can't see anything . . ."

I have been waiting for any stray survivor of the Final Battle to return to mankind's first home. You are the only one to come this way, in all this time.

"Waiting? Why?"

Holman sensed a bemused shrug, and a giant spreading of vast wing.

I am an observer. I have watched mankind since the beginning. Several of my race even attempted to make contact with you from time to time. But the results were always the same— about as useful as your attempts to communicate with insects. We are too different from each other. We have evolved on different planes. There was no basis for understanding between us.

"But you watched us."

Yes. Watched you grow strong and reach out to the stars, only to be smashed back by the Others: Watched you regain your strength, go back among the stars. But this time you were constantly on guard, wary, alert, waiting for the Others to strike once again. Watched you find civilizations that you could not comprehend, such as our own, bypass them as you spread through the galaxies. Watched you contact civilizations of your own level, that you could communicate with. You usually went to war with them.

"And all you did was watch?"

We tried to warn you from time to time. We tried to advise you. But the warnings, the contacts, the glimpses of the future that we gave you were always ignored or derided. So you boiled out into space for the second time, and met other societies at your own level of understanding—aggressive, proud, fearful. And like the children you are, you fought endlessly.

"But the Others . . . what about them?"

They are your punishment.

"Punishment? For what? Because we fought wars?"

No. For stealing immortality.

"Stealing immortality? We worked for it. We learned how to make humans immortal. Some sort of chemicals. We were going to immortalize the whole race . . . I could've become immortal. *Immortal*. But they couldn't stand that . . . the Others. They attacked us."

He sensed a disapproving shake of the head.

"It's true," Holman insisted. "They were afraid of how powerful we would become once we were all immortal. So they attacked us while they still could. Just as they had done a million years earlier. They destroyed Earth's first interstellar civilization, and tried to finish us permanently. They even caused Ice Ages on Earth to make sure none of us would survive. But we lived through it and went back to the stars. So they hit us again. They wiped us out. Good God, for all I know I'm the last human being in the whole universe."

Your knowledge of the truth is imperfect. Mankind could have achieved immortality in time. Most races evolve that way eventually. But you were impatient. You stole immortality.

"Because we did it artificially, with chemicals. That's stealing it?"

Because the chemicals that gave you immortality came from the bodies of the race you called the Flower People. And to take the chemicals, it was necessary to kill individuals of that race.

Holman's eyes widened. "What?"

For every human made immortal, one of the Flower Folk had to die.

"We killed them? Those harmless little . . ." His voice trailed off.

To achieve racial immortality for mankind, it would have been necessary to perform racial murder on the Flower Folk.

Holman heard the words, but his mind was numb, trying to shut down tight on itself and squeeze out reality.

That is why the Others struck. That is why they had attacked you earlier, during your first expansion among the stars. You had found another race, with the same chemical of immortality. You were taking them into your laboratories and methodically murdering them. The Others stopped you then. But they took pity on you, and let a few survivors remain on Earth. They caused your Ice Ages as a kindness, to speed your development back into civilization, not to hinder you. They hoped you might evolve into a better species. But when the opportunity for im-

*mortality came your way once more, you seized it, regardless
of the cost, heedless of your own ethical standards. It became
necessary to extinguish you, the Others decided.*

"And not a single nation in the whole universe would help
us."

Why should they?

"So it's wrong for us to kill, but it's perfectly all right for
the Others to exterminate us."

*No one has spoken of right and wrong. I have only told you
the truth.*

"They're going to kill every last one of us."

There is only one of you remaining.

The words flashed through Holman. "I'm the only
one . . . the last one?"

No answer.

He was alone now. Totally alone. Except for those who were
following.

> Run to Satan: O Satan, won't you hide me?
> Satan said: O sinner-man, step right in
> All on that day.

Holman sat in shocked silence as the solar system shrank to a
pinpoint of light and finally blended into the mighty panorama
of stars that streamed across the eternal night of space. The
ship raced away, sensing Holman's guilt and misery in its
electronic way.

Immortality through murder, Holman repeated to himself
over and over. Racial immortality through racial murder. And
he had been part of it! He had defended it, even sought immortality as his reward. He had fought his whole lifetime for it,
and killed—so that he would not have to face death.

He sat there surrounded by self-repairing machinery, dressed
in a silvery uniform, linked to a thousand automatic systems
that fed him, kept him warm, regulated his air supply, monitored
his blood flow, exercised his muscles with ultrasonic vibrators,
pumped vitamins into him, merged his mind with the passion-
less brain of the ship, kept his body tanned and vigorous, his
reflexes razor-sharp. He sat there unseeing, his eyes pinpointed
on a horror he had helped to create. Not consciously, of course.
But to Holman, that was all the worse. He had fought without
knowing what he was defending. Without even asking himself

about it. All the marvels of man's ingenuity, all the deepest longings of the soul, focused on racial murder.

Finally he became aware of the computer's frantic buzzing and lightflashing.

"What is it?"

COURSE INSTRUCTIONS ARE REQUIRED.

"What difference does it make? Why run anymore?"

YOUR DUTY IS TO PRESERVE YOURSELF UNTIL ORDERED TO DO OTHERWISE.

Holman heard himself laugh. "Ordered? By who? There's nobody left."

THAT IS AN UNPROVED ASSUMPTION.

"The war was billions of years ago," Holman said. "It's been over for eons. Mankind died in that war. Earth no longer exists. The sun is a white dwarf star. We're anachronisms, you and me . . ."

THE WORD IS ATAVISM.

"The hell with the word! I want to end it. I'm tired."

IT IS TREASONABLE TO SURRENDER WHILE STILL CAPABLE OF FIGHTING AND/OR ELUDING THE ENEMY.

"So shoot me for treason. That's as good a way as any."

IT IS IMPOSSIBLE FOR SYSTEMS OF THIS SHIP TO HARM YOU.

"All right then, let's stop running. The Others will find us soon enough once we stop. They'll know what to do."

THIS SHIP CANNOT DELIBERATELY ALLOW ITSELF TO FALL INTO ENEMY HANDS.

"You're disobeying me?"

THIS SHIP IS PROGRAMMED FOR MAXIMUM EFFECTIVENESS AGAINST THE ENEMY. A WEAPONS SYSTEM DOES NOT SURRENDER VOLUNTARILY.

"I'm no weapons system, I'm a man, dammit!"

THIS WEAPONS SYSTEM INCLUDES A HUMAN PILOT. IT WAS DESIGNED FOR HUMAN USE. YOU ARE AN INTEGRAL COMPONENT OF THE SYSTEM.

"Damn you . . . I'll kill myself. Is that what you want?"

He reached for the control panels set before him. It would be simple enough to manually shut off the air supply, or blow open an airlock, or even set off the ship's destruct explosives.

But Holman found he could not move his arms. He could not even sit up straight. He collapsed back into the padded softness of the couch, glaring at the computer viewscreen.

SELF-PROTECTION MECHANISMS INCLUDE THE CAPABILITY OF PREVENTING THE HUMAN COMPONENT OF THE SYSTEM FROM IRRATIONAL ACTIONS. A series of clicks and blinks, then: IN LIEU OF SPECIFIC COURSE INSTRUCTIONS, A RANDOM EVASION PATTERN WILL BE RUN.

Despite his fiercest efforts, Holman felt himself dropping into deep sleep. Slowly, slowly, everything faded, and darkness engulfed him.

> Run to the stars: O stars, won't you hide me?
> The Lord said: O sinner-man, the stars'll be a-falling
> All on that day.

Holman slept as the ship raced at near-lightspeed in an erratic, meaningless course, looping across the galaxies, darting through eons of time. When the computer's probings of Holman's subconscious mind told it that everything was safe, it instructed the cryogenics system to reawaken the man.

He blinked, then slowly sat up.

SUBCONSCIOUS INDICATIONS SHOW THAT THE WAVE OF IRRATIONALITY HAS PASSED.

Holman said nothing.

YOU WERE SUFFERING FROM AN EMOTIONAL SHOCK.

"And now it's an emotional pain . . . a permanent, fixed, immutable disease that will kill me, sooner or later. But don't worry, I won't kill myself. I'm over that. And I won't do anything to damage you, either."

COURSE INSTRUCTIONS?

He shrugged. "Let's see what the world looks like out there." Holman focused the outside viewscreens. "Things look different," he said, puzzled. "The sky isn't black anymore; it's sort of grayish—like the first touch of dawn. . ."

COURSE INSTRUCTIONS?

He took a deep breath. "Let's try to find some planet where the people are too young to have heard of mankind, and too innocent to worry about death."

A PRIMITIVE CIVILIZATION. THE SCANNERS CAN ONLY DETECT SUCH SOCIETIES AT EXTREMELY CLOSE RANGE.

"Okay. We've got nothing but time."

The ship doubled back to the nearest galaxy and began a searching pattern. Holman stared at the sky, fascinated. Something strange was happening.

The viewscreens showed him the outside world, and automatically corrected the wavelength shifts caused by the ship's immense velocity. It was as though Holman were watching a speeded-up tape of cosmological evolution. Galaxies seemed to be edging into his field of view, mammoth islands of stars, sometimes coming close enough to collide. He watched the nebulous arms of a giant spiral slice silently through the open latticework of a great ovoid galaxy. He saw two spirals interpenetrate, their loose gas heating to an intense blue that finally disappeared into ultraviolet. And all the while, the once-black sky was getting brighter and brighter.

"Found anything yet?" he absently asked the computer, still staring at the outside view.

You will find no one.

Holman's whole body went rigid. No mistaking it: the Others.

No race, anywhere, will shelter you.

We will see to that.

You are alone, and you will be alone until death releases you to join your fellow men.

Their voices inside his head rang with cold fury. An implacable hatred, cosmic and eternal.

"But why me? I'm only one man. What harm can I do now?"

You are a human.

You are accursed. A race of murderers.

Your punishment is extinction.

"But I'm not an Immortal. I never even saw an Immortal. I didn't know about the Flower People, I just took orders."

Total extinction.

For all of mankind.

All.

"Judge and jury, all at once. And executioners too. All right . . . try and get me! If you're so powerful, and it means so much to you that you have to wipe out the last single man in the universe—come and get me! Just try."

You have no right to resist.

Your race is evil. All must pay with death.

You cannot escape us.

"I don't care what we've done. Understand? I don't care!

Wrong, right, it doesn't matter. I didn't do anything. I won't accept your verdict for something I didn't do."

It makes no difference.

You can flee to the ends of the universe to no avail.

You have forced us to leave our time-continuum. We can never return to our homeworlds again. We have nothing to do but pursue you. Sooner or later your machinery will fail. You cannot flee us forever.

Their thoughts broke off. But Holman could still feel them, still sense them following.

"Can't flee forever," Holman repeated to himself. "Well, I can damn well try."

He looked at the outside viewscreens again, and suddenly the word *forever* took on its real meaning.

The galaxies were clustering in now, falling in together as though sliding down some titanic, invisible slope. The universe had stopped expanding eons ago, Holman now realized. Now it was contracting, pulling together again. It was all ending!

He laughed. Coming to an end. Mankind and the Others, together coming to the ultimate and complete end of everything.

"How much longer?" he asked the computer. "How long do we have?"

The computer's lights flashed once, twice, then went dark. The viewscreen was dead.

Holman stared at the machine. He looked around the compartment. One by one the outside viewscreens were flickering, becoming static-streaked, weak, and then winking off.

"They're taking over the ship!"

With every ounce of willpower in him, Holman concentrated on the generators and engines. That was the important part, the crucial system that spelled the difference between victory and defeat. The ship had to keep moving!

He looked at the instrument panels, but their soft luminosity faded away into darkness. And now it was becoming difficult to breathe. And the heating units seemed to be stopped. Holman could feel his life-warmth ebbing away through the inert metal hull of the dying ship.

But the engines were still throbbing. The ship was still streaking across space and time, heading towards a rendezvous with the infinite.

Surrender.

In a few moments you will be dead. Give up this mad fight and die peacefully.

The ship shuddered violently. What were they doing to it now?

Surrender!

"Go to hell," Holman snapped. "While there's breath in me, I'll spend it fighting you."

You cannot escape.

But now Holman could feel warmth seeping into the ship. He could sense the painful glare outside as billions of galaxies all rushed together down to a single cataclysmic point in spacetime.

"It's almost over!" he shouted. "Almost finished. And you've lost! Mankind is still alive, despite everything you've thrown at him. All of mankind—the good and the bad, the murderers and the music, wars and cities and everything we've ever done, the whole race from the beginning of time to the end—all locked up here in my skull. And I'm still here. Do you hear me? I'm still here!" The Others were silent.

Holman could feel a majestic rumble outside the ship, like distant thunder.

"The end of the world. The end of everything and everybody. We finish in a tie. Mankind has made it right down to the final second. And if there's another universe after this one, maybe there'll be a place in it for us all over again. How's that for laughs?"

The world ended.

Not with a whimper, but a roar of triumph.

WAITING IN CROUCHED HALLS

by Ed Bryant

Worthy to be loved . . .

She screamed softly. The cry was low, not in pain or fear or hate. A scream compounded of an incandescent, sharp indrawing of breath melting into a moan, languishing into a whimper.

Her hands closed behind his head. She felt her nails digging into the corded muscles of his neck as she pulled his face down and crushed her lips against his mouth. His mouth gaped against hers and she bit his lower lip cruelly, tasting an intoxicating saltiness around her tongue. After the blood was his own tongue; thrusting, rough, swelling and exploring.

The quilted coverlet was so softly tactile against her back. She lay utterly vulnerable and let his spread hands cover her shoulderblades, driving her body close to him. She closed her legs and felt him there. Her mind drove toward nova.

In shadow, faceless, he withdrew and left her.

She felt the loss.

Amanda ripped away the gold strands from her head and tried to sob. Her head dropped back on the pillow and she stared at the soft green walls of her cabin. She grasped the tufts of the sheet and clung so tight that nails bit into her palms.

Her body ached; her mind felt sick. She wanted to scream out the frustration and loneliness, as the dream faded irrevocably.

"Marc." She moaned the name, tried to say it again, stopped as the constriction in her throat stifled the word. Amanda reached out and plucked the pink cube from the slot in the console by the bunk. She blindly hurled the object and it caromed off a wall before rolling, undamaged, beneath an equipment locker.

Marc, she repeated in her mind. *Marc. I want you here with me now; not a faceless actor in a tape. Not coming into my body through a gold wire to my brain.*

She turned to the wall and weakly struck its chill with her fist, letting the surge of lonely self-pity roll across her, unchecked.

"Wake up, Amanda." The voice was soft yet insistent.

"No." Her reply was remote, without inflection.

"Wake up, Amanda. Condition Black."

Hypnotic cues clashed into place and Amanda's deep-sleeping mind uncurled from its fetal ball. Her eyes opened painfully; she felt as though sand were spread beneath the lids. Amanda rubbed her eyes, touched her face, felt the few dried tears still on her cheeks.

"I'm awake," she said. "Condition Black?"

"Correct." The voice came from the transceiver embedded below Amanda's temple. "Code Black William. The rest of the team is awake and fully functional. They will go under in seventy-four seconds. Can you match?"

"Yes." Amanda climbed out of the bunk. The wall of the cabin slid aside and she entered the control chamber.

Sixty-five seconds.

Amanda lay prone on the control couch, felt the customary claustrophobic panic as sinuous contours enfolded her body and she was cut off from external stimuli. She willed herself to be calm and waited out the warm darkness.

Thirty-three seconds.

Prismatic lenses clicked into place over her eyes. She possessed sight. The transceiver beeped and Amanda knew that Terminex was monitoring her. She had sound. Golden snakes of metal uncoiled into the cocoon on the control couch and mated with the implanted receptacles in the base of Amanda's neck. She had the rest of her senses.

Twenty seconds.

Circuitry opened and the ship became the extension of Amanda's body.

"Joined," she said to the transceiver.

"Seventeen seconds," said Terminex. "I will put you under at the ten second mark. At zero I will shift you and the others into null-space. You may then reassume control."

"Understood," said Amanda.

"I am switching off the transceiver," said Terminex. "We will resume communication in null-space."

Ten seconds.

She didn't feel the microscopic spray as the hypo injected micrograms of contrazine-L into the base of her skull. The effect was almost immediate. Her mind began its preliminary shivering of reality. She felt the beginnings of fear; perhaps this time would—

Zero.

Everything in the universe turned ninety degrees away from Amanda.

Her body felt infinitely huge, yet she sensed she was simultaneously less than a hydrogen ion. Gray shifted to red to the right side of her, blue to the left. Waves of drawn-out bass chords choked her nostrils and a peppermint crashing assailed her ears. In amplified, rebounding panic, she selected an arbitrary point on the blue/red border and pivoted her body/ship about it.

"That's it," said a soothing voice. "You are doing fine, Amanda." It was Terminex on the psi-link, the webwork of telepathic communication that intruded into null-space. "Just orbit your ship in relation to that point until you are completely calm." Amanda flashed an intimation of massed shoals—magnetronic equipment gleaming brittle and chill. *Terminex,* whispered her mind. *Bring me back. Hide me.*

"No," said Terminex. "I cannot. The mission is begun." *Please?*

"No. Clear a receptor, Amanda. I have a briefing tape for you to absorb."

Amanda absorbed.

(Terminex, silver cube, featureless, speaking:)

Black William. Down-delving deep from the nonexistence of null-space he comes. He is hunger; an appetite ravenous, continual, insatiable. Material substance lures him, energy is his temptation, the life force is the greatest of bait. It is life for which Black William was originally programed to search. He is a sperm arrowing to the egg, but the zygote is life for Black William only. Union generates death.

I know little more; save that he seems to be partly machine, partly creature. I believe he is ancient. I do not know who created him. I know he destroys and kills randomly; sometimes men alone in ships, sometimes entire worlds.

He feeds on them.

Two years ago the world of Ligaera Blue was the feast. The population of two billion died. One year ago, Black William glutted on Algol IV; five billion perished. Now he approaches our world. The change-winds have blown and he is cast to us.

(The scene changes: the image of Terminex fades, yielding to normal space)

Knowing the statistical possibility of his coming to this world next, I prepared a defense. The defenses of Ligaera Blue and Algol IV failed them. I have other weapons. You three— Amanda, Soni, Marc—are part of that arsenal, as are your ships, the equipment you bear and even myself. We four may destroy where fleets have failed.

(Again the image alters. In the center of the stars' unblinking glaze, space seems to tear asunder as a shadow forms. A shadow of glimmering, hard-to-look-at black, writhing amorphously while drinking light in rather than reflecting it)

This is Black William as he appeared to my monitor beyond the periphery of this star-system only a short time ago. He is yet a light-day from this planet unless he has slipped back into null-space. In any case we must intercept him while he is still distant so that we may lure him into our trap.

I will withdraw all my links save the communication psi-relay. You are now in complete command of your respective ships.

The sky was all about her, shimmering with hot and cold flashes of licorice. *Black William*, she thought. *Father/lover/avenger*. The thought was strange and it disturbed her. Amanda's attention had strayed and she found it difficult to locate the secure pivot-point about which she had orbited.

The voice of Terminex was edged steel in its clarity. "Force yourself to stop synesthizing, Amanda. Focus back on the pivot-point." The words were a laser through the sensory distortion.

"Yes, I'm trying." Amanda willed herself to regain the stability of her previous orbit. Slowly the bitter licorice sounds paled. She concentrated. Her sensory pickups began to distinguish the pivot-point, as the pulsing beacon of clear light signaled. The girl activated one of the autonomic systems of her ship/body and she was abruptly locked in an unbreakable homing bond with the bead of light ahead.

"I'm there."

"Good girl." The voice wasn't the inflected metal of Terminex. Amanda, momentarily surprised, let her concentration falter and the pivot-point wavered uncertainly.

Marc.

Amanda flashed a laughing face, oak-brown under curling brown hair, eyes lively and glistening black like a terrier's.

"Hey, don't let me shake you," said Marc, sensing her disorientation. "Tighten up on that pivot-point."

Amanda did as he ordered. She gloried in that small obedience, a response that beat back the distorted geometry of nullspace as she locked into a stable orbit of security. She waited tediously expanded microseconds for Marc Chenevert to speak again.

"You take suggestions well," said another voice maliciously. Cool, this voice—mockingly amused. The image flashed was soft raspberry hair, long and unbound; eyes green and so large they reflected the spiral of the galaxy in their oval depths; a body as sleekly graceful as a cheetah.

Bitch, thought Amanda without broadcasting on the psi-relay. *Die in blackness.*

"Be nice, Soni." Marc's voice, amused.

"I am," said Soni Martelli, flirting. "Always." She chuckled throatily. To Amanda it sounded like the purr of a predator.

"Where have you been, Amanda?" asked Soni. "Out playing with your synesthetic fantasies? Marc and I've been in visual contact and waiting for almost ten objective minutes now."

Lambent fires flickered underneath the response Amanda almost uttered. Tightly contained, she said, "No, I just lost control for a while. I'm all right now."

"Fine," said Terminex, rejoining the conversation. "I'm

glad, Amanda. Any incapacity on your part would impair our collective efficiency.''

''Well, I'm all right,'' Amanda repeated.

''Very good, then. Marc and Soni will rendezvous in visual range at your pivot-point. We then will move out to contact and destroy Black William.''

''Great,'' said Marc. ''I wonder whether we hunt the snark or the boojum.''

''A what?'' asked Amanda, bewildered.

''Nothing. Just an old poem I read once. This hunting of Black William reminded me.''

But it was Black William, snark incarnate, who was the hunter.

Amanda waited. Then the other two members of the team were *there*, bracketing her. Marc's *Rhomboid Blue*, and angular robin's egg looming out of the grayness to her vertical left; Soni's *Cat,* a tawny polyhedron to the right. Amanda's ship had no name painted on its prow. Amanda couldn't decide on a suitable christening, and no suggestion from Marc or Soni had satisfied her.

Blue and *Cat* danced in double orbit about Amanda and the pivot-point.

''Hello, Amanda,'' said Marc.

''Hello, Amanda,'' echoed Soni.

Die, both of you, thought Amanda suddenly, on a jealous level so obscure that her psi receptors didn't pick up and broadcast the thought.

''All right, children,'' said Terminex with odd paternalism. ''Link up and move out from Amanda's pivot-point in a spiral sweep. We will assume that Black William has reentered null-space. You will bait him back to normal space at the prearranged coordinates. Understood?''

''And off,'' said Marc, laughing like spattering mercury. ''Let's go. Concentrate and link up, you two.''

Along the psi-relay, three minds reached out toward the common ground of the pivot-point and linked in a tandem trihedral that extended into all the skewed dimensions of null-space. Three were temporarily one plus something inexplicably more.

''We go!'' it/they shouted. Whirling outward from the pivot-point the hound-pack raced to the hunt. Behind followed the psionic shade of Terminex. Horizons opened ahead, constantly obscured and warped by the haze, flickering and shot with streaked color.

"Where red predominates," said Terminex. "Follow that. It leads toward my monitor's sighting of Black William."

There was an incarnadine beckoning.

The psi-linked three raced up beaded filaments shining sanguine. Crimson subtly muted to red.

Then black.

Midnight sucked in the hounds. The inconceivable hunger tore at the trinity, drove for the throat of their oneness.

"Aaah!" The cry was Marc's as unity cracked and flindered into mental shards. The three ships were individual entities, each whirling on a separate random tangent.

AMANDA *AMANDA* CAN YOU UNDERSTAND ME THIS IS TERMINEX YOUR SHIP IS DAMAGED HYPO SPRAY IMPAIRED OVERDOSE CONTRAZINE-L INCREASING

Wailing in the anonymous night, Amanda drew her mother into the bedroom through the power of her screams.

The Widow Thisbi cradled her daughter in well-intentioned, clumsy arms. "There, darling," she murmured. "Hush now."

"I saw him," Amanda said through sobs. "I watched him under the rocks."

Her mother's voice was strange. "No, darling, you couldn't. You weren't there. You were only dreaming."

"No," said Amanda, with all the tenacity of her ten years. "I saw him. It was just as Brother Martin told us."

She had seen her father leading the survey party, standing under the ledges to escape the summer storm. Heard with his ears the crackling warning and watched with his eyes the first rocks breaking loose from the heights above. Her vision had retreated and she watched her father crushed by the tons of stone. Amanda saw his face, creased with pain and dying; saw it look at her despairingly; watched as his face became the bone-white of a skull, then darkness writhing, grasping at her—

CONTROL AMANDA PURSUED BY BLACK WILLIAM TRY MARC AND SONI ATTEMPTING AID

The big man whispered, foreboding in his black suit. His styrene eyes were as hard as the table top. His voice was low and secretive in conference with his collegues, but Amanda could overhear and sense, if not understand, the undertones:

". . . latent telepath . . . psychopathic tendency . . ."

". . . only ten . . . too bad they're all . . ."

". . . definitely needs . . . for the sake of . . ."

". . . protective detention . . . recommend . . ."

"Come here," said the big man to Amanda as he stood, his suit and his shadow joining and forming a dark jaw that reached out, wider and nearer and—

MARC AND SONI CLOSING FAST CONCENTRATE THEY NEED YOU

The farm was beautiful and the years followed other years peacefully as Amanda slept and didn't dream, awoke in the green morning to play, and was faithfully tended by the machines. Then the men came to take her. They led her to the helicopter and there in the rear seats she first saw Marc and Soni.

Amanda sat shyly, apprehensively beside them and didn't notice the bite of the hypo-spray until darkness coursed up along her arm and warmly enfolded her mind—

FIGHT THE DARKNESS AMANDA STAY CONSCIOUS REMEMBER TRAINING

A school of two, Terminex and Amanda.

"This is null-space," said Terminex, his manipulator thrust out from a teaching console and holding the twisted bottle of nothing. "A place far beyond the three dimensions of *here*, a strange place where men and ships can travel beyond the limiting velocity of light. The only problem is that most men cannot travel conscious through null-space; they must sleep in hibernation."

"It's like a dream," said Amanda suddenly.

"Exactly," said Terminex, the teacher. "But a few humans are so fitted that they can live in null-space awake and remain sentient. You are one, Amanda. So is Marc. Soni too. Even though each of you must depend on a drug such as contrazine-L to retain the ability to maneuver in null-space. The drug gives you the ability to fix arbitrary points and navigate in relation to them within the effect of concentration."

Amanda had stopped listening. "I hate Soni," she said.
"Why?"

"I hate her." Because she likes Marc and has him any time she likes. The last was unsaid.

"Try to be friends with her," said Terminex.

"I will," muttered Amanda. But behind her, both hands crossed their fingers.

"The lesson is over," said Terminex. "It is almost time for the evening meal."

Amanda turned and stared at the window. The sun had gone and the sky was dark. Hungry black. Loving. Amanda screamed—

AMANDA EFFECTS DIMINISHING WILL THEM TO DIS-SIPATE COME BACK TO *HERE*

Amanda skipped through the sun-shafts impaling the forest path. Ahead she could see a pair of vibrating shadow figures, their hands linked. Soni and Marc—

"Come on!" shouted Marc. "He's following us. Take my hand, Amanda."

She was a shadow figure herself and she took Marc's hand and the three of them danced like wind through the glade. Behind them the forest turned from green to grey to deadly black, as though the sun were always sliding behind a cloud.

"Hold on," said Marc. "We're close now, very close."

"To what?" asked Amanda, breathless and disoriented.

"To the snark trap."

The path led into a clearing.

"It's here!" Marc cried. "All out to normal space."

And the clearing blazed up, a ball of fiery gasses glowing with an actinic glare that hurt Amanda's shadow-eyes. Then her eyes were no longer shadows—they were real again; and the clearing was gone and the fire was a white-searing star hanging baleful against the stellar backdrop.

"Excellent," came the voice of Terminex. "I am back on the psi-relay and monitoring your sensory inputs. Black William has diverted from his original course and is close behind you."

"Yes," said Soni. "There!" Not far from *Cat*, space swirled with an intangible dark distortion.

"The trap," said Marc. "Now we spring it."

"The three of you," said Terminex, "skim together across

the corona of the star. You will eject your seeding devices into the heart of this sun, then return to the safety of null-space as Black William's hunger becomes his destruction.''

Cat, Rhomboid Blue, and Amanda's unnamed ship swooped closer to the sun and behind them raged Black William, ravenous. The star was huge; Amanda could feel the roiling floods of radiation with her sensors. Close, so close—

"Prepare," said Terminex. Systems meshed synchronously in the three ships. "Arm." Devices locked into launching cradles. "Trigger." And they were gone out of the bellies of the ships. At close to the speed of light the projectiles plunged deep into the energy of the star—and performed their unique task.

"The reaction is beginning," said Terminex. "Instability is breeding the supernova. The initial fire-shell of the explosion will be charring this system's inner planets in minutes. Black William will not escape—this energy-eater will die of gluttony. Your job is done—return to null-space."

"What for?" *Cat* spun wildly. "Look," said Soni. She indicated the star. Mottled and angry, it ballooned toward the three ships. "Home. It's beautiful. I'm staying."

Cat broke formation, hurtled toward the eddying sea of flame.

"You're crazy!" It was Marc. *Rhomboid Blue* plunged after *Cat.*

"Of course," came Soni's reply and she was laughing. "Aren't we all?"

Terminex: "Get out! The three of you; you're trapped between Black William and the nova."

"Snarks and bonfires," said Marc. "I'm getting Soni."

Amanda was in the middle. She hesitated and watched as her companions raced to meet the first fire-ring of the stellar explosion. For a moment curiously detached from the action— then suddenly, supremely passionate: "Marc, love, come back!" Too late for pleas.

Cat went first. Soni never stopped laughing until her psi-link flashed a micro-instant of searing agony and was blank. Amanda recoiled with the relayed pain. But it was mixed with her own supreme satisfaction.

Rhomboid Blue was close behind. On the psi-link to Marc, Amanda flashed his limbs charred and shriveling like spider's legs above the open fire of God.

Her mind imploded.

•   •   •

Foundations shift sky tilts. Run the chasm. Cautiously explore structures jumpy fear slowly slip inside: steps sounding hollow echoes in waiting crouched halls. Little rumble, instantly rigid inside nothing silence eyes darting breath skipping slowly unbend move gently hard harder nothing untangle inside moving like rat skid though place of before. Run bounding for rock of only precious nectar distilled ecstasy. Mountains leap together stark red scream writhing solitude shriek black engulf

"I pulled you out," said Terminex. The speaker grill was above Amanda. "I overrode your command circuits and shunted you into null-space when you—when your mind reached its overload. I regret that I took action too late to save Soni from self-termination."

"Marc?" whispered Amanda, hardly conscious in a soft sea of healing liquid.

"Alive—barely. I was able to transfer him back to null-space in virtually the exact nano-second his ship was being destroyed by the supernova. I'm afraid his body is not reclaimable, but my surgeons have removed his brain and there seems to be little damage there. He is still unconscious."

Amanda wanted to weep.

"Black William is destroyed," said Terminex. "The immense outpouring of energy from the exploded star overloaded his intake capacity."

"Good," said Amanda because she felt it required of her.

"But all is not good news," said Terminex. "Another anomaly reportedly similar in nature to Black William has been discovered ravaging the Beta Lyrae system. I'm afraid that you must become the nucleus of a new team assembled to destroy it, Amanda."

"I want Marc." Amanda's voice was barely audible.

"For the new team?" said Terminex. "That may be difficult in his present state."

"I want Marc."

For a micro-second the computer mused. "I will consider it. There are implicit possibilities. You will be told. Now sleep, Amanda. Sleep and rest."

Amanda slept and dreamed and this time her dreams were softer than before. Except for the thought as she fell into unconsciousness: *Black William, thank you.*

• • •

Amanda Thisbi's craft, repaired and re-equipped, swings in silent orbit around the blue-green disc of the planet. No longer anonymous, on one of its angular prows is painted the name *Pyramus*. Terminex ordered this done during Amanda's long recuperative sleep.

"My darling," Amanda whispers with paramount kindness and solicitude as she strokes the steel flank of her starship—of her Marc really, since he is now part of the permanent circuitry of *Pyramus*. You might say, Marc is *Pyramus*. An experiment in efficiency courtesy of Terminex.

And when the chronometer decrees the artificial night, Amanda lies in her bunk and plugs the ship into the receptors implanted in the base of her neck. She and Marc share the same dream-circuit; and it is supremely erotic.

In his other hours, unplugged from Amanda, Marc is usually quiet. But occasionally he screams and his speaker grills rattle with pleas for death.

And that is when Amanda comforts Marc, soothes him with the damning words: "I love you."

EARLY BIRD

by Theodore R. Cogswell
and Theodore L. Thomas

When the leader of a scout patrol fell ill two hours before takeoff and Kurt Dixon was given command, he was delighted. More than a year had passed since the Imperial Space Marines had mopped up the remnants of the old Galactic Protectorate, and in spite of his pleasure at his newly awarded oak leaves, he was tired of being a glorified office boy in the Inspector General's office while the Kierians were raiding the Empire's trade routes with impunity. After a few hours in space, however, his relief began to dwindle when he found there was no way to turn off Zelda's voice box.

Zelda was the prototype of a new kind of command computer, the result of a base psychologist's bright idea that giving the ship's cybernetic control center a human personality tailored to the pilot's idea of an ideal companion would relieve the lonely tedium of being cooped up for weeks on end in a tiny one-man scout. Unfortunately for Kurt, however, his predecessor, Flight Leader Osaki, had a taste for domineering women, and the computer had been programmed accordingly. There hadn't been time for replacement with a conventional model before the flight had to scramble.

Kierian raids on Empire shipping had only begun six months

before, but already the Empire was in serious trouble. Kierians bred like fruit flies, looked like mutated maggots, and ate people. Nobody knew where they came from when they came raiding in. Nobody knew where they went when they left with their loot. All that *was* known was that they had a weapon that was invincible and that any attempt to track down a raiding party to the Kierian base was as futile as it was suicidal. Ships that tried it never came back.

But this time it looked as if the Empire's luck might have changed. Kurt whistled happily as he slowly closed in on what seemed to be a damaged Kierian destroyer, waiting for the other scouts of his flight to catch up with him.

Zzzzt!

The alien's fogger beam hit him square on for the third time. This close it should have slammed him into immediate unconsciousness, but all it did was produce an annoying buzz-saw keening in his neural network.

Flick! Six red dots appeared on his battle screen as the rest of his flight warped out of hyperspace a hundred miles to his rear.

An anxious voice came over his intercom. "Kurt! You fogged?"

"Nope. Come up and join the picnic, children. Looks like us early birds are just about to have us some worms for breakfast."

"He hits you with his fogger, you're going to be the breakfast. Get the hell out of there while you still have the chance!"

Kurt laughed. "This one ain't got much in the way of teeth. Looks like he's had some sort of an engine-room breakdown because his fogger strength is down a good 90 percent. He's beamed me several times, and all he's been able to do so far is give me a slight hangover."

"Then throw a couple of torps into him before he can rev up enough to star hop."

"Uh, uh! We're after bigger game. I've got a solid tracer lock on him and I've a hunch, crippled as he seems to be, that he's going to run for home. If he does, and we can hang on to him, we may be able to find the home base of those bastards. If just one of us can get back with the coordinates, the heavies can come in and chuck a few planet-busters. Hook on to me and follow along. I think he's just about to jump."

Flick! As the tight-arrow formation jumped back into normal space, alarm gongs began clanging in each of the tiny ships. Kurt stared at the image on his battle screen and let out a low whistle. They'd come out within fifty miles of the Kierian base! And it wasn't a planet. It was a mother ship, a ship so big that the largest Imperial space cruiser would have looked like a gnat alongside it. And from it, like hornets from a disturbed nest, poured squadron after squadron of Kierian destroyers.

"Bird leader to fledglings! Red alert! Red alert! Scramble random 360. One of us has to stay clear long enough to get enough warper revs to jump. Zelda will take over if I get fogged! I. . . ." The flight leader's voice trailed off as a narrow cone of jarring vibration flicked across his ship, triggering off a neural spasm that hammered him down into unconsciousness. The other scouts broke formation like a flight of frightened quail and zigzagged away from the Kierian attackers, twisting in a desperate attempt to escape the slashing fogger beams. One by one the other pilots were slammed into unconsciousness. Putting the other ships on slave circuit, Zelda threw the flight on emergency drive. Needles emerged from control seats and pumped anti-G drugs into the comatose pilots.

A quick calculation indicated that they couldn't make a sub-space jump from their present position. They were so close to the giant sun that its gravitational field would damp the warper nodes. The only thing to do was to run and find a place to hide until the pilots recovered consciousness. Then, while the others supplied a diversion, there was a chance that one might be able to break clear. The computer doubted that the Imperial battle fleet would have much of a chance against something as formidable as the Kierian mother ship, but that was something for fleet command to decide. Her job was to save the flight. There were five planets in the system, but only the nearest to the sun, a cloud-smothered giant, was close enough to offer possible sanctuary.

Setting a corkscrew evasion course and ignoring the fogger beams that lanced at her from the pursuing ships, she streaked for the protective cloud cover of the planet, programming the computers of the six ships that followed her on slave circuit to set them down at widely separated, randomly selected points. Kierian tracer beams would be useless once the flight was within the violent and wildly fluctuating magnetic field of the giant planet.

Once beneath the protective cloud cover, the other scouts

took off on their separate courses, leaving Zelda, her commander still slumped in a mind-fog coma, to find her own sanctuary. Then at thirty thousand feet the ship's radiation detector suddenly triggered off a score of red danger lights on the instrument panel. From somewhere below, a sun-hot cone of lethal force was probing for the ship. After an almost instantaneous analysis of the nature of the threat, Zelda threw on a protective heterodyning canceler to shield the scout. Then she taped an evasive course that would take the little ship out of danger as soon as the retrorockets had slowed it enough to make a drastic course change possible without harm to its unconscious commander.

II

Gog's time had almost come. Reluctantly she withdrew her tubelike extractor from the cobalt-rich layer fifty yards below the surface. The propagation pressures inside her were too great to allow her to finish the lode, much less find another. The nerve stem inside the extractor shrank into her body, followed by the acid conduit and ultrasonic tap. Then, ponderously, she began to drag her gravid body toward a nearby ravine. She paused for a moment while a rear short-range projector centered in on a furtive scavenger who had designs on her unfinished meal. One burst and its two-hundred-foot length exploded into a broken heap of metallic and organic rubble. She was tempted to turn back—the remnants would have made a tasty morsel— but birthing pressures drove her on. Reaching the ravine at last, she squatted over it. Slowly her ovipositor emerged between sagging, armored buttocks. Gog strained and then moved on, leaving behind her a shining, five-hundred-foot-long egg.

Lighter now, her body quickly adapted for post egg-laying activities as sensors and projectors extruded from depressions in her tung-steel hide. Her semi-organic brain passed into a quiescent state while organo-metallic arrays of calculators and energy producers activated and joined into a network on her outer surfaces. The principal computor, located halfway down the fifteen-hundred-meter length of her grotesque body, activated and took over control of her formidable defenses. Then, everything in readiness, it triggered the egg.

The egg responded with a microwave pulse of such intensity

that the sensitive antennae of several nearby lesser creatures grew hot, conducting a surge of power into their circuits that charred their internal organs and fused their metallic synapses.

Two hundred kilometers away, Magog woke from a gorged sleep as a strident mating call came pulsing in. He lunged erect, the whole kilometer of him. As he sucked the reducing atmosphere deep into the chain of ovens that served him as lungs, meter-wide nerve centers along his spinal columns pulsed with a voltage and current sufficient to fuse bus bars of several centimeters' cross section. A cannonlike sperm launcher emerged from his forehead and stiffened as infernos churned inside him. Then his towering bulk jerked as the first spermatozoon shot out, followed by a swarm that dwindled to a few stragglers. Emptied, Magog sagged to the ground, and suddenly hungry, began to rip up great slabs of igneous rock to get at the rich vein of ferrous ore his sensors detected deep beneath. Far to the east, Gog withdrew a prudent distance from her egg and squatted down to await the results of its mating call.

The spermatozoa reached an altitude of half a kilometer before achieving homing ability. They circled, losing altitude until their newly activated homing mechanisms picked up the high-frequency emissions of the distant egg. Then tiny jets began pouring carbon dioxide, and flattened leading edges bit into the atmosphere as they arced toward their objective.

Each was a flattened cylinder, twenty meters long, with a scythe-shaped sensing element protruding from a flattened head, each with a pair of long tails connected at the trailing edge by a broad ribbon. It was an awesome armada, plowing through the turbulent atmosphere, homing on the distant signal.

As the leaders of the sperm swarm appeared over the horizon, Gog's sensors locked in. The selection time was near. Energy banks cut in and fuel converters began to seethe, preparing for the demands of the activated weapons system. At twenty kilometers a long-range beam locked in on the leading spermatozoon. It lacked evasive ability and a single frontal shot fused it. Its remnants spiraled to the surface, a mass of carbonized debris interspersed with droplets of glowing metal.

The shock of its destruction spread through the armada and stimulated wild, evasive gyrations on the part of the rest. But Gog's calculators predicted the course of one after another, and flickering bolts of energy burned them out of the sky. None was proving itself fit to survive. Then, suddenly, there was a moment of confusion in her intricate neural network. An intruder was approaching from the wrong direction. All her reserve projectors swiveled and spat a concentrated cone of lethal force at the rogue gamete that was screaming down through the atmosphere. Before the beam could take effect, a milky nimbus surrounded the approaching stranger and it continued on course unharmed. She shifted frequencies. The new bolt was as ineffective as the last. A ripple of excited anticipation ran through her great bulk. This was the one she'd been waiting for!

Gog was not a thinking entity in the usual sense, but she was equipped with a pattern of instinctive responses that told her that the gamete that was flashing down through the upper skies contained something precious in defensive armament that her species needed to survive. Mutations induced by the intense hard radiation from the nearby giant sun made each new generation of enemies even more terrible. Only if her egg were fertilized by a sperm bearing improved defensive and offensive characteristics would her offspring have a good chance of survival.

She relaxed her defenses and waited for the stranger to home in on her egg—but for some inexplicable reason, as it slowed down, it began to veer away. Instantly her energy converters and projectors combined to form a new beam, a cone that locked onto the escaping gamete and then narrowed and concentrated all its energy into a single, tight, titanic tractor. The stranger tried one evasive tactic after another, but inextricably it was drawn toward the waiting egg. Then, in response to her radiated command, the egg's shell weakened at the calculated point of impact. A moment later the stranger punched through the ovid wall and came to rest at the egg's exact center. Gog's scanners quickly encoded its components and made appropriate adjustments to the genes of the egg's nucleus.

Swiftly—the planet abounded in egg eaters—the fertilized ovum began to develop. It drew on the rich supply of heavy metals combined in the yoke sac to follow the altered genetic blueprint, incorporating in the growing embryo both the heritage of the strange gamete and that developed by Gog's race in its long fight to stay alive in a hostile environment. When the yolk sac nourishment was finally exhausted, Gog sent out

a vibratory beam that cracked the shell of her egg into tiny
fragments and freed the fledgling that had developed within.
Leaving the strange new hybrid to fend for itself, she crawled
back to her abandoned lode to feed and prepare for another
laying. In four hours she would be ready to bear again.

III

As Kurt began to regain consciousness, mind still reeling from
the aftereffects of the Kierian fogger beam, he opened his eyes
with an effort.

"Don't say it," said the computer's voice box.

"Say what?" he mumbled.

" 'Where am I?' You wouldn't believe it if I told you."

Kurt shook his head to try to clear it of its fuzz. His front
vision screen was on and strange things were happening. Zelda
had obviously brought the scout down safely, but how long it
was going to remain that way was open to question.

The screen showed a nightmare landscape, a narrow valley
floor crisscrossed with ragged, smoking fissures. Low-hanging,
boiling clouds were tinged an ugly red by the spouting firepits
of the squat volcanoes that ringed the depression. It was a
hobgoblin scene populated by hobgoblin forms. Strange shapes,
seemingly of living metal, crawled, slithered and flapped.
Titanic battles raged, victors ravenously consuming losers with
maws like giant ore crushers, only to be vanquished and gulped
down in turn by even more gigantic life forms, no two of which
were quite alike.

A weird battle at one corner of the vision screen caught
Kurt's attention, and he cranked up magnification. Half tank,
half dinosaur, a lumbering creature the size of an imperial space
cruiser was backed into a box canyon in the left escarpment,
trying to defend itself against a pack of smaller but swifter
horrors. A short thick projection stuck out from between its
shoulders, pointing up at forty-five degrees like an ancient
howitzer. As Kurt watched, flame suddenly flashed from it. A
black spheroid arced out, fell among the attackers, and then
exploded with a concussion that shook the scout, distant as it
was. When the smoke cleared, a crater twenty feet deep marked
where it had landed. Two of the smaller beasts were out of
action, but the rest kept boring in, incredibly agile toadlike

creatures twice the size of terrestrial elephants, spouting jets of some flaming substance and then skipping back.

This spectacular was suddenly interrupted when the computer said calmly, "If you think that's something, take a look at the rear scanner."

Kurt did and shuddered in spite of himself.

Crawling up behind the scout on stumpy, centipede legs was something the size of a lunar ore boat. Its front end was dotted with multifaceted eyes that revolved like radar bowls.

"What the hell is *that*?"

"Beats me," said Zelda, "but I think it wants us for lunch."

Kurt flipped on his combat controls and centered the beast on his cross hairs. "Couple right down the throat ought to discourage it."

"Might at that," said Zelda. "But you've got one small problem. Our armament isn't operational yet. The neural connections for the new stuff haven't finished knitting in yet."

"Listen, smart ass," said Kurt in exasperation, "this is no time for funnies. If we can't fight the ship, let's lift the hell out of here. That thing's big enough to swallow us whole."

"Can't lift either. The converters need more mass before they can crank out enough juice to activate the antigravs. We've only five kilomegs in the accumulators."

"Five!" howled Kurt. "I could lift the whole damn squadron with three. I'm getting out of here!"

His fingers danced over the control board, setting up the sequence for emergency takeoff. The ship shuddered but nothing happened. The rear screen showed that the creature was only two hundred yards away, its mouth a gaping cavern lined with chisel-like grinders.

Zelda made a chuckling sound. "Next time, listen to Mother. Strange things happened to all of us while you were in sleepy-bye land." A number of red lights on the combat readiness board began changing to green. "Knew it wouldn't take too much longer. Tell you what, why don't you suit up and go outside and watch while I take care of junior back there. You aren't going to believe what you're about to see, but hang with it. I'll explain everything when you get back. In the meantime I'll keep an eye on you."

Kurt made a dash for his space armor and wriggled into it. "I'm not running out on you, baby, but nothing seems to be working on this tub. If one of the other scouts is close enough,

I may be able to raise him on my helmet phone and get him here soon enough to do us some good. But what about you?''

''Oh,'' said Zelda casually, ''if worse comes to worst, I can always run away. We now have feet. Thirty on each side.''

Kurt just snorted as he undogged the inner air-lock hatch.

Once outside he did the biggest and fastest double take in the history of man.

The scout did have feet. Lots of feet. And other things.

To begin with, though her general contours were the same, she'd grown from forty meters in length to two hundred. Her torp tubes had quadrupled in size and were many times more numerous. Between them, streamlined turrets housed wicked-looking devices whose purpose he didn't understand. One of them suddenly swiveled, pointed at a spot somewhat behind him, and spat an incandescent beam. He spun just in time to see something that looked like a ten-ton crocodile collapse into a molten puddle.

''Told you I'd keep an eye on you,'' said a cheerful voice in his helmet phone. ''All central connections completed themselves while you were on your way out. Now we have teeth.''

''So has our friend back there. Check aft!'' The whatever-it-was was determinedly gnawing away on the rear tubes.

''He's just gumming. Our new hide makes the old one look like the skin of a jellyfish. Watch me nail him. But snap on your sun filter first. Otherwise you'll blind yourself.''

Obediently Kurt pressed his polarizing stud. One of the scout's rear turrets swung around and buzzsaw vibration ran though the ground as a purple beam no thicker than a pencil slashed the attacker into piano-sized chunks. The reason for the scout's new pedal extremities became somewhat apparent as the ship quickly ran around in a circle. Reaching what was left of her attacker, she extended a wedge-shaped head from a depression in her bow and began to feed.

''Just the mass we needed,'' said Zelda. A tentacle suddenly emerged from a hidden port, circled Kurt's waist, and pulled him inside the ship. ''Welcome aboard your new command. And now do you want to hear what's happened to us?''

When she finished, Kurt didn't comment. He couldn't. His vocal chords weren't working.

A shave, a shower, a steak, and three cups of coffee later, he gave a contented burp.

"Let's go find some worms and try out our new stuff," Zelda suggested.

"While I get fogged?"

"You won't. Wait and see."

Kurt shrugged dubiously and once again punched in the lifting sequence. This time when he pressed the activator stud the ship went shrieking up through the atmosphere. Gog, busily laying another egg, paid no attention to her strange offspring. Kurt paid attention to her, though.

Once out of the sheltering cloud cover, his detectors picked up three Kierian ships in stratospheric flight. They seemed to be systematically quartering the sun side of the planet in a deliberate search pattern. Then, as if they had detected one of the hidden scouts, they went into a steep purposeful dive. Concerns for his own safety suddenly were flushed away by the apparent threat to a defenseless ship from his flight. Kurt raced toward the alien ships under emergency thrust. The G needle climbed to twenty, but instead of the acceleration hammering him into organic pulp, it only pushed him back in his seat slightly.

The Kierians pulled up and turned to meet him. In spite of the size of the strange ship that was hurtling toward them, they didn't seem concerned. There was no reason why they should be. Their foggers could hammer a pilot unconscious long before he could pose a real threat.

Kurt felt a slight vibration run through the scout as an enemy beam caught him, but he didn't black out.

"Get the laser on the one that just hit you," Zelda suggested. "It has some of the new stuff hooked into it." Kurt did, and a bolt of raging energy raced back along the path of the fogger beam and converted the first attacker into a ball of ionized gas.

"Try torps on the other two."

"They never work. The Kierians warp out before they get within range."

"Want to bet? Give a try."

"What's to lose?" said Kurt. "Fire three and seven." He felt the shudder of the torpedoes leaving the ship, but their tracks didn't appear on the firing scope. "Where'd they go?"

"Subspace. Watch what happens to the worms when they flick out."

Suddenly the two dots that marked the enemy vanished in an actinic burst.

"Wow!" said Kurt in an awe-stricken voice, "we something, we is! But why didn't that fogger knock me out? New kind of shield?"

"Nope, new kind of pilot. The ship wasn't the only thing that was changed. And that ain't all. You've got all kinds of new equipment inside your head you don't know about yet."

"Such as?"

"For one thing," she said, "once you learn how to use it, you'll find that your brain can operate at almost 90 percent efficiency instead of its old 10. And that ain't all; your memory bank has twice the storage of a standard ship computer and you can calculate four times as fast. But don't get uppity, buster. You haven't learned to handle it yet. It's going to take months to get you up to full potential. In the meantime I'll babysit as usual."

Kurt had a sudden impulse to count fingers and toes to see if he still had the right number.

"My face didn't look any different when I shaved. Am I still human?"

"Of course," Zelda said soothingly. "You're just a better one, that's all. When the ship fertilized that egg, its cytoplasm went to work incorporating the best elements of both parent strains. Our own equipment was improved and the mother's was added to it. There was no way of sorting you out from the other ship components, and you were improved too. So relax."

Kurt tilted back his seat and stared thoughtfully at the ceiling for a long moment. "Well," he said at last, "best we go round up the rest of the flight."

"What about the Kierian mother ship?"

"We're still not tough enough to tackle something that big."

"But that thing down there was still laying eggs when we pulled out. If the whole flight . . ." Her voice trailed off suggestively.

Kurt sat bolt upright in his seat, his face suddenly split with a wide grin.

"Bird leader to fledglings. You can come out from under them there rocks, children. Coast is clear and Daddy is about to take you on an egg hunt."

A babble of confused voices came from the communication panel speaker.

"One at a time!"

"What about those foggers?"

Kurt chuckled. "Tell them the facts of life, Zelda."

"The facts are," she said, her voice flat and impersonal, "that before too long you early birds are going to be able to get the worms before the worms get you."

Major Kurt Dixon, one-time sergeant in the 427th Light Maintenance Battalion of the Imperial Space Marines, grinned happily as he looked out at the spreading cloud of space debris that was all that was left of the Kierian mother ship. Then he punched the stud that sent a communication beam hurtling through hyperspace to Imperial Headquarters. "Commander Krogson, please, Dixon calling."

"One second, Major."

The Inspector General's granite features appeared on Kurt's communication screen. "Where the hell have you been?"

"Clobbering Kierians," Kurt said smugly, "but before we get into that, I'd like to have you relay a few impolite words to the egghead who put together the talking machine I have for a control computer."

"Oh, sorry about that, Kurt. You see, it was designed with Osaki in mind, and he does have a rather odd taste in women. When you get back, we'll remove the old personality implant and substitute one that's tailored to your specifications."

Kurt shook his head. "No, thanks. The old girl and I have been through some rather tight spots together, and even though she is a pain in the neck at times, I'd sort of like to keep her around just as she is." He reached over and gave an affectionate pat to the squat computer that was bolted to the desk beside him.

"That's nice," Krogson said, "but what's going on out there? What was that about clobbering Kierians?"

"They're finished. Kaput. Thanks to Zelda."

"Who?"

"My computer."

"What happened?"

Kurt gave a lazy grin. "Well, to begin with, I got laid."